DEATH
OF A
TSAR

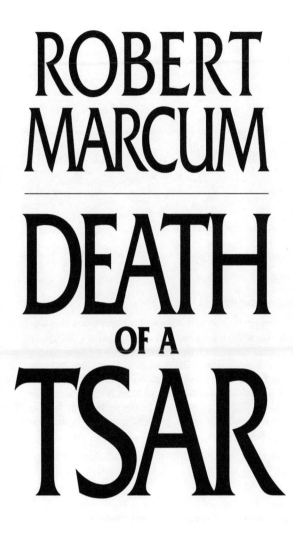

ROBERT MARCUM

DEATH
OF A
TSAR

DESERET BOOK COMPANY
SALT LAKE CITY, UTAH

Library of Congress Cataloging-in-Publication Data

Marcum, Robert.
   Death of a tsar / Robert Marcum.
     p.   cm.
   ISBN 0-87579-914-0
   1. Political corruption—Russia—Fiction. 2. Americans—Russia—
Fiction. 3. Mormons—Russia—Fiction. I. Title.
PS3563.A6368D4   1994
813'.54—dc20   94-22709
                                                       CIP

Printed in the United States of America

10 9 8 7 6 5 4 3 2 1

This book is dedicated solely to my wife.

Janene, I love you, and thank you
for putting up with the endless hours it takes
to create these stories.

Characters

Samuel Andrews	Creator of ALLIANCE.
Dimitri Bakatin	Former KGB agent turned businessman; owes allegiance to his old boss, Vladimir Tupolev.
Marina Bakatina	Wife to Dimitri Bakatin; sister to Nickolai Poltav.
Lavrenti Beria	Butcher of the KGB under Stalin; former ally with Vladimir Tupolev.
Iuri Bondorenko	KGB agent loyal to his friend Ivan Kulikov.
Alexander Bychevsky	Chairman and chief of state for the White Guard; his life has but one purpose—to see the heir of Nicholas II return to the throne of Russia.
Vostya Dubenky	Assistant to Nickolai Poltav whose loyalties have no limits.
Vasily Ignatov	Lieutenant in the White Guard and driver for Volodya Vilechenko.
Rand King	American diplomat pulled into dangerous events by the lovely Galya Starkova.
Robert Kitrick	American soldier whose brief military career changes history.
Ivan Kulikov	KGB agent loyal to the empire of Vladimir Tupolev and with a penchant for murder.
Nora Larsen	Betrayed member of the Norwegian underground whose war diary reveals a dark past.
Rikki Mogilev	Restorationist who works on the diary.
Nickolai Poltav	Brother-in-law to Dimitri Bakatin, former KGB agent who now heads Boris Yeltsin's anti-crime department and seeks the diary in order to stop Vladimir Tupolev.

Ted Powell	Rand King's assistant at the American consulate with a love for money.
Aleksei Shelepin	Dimitri Bakatin's assistant, a weasel in the woodpile.
Elina Sorenson	Linguist, friend of Rand King.
Grisha Stachek	Friend of Nickolai Poltav at the Waldorf Astoria.
Rustam Starkov	Galya Starkova's cousin, LDS branch president with a hidden past.
Galya Starkova	Journalist, guardian of the diary.
Natalya Starkova	Rustam Starkov's wife.
Vladimir Tupolev	A survivor; former military general and past head of the old KGB; his power is exceeded only by that of Boris Yeltsin; his clouded past proves to be his worst enemy.
Larissa Vavilova	Former ballerina blacklisted by the KGB.
Volodya Vilechenko	Intelligence director for the White Guard whose obsession with the past leads to an unwanted future.
White Guard	At the death of Tsar Nicholas II, a number of clandestine organizations came into being for the sole purpose of protecting the royal family and returning them to the throne of Russia. The White Guard is a fictional name for one of the more prominent and permanent of these organizations.
Yuri Yezhov	Amateur archaeologist who discovers Nora's diary only to die for its secrets.
Sasha Zagladin	Ivan Kulikov's confidant who changes loyalties for money.
Georgi Zhelin	Minister of security, son-in-law of Vladimir Tupolev; for him, power is the name of the game.

Chapter One

GALYA STARKOVA STARED AT THE SIGHTS through the open window of the bus, her hand fanning her face with a piece of paper. It was an unusually warm night in St. Petersburg, and the bus with its thin metal roof and wall-to-wall bodies was like a furnace. But it was only a minor irritation for Galya. For the past twenty-five years she had lived and worked in the Siberian Plain, and to return to Petersburg, the city of her childhood, was a dream come true.

With long, thin fingers Galya brushed back the damp bangs of her brown hair as the bus crossed the Neva on the Aleksandra Bridge and turned right into Nevsky Prospekt. Her dark, brown eyes danced with light at the city's main street as memories flooded over her. She and her parents had walked this street many times, shopping, visiting museums.

The bus stopped at the light at the corner of the canal Griboedova and Nevsky. As Galya looked to her left, her vision was filled with the columns and rotunda of Kazansky Cathedral, turned into a museum on the history of religion and atheism by the revolutionaries. She and her father had visited the museum when Galya was only seven and was struggling with the death of a friend from pneumonia. Her father had used the displays, most of which concentrated on the atheistic viewpoint, to show her the reasons he believed in God. From there they had gone to St. Isaac's Cathedral, where he had used the pictures, the icons, the beauty to instill in her feelings about God that she had never for-

9

gotten and that had given her strength during the difficult life the regime of Communism had handed her. It was on that visit that he had given her the small Bible she still carried, still read, still sought answers in. It was in her suitcase along with books by Tolstoy, Pushkin, and Dostoyevsky, all that was left of her father's once considerable library.

Anatoly Starkov had been a freethinker, a man whose thirst for knowledge was like a thirst for water. And Anatoly wasn't satisfied to read only those books on the party's established list. Copies of manuscripts by dissidents like Trotsky (Stalin's hated foe), Solzhenitsyn, and Pasternak, along with foreign authors, when he could get them, and emigrés living in Paris and London also helped fill her father's library. All of those were gone now, had been for years—taken by the KGB along with her father.

What they had not taken was the love for truth her father had instilled in her heart. He had taught her to think from the point of absolutes rather than by whim, as the Communists always seemed to do. "Truth," he said, "is constant. Find absolute truth, and don't get thrown by the relative truths men often espouse. Then build on those absolutes; the rest will take care of itself." She had tried. Through more than twenty-five Siberian winters, through the death of both her parents, through the struggle to survive, she had tried. With the Communists it was not an easy thing.

As the light changed and the bus moved forward, Galya looked quickly to her right and caught a glimpse of St. Saviour's Church on the Blood, its restored mosaic domes and golden crosses bright even in the late evening of Petersburg's white nights—the time of night when the sun lay low on the horizon but refused to set, giving a yellow tint to everything it touched.

The church had been built on the site where Alexander II was assassinated by members of an early revolutionary group, the People's Will, in March of 1881. Galya remembered her father's denunciation of the act, saying that terrorism was unacceptable as a tool of revolution. But then, her father hadn't liked a lot of things about his country's past, and particularly about its revolutionaries.

Galya's heart ached with memories. It had been so long!

Things hadn't really changed that much. More worn and dirty, some of the buildings she remembered as a child were now under renovation, like Gostiny Dvor, the city's biggest department store, its facade torn down and being replaced. To look at it all, one wouldn't know that the country and the city were in the midst of political upheaval and economic challenges the likes of which had not been seen since 1917.

The bus pulled over, and two of its passengers exited onto the nearly deserted late-night street. It wasn't a normal bus, running a normal route, but a bus for hire. Originating in Novosibirsk and carrying people anxious to get to Volgograd, Moscow, and Petersburg, this city was its final stop.

Galya quickly moved into the seat vacated by one of the departing passengers. She had been standing for more hours than she could count. Getting off the bus at Bologoye to use the bathroom, she had returned to find her seat occupied by an older man who had paid the driver enough to let him join them for the rest of the journey. She had noticed two other passengers who had recently boarded the bus, making even standing in the aisle a hardship.

She couldn't blame the driver. Even though the bus was supposed to be chartered, they had picked people up all along the way, delivering them to the next city or taking them clear to Moscow. It was standard practice for bus drivers and well understood by everyone. Under the Communist system, it had become a way of life. Picking up extra rubles as the driver did by overcrowding a leased bus, or stealing from the state store you worked for so you could sell the items on the black market for extra cash, was common practice. It was needed in order to survive.

She glanced over her shoulder. The old gentleman was still sitting in her original seat at the back. He returned her smile.

At Bologoye, when he had seen that he was in her seat, he had tried to stand and let her have it back. Seeing his age, she had refused. There was a pecking order of sorts on Russian buses. Small children and old people sat first. The young and strong stood or found a place on the floor where they could sit out the journey. Galya had grown up with that tradition but had seen it change over the years. The young weren't as respectful of their elders as they used to be. Many times she had seen older people, feeble, even sickly, forced to stand because indolent, disrespectful young men and even women ignored the hardships of others. She blamed it on the cynicism and selfishness the Communist system had taught her people over the years. When the system offered you nothing more than it had offered its citizens for more than seventy years, nothing but bare-bones existence and little chance of having anything better, you lost hope. Where hope was lacking, hate, selfishness, and meanness took its place.

She had wondered about the old gentleman, about who he was, what stories he could tell. Even though he had boarded the bus in a small farming town, he didn't look like a villager. And though his hands were calloused, they were well manicured. His face, darkened from working in the sun, had a wise, thoughtful look about it, especially in the deep-set, dark, but shining eyes— not the blank stare of the farmer who trudged through life hoeing out an existence on a collective farm. His clothing bespoke a man who wasn't concerned with appearances while still being clean and neat. His gray moustache and beard were evenly trimmed, his hair washed and combed though still bordering on the unruly. The fact that he carried no luggage told Galya he probably lived in Petersburg and had been away on a day-long visit, possibly to see relatives or visit friends. He did have a bag, a plastic transparent one that contained a package, several books, bread, cheese, and two apples.

Galya, with typical journalistic fervor, had caught herself wondering what those eyes had seen in their long lifetime, how the mind behind them perceived the events that had created a Communist Russia, and how he felt about its sudden collapse.

The rest of the trip she had wanted to talk to him, tried to get closer, but the crowded conditions hadn't allowed it. Now she made up her mind that she would introduce herself when they got off the bus, find out if he really did live in Petersburg. Maybe she could talk to him, get an interview, if he proved to be as interesting a person as her mind said he might be. She was a journalist, a well-known author in her own right, who was about to start writing for one of the country's best-known newspapers. She had interviewed hundreds of people like him, and if she had learned anything, it was that such people had a story to tell. Possibly this man's would be more interesting than all the others.

She glanced around at the rest of the passengers in the bus. By now she had made mental notes on most of them. Some had even become acquaintances. Vera Khlopova, expecting her first child, was joining her husband in Murmansk, where he was working on construction now. She would take a train from Petersburg to the northern port city. Young, talkative, excited about the future, even though inflation was rampant and politics volatile, Vera seemed full of hope—rare in these hard and confusing times when Russia was trying to find a new path while still showing some reluctance at leaving the old one.

Galya found herself admiring Vera's exuberance and positive outlook. But then, leaving a Siberian village that had never had indoor plumbing, where a young woman's teeth began falling out at twenty and where having babies was confronting death itself, Vera probably saw a lot to be positive about.

Vera was the daughter of a former politico who had been sent to Siberia because he had gotten on the wrong side of the argument between Brezhnev and Krushchev. When Brezhnev won the struggle, he carried out a minor purge of his own, sending his supposed enemies to positions in faraway places. It wasn't popular then to have political enemies executed as Stalin had done so blatantly, nor was it accepted to work them to death in Siberian gypsum mines. But demoting them to villages and provinces in which they would work the rest of their days, then die in anonymity, had become the punishment of choice. It meted out the punishments the Communists seemed to thrive on without depleting the shrinking work force.

Aleksander Glinka, the owner and driver of the bus, Dimona Plakov, a steel-mill janitor, and half a dozen others all had similar stories of hardships given by the old regime, hardships they had neither earned nor wanted but to which they had put their shoulder and won the victory. This bus from Siberia was full of such people.

The fuzzy-sounding, cheap loudspeaker hanging precariously on the front wall of the passenger section erupted as Glinka informed them they should prepare to leave the bus—they were almost there.

Galya pulled a light jacket from her bag and tried to stand and put it on. A man standing in the aisle next to her gave her a helping hand.

"Thank you," she said with half a smile.

He nodded, then looked away as if he hadn't really intended to help at all.

The man, who had earlier given her his name only as Nickolai, had boarded the bus at the same time as the old gentleman, a last-minute, unwanted addition to their crowded condition who must have paid an exorbitant amount to Glinka in order to get on. At an age that Galya estimated between forty-five and fifty-five, he had the hardworking physique of a much younger man and had been happy and strong enough to stay near the front of the bus and stand in the aisle. Galya had ended up next to him.

Nickolai was dressed in a suit coat a size too small for him and a tie that hung loose around a white shirt with a dirty collar. His shoes looked fairly new but were scuffed and unpolished, his suit unpressed. His hair was dark brown with gray at the temples, mussed and a bit greasy. He looked and smelled as if he had been traveling for some time without sleep or a bath. But for some reason Galya didn't think this was the way Nickolai usually dressed or looked. He seemed uncomfortable with the tightness of the jacket and embarrassed about his appearance and odor. Galya had tried to imagine his past occupation, but without much success. Possibly he was retired from the military, where things had been good for him, but he was now forced to live on the government's meager pension.

Other than the basic introductions, they hadn't said much to one another. He seemed preoccupied whenever Galya tried to start up a conversation. At the first opportunity, he had moved far enough away to prevent further talk. She had taken the hint.

Galya looked through the front window of the bus as it turned into St. Isaac's Square, where the last passengers would disembark near the Astoria Hotel and go their separate ways. St. Isaac's Cathedral, as majestic as ever, stood in front of them, the monument to Nicholas I in the foreground. The Astoria was to the right, along Maiorova Prospekt.

The bus came to a halt next to the hotel but a hundred feet from its doors so as not to get in the way of its paying foreign clientele and embarrass the management. Galya caught herself sighing with relief. It had been a long, hard trip, and she was glad it was finally over. The remaining passengers quickly gathered their personal items and left the bus. The driver flung open the small luggage compartment near the back wheels for those who had come from a far distance, then stepped aside, letting them sort out their own things. All were irritable, a product of the exhaustion that comes with such a long and grueling trip.

As she stepped forward to get her bag, she noticed that the old man who had taken her seat at Bologoye was still there. His face was pale, his eyes filled with concern. He seemed to be watching something behind her, and she turned to look. Two men in dark suits were coming down the walk toward the bus. As one of them was forced to dodge a passenger, his suit coat opened, and Galya saw that he was armed—a 9mm Makarov pistol in a brown leather holster. She felt a chill go up her spine. She knew these men. Everyone knew them, but she better than most. Her eyes darted back to where the old man had been staring out the window only to find the window empty, the old man already moving quickly toward the front of the bus. Why was he afraid? Why did he think these men were after him? There were others who looked like better candidates for interrogation by the Ministry of Security, the new name for the supposedly reformed KGB. The man who called himself Nickolai, for one, she for another.

Her breath caught, her chest tightening. Maybe they *had* come for her. She had written the book—her experiences and her research about the old KGB had lain the organization's crimes in front of the world for all to see. During a feeble attempt at changing their image by changing their name, leaders of the new Ministry of Security, the MB, were not happy about her first book's becoming an international best-seller. She was the better candidate—the best candidate—to be greeted and held by these men.

But they had seen her, their eyes stopping only long enough to admire. Then they continued their search. It wasn't her they were after—it was the old man.

They were still thirty feet away as the old man stepped off the bus. Their view of him was blocked by a crowd of people gathering their luggage and greeting friends and relatives. Galya worked her way toward where he stood, forgetting her luggage, drawn to him by the fear that she knew he was feeling—that she had felt—and by the hate she had for those who pushed and shoved to find him.

Others began feeling the presence of the two men and grew quiet. People, hurriedly, but with measured movements, picked up their luggage and began moving away. Galya knew what they were feeling. Even now, three years after the fall of the Communist regime, their hearts were begging that it wasn't to be them, that they would be able to move away, that these men would not call their name. Even though many changes had taken place in her country, people were still afraid—afraid the old system had never really gone away but just lay dormant, ready to inflict pain once again.

With her side vision, Galya saw one of the men point toward the bus, then move in her direction. People moved aside as if an unseen hand had grabbed each of them and jerked them out of the path of the two agents. Galya felt the bile in her stomach, the fear. She had to do something, had to help him, protect him. She stepped past the last person between her and the old gentleman and squeezed his arm.

"Are you in trouble?" she asked.

The old man's wrinkled face was dripping with sweat. His eyes met hers for only a moment, then focused on the men as they worked their way through the crowd.

"I can help, if you will let me."

He hesitated, then reached inside his bag and pulled out the package wrapped in brown paper. He shoved it into Galya's bag, the agents' view of his actions blocked by her body. His sad, frightened eyes met hers, pleading and thanking her at the same time.

"We will find you, Miss Starkova," he said weakly. "Keep it for us until we find you." He glanced at the searching agents, and a hard determination replaced his look of fear. As he grabbed his bag and started away, she froze, her mind muddled, her eyes darting first to where the package lay in her bag, then to the old man as he tried to get away, weaving his way through the luggage and the people that stood next to the bus.

"You! Stop!"

The words drew Galya's eyes to the two agents. One was reaching inside his suit coat; the other was shoving a woman aside as she tried to dart away but only stepped into his path. The old man glanced over his shoulder at them as he forced his tired old legs to carry him away. Galya saw the truck and screamed: "Don't! The truck! Look out!"

The old man faced the sky-blue truck, but his old bones were unable to move him out of harm's way in time. Galya saw the front fender hit him in the stomach and fold him over like a paper doll. She looked away, the screaming of thick rubber on pavement loud in her ears. When she looked back, she saw the old man's body protruding from behind the rear wheel of the vehicle, his arm bent grotesquely over the top of his shoulder blades. The white shirt was covered in red. She felt sick to her stomach, dizzy, and had to lower herself to the bottom step of the bus's open door.

One of the two men walked quickly to the body, staring down, then pulled his jacket aside and placed his handgun in his belt. The other stooped to look under the vehicle, then crawled beneath it to retrieve the old man's package. The driver, pale and frightened, slid out of the truck and onto the street, then stood waiting as one of the agents, the one without the old man's bag, walked over to him. Galya watched as the second man rifled through the old man's possessions, discarding them on the street as each proved not to be what he was looking for. It was then that her own eyes returned to her bag where the wrapped package lay. She realized she had to get away.

She rose, forcing the sickness back into the pit of her stomach, trying to keep the dizziness from making her faint. She bumped into an old woman who cursed her for her ineptitude. Galya apologized but stumbled on. The heel of her shoe caught on a piece of discarded luggage. She fell but quickly picked herself up and began moving down the side of the bus, out of sight of the two men she knew would want the package, away from the lifeless body of the old man.

She lifted her bag, pressing it tightly against her chest as she glanced over her shoulder, wondering if they had seen her as she walked away from the bus and the entrance to the hotel. But they were busy, the one going through the papers of the driver, the other cursing as he went through the old man's possessions again. It struck her how empty the street seemed now, even for the late summer night. The thoroughfare was wide here, and yet so little life was visible. Only a single passenger from the bus remained in sight, the others all doing as she had done, quietly disappearing, afraid the old man's sin, whatever it was, would somehow spread to them like an infectious disease. Even under perestroika and Yeltsin's reforms, some things hadn't changed.

As Galya turned to go, the one remaining passenger caught her eye—the man who called himself Nickolai. And he wasn't watching the agents, wasn't looking at the morbid scene in which a man's life had been snuffed out like a flame on a candle. He was watching her.

She stared back, unable to move, the sudden realization a shot of paralysis. Nickolai had boarded the bus with the old man, had avoided being seen by him, was following him. That was why he was uncomfortable in his old clothes and unkempt appearance. He was KGB, a man trained in watching people, in becoming part of the crowd, dressing and acting like a nothing, just another struggling Russian on the street.

He had taken a step toward her when one of the agents caught hold of his arm, unaware of Galya just a hundred feet away. As Nickolai glanced down at the agent's identity papers, he turned away from Galya and toward the wreck as if being asked a question.

When he turned back, Galya was gone.

In her hasty appraisal of the large square, Galya hadn't seen the man watching from a bench near the monument of Nicholas I. He was dressed in a white suit and matching hat, his white moustache and beard well trimmed. Glasses, round and framed in metal, sat atop an aquiline nose and gave clarity to his deep blue eyes. As Galya ran from the scene, then boarded a trolley bus that was taking on a few scant passengers in the lateness of another white night, he took a handkerchief out of his pocket, removed his old-style fedora, and wiped the inside of the leather band. Placing the hat back on his gray hair, he got to his feet and, using a cane of mahogany tipped with steel, stepped to the curb. A black Mercedes with dark tinted windows was immediately in front of him, and he opened the door and slid inside. He pointed down Gertsena Prospekt to where Galya's bus was just turning right.

"Follow the trolley bus, Vasily." From his position the crowd was thin, and he had watched helplessly as old Yuri had dropped the package into the woman's bag, then attempted an escape. It had sickened him to see, to hear, the crushing blow that had taken the aging gentleman's life. "I am sure he gave the package to the woman who just entered the bus. Keep your distance but do not lose her."

Vasily pulled the Mercedes away from the curb. "What about the archaeologist?" he asked.

"Dead."

Volodya Vilechenko removed his glasses and began wiping them free of dust, deep in thought. The archaeologist. Yuri Yezhov. A simple man who had become a good friend to their cause. A historian, an archaeologist of more than amateur status, Yezhov had begun a search based on nothing more than a scrap of information and had come up with the diary. For years Volodya had wondered, searched, never sure if it would turn up. Sometimes he was afraid that it might; other times he wished he could just leave it alone—forget it had ever existed. But he couldn't. The nagging doubt wouldn't let him.

He had asked the movement's ruling committee to make one

last attempt to find the diary before proceeding with their plans. It was only good sense, he had said, essential to peace of mind. If it turned up after they began their plans, it would destroy them. They must be sure.

The chairman, Alexander Bychevsky, had opposed the move as time consuming and a waste of energy. Alexander's position had been simple—if the diary had not turned up by now it never would, so why waste time with a foolish search that would only divert their attention from a return to power? But Volodya had been successful in getting the committee to back his position. Alexander had been unhappy about what he called Volodya's "obsession with the past," and there had been a good deal of tension between them since. But Volodya had pursued the diary one more time. They had launched the search. And Yezhov had found it.

Now Yezhov was dead, the diary gone. He removed his glasses and rubbed his tired eyes. Obviously Vladimir Tupolev had discovered they were looking for the diary again. The question was how. Tupolev was powerful, but unless he had a co-conspirator inside their organization, there was no way he could have known about Yezhov. The thought made him nervous, the doubt returning like a cold wind. Volodya knew his people. None of them were traitors. The leak about Yezhov's discovery had to have come from within the committee.

He placed his glasses back on the bridge of his nose. He should have taken more precautions, but he hadn't wanted to accept the possibility that the traitor would go so far as to inform the very man all of them hated so passionately.

He cursed himself for his miscalculation. It had cost Yuri Yezhov his life, and the movement could be in serious jeopardy. He had hoped to keep everything inside the movement, to let the diary reveal the past and resolve the problems it might present to them without endangering the plans they had been so long in bringing to fruition. But the traitor was a fool, a mistrusting, self-ish fool, who now gave Volodya no choice but to pursue him with zeal. Hopefully he could get the diary back, quickly, and no long-reaching effects would keep them from their greater goal of returning the Romanovs to the rightful rule of Russia, even if the traitor had to be unmasked to the committee and destroyed.

"Don't lose her, Vasily," he said to the driver. "She could ruin everything."

Galya sat in an empty seat in the rear of the bus trying to catch her breath, her mind a mass of confusion, fear, and endless questions. She held her bag in her lap, her fingers holding the top of it closed around the old man's package so tightly that her knuckles were white.

The man had died. The agents hadn't found what they were after, because what they were after was inside her bag. The KGB agent, Nickolai, had followed him, had almost come after her. But he hadn't come after her. Why? What had happened? She nearly groaned aloud. What was it all about?

She felt drops of sweat on her forehead and forced herself to let go of the bag long enough to remove a handkerchief and wipe her brow. The bus moved to the curb for a stop, and she found herself instantly on her feet, peering at the road behind them. If he was truly KGB, he would come. A black Zhiguili or Volga would pull to the curb behind them. Then agents would board the bus and forcibly remove her.

There was no Zhiguili, no Volga, no agents. A black Mercedes stood at the curb some distance away, but it was a chauffeured car with a man in its rear seat. There were many such cars in Russia nowadays—a sign of the new class rising from the dust of the old Communist bureaucracy—the part of the transition of Russia to a new government that Galya Starkova abhorred as the old, corrupt bureaucracy became the new corrupt rich.

She collapsed back into the seat as the bus's doors closed and it moved into the street. It was then she remembered her luggage. All of it was back there, back at the bus stop! Everything she owned was inside those two dilapidated pieces of luggage held together with old string and wire.

Was there anything inside that might lead them to her?

As the bus came into the square in front of the Winter Palace,

she searched her brain for what she might have left behind. Her
passport, all her personal papers she had in the bag on her lap.
Clothing, personal items, a copy of her book so recently published were inside the luggage, along with her father's books. Did
they have his name in them? No, and the copy of her book could
have been purchased by anyone; it was popular in Russia. No,
there was nothing. At least she didn't think so. But she wasn't
KGB. They would find something in time. It was always a matter
of time. Usually she had been able to avoid such confrontations
with the KGB. She had played the game well enough to avoid
them even though she hated them passionately. Now they might
find something they could use against her.

The thought frightened Galya, but not into submission. She
would never submit. But it frightened her to think she might have
given them the ammunition with which to destroy her work
against them.

KGB. Now the MB, the Ministry of Security. Under Yeltsin it
was dispersed but not diminished—140,000 men and women,
five times the size of the American FBI. The new face the government was trying to put on the organization had a purpose.
Crime and corruption were running amok in Russia's attempt to
evolve a free-market economy. Law enforcement was needed,
and the police were not enough. Now Yeltsin was trying to make
the old oppressor of the people into the new savior.

Everyone knew them. Everyone knew their past, their allegiance to totalitarian rule, and their attempts to subvert first
Gorbachev, then Yeltsin and return the country to the government
under which the old organization had thrived. No one trusted
them. No one would ever trust them. Everyone knew that members of the organization, particularly leaders, were using their
positions to get rich by protecting criminals and dealing in criminal activity themselves. Too many average citizens had suffered
losses of family and friends at the hands of the KGB over the past
seventy years. The name had been changed before, but the intent
had never changed. The thin makeover wasn't working, and most
Russians refused to refer to the new "MB" by its makeover title.

To the common people, it was the KGB, would always be the KGB.

Now they were supposed to be the crime-stoppers, the ones that would end the extortion, mayhem, and murder instituted by the new Mafia that was springing from the Russian land like weeds from a garden. Galya knew better, and it disgusted her to think that Boris Yeltsin was forced to make deals with them in order to survive.

Galya knew that organized crime in her country was an effect of larger political problems created by the greed of those within corrupt but still-powerful organizations like the KGB. You didn't get rid of the one until you got rid of the other. In doing research for her book, Galya had learned of more than five hundred organized crime families in Russia and thousands of other smaller gangs. Of the ten most prominent families, all had KGB ties that gave them the ability to use the old intelligence organization's national and international connections to enhance their businesses and get rich. From what Galya had learned, each family's enforcement branch was heavily staffed by both retired and non-retired KGB officers who used the Ministry's technology and resources to protect the families they served. That meant there were hundreds of agents inside the MB, all serving organized crime. They weren't about to put the hand that fed them out of business. The only hope was that in their drive for control they would destroy one another.

Galya stood and checked behind the bus. Nothing. She sat again, wiping the thin layer of sweat from her forehead. She knew them. She knew about the hard fist of the KGB firsthand. But she had dealt with them and survived. If they came, she would do it again. Right now, she needed a safe place to hide, a chance to think behind locked doors, out of sight.

The bus stopped at the small park on the side of the Winter Palace to take on late-night passengers, then moved north across the Dvortsovy Bridge toward Vasilevsky Island. At the other side, it turned left on University Street, drawing ever closer to the stop near her cousin's apartment complex.

Her eyes went to the package, then to the passengers in the

packed bus. All looked busy with their own thoughts. None looked to be KGB, but then, such men didn't always dress in suits and ties, either. Her hand slipped inside the bag and felt the rough paper, the old string wrapped around the package. Her fingers searched the paper, looking for some clue of what it held. She thought she could feel the pages of a book.

The bus came to a stop in front of a blue and white building Galya recognized as the Institute of Ethnography. Good. If she got off at the next stop, she would be only a short walk from her cousin's apartment.

She removed her hand from her bag and clutched it shut with both fists while sliding down in the seat enough to lay her head against the iron rod that ran around the top of it. She would be out of sight in a few minutes, away from prying eyes. She would get a look at the package then so she could decide what to do with it. If the KGB wanted it so badly, possibly there was a story in it— one she could use to further discredit them, to show the world they hadn't changed, would never change.

She began to relax. Possibly they would come, but not before she could discover the secret of the package, take steps to protect herself. They had only her luggage. They didn't know her name. It would take some time to—

She sat straight up, immediately looking behind the bus, sure she would see them, sure the man she knew only as Nickolai would be in a black Volga only a few feet away. She had forgotten: Nickolai *did* know her name!

Chapter Two

AS GALYA STEPPED FROM THE BUS, she saw a small park across the street, with a monument of some kind in its center. To her left was Universitetskaya Street and the Neva embankment. She shifted her bag nervously from one hand to the other. The street was quiet, empty, the pale yellow of the white nights her only company.

She crossed the street and went into the park. No cars had passed by, none had stopped, but she decided she'd wait a few minutes before beginning the search for her cousin's apartment. She was exhausted. The long trip and the old man's death had drained her of energy. Her brain seemed numb, foggy.

She stood in front of the monument and looked at the words on the plaque without really reading them—something about a victory of the Russian troops over the Turks in the 1700s. Russians made monuments to everything.

The apartment building should be the one she could see straight through the back of the park. She let her eyes wander around her, checking the terrain. Nothing new, no perceived enemies. But something wasn't right; she felt watched, uncomfortable. It was probably just the aching of her tired bones and gray matter. She shoved aside the feeling. They hadn't followed. She could go now. She must go now, must get off the street before she collapsed on it.

She lifted her bag and hung the strap over her shoulder, then headed for the building. As she got closer, she could see that it was old but had had some renovation in the past ten years. It was a pale yellow with white trim.

Checking again for anyone following her but finding no one, she moved toward the narrow street where the entry lay. Pulling the instructions from her pocket, she reread them. The outside door was secured with a lock system that required a code by which she could contact her cousin in his apartment, and he would then open the door. She read the numbers on her instructions, then pushed the buttons. A beeping sound came through the small speaker, then a voice. She pulled on the handle and the door opened. Going through a short, dimly lit hall with no windows, she began climbing the stairs to the fourth floor. Her cousin's apartment was number 8—the top floor. With the outer door clicking shut, she felt more at ease. Safe. Climbing the stairs, she passed the landing of apartments 1 and 2.

The cousin she sought was the son of her father's brother. She was quite nervous about making contact. She had written and received a pleasant enough response, but they hadn't seen each other since childhood, before her parents were sent to Novosibirsk by the government, the circumstances of which had separated their families in more than just physical distance.

Galya's father had been an engineer and physicist, a very talented one, whose work was highly respected in the Soviet Union and abroad, but he was also a political rebel who didn't easily buckle under to Russian authority. When Galya was young and they lived in Petersburg, called Leningrad in those days, he had worked at one of the government's nuclear facilities in nearby Kolpino. He had been deeply concerned about the plant's safety and the lack of proper care in disposal of waste. When he was told to shut up by the plant head, then by the central nuclear planning board in Moscow, he had refused, smuggling information about the facility to colleagues in Germany. It had caused such a stir in the world community that scientists and governments alike demanded, at the very least, an investigation, at the most that the plant, and all others like it, be temporarily shut down.

Galya could still remember the day the men came to their nice apartment and took them and their belongings away for her father's "rehabilitation." She remembered her father telling her that they were moving to Novosibirsk, in the east. When she had asked her mother what it was like in Novosibirsk, the only answer had been, "I don't know, but we will survive it—we will survive it." The fearful look on her mother's face had made Galya bite her lip with apprehension and dread—she didn't know what to expect.

Novosibirsk, the city on the edge of the west Siberian plain, had no nuclear plants, no jobs for men like her father. Not then. It was a factory town in those days, a substantial one, but one that offered no future for a nuclear physicist. Instead he was to work in a factory that made hydroelectric turbines, not as one of the plant's foremen, not even as one of its designers or scientists, but as a simple worker. Humbling people, reducing their status, was an integral part of the party's rehab program. Make them grovel. Make them wish they had never questioned the state.

But it hadn't made her father grovel; it had only made him more determined. For the first five years he did his job well, kept his mouth shut, and, when given the opportunity, offered suggestions that made the plant more efficient, its product better. One of his ideas, a tool for making internal parts for the turbines, so impressed the leaders that they gave him a promotion. From there he moved into the plant's design section, eventually becoming its head. But he was never allowed to leave Novosibirsk. The government might be willing to use his multiple talents, but they were not willing to forgive his sins. Not yet.

Under the old regime when people came into disfavor, as her father had, it didn't affect just them or even their immediate family. Often the disfavor went to the extended family and friends as well—especially if the sinners were unrepentant, as her father had been, refusing to declare the study he had smuggled to the West a forgery. Because of that, Gregor, her father's brother, who held a good government job, had lost it, and his apartment. When he had questioned the decision, he was nearly sent to Siberia himself. Gregor Starkov had never forgiven his brother for putting him and his family in such a situation, and they had not written

or spoken to one another since the day Galya had followed her
father out of their apartment to go to Siberia.

As Galya grew up, she watched Novosibirsk turn into a big,
bustling city, nearly the size of Berlin, Germany. It grew because
the government, no longer interested in having Siberia exist under
a "slave economy" as Stalin had wanted, began offering incentives to people willing to put up with the climate and fight the
flow of western migration—incentives such as better housing,
better pay, longer vacations, and better pensions. Before Galya's
family arrived, Krushchev's incentive program for the city on the
Ob River, in the foothills of the Altai Mountains, was helping it
become one of the economic and academic centers of eastern
Russia.

And her family grew with it. After her father worked his way
up the factory ladder to become the head of the design department, he went from there back into the scientific community.

Eighteen miles south of Novosibirsk and also on the banks of
the Ob River lay the town of Akademgorodok, or Academic City.
When Galya and her family arrived it was just getting started, but
as Novosibirsk became the economic capital of eastern Russia,
Akademgorodok became its intellectual, scientific capital.

Akademgorodok was and is a university research center with
more than thirty branch institutes of study—the think tank of eastern Russia's scientific community. With his return to science at
Akademgorodok, her father had arrived at his Shangri-la.

Akademgorodok was peopled largely by younger scholars
and discontented freethinkers who had been willing to give up the
cultural attractions of Moscow and Leningrad for more opportunity and freedom. Because the city was almost two thousand
miles from Moscow, and therefore from the Kremlin's official
snoops, and because the city's founder had been smart enough to
locate it far enough away from the overlords housed at
Novosibirsk, Galya's father felt freer, and happier, than he ever
had before. He began to write again.

In 1972, one year after Galya's father had been declared
rehabilitated and given privileged status again, and while
Brezhnev was leader of Russia and squeezing it for all it was

worth, he had wrangled a trip with other scientists to several of Russia's nuclear facilities, including Chernobyl. What he saw appalled him, frightened him, and made him angry. When he returned, Galya watched him become moody, fight with her mother so often that Galya dreaded being home, and finally erupt by writing a scathing paper about what the government was doing, the danger to the people, and the danger to the world. The paper also gave a solemn warning: If something wasn't done, the Soviet Union and her nuclear plants would destroy the world as the Russians knew it without the United States or any other world power ever firing a single shot.

The paper never reached anyone outside the Soviet Union, but it literally rocked the Union's power structure. Her father had done it again; this time, there would be no leniency.

On September 22, 1973, when Galya was just eleven years old, Anatoly Starkov was taken away.

Galya noted how clean the stairway was, even though it smelled a bit of animal urine. As she reached the second level, the unpleasant odor became strongest just outside the door of an apartment in which a dog barked harshly. From the smell of the area around the door, the owner didn't take the time to go down two flights and take the animal for a walk. She held her breath and kept climbing. She had been in worse. Many apartment house entry halls were much dirtier, smelled like waste bins, and were dark and damp—the result of years in which people had simply refused to accept responsibility for anything outside their own little domains. Much of Russia's infrastructure, her buildings, parks, and public facilities were suffering under the same neglect—the people's way of rebelling against a system they no longer believed in and refused to sustain.

Galya remembered the day her father was taken. The hours turned into days without hearing a word from or about him. The waiting was horrible, frightening. Finally, after seven of these

painful twenty-four-hour periods, she and her mother visited the
authorities in Novosibirsk. They were met by a very high and
very hard bureaucratic brick wall, which they were unable to circumvent or penetrate.

For the first time in her life Galya sensed panic in her mother
as they went from place to place, trying to learn what had happened. No one was talking—not friends and fellow scientists, not
officials, no one. It seemed as if the system, the monster of Soviet
fascism, had simply opened up and swallowed her father, and he
was gone forever.

After two months, Galya's mother was beside herself with
worry and exhaustion. They had run out of rubles, and food was
scanty to nonexistent. Galya was too weak even to go to school,
something that made her mother even more fearful because Galya
loved school more than anything else and had rarely missed a day
in all the years she had been attending.

Then the letter came announcing that Uncle Gregor had died,
only two months, almost to the day, after her father had disappeared. It was a decent letter sent by her aunt Katarina to Galya's
mother. The two women had been best friends growing up, but
because of what had happened in Leningrad, what Galya's father
had done, their prideful husbands had kept them apart, refusing
to make amends with each other and affecting the well-being of
their families. Katarina wanted only that Galya's mother know
that now she wished to correspond, to share pictures, to help their
children understand and know one another. Galya's mother had
simply wept.

It was in midsummer that the man from Moscow had come.
His name was Mikhail Klishtorny. He was KGB.

At first he seemed kind, even caring. Seeing that their food
supplies were low, he brought groceries and replenished them,
then gave her mother twenty rubles to get medicine for a cold
Galya had contracted.

On his fourth visit he asked questions.

"Where was your husband born?" Klishtorny asked.

"Leningrad, during the Great Patriotic War," Galya's mother
had responded.

"Do you have his papers?"

"He had them on him when he was . . . when he left."

"They were forgeries. Your husband was an enemy of the people, a spy sent here from London, England," Klishtorny said matter-of-factly.

Galya's mother's jaw dropped, but she closed her mouth quickly.

"That cannot be. He is a scientist. He studied at Moscow University. His father was a scientist as well, with an unsullied reputation. He worked for the people for many years."

Klishtorny's eyes narrowed. "Sergei Starkov, the man your husband called his father, was a true patriot—we do not doubt that. His work on our nuclear weapons system is well known. Did you ever meet him?"

"No, he was dead before Anatoly and I met. He—"

"It is not likely you would have ever met him," Klishtorny said harshly. "Your husband was not his son."

Galya had never seen her mother so upset. "This is a lie . . . " she started to say. Then, glancing at Galya, she regained her control.

"Your husband never knew Sergei Starkov. Your husband was a spy with forged papers. The real Anatoly Starkov died in an automobile accident the year you married this impostor."

Galya's mother's eyes darted from side to side, looking for an argument. She bit her lip, her hands grasping the sides of the chair so she could gain control of her emotions. Galya had seen that look only once before, when a man had tried to steal from them in the streets of Novosibirsk during their first hard winter. Even though Galya had been just a small child, she remembered that look because it had frightened her. Klishtorny seemed unaffected.

"Your husband's real name was Benson, Felix Benson. He was sent here to spy on our people, to discredit our nuclear facilities with his lies. We know this from his writings and from our own spies in England."

Klishtorny had his chin down but was watching over the tops

of his reading glasses. His eyes went back to his notes. "You must have known of his deception."

Klishtorny stood. Galya would never forget his next words. "You must share his guilt. You and the child. You are both enemies of the people. To save yourselves you must denounce this impostor. You must reveal his sins to the people and testify against him at his trial."

Galya's mother erupted. "These are all lies! You wish to discredit my husband, to destroy him! You make these lies up so that you can accomplish your purpose! You, and all like you, are corrupt and evil. Evil! Even Stalin does not hold a candle to you! Get out of my house!"

Galya remembered stepping back from her chair, afraid of what was about to happen. Her mother stood like a woman possessed, her face full of hatred, her shaking hands reaching for Klishtorny, shoving him viciously toward the door.

The KGB demon turned back as he opened it, a slight smile on his face. "You will never see your husband again. He has been declared an enemy of the state and will be executed. You can only save yourself and the child by denouncing his traitorous acts. If you do not, you will be asked to move from here." He glanced at Galya, then back to her mother. "Both of you will share his guilt. I will see that you go someplace that will cool your hot temper and turn this beautiful girl's face to stone." He closed the door behind him.

Her mother had collapsed into the chair, her face pale. All she said was "What have I done?" over and over again.

———

Galya reached the landing of apartment 8 and pushed on the buzzer.

———

It had all been so strange to her, what had happened that day. Her father never returned to them, nor did Mikhail Klishtorny. But only two days after the awful man left, the local KGB officers came and began hauling their things away. They found her father's books in the small bedroom where they lined the walls. Galya had managed to sneak five or six into a bag as they made trip after trip, removing the books to the courtyard, where they burned them. She could still see the flames licking at the leaves of the overhanging trees as all those wonderful books disappeared before her eyes. She would never forgive them for that. Never.

The next day the men came back and removed her and her mother from their apartment, giving it to strangers who looked away, embarrassed that they were reaping the benefits of someone else's misfortune, but not enough to keep them from immediately asking the agents if they could keep everything that was left behind. Galya and her mother had only enough time to pack their personal belongings. The KGB's main business was to turn neighbor against neighbor. It was their main source of information, and such tactics were used to reward the cooperative and deny rights to those the KGB labeled belligerents.

Galya pressed on the door buzzer again, listening for sounds inside. A voice, hardly audible, spoke in Russian. "Who is there?"

Galya smiled. "It is Galya Starkova from Novosibirsk. Is cousin Rustam Starkov there?"

The door was quickly unlocked, and a woman, older than Galya had expected, stood in front of her, a forced smile on her face.

"Galya," she said. "We weren't expecting you just yet." She motioned for Galya to join her in the small hallway of the apartment, then quickly closed and double-locked both doors. Galya noticed the haunted, fearful look and nervousness—a natural condition of Russian people who had never been able to adjust to the constant pressures of a survival society. Galya had seen such women break into small pieces emotionally and found herself feeling remorse for having invited herself into her cousin's home. Especially now. Especially with the package. She shoved aside the regret as a middle-aged man with prematurely graying hair appeared in a doorway. His six-foot, lithe frame was dressed in pajamas and a light blue robe. The woman went to his side.

"Rustam, this is Galya Starkova, your cousin."

The man's eyes lit up. "Galya! Galya Starkova." He walked to her, hugging her and kissing her on both cheeks.

"Welcome! Welcome!" He kissed her again, then turned to his wife. "This is my wife, Natalya." Rustam put his arm around the frail woman's shoulders and pulled her tight, trying to dispel the unsettled look in his wife's eyes. It didn't seem to help.

Rustam felt the tension in the shoulders and released his wife, taking Galya's bag and placing it near the table.

"Natalya, I am pleased to meet you," Galya said, trying to ease the anxiety emanating from her cousin's wife. "I hope you don't mind . . . "

"No," Natalya said stiffly. "I am glad you have come. We just did not expect you now. A surprise is all."

"I sent a letter, after the first one, accepting your invitation to come and telling you when I would arrive," Galya said to Rustam. "I'm sorry you did not receive it." Galya knew the reason. The KGB had made a habit of disrupting her mail ever since the publication of her book—one of the ways they used to reassert their waning control on people who challenged them. It was then Galya had been forced to use her prepared method of protecting herself from them. Earlier she had sent the head of the local KGB copies of documents implicating him in a number of black-market enterprises for which he could be ruined if his involvement were made public. He had responded to her black-mail with the usual macho enthusiasm, pulling her in and threatening her, then releasing her unharmed. The man knew the documents would be released within hours if he did anything to Galya, but he had tried to intimidate and threaten anyway. To some degree it had worked. She had left the building shaken by his detailed description of what he would do to her if the documents ever saw the light of day. But she had left him with the knowledge that she would not cower before his bullish methods and that if she so much as sensed a KGB presence in or near her residence, his career would be over. She had no further trouble after that. She couldn't help but wish she had some such hold over the agents responsible for finding the package presently residing in the bottom of her bag. Blackmail, force, the only thing such men understood.

Galya knew that under the old system such methods would seldom have worked. Then they controlled the press, and for any-one to threaten the use of that means to discredit them was laugh-able. Now things were different. People could air their grievances, embarrass the powers that be, and even unseat them from their thrones of power. But it was dangerous to play such games. You could only go so far, only to a point at which they felt letting you live was better than killing you. If you went beyond that point you lost everything, and others would pick up the pieces of what remained.

Rustam waved a thin hand in the air. "Never mind. You are here, and we are glad you have come. We will make the room." He glanced at his wife, whose face showed passive anger, then back to Galya. "You look tired. Please, sit. Natalya will make some tea."

Natalya went into the small kitchen and put a kettle on for tea. Rustam seated Galya on one of the straight-backed chairs, then pulled another to the table.

"Why have you come to Petersburg?"

"I have a new job, working for *Petersburg News*."

Rustam seemed pleased. "It is a good paper. You will need a permanent place to stay. Do you have the proper papers, your per-mit to reside in Petersburg?"

Galya nodded. "Yes. The paper has taken care of everything. They have a small, one-room apartment for me, but it will not be vacant for two weeks. I wanted to do some sight-seeing, possibly travel to Berlin to meet with my publisher there. And to see you." She paused. "I was sorry to hear about your mother."

Rustam smiled a thank-you. "You have a publisher in Berlin?"

"Yes. They are responsible for my book in the international market. When your mother came to Tomsk to see me that first year after my mother's death, she was a great comfort. I have been thankful every since."

Rustam nodded. "Mother wanted very badly for our families

to forget the past, wanted us to be family again. She would be pleased that you are here."

"And you? How do you feel?"

"I used to hate your family. My father spoke only harshly of your father and the trouble he made for everyone with his unwillingness to bow before our Communist overlords." He smiled. "Since growing up, since serving in the army, I have come to understand your father's feelings—and agree with them. I feel only admiration for his willingness to sacrifice all to save our country untold hardship." He shrugged. "Your father was right about Chernobyl, and the other facilities. They will kill us all one day." He glanced toward the kitchen. "My father was very much like Natalya. They allow the pain of the past to dictate how they think, how they act, how they live."

"All of us do, to some extent," Galya said, letting him know she understood Natalya's coldness.

Natalya entered the room with a tray and cups of tea—and with both sugar and sweet cream. Such things were hard to come by in far-off Siberia where Galya lived. It had always been that way. The center of society was in Moscow and Petersburg. As you moved away from the center, things got harder, food and other commodities more scarce. But even in Petersburg there was an understood hierarchy to things. Only the connected could get what they needed and wanted easily. Were these items more plentiful now, or did Rustam have the connections? She looked around her. Modest, but comfortable. There were some signs of travel abroad, and Western influence could be seen in the furnishings. Rustam was, or had been at one time, connected, and she couldn't help but wonder how.

"Thank you, Natalya," Galya said, taking the cup of offered tea while shoving her curiosity aside.

"This is your first time to Petersburg then?" Rustam said, leading the conversation in a more pleasant direction.

"Yes. At least since I was a child." She wanted to tell them about the number of times she had tried to come, only to be refused by authorities. Only in the past few years had people with her past and parentage been able to travel about freely, and then she hadn't been able to because of her work. The book, getting it done, getting it published, had been too important to upset it all with a change. She caught herself walking to the window for the fifth time and staring down into the street.

"What is it?" Rustam asked. "You are wearing out our old floor between the table and window."

"Nothing. Nervous energy, I guess. I . . . " She took a deep breath, then lay her cup and saucer on the table. "No, that is not true. There is a problem, and it could mean trouble for you. It was callous of me to come here." She sat down and began to explain. When she had told them what had happened to the old man, Natalya looked pale and went to the window herself, staring into the street.

When Galya finished, Rustam's face was wrinkled with concern. "Where is this package now?" he asked.

Galya went to her bag and removed it, placing it on the table.

Natalya methodically pulled the heavier curtains over the window, then returned to the table, staring at the book-sized parcel before them.

"You should have given it to them," Natalya said. "You of all people. Because of your book they already think of you as their enemy. To take something you know they are after is asking for trouble." She stood erect, facing Galya, her arms folded across her chest, her face drawn. "We are not wealthy people, but we are comfortable, and we have privileges that have taken years to obtain. One word to the manager of Rustam's design facility and we will lose it all. It still works that way, Galya. They can still hurt us." She glanced at Rustam. "My husband's new religious beliefs have already caused us problems. With this, it can only get worse." She went back to the window.

Rustam ignored his wife's coldness and spoke in an unruffled tone. "Your book is considered by the Ministry of Security to be dangerous anti-Russian propaganda. Leaders within the MB have denounced it over national television. They say you concocted the stories, that you have no proof."

"They can't just arrest me, Rustam, at least not at first. They must try to discredit me some other way. Their lies are not working. My book is growing in popularity."

"You do not need to defend your position to me, Galya. My own experience, the experiences many Russians have had, tells us you are right. Books like yours reveal the evil in such an organization and create in the minds of our people the need for even more change. But in the desperate attempt of the KGB to survive and continue their dirty business, they now believe you must be discredited, and, as you said, that is what they will try to do. If they find out you took evidence from the scene of a crime, it will give them opportunity to make an example of you. By making you a criminal, they can have your book removed from the shelves of stores in this country and will force you into oblivion. At the very least, you will lose your job, Galya, one in which you can do much good. Is this package worth that?" He focused his eyes on the bundle on the table.

Galya could see that Rustam's concerns were not the same as Natalya's, not for his own safety but for that of the work she had tried to do. It was an important work, but the package was linked to it, she could feel it. She couldn't give it up without first finding out what it was, why the KGB was involved at all. And she could not stand the thought of giving in to them. Russians had done that for too long. Now they must fight this plague until it was completely gone.

"I don't know, Rustam. Until I open it I will not know if it is worth so much."

"Is what you say in your book true?" Natalya asked stiffly. "Has the transition from KGB and the old tactics to a new Ministry of Security been a smoke screen? Is the new MB the same old KGB or not?"

Galya was stung by the use of her own words against her.

"I thought so," Natalya went quickly on. "It is as you said in your book—they have not changed anything but the name."

Natalya was right. There were no more blatant executions of people now. Everything was much more subtle. A word here, a lost privilege there, a paper placed in your work file that eventually put you in a bad light. The KGB wielded power because its people were still connected to the petty bureaucracy at the grass roots of Russian society, the ones who made the people grovel for everything. They used that connection to deny the average people what they needed, and even though perestroika had ushered in a new era, change was slow in coming. Some wondered if it ever would.

"Maybe you don't care what they can do, but it frightens me—has always frightened me," Natalya said.

Rustam gave his wife a quick glance, a look of both love and frustration in his eyes. "Natalya, this is not the issue. Our safety—"

"No, Rustam, she is right," Galya said. "I should not have come to you under these circumstances. To endanger you is wrong." She stood. "I must leave." Galya was upset for her thoughtless actions. Even though she had no proof that the package was directly related to the KGB, it was their agents who had come, she was sure of that. If they wanted the package so badly as to draw weapons on an old, unarmed man, they were dangerous to her and thus to Rustam and Natalya. She should have thought it through more carefully.

Natalya's face was filled with both relief and guilt. Galya had seen that look many times on the faces of Russians torn between protecting themselves and fighting for their right to do as they wanted without fear of retaliation.

"Get rid of it, that is all I ask," Natalya said in an attempt at reconciling her own inner struggle. "You are welcome, but you must get rid of the package. They cannot prove you took it, and without proof they can do nothing to any of us. Please, Galya, just get rid of the package."

Galya placed the package back in her bag, then picked it up. Natalya's eyes avoided hers. Galya turned to Rustam. "The old man died for this. I must find out why." She turned to Natalya. "I am sorry, but I cannot give it back, and I cannot just throw it in the Neva. I must see where it leads."

"Your silly curiosity will get you killed, Galya Starkova. It is better to leave such things alone. You are playing with dangerous people," Natalya said, her finger wagging.

Rustam's look at his wife was now a glare. "She has no place to go. She must stay here." He raised a hand against Natalya's sudden movement as she turned to protest. "We do not even know there is a danger. This package could be a book of poetry. You react from fear. I have always told you it is that, not the KGB that holds us prisoner. Natalya . . . " He took a deep breath. "She stays here with us."

Natalya went to a chair and sat down, resigned, confused, angry. Galya perceived that her reaction was more at her own cowardice than at Rustam's decision.

Galya kissed him on the cheeks. "I thank you, Rustam, but I cannot stay. It was thoughtless of me not to consider the dangers. I have dealt with these people before successfully, but that was in a far-off place, with different people. My success has made me careless. Please forgive me. I will come back in a few days when things are resolved. I have money for a hotel. It is all right." She picked up her bag and started for the door.

Rustam took her by the arm and turned her back. "A hotel is wrong."

Galya knew what he meant. Unless you paid many American dollars at the expensive ones, you got nothing but filthy sheets to sleep in and cockroaches for company. And they offered no protection from the kind of people she was running from. But she couldn't stay. Natalya's fear alone would be more than Galya wanted to handle.

"If you will not stay with us, there is another solution, a woman who can help you. Do you have a pencil and paper? I will give you the address."

Galya removed both from her bag and quickly wrote down the address. She kissed her cousin on each cheek and promised to be in touch, then left the apartment. As she descended the stairs, she felt alone, her heart pounding. She glided down the first two flights as quickly as she could, anxious to be away, hopeful that her presence in the building had gone unnoticed and would bring Natalya and Rustam no trouble. As she came to the last landing and turned to go down the few steps that remained, an alarm went off in her head, and she stopped in mid-stride. The fifty feet of windowless hallway to the entrance door was dark. Before it had been at least dimly lit. She knew it! Remembered it! She saw the switch on the wall and approached carefully, flipping it twice. Nothing.

Her heart felt as though someone was squeezing it, and she turned to race back up the stairs when she saw the man appear out of the blackness.

He was up the first set of stairs and had hold of Galya's arm before she could get away. She tried to jerk free of his strong grip as he began pulling at her bag. Desperate, she used her fingernails, raking the side of his face and leaving four evenly spaced red lines in his cheek. He screamed and grabbed for the wound, letting go. She leaped away and started up the stairs again, this time screaming at the top of her lungs. The dog on the second floor barked and scratched at his door, creating some indecision in the assailant's mind and giving Galya the chance to distance herself from him. When he started after her, she was at the door where the dog was, knocking, screaming, the animal on the other side in a frenzy. As the man appeared at the landing, a single set of steps separating them, a voice came at the door, cursing and telling her to shut up and go away.

The assailant smiled as he came up the stairs. "I am not going to hurt you. I only want . . . "

Galya didn't hear the words; her eyes and mind focused on the knife in his hand. She fumbled through her bag, her fingers searching for something, anything, she could use as a weapon. As the man reached for her hand, the door behind her opened and the snarling snout of a Doberman shoved its way through the crack. Galya moved away giving the door a chance to open as the startled assailant hesitated, then launched himself down the stairs with the hound at his heels. As the sound of the man's leather soles became weaker and the Doberman's snarls more distant, Galya let herself slip down the wall and to the floor. She saw a man standing over her but couldn't make out his features, and his words sounded dull and distant. Her vision blurred around the edges, then blackened. She tried to fight it, tried to stay conscious, but felt herself slipping, then lose the battle.

Chapter Three

THE CAR TURNED OFF DVORTSOVAYA and passed under the arch between the Old Hermitage and the Winter Palace. Two men dressed in casual street clothes but with automatic weapons stood on each side of the archway. Part of the movement's elite bodyguard unit, the two saluted as the car passed by. Volodya Vilechenko returned the salute from behind the wheel. His driver was at the doctor's office, getting a few stitches for a nasty dog bite.

As the black Mercedes came to a rest near a side entrance to the Winter Palace side of the courtyard, two additional guards came down the steps. Vilechenko was already out of the car and moved quickly toward them, touching his fingers against his white fedora in salute as they passed him.

Members of the tsar's personal guard were dedicated soldiers sworn to secrecy about their duty and selected for their willingness to die in defense of the man they had sworn to protect. As the movement's defense minister, Vilechenko had selected and trained them himself. He was proud of them for their loyalty and expertise. For years such men had given physical protection to the heirs of the tsars and kept the royal family safe. A number, twenty-two at last count, had died in that service over the years. Vilechenko was their leader and had often wondered how many would be so willing to die if they knew . . .

But they didn't know, would never know. That much had been planned and done well.

Volodya had no false illusions about the tsar's bodyguards.

Even though he was responsible for their training, even their very existence, their loyalty was to someone else. Alexander Bychevsky was the acting chief of state, and the guards would do as he told them. Volodya found it ironic that the troops he had trained might be his executioners if he failed to deliver the diary that seemed now to elude him. He could only hope that Alexander would give him more time, an opportunity to undo the damage his carelessness had done. Volodya felt he had a fifty-fifty chance.

On entering the building, Volodya passed through another set of doors and came into a large, formal entryway, stairs going both right and left to the second floor. He turned left. Taking the steps two at a time, he passed another half-dozen guards, these dressed in full uniforms of the tsar's army and standing at attention. Turning to his right and entering a large room, Volodya walked across the rich parquet floors toward the far door, his leather heels echoing off the high windows and sculpted walls. The paintings on the ceilings looked through the large chandeliers like sentinels, their colors, freshly restored to original richness, shrouded in shadow.

As he approached the second set of doors, a guard stepped aside and let him enter, then closed the door and took up his position again. Vilechenko entered a small room, well furnished from the Hermitage's huge stores of Chippendale, Georges Jacob, and Roentgen furniture. Paintings of Tsar Nicholas II and his family graced the walls at the front of the room, while artwork by Rubens, Leonardo Da Vinci, and Raphael hung between the windows. Rembrandt's portrait *An Old Man in Red* hung on the wall near the door, his *Return of the Prodigal Son* next to it.

The fact that the future tsar's family inhabited a small portion of the Winter Palace was unknown to the Russian people. In fact, the very existence that a descendant of the family still lived was unknown, a well-kept secret for more than seventy years.

The future tsar's residence consisted of ten rooms blocked off from the rest of the building, known as the Hermitage and presently serving as a museum. For now, the heir and his family had access to the building and its wealth of artwork because

Volodya Vilechenko was, officially at least, curator for this and other state museums and sites—his "day job," as other members of the organization jokingly reminded him. Soon their movement hoped to return the Winter Palace to its prerevolutionary glory in which at least a portion of it would house the royal family.

Various works of Russian artists graced the mantle, tables, and shelves throughout the rest of the room. A man stood near Ivan Kulibin's *Clock,* admiring its small, egg-shaped beauty as it played strains of music. Vilechenko glanced at his watch. Quarter to four. On time. The other man turned and faced him.

"Kulibin was one of our best artisans, Volodya. Music on the quarter hour, then the miniature figures that exit through such tiny doors, enacting the resurrection of Christ on the hour. I am in awe of his talent."

Alexander Bychevsky walked to a position directly in front of Volodya, his own dark-gray suit a contrast to that of the white encasing Vilechenko's stately frame. "Did you locate the woman?"

At seventy-five, the man in gray was approximately the same age as his counterpart in white but looked younger. His hair was gray like Vilechenko's but was tinged with streaks of its original brown color. It was combed straight back, accentuating a receding hairline. His eyes were green, and he sported a moustache the same color as his hair. At five feet eight inches, he was at least four inches shorter than Volodya, and thirty pounds lighter. Although broad in the shoulders, he had a thin quality to him that was accentuated by his narrow jaw and face. He turned and went to the Victorian couch. Volodya followed, and they sat facing each other.

"No, Alexander, not yet. The wound to my driver was a deep one, and he was bleeding badly. I had to take him directly to one of our people at the hospital. When I returned, the woman was gone. We are still watching the cousin's apartment in hopes that there will be further contact. Others are searching as well."

"And how is Vasily?"

Volodya smiled. Vasily was Alexander's nephew, young, fanatically dedicated to the cause. His decision to approach the

Starkova woman in the manner of an adversary was a young and foolish one, and contrary to Volodya's instructions. The young man had made a bigger mess of an already acute one.

"He is greatly pained by the experience. He acted contrary to my instructions but is repentant. He really had no intention of hurting the woman. He thought he could cut the strap of her bag so he could remove it easily. In the darkness she panicked. He wants to return to full service tomorrow but finds it difficult to sit at present." Volodya really couldn't help but smile. Seeing young Vasily burst from the door with the dog hanging from his backside had been too humorous for words.

Alexander seemed relieved at Volodya's defense of his nephew's actions. "Good, but his decision was foolish. I will still take steps—" He caught himself overstepping his bounds. "*You* must take steps . . . some sort of discipline—possibly something without removing him from his present position but still effective . . ."

"I will take care of it, Alexander," Volodya said.

Alexander looked away, dismissing the subject and the tension between them. "You will find her?"

"Of course, and the diary. These things are under control; they are not the reason I have come. There is another concern."

"You mean the KGB agents at the bus?"

"I mean those whom the agents work for and the threat they are to us."

"At which hour, which day? The services they sell are open to anyone with the right money," Alexander said in a flat, almost bored tone.

"Not these. It is well known in the KGB that they work for Vladimir Tupolev."

Alexander's posture didn't change. "Tupolev? How could the one man we least want to discover our intentions have found our archaeologist? You must be mistaken."

"My sources are very good."

"If they are so good, why weren't you informed of Tupolev's interest beforehand?" Alexander asked impatiently. He waved a hand of dismissal before Volodya had a chance to answer. "Never mind. The damage is done."

Alexander stood and went to the mantle. He looked carefully at the *Peacock Clock* resting there. The clock was made in London, a gift from Prince Grigory Potyomkin for Catherine the Great. The peacock was perched on a tall, oak-tree stump with two spreading branches fastened to a base. A cage with tiny bells and an owl of silver were suspended from one of the branches by a cord. Below the cage was a squirrel nibbling a nut. On the other side was a life-size cockerel on a small stump. In the foreground were mushrooms, leaves, acorns, and even a pumpkin, with snails and lizards, and two squirrels in the branches. When the clock was wound, all the figures moved on the hour. First the owl turned its head, rolled its eyes, and stamped its foot while the cage revolved and the little bells tinkled. When the sound of the bells ceased, the peacock spread its tail, turned to display its plumage, and gracefully bowed its head. Finally the cockerel sprang into action, arching its neck, opening its beak, and crowing. It was an amazing piece of work, one Alexander had loved all his life. He checked his timepiece, waited a few seconds, and watched as the clock hit the hour. When it had gone through its complete program, he returned to the couch.

"You are telling me that Tupolev knows about the diary, that it still exists?" he asked.

"It is probable," Volodya answered.

"Do we know how he discovered Yuri Yezhov's quest?" Alexander asked.

"No, but Tupolev has many sources," Volodya said, avoiding discussion of his real feelings.

"We should have left well enough alone, Volodya. Now we are in great danger."

"I take full responsibility. I am the one who encouraged the ruling council to make one last search."

"Even Tupolev had stopped searching." Controlled frustration tinged Alexander's voice. "Now he searches again. He is afraid our having the diary will give us even greater control of him. He is tired of our demands."

"We already know enough about his past to destroy him, and he knows it. Our getting the diary will not change that. His reasons run deeper. Possibly he suspects that our claim to the throne is based on deception and believes the diary will help prove his suspicions."

"Yes, yes. I am sure he does. And if the diary speaks of what happened . . . "

Volodya's face showed his understanding of the gravity of the situation. "I know. Then he would have the upper hand. He could destroy our attempt at returning the Romanovs to the leadership of Russia."

"It was stupid, Volodya. Well enough should have been left alone," Alexander said, frustrated.

Vilechenko didn't respond. They had been on opposite sides of the matter; now it seemed that all of Alexander's fears of what might happen were well founded. What could he say when it seemed his position had been the wrong one?

"I do not understand your obsession, Volodya. For years you have refused to let it go and support our decision. Now your actions have jeopardized everything."

"As I have told you many times, we must make sure. I still have my doubts that the boy—"

"The boy is dead, Volodya! There can be no other explanation. He has never come forward, never been found! We did the right thing—the only thing that would keep the family intact and prepare them for the heir's return to lead Russia in her greatest need! The only thing!"

Volodya felt the anger push the blood into his head. "That, Alexander, is *exactly* the point—has always been the point! The diary might tell what happened, might tell the world he was killed. If the diary were to turn up later, after putting Peter on the throne of Russia, our enemies would crucify us and the movement. Nothing would save us then! Nothing! It is better to get the diary, learn its secrets if there are any, then burn it, be rid of any chance of discovery!" He paused, getting control. "It is the only way to safeguard the royal family completely!" He paused again. "I realize the loss of the diary is an unfortunate side effect of—"

"Unfortunate? If the diary falls into Tupolev's hands, or any-one else's, and it reveals what happened, you have doomed every-thing we have worked for, that thousands have worked for, for better than seventy years! It is exactly why we should have left well enough alone!" Alexander was shouting now. "The diary would have rotted in the ground, where it could do no harm to us! No harm!" He tried to get a handle on his emotions. "Nora was no fool, Volodya. She would not have been so stupid as to put such deadly information in the diary. Never!"

Volodya looked away, refusing to make eye contact. "There is still the vault. The diary is the only known record of where the vault is and how to open it. It contains millions in the family's lost wealth. We need the diary to find the vault."

"It was emptied by the same man responsible for the failure of our mission back then."

"We don't know that. He has never said so."

"Hah! The man lives like a king! Where did he get the money? And do you think he would tell you the truth? We black-mail him, Volodya. He does only what we force him to do. Surely you can't believe he would be honest with us!"

"He sold weapons to third-world nations. We know he stole millions of dollars worth of goods and matériel from the state and sold them on the black market. Millions. That is when he made his money! Not from the vault," Volodya replied.

"He was rich before that. Many of the pieces we know were in the vault are now in the hands of this museum, Volodya! You purchased them! How did they free themselves? How? I do not understand you! Why are you so blind to this? He emptied the vault and sold the items on the black market. It is the way *he* gained his wealth. Nothing is left. The vault is of no consequence anymore!"

Volodya took a deep breath. They had had this argument so many times. He was sure the man who had betrayed them to the Russians at the time of the attempt to kill Stalin had never opened the vault. He had no way of doing so. The instructions for entry were coded inside Nora's diary. If, when Tupolev had changed sides, he had taken the diary, why was he looking for it now? It made no sense.

As to how the objects had "freed themselves," Volodya had other ideas. A second traitor—a thought that had given him nightmares of doubt for better than twenty years.

"We don't *know,* Alexander! *You* are the only sure one. Only the opening of the vault will tell us if Tupolev desecrated it. Only then will the evidence be sure. Only then will we know our movement cannot be compromised. I would think you would want such assurances."

Alexander glared at his old friend, then stood and went to a window, staring at the Neva without seeing it, calming himself.

Volodya had known Alexander since they were children. Their fathers had been loyal to the tsar, and their fathers before them. In fact, it was Alexander's father who had traveled to America to meet with members of the guard who had fled to that country at the death of Tsar Nicholas II. They began even then, only one year after Stalin took over from Lenin, to make plans for the assassination of the Butcher, hoping to save as many Russians from his murderous methods as they could—hoping they could return power to Nicholas's heirs, reclaim the family's property and valuables before it was too late. From those meetings, there had been two attempts to kill Stalin. Both had failed. Alexander's father had died in the second attempt, the one in 1938, and Alexander had been asked to carry on his father's work and lead the White Guard movement.

Volodya had always supported Alexander. They had been friends, associates, all their lives. They had fought together, planned, overcome, and nearly died together. ALLIANCE had nearly gotten them both killed, but they had survived, and by the sheer will of their personalities they had pulled their decimated numbers back together again. By will and deception. But the deception had been for the good of the movement. Anyway, it wasn't the actual deception of members of the movement that bothered Volodya. He knew it was necessary for the salvation of Russia. But all of it could be undone if the diary or the vault were found by others and somehow used against them. That was his greatest fear.

Now he, Volodya, had put everything at risk! It made him sick to think about it, but he couldn't help himself. The nagging doubts, the little pieces of missing puzzle were an obsession. He had to know.

After several long moments, Alexander turned. "You have opened Pandora's box, friend Volodya. I hope you know how to close it before our old nemesis destroys what we have accomplished."

Volodya stood. "I have people searching for the woman and watching Tupolev and Zhelin. I promise you the return of the diary."

Alexander watched his friend. For years Volodya had been obsessed by the diary. He had tried to get him to back away, channel his energies in meaningful directions—tried to get him to realize that the best thing that had happened to them was its disappearance. All of Alexander's attempts had been unsuccessful. Why? Did Volodya know something he wasn't sharing?

The thought upset Alexander's stomach. Some things were better left unknown—for the good of everyone. If only Nora had died in the city! Volodya would never have known of the diary's survival, and all of this could have been avoided.

Guilt washed over him even as he had the evil thought. He had loved Nora—quietly and from a distance, but he had loved her. It wasn't her fault the boy had made his decision—had messed it all up! It wasn't Nora's fault the boy had died!

He felt himself shudder at the memory and threw it quickly aside. Harboring such thoughts could do no good. What was done was done. They must move on.

"You will bring the diary here, immediately."

"Immediately," Volodya said flatly while moving to the door.

"And Volodya." Alexander looked after his old friend. "If you fail, if Tupolev gets the diary, I will have no choice. You will be brought before the council. You will be tried for your failure."

Volodya glanced back at his friend as if to say something, then went through the door and closed it behind him.

Alexander went to the window again.

ALLIANCE. How he wished he had never heard the name.

He stood for long minutes until he saw Volodya's car enter the street and turn right. He loved the man like a brother, but even Volodya couldn't be allowed to interfere with the return of the Romanovs. Nothing could interfere. Too great a price had already been paid, and the future of Russia was at stake. The boy had died because he had lost that vision to the passion of a moment. He, Alexander Bychevsky, had picked up the pieces and put it all back together again. He would not allow anything, even the life of his old friend, to detour them from their appointed road now!

"You have made a very big mistake, friend Volodya. With your insatiable curiosity and nagging doubts, you have set your foot on a different path. If it conflicts with mine . . . "

He walked to the phone and dialed a number. Volodya would bear watching. There were several who could do the task.

Chapter Four

GALYA AWAKENED IN A DARK ROOM, the warmth of blankets against her body. She snuggled deeper into them, wanting to go back to sleep, to keep the thoughts of yesterday at bay until they were nothing but old memories.

After a few minutes she gave up, the assailant, knife in hand, invading the darkness and coming to life again. She reached over and switched on the lamp, half expecting him to be sitting on the end of the bed.

The bed was shoved against one wall of a narrow room. Reaching out with her hand, she could touch the other wall, lift the peeling paint from it. Near her head was a small end table jammed between the bed and the wall. On top of it was the lamp and an old radio with the glass face broken out of it. Next to it Galya saw a small, wind-up alarm clock that ticked so loudly she wondered how she had been able to sleep. Its black hands both pointed at ten.

Throwing off the covers, she planted her feet on the thread-bare rug on the floor. Then her mind became clear. The memory of the heavy-set man stooping over her when she lost consciousness wasn't a pleasant one.

The door to the room opened, and Rustam stood in the space. He smiled as she quickly tried to straighten her mussed hair.

"Good morning," Rustam said.

"Yes. Good morning," Galya returned. "Where am I? You didn't . . . I am not at your apartment, am I?"

"A different place, Cousin." Rustam smiled. "The address I gave you, and safe for now. Would you like to take a hot bath?"

Galya was relieved. "Very much. How did you get me here?"

"You are really quite light, and I have a car. The bathtub is just across the hall." He started to leave.

"The man . . . the one who tried . . . "

Rustam turned back. "Escaped." His lips showed a row of even teeth that were already discoloring. "But Boris made him think twice about returning."

"Boris?" Galya asked while standing to stretch.

"The Doberman. He had part of the man's pants in his teeth when he returned. There was blood on them." He paused. "Can you remember? We have had this problem before. A neighbor was attacked by thieves who seem to know how to open the outer door. I am sorry . . . "

Galya nodded. "I know. It is all right, Rustam. Really. I am fine. I was afraid it might be one of the men from the bus stop at first, but he wasn't dressed right. He was after my bag. You are right; it was probably just thieves. You should have the door checked." She forced a smile, not sure she was fully convinced of her own words.

He shrugged, unsure of what to say. The lock had been fixed, and their troubles had stopped. So he found it curious that it had happened now, to Galya, when the KGB was looking for her. But she said it wasn't the same men. He shoved it aside.

"We will have something for you to eat as soon as you are ready." He left the room.

The bathroom was small, but the kalonka was already lit, the hot, steaming water running into the stained tub. After brushing her teeth with some paste on her finger, she undressed and carefully eased herself into the water, letting the hotness of it take away some of the aches she still felt in her muscles. Her mind drifted to the attack, but she pushed the thought aside, replacing it with old memories—memories of her mother.

The day after the confrontation with the KGB agent from Moscow, Klishtorny, the man who told them they would never see Galya's father again, she and her mother were taken directly to the Novosibirsk train station, where one of the two agents accompanying them bought tickets. They went two hundred miles north, where the agent left them with officials of another small city on the Ob River.

Guryevka was a village made up largely of ruined houses with thatched roofs positioned along the side of a ravine. The houses had whitewashed walls, small windows that couldn't be opened, large vaulted stoves, and dirt floors. She remembered that the window glass was thin and wavy, hard to see through, but shuttered in the winter anyway, the harsh winds too much for the brittle sheets of glass.

Galya and her mother were replacing a man who died during the winter and whose body had lain frozen for several months before it was discovered. Unfortunately, the neighbor told Galya, he had died in the room of the house inhabited by the animals, and when the pigs had gotten hungry they had started on the old man. Galya had scrubbed the room until her hands were raw.

They did have a vegetable garden and could gather berries from the woods, but for the most part people in Guryevka lived on sugar (when they could get it), bread, butter, and eggs, all produced locally. Galya and her mother had no chickens for eggs, no cow to milk, and very little money to buy sugar and wheat for bread in Krivosheino.

Krivosheino was five miles distant from Guryevka. It had two streets, both muddy, and wooden sidewalks. It also had two stores, whereas Guryevka had none, and the military headquarters of the district was housed there. From the military headquarters near the outskirts of town, Galya's mother received her meager pay for work done on the railroad being built from Tomsk, some hundred miles to the south, to Nizhnevartovsk in the north. There was also a school in Krivosheino.

They used their meager funds to buy what they could against the coming winter, but it wasn't enough. If it hadn't been for the goodness of the people of Guryevka, they would have starved or frozen to death. When they ran out of firewood, they lived with neighbors, sharing their food and the food of others in order to survive. It was that winter that Galya first understood the meaning of hunger, and of kindness. Children grew thin in winter as a normal course of things, but even thinner when having to spread their scanty supplies among two more hungry people. Galya ate as little as possible, becoming nothing more than skin on bones, and her mother ate even less. Of course, there was no work and no money, but even in Krivoshieno supplies were scarce, so money meant nothing. Somehow they survived that winter, and they knew that they would not survive another unless they found other ways to buy or find what they needed. Galya was sure of one thing—they would never take another bite of food from the children of Guryevka in order to live. She and her mother swore they would die first.

For the next nine years they worked eighteen hours a day to survive. Although the town was not far from her old home in Novosibirsk, for Galya it was like living on another planet. All the nice things, the conveniences she had learned to take for granted, were gone. Now there was only hard work and school. During the spring, summer, and fall, her mother worked long hours on the railroad to earn food passes allowing her to buy flour and other essentials from the railroad bosses who came into Krivoshieno for the working season. They never seemed to be short of food, with fresh supplies coming in weekly as long as they were there. Galya understood the system. Black market, it was called, and it was illegal, but officials paid no attention simply because everyone's survival, including their own, depended on this method of supply.

During the working season, Galya's mother had no time for housekeeping, gardening, and food preparation, so these became Galya's responsibility. Sometimes her mother was gone for five days to two weeks at a time, working at some distance from Guryevka, and Galya was left alone. But she carried on, working hard, learning from her neighbors how to produce food on the small garden plot next to their house.

Her day began at sunrise. If her mother was there, Galya would prepare a meal for her and send her off to work. Then she would sweep the dirt floors and scrub the few dishes before going off to school, held during all seasons except the very worst of winter. Returning in late afternoon, she would tend to their garden, then go to the woods and pick berries, which they dried in the summer heat and stored for winter use in a hole in the ground beneath the stone floor of their house, along with what vegetables and other items they could raise or purchase.

It was a glorious day when they were able to purchase their own chickens, then a cow for fresh milk. An old farmer who lived alone had passed away, and Galya's mother convinced the authorities at Krivosheino that the animals were too sickly, and they did look sickly, to be of much use or value, and that she and Galya wold be doing the state a favor in purchasing them for the exorbitant amount of fifty rubles. The leader of the Communist party, an old drunk with only half his teeth in his head and a sweet feeling for Galya's mother, was convinced, and they had their chance at fresh milk and eggs.

A neighbor who knew herbs and good places to feed the cow to make her fat helped them get the animal into production again, and by winter they were content at receiving a pitcher of milk a day and half a dozen eggs.

They burned wood in the old stove in the winter, but it had to be cut and laid up in the summer. One day a week Galya and her mother would go into the forest and cut as long as their strength would hold out, then use a few of their precious rubles to pay a man to haul the wood in his horse-drawn wagon. Although they had to ration the amount burned each day, and on the coldest nights slept in their clothes and with each other, they survived.

When winter came, work on the railway all but stopped, and so did the rubles the work brought to them. For Galya it was good to have her mother at home, but to keep themselves alive they had to find ways to get additional food for their larder.

Galya and her mother knew how to sew. Using some of their last remaining rubles, they purchased linen and white thread. Then, mixing the dried berries with water and boiling them, they made a rich, red dye for embroidering colorful tablecloths.

Although by Novosibirsk standards most of the people in Guryevka and Krivosheino were poor, the women of both villages were hungry for something beautiful with which to adorn their bleak, well-worn, and colorless houses. The tablecloths Galya and her mother made were just what they wanted. That made them good items for bartering for food and a few other items needed for survival. Making them also gave Galya and her mother something to do during the long winter days.

Galya learned to love the hours spent in the Krivosheino schoolhouse. When, because of the need to care for the garden or the animals or the necessity to cut and gather wood for winter, she could not walk the five miles to lose herself in the wonder of her books, she almost became physically ill. She worked hard at her studies and read over and over again the few of her father's books she had been able to salvage from the monstrous hands of the KGB, losing herself in their mystery.

For Galya, Guryevka became her home. She made friends, excelled in school, and, because of the hard work and determination required for survival, became very confident and independent. Her mother, on the other hand, slowly deteriorated. Her bitter hatred of what had been done to her and her husband festered until, over the years, it began to consume her.

At first Galya and her mother never fought but worked together for survival. But as days turned into years without word of Anatoly, without any response to her pleas for information and leniency, Galya's mother began to change.

First it was her temper, roiling over her and spilling out on Galya like scalding water. Galya bit her tongue and took the abuse as best as she could until, finally, she could take it no more and screamed back, then struck her mother, something for which she would be forever sorry.

Then came silence, depression. It was in the ninth year, the winter. Galya watched her mother become more and more sullen, sleeping long hours, unwilling to help around the house, do the embroidery, or share in the cooking. But Galya tried to understand and pick up the slack.

Then her mother stopped eating. After that Galya could do nothing but watch her mother die. There were no doctors, no psychiatrists, no one to help pull her mother through. Galya pleaded and begged, yelled and screamed, but her mother just lay there, a blank look on her thin face. Neighbors came to help, but when they saw the ailing woman, they only shook their heads and spoke in hushed tones to one another. They had seen this condition before, and it was always the same.

Galya, who was raised a Christian, prayed every day that the warm sun of spring would come early this year, that its rays would strike through the window and raise her mother from her deathbed. But God chose not to answer. Each day cold winds and freezing temperatures moved her mother closer to the grave. Finally, Galya quit praying, accepted the inevitable, and waited.

On the first day of May, Natasha Starkova died.

It was nearly a month before Galya could dig a grave through the snow and frozen permafrost. Until then she wrapped her mother in a blanket and placed her remains near the door where she could keep watch for wild dogs and other predators. It was the worst month of Galya's life. Not that she remembered much except the crying, the anguish, the hatred for God, who didn't seem to care, had never seemed to care, at least for her and her family. It was a month of horrible soul searching, but at the end of it Galya knew just one thing—she must leave Guryevka. Whatever it took, she would do.

Six months later, Galya left Guryevka and went to Tomsk to the university. She had performed well in the Krivosheino school, graduating first in her class despite the hardship of missing so much time because of their circumstances and her mother's death. At first she didn't think she would be allowed to leave. Because she and her mother had been sent to Guryevka at the orders of the Moscow KGB, permission had to be obtained from the Kremlin. Galya waited nearly all summer, continuing her work, preparing for winter, refusing to get her hopes up, planning an alternative escape through marriage to a man she loathed—an official of the party in Krevosheino with enough power to get them to a larger city but who was everything Galya had come to hate. She was within hours of telling him she would marry him when the letter came, preventing the mistake of a lifetime. Two weeks later she was in Tomsk. She never did really understand why she was allowed to leave. The letter didn't give reasons, just permission. But she assumed that the Kremlin did not hold her responsible for her parents' supposed crimes, and that, coupled with her excellent work in school, gave her the freedom she desired.

She visited her mother's grave the day she left. She loved her mother more deeply than she could ever have supposed. They had literally been everything to each other for nine years—friends, family, everything. She hated to leave her behind.

By the time Galya left Krivosheino, she had learned to play the system. She knew what to say and when to say it. She could bow and kowtow with the best of them, keeping her emotions, her hatred, buried deep inside, refusing to let even close friends see it. The state had taken her parents. She hated it for what it had done, but she knew that she could never reveal her story, never get the vengeance she sought while in Guryevka. For that she must be elsewhere, in the centers of power, in positions where it would be possible to get even. She must learn to play the game better than her enemies, better than the KGB and the party bureaucracy they served. She joined the party, went to the meetings, played the games a good party member would play, and climbed the ladder of party success, opening more doors of opportunity to get the education, then the positions she wanted. All the time she kept notes of names, places, events. She copied documents verifying what was going on, how the bureaucrats used the system for their own advantage. She had information on men and women alike that later, when revealed, could destroy them and show the party for what it was.

Then came the connection to the Novosibirsk KGB office.

Galya had returned to Akademagoroduk as an assistant professor of mathematics. While there she renewed acquaintances with some of her father's old friends, men and women whom she trusted and in whom she confided the story of what she was attempting to do. One of them put her in touch with a young member of the KGB who had become disenchanted with his organization and might be a willing participant in any undertaking that would bring down their power-hungry overlords. She found him very cooperative. That was when she began writing her book.

She documented murders, plunder for personal gain, conferences between local and national leaders as they set up black-market operations in which they stole millions from the state, and the institution of a direct line to the Far East in which Japanese and American goods were smuggled into Russia and sold on the black market to the rich Communist leaders. For Galya, it was corruption at its worst and a story that must be told.

On the surface Galya wrote articles and short stories about the hardships of Siberian life and about historical characters who lived and survived there. Because intellectual restrictions had been temporarily loosened in order to impress the West, and because of the movement within the country toward a return to nationalism and roots, her articles were well received in the loose academic environment of Akademgorodok, then across the country. Many who had shared such hardships considered Galya their voice and advocate. Galya had done her best to represent them well, but secretly she was preparing another story: the truth about the KGB and its atrocities, to be smuggled out of Russia and published in the West.

She remained at Akademgorodok, intellectually involved, working on her book. Of course this secret research put her in grave danger. The people about whom she wrote would not take kindly to her revelations. The least she could expect was another stint in a place like Guryevka. Galya didn't mind. She had survived it once, she could again—especially knowing that her work was in print for all to see.

Then had come a miracle—Gorbachev's perestroika and the beginning of the end for the Communist hold on the people's souls. It had come at a good time, just as she was finishing her book. Challenges remained, but over a two-year period all had been surmounted and conquered. The book had become a best-seller in the international market.

When Galya finished soaking, she hurriedly washed her hair under the tap, dried with a thin towel, and redressed. Her clothes smelled of travel and sweat, but she had no others. All she owned were in the two suitcases left behind when she ran from the bus. Members of the KGB were probably already distributing them to friends and relatives. She smiled. No. One thing was certain—her clothes were too poor for such people. They would be discarded as rags.

She had intended to spend her savings on furniture and dishes, but now some would have to go for new clothes. Her decision to keep the package could be expensive.

After applying what little makeup she used, Galya combed out her wet hair and cleaned up the bathroom. Then she joined the others in the kitchen.

Small even by Russian standards, the table was shoved into a tiny alcove carved out of the wall near the window. There was room for two people to sit comfortably, but four small stools were crowded into the space. A woman Galya had never met before stood a few feet away at the stove cooking cutlets.

Rustam sat his teacup down and stood, introducing Galya to the cook.

"This is Larissa. She is your hostess, and a friend."

Larissa smiled. "Sit. I will have this finished in a moment."

Larissa was probably in her mid-forties, tall, thin, with dark hair that hung to her shoulders. Her complexion was smooth, and it took very little makeup to make her large, sad eyes beautiful.

"Larissa was with the Kirov for many years," Rustam said.

Galya remembered now. "Larissa Vavilova! You were wonderful to watch. I saw you on television many times."

Larissa seemed pleased at the recognition as she placed a plate of cutlets and potatoes in front of Galya. On the table were cheese, bread, juice, and vegetables cut into slices. Seeing the condition of the apartment and the bare cupboards, Galya wondered where it had all come from.

Larissa pulled up a chair with a plate of her own, seeming to read Galya's mind.

"Your cousin is a savior. This is not the only time he has filled my table to overflowing," Larissa said. Rustam turned slightly red and reached for a piece of bread.

"You disappeared from the ballet," Galya said.

"I refused to go to bed with one of the heads of the cultural ministry." She shrugged. "He considered the women of the ballet his personal harem. At first there was nothing he could do about my rejection of his advances—my success was a deterrent. But when my age and a broken ankle allowed others to take my place, he had his vengeance for my rejection." She paused. "I lost my position."

"The papers said only that you were ill. Then there was nothing," Galya said.

Larissa smiled. "I was sent to Murmansk—a small, insignificant theater there. My new partner was clumsy, drunk half the time. While doing a difficult move he dropped me." She lifted her arm. Galya hadn't noticed the slightly deformed elbow. "It ended my career."

"They gave her a pension," Rustam said with disgust. "A measly forty rubles a month. Once you incur the wrath of the party . . . " He put the bread to his mouth as if to keep himself quiet.

Larissa smiled at him. "It wasn't so bad, Rustam. I met Konstantin. We were happy."

"Konstantin?" Galya asked.

"My husband. My married name is Nogin, but since his death I have returned to my own name." She paused. "He was in the navy. A good man, captain of his ship. He knew our marriage would make things difficult for him, but we married anyway. There were no more promotions for him, but we were happy." Larissa's eyes saddened, but she seemed to want to talk. It was that way in Russia now, people talking about the old system, how it had hurt them. It had a cleansing effect.

"He was transferred to the Black Sea Fleet when our leaders went to war with Afghanistan. I was not allowed to go. Six weeks after I had our son, I was called to party headquarters." Larissa's eyes glazed over as if looking at something in the distance, beyond the walls of the apartment. "It was a cold day, even in the buildings. I waited for hours, knowing, feeling something terrible had happened. Finally a woman called me to the counter. Her eyes never met mine; she never smiled. Shuffling through papers, she yanked one free and handed it to me, then waved me away. It was a letter announcing my husband's death."

There was a long pause as they all reached back into their own experiences, remembering. They would always remember. The scars ran deep for every Russian who fought being controlled.

"I nearly dropped the baby," Larissa said.

The baby. Galya saw no signs of a child in this tiny apartment, no signs of anyone but Larissa, but she was afraid to ask, and Larissa seemed to be finished, unable to say more. The dancer stood and went to the stove, pouring hot water into a cup through a strainer full of what looked like mint leaves. Galya wondered how many cups of tea those leaves had tried to flavor.

Rustam brooded over his empty plate. Galya could sense the anger. She was beginning to see her cousin now—the official Rustam Starkov and the unofficial one. The first played the games of survival while the second found ways to rebel by providing funds and support for the unfavored. It was his way of thumbing his nose at the system in which he was still forced to function. It was a game Russians had played for three hundred years. As she sipped the last of her tea, Galya wondered if Natalya knew of this side of her husband, but she doubted it. She would either forbid it or leave him for it.

She felt guilt for her judgment. She didn't know Natalya Starkov, didn't understand where the fear that inhabited the woman's soul came from. Until one understood those things, one was incapable of judging another's actions.

"After Gorbachev was replaced by Yeltsin," Larissa said, "I left Murmansk to come to Leningrad. I had a limited passport, but they still let me go. I kept thinking they would remove me from the train before it left the station, that they were just playing games with me. I was in a compartment with a family of three. They seemed as frightened as I was. We all breathed a sigh of relief when the train started to move. When the last of the apartment buildings, then the small homes on the edge of the city disappeared behind us, the air in the compartment seemed to change. It smelled fresh—the scent of freedom." She placed her teacup on the table and sat on the stool. "Rustam was waiting at the station when I arrived." Her dark eyes showed the feelings she had for Galya's cousin. "He is a true friend."

Galya smiled at the red in Rustam's face. In a nation where nothing worked anymore, where people were tired of sacrificing themselves for something most of them had stopped believing in years ago, friendship was the one true commodity people had left to offer one another.

"Konstantin was my friend." Rustam shrugged. Galya realized how little she knew about her cousin. Her mind struggled to find information, and she realized there wasn't any. Distance and the system had separated them, kept them from one another. She suddenly had another reason to hate it. It hadn't just affected her own small family, her parents. It had denied her this family, her cousins, aunts, and uncles, deprived them all of each other. Oh, how she hated it!

"We met when he was stationed in Leningrad," Rustam said. "We both belonged to an underground group called Pozhar then. When he was transferred to Murmansk, I visited him many times, and Natalya and I were at the wedding. I was Konstantin's best man."

Pozhar. Fire. A group considered ultra-nationalist. Anti-Communist to the core, it had survived political purges because of its ability to hide its real intentions under a mountain of propaganda that made it look just the opposite. Pozhar had effectively used the party's own methods to keep the party from discovering its true intentions.

Galya knew that Pozhar wanted, even back then, to remove Russia from the Union because they felt the other parts, such as the Ukraine and the Baltic states, were sucking Russia dry of resources. She knew they wanted platforms that would encourage more births and fewer abortions and divorces. A moral renaissance they called it, with a return to religion and the country's roots. They admired Pushkin, Lermontov, and Dostoyevsky, just as Galya had. That was why she had been encouraged by their growth.

But then things had gone bad. Fanatics had taken control, crying for a purification of the country and the blood. They blamed all their ills on the Jews and, like Pamyat, another nationalist movement, spent most of their time searching for mythical enemies. Both groups disseminated information about mysterious groups bent on the annihilation of the Russian people. The great Satan had become world masonry, Zionism, and imperialism.

Larissa smiled. "Neither of us belongs to Pozhar now. We have other interests, less subversive." She smiled. "At least we think so."

Galya looked into the woman's dark eyes, curious about the statement, about what group Larissa might mean.

"We wondered for many years if anyone wanted Russia to survive. If anyone had any solutions. With Gorbachev things began to change, and we changed. We found something better than Pozhar," Rustam said.

There were few in Russia who didn't wonder if Russia would survive her latest revolution. Few believed in Communism anymore, but some hung onto it simply because nothing better had been offered. Their attempts at capitalism and Western democracy were failing miserably. No one knew how to operate a democracy, not even Yeltsin, and the people were afraid to make the changes necessary for it to succeed, especially the petty bureaucrats who knew they would have to give up what power, control, and access they had gained over the past seventy years. To compensate, they were trying to adjust socialism to a more democratic form, but that was like splitting an apple into hundreds of parts, and, so far, it had done nothing but create chaos. Now there were hundreds of groups, all out to get a piece of the pie. It pained Galya, but ultra-nationalism like that professed by Pozhar was becoming extremely popular. Some, like Vladimir Zhirinovsky, watered it down for international consumption, but underlying principles included racism, nuclear rearmament, and a return to the worst that Communism had to offer. He and others like him used people's problems to keep democratic reform at bay while trying to get a return to the old system under a new name, a system that would push Russia back into its own dark ages.

Larissa glanced at Rustam. "Your cousin told me about what happened at the bus, about the package. Do you still have it?"

Galya looked up, the question forcing her mind onto a different track. Reaching for the bag by the side of her chair, she took out the package. Larissa and Rustam shuffled the dishes to the sink, making room.

Galya inspected the brown wrapping. It was about the size of a small book, four inches wide, six high, an inch thick, tied with dirty pieces of string. She began untying the knots.

As she folded back the paper, she found herself holding her breath. Galya knew what she was looking at was important to someone with connections to the KGB. All her senses tingled with expectation as she lifted the prize from its package.

It was a book. The front cover was olive green, old and dirty. The back cover was missing, and a large number of pages were gone as well. She opened it carefully. As she did so, several pictures fell into her lap. She picked them up and laid them on the table, then went back to her investigation of the contents. Rustam leaned over and peered at the writing.

"It is not Russian," he said.

"No, I think it is a Nordic language. Possibly Finnish or Norwegian. It is in longhand, a diary. See, at the top of the page is a date." She turned a page. It crackled with stiffness. The book was badly water damaged, and many of the pages stuck together enough that Galya was afraid to try separating them. "Some Russian names." She pointed at two different places on one of the pages. "And here." She pointed. "The name of Leningrad."

"The old man on the bus, he was Nordic then?" Larissa asked.

Galya shrugged. "Maybe, but I don't think so. He seemed very Russian to me."

"Then this is not his diary?" Larissa queried.

"No, I think it is a woman's writing." She turned back to the inside front cover. There was Norwegian writing. A name. "Nora . . . " She squinted at the barely legible words. "Nora Larsen," she said, a tinge of excitement in her voice. "And here.

Yes, Tromso, Norway." She sat the book carefully on the table and picked up the pictures.

The first was a group picture, aged and of brownish tint. Its corners were broken off, and it showed wear from a good deal of handling. A dozen people stood in front of an old shack, a tall, snow-covered mountain in the background. There were very few trees, and the snow looked deep. Most of the group were men dressed in white camouflaged winter gear with backpacks of the same color. Each had a set of skis leaning against one shoulder, and all were armed with rifles. A woman stood in the same gear at the center of the picture, her blond hair falling onto her shoulders.

"This man. He is American," Rustam said. "You see. The hat. The insignia is of the American army air force."

Galya nodded.

"And this one," Rustam went on. "And these two, they are Russian." One young man of slight build stood on the other side of the girl next to the American. The other two stood behind him, each looking over a shoulder. "All the rest are Norwegian."

"How can you tell?" Galya asked.

"Training, Cousin. I was in the Russian military for five years. We learned to recognize insignias, the weapons, the gear of every foreign nation. These are all World War II uniforms," he said. Galya sensed a change in Rustam's voice and could tell the military hadn't been a pleasant experience for him.

Galya moved to the next picture, of a couple in front of a small house. They wore leather coats with a wool lining and civilian clothes. The woman stood in front of the man, his arms around her waist and his chin near her left shoulder.

"The American and the woman," Rustam said.

"Nora Larsen," Galya added. She turned the picture over. There was a date, March 1941, and another name. "The American is Kitrick. Robert Kitrick."

"They look very happy," said Larissa.

"I wonder what this American was doing in Norway in March of 1941," Galya mused. "The Americans were not in the war then."

"But the Norwegians were under siege by Hitler," Rustam said. "Possibly the American was there to help them in their fight. Train them. They did such things, I am sure."

"What about the Russians?" Galya asked, going back to the first picture.

Rustam sat back in his chair. "Umm. With an American. A complication. March 1941. Russia, Stalin really, had turned on the United States, vehemently denouncing them for everything they did. Russia and Germany were still allies even though there were signs that some Russians knew Germany was going to break the agreement. It was just a matter of when. Trouble was, no one could get Stalin to listen until it was too late. That was in June." He paused. "Puzzling. Stalin was very much anti-American at this point, and I find it difficult to believe he would have sent these men in the picture. Possibly they were traitors or were working on their own. Possibly they aren't Russian at all, just dressed as Russians for a mission of some kind."

"Too many possibilities." Galya went to the next picture, of the woman and a different young man. Galya was captured by the youthful but stately good looks of the man—actually more of a boy, even though he seemed to have acquired a thin blond moustache. She turned the picture over.

"Nora and . . . " It was in Norwegian.

"Wilhulm. William." Rustam had picked up the diary. "You need someone who can read Norwegian."

Galya nodded as she took the book, placing the pictures back inside.

"Why would this be of interest to the Ministry of Security?" Larissa asked.

Galya shrugged, her mind already working on how she would approach the day. She must steer clear of the places the KGB might look for her. By now they would know her name, would be starting to search if they suspected she might know something. She would have to be careful about where she went, whom she talked to. She placed the diary back in her bag, then removed it again. "Do you have a smaller bag, Larissa? My travel bag is too bulky."

Larissa went into the room across the hall, a bedroom, and returned almost immediately with a leather purse with a heavy leather strap. She took the few things of value out of it, dumped the rest in the garbage, and handed it to Galya, who stuck her own papers inside along with the diary.

"You need a restorationist to open the rest of the pages," Rustam said. "I know such a man."

"Can he be trusted?" Galya asked.

Rustam nodded. "A good friend. We have been through much together." He glanced at Larissa. "He works for the Hermitage."

"Rikki Mogilev," Larissa said with approval. "Yes, if anyone can work with the diary, it will be Rikki."

"I will take you," Rustam said.

Galya started to protest. Rustam waved his hand as if swatting away a fly. "I have to meet with Rikki on another matter. I am not expected at work until later today." He stood, as if it were settled, and Galya didn't pursue it.

Larissa kissed him on the cheek. "I will see you at the meeting tonight. Thank you again for the food."

Rustam smiled. An outsider might misread the relationship, but Galya understood. In Russia, real friends, people you knew you could trust with your life, were few. But when they were found, the relationship was one of total commitment—a spiritual rather than physical bond. You had so few in which you could place such trust, such friendship, that when you found such people you bound yourself to them in such a way that only death would break the connection.

"I must go to the American consulate as well," Galya said. "Can you drop me off after we meet your friend?"

"Of course. It is near Rikki's place. But what can you accomplish there?"

"If Robert Kitrick is still alive, the Americans can find him. I wish to talk to him. I want to know why he came to Russia."

Chapter Five

NICKOLAI STOOD ON THE CORNER, deep in thought, his eyes focused on the old building across the street. A direct confrontation would be dangerous, could get him killed. Was it worth the risk? What other choices did he have? He had followed Yezhov on a hunch, and the hunch had paid off, but in what way? What had Yezhov been carrying? All his informant had said was that Dimitri Bakatin was after something for Tupolev, something important, possibly illegal. He had wanted to catch Bakatin and Tupolev red-handed, had decided to follow Yezhov, find out what he was after and whether it involved illegal contraband. If it did, and if he could get photographs of an exchange, then he could arrest everybody and sort it all out. For days he had watched the amateur archaeologist search the remains of an old house at Bologoye, watched him find something in the floor of a nearby church—something Nickolai had determined must be state property and, therefore, the illegal contraband he had hoped to catch the old man delivering to Tupolev. He had followed Yezhov back to Petersburg.

All for nothing.

Now he wished he had arrested Yezhov. It would have saved the old man, and instead of having nothing, Nickolai would at least have had the package.

The two men who had come after Yezhov at the bus, Kulikov and Bondorenko, had been KGB. Their appearance shouldn't have surprised him, but it had. He had been tired. It had been a long trip, and they had caught him lax and unprepared. By the time he had seen what was happening, it was too late. Yuri Yezhov was dead, the package gone, his opportunity to nail Tupolev and Bakatin gone with it. He had messed up—a costly mistake, one he now had to work around, and a direct confrontation with Dimitri Bakatin was the only way.

Vladimir Tupolev was corrupt, a man with no scruples, no morals, who had, in the past, used his power and position to put away inestimable wealth at the expense of the Russian people. Nickolai estimated it in the hundreds of millions.

Nickolai didn't know all the ways Tupolev had become wealthy under the old regime but suspected that they included selling secrets to foreign governments and selling military weapons, stolen from Russian bases, to third-world countries. Like others who used their power to get wealth, he stashed his ill-gotten gains in foreign bank accounts, much as the Mafia bosses of Sicily or the United States.

Now, under perestroika, Tupolev was using his wealth to buy up companies that the government wanted privatized, and then, with the access his power gave him, influencing government officials in the national ministries to sell him natural resources such as oil, gas, and lumber along with the facilities needed to refine them into usable products. He then shipped them to his own plants for use or sold them on the black market, making tremendous profits.

In fact, Tupolev, through his son-in-law, Georgi Zhelin, controlled important elements within the KGB and used its resources to expand and protect his empire. Zhelin used the KGB's extensive resources to keep track of enemies and potential enemies, as decided by Tupolev, protecting their new kingdom. Anyone who questioned his conduct was bought off, was threatened, or simply disappeared.

That was how things worked in the abyss between the old command economy and the new markets of democracy—a free-for-all, with the powerful and rich like Tupolev walking away with all the spoils.

Now Tupolev was expanding. As others moved into the privatization business, he offered them greater access through his

connections and the protection Zhelin could give them under the
Ministry of Security, taking 20 percent of their profits for his services. Dimitri Bakatin, the man Nickolai was about to pay a visit,
was one of these, and he had become a millionaire doing it. So
had half a dozen others. Under present law it was all legal.

But over the past year, Vladimir Tupolev had stepped over
the line of even the new Russian economic free-for-all. He had
extended his access to organized crime and had even allowed
Zhelin to protect their operations from arrest and prosecution. The
police force found it nearly impossible to get at these new Mafia.
If they did, judges, influenced by Tupolev's money or Zhelin's
strong-arm tactics, either reduced sentences or dismissed them
altogether. In the process, Tupolev and Zhelin charged a hefty fee
or took a piece of the operation they were going to protect. By
doing so, they had garnered a healthy handful of organizations
that controlled the Russian black market. Drugs, firearms, prosti-
tution, and a myriad of other ills were quickly coming under Old
Man Tupolev's influence.

In Nickolai's mind, everything bad about Communism was
being kept alive by the Tupolevs of Russia, being used to widen
their power base and keep real change at bay while they lined
their own pockets. That caused untold pain and suffering to the
Russian people, destroying the chance for the nation to move out
of the past and into the future. In Nickolai's mind, at least part of
the answer was simple: Vladimir Tupolev had to be stopped.

But, so far, Nickolai had found nothing on which to hang an
indictment. Zhelin and his people in the MB protected their men-
tor like a pack of dogs, insulating him from people like Nickolai
Poltav or anyone else foolish enough to try to get something on
their master.

Nickolai was forced to grab at thin strands and endless
straws. The chance he had taken on Yezhov was that kind of
chance. Going after Bakatin was the same—except that he knew
Bakatin could be used because he was as greedy as Tupolev.

According to his sources, Kulikov and Bondorenko were taking orders from Bakatin, an assignment from Zhelin or from
Tupolev himself. It was cleaner that way, the top insulated from

the actual crime or dirty work. It kept the MB from being directly implicated in something as illegal as kidnapping so that Yeltsin couldn't discredit Zhelin and remove him from leadership.

The two agents were probably even on Bakatin's payroll, a second job as security personnel for his numerous properties. Moonlighting was legal and covered a myriad of sins that were taking place right before the public eye.

Dimitri Bakatin was hooked to Tupolev by the twin umbilical cords of fear and money, and it would take a powerful motivator to get him to cut himself free of the old man. Bakatin had to believe that he could live, breathe, and grow on his own at a greater pace than even the old man could give him. Nickolai intended to fill Bakatin's head with such dreams of grandeur and see what happened—just another way of getting at Vladimir Tupolev.

Nickolai took a deep breath. The summer air was a mixture of the sweet smell of spring flowers and the stale odor of factories that circled the city. But it was the same everywhere in Russia—the smell of the new mingled with the stench of the old.

He should have stayed in retirement, regardless of what his old friend Boris Yeltsin wanted. What he asked was an impossible job. But Yeltsin knew him, knew his past, knew Nickolai wanted Tupolev for more than corruption. He wanted him for cold-blooded murder: Vladimir Tupolev had been responsible for the killing of Nickolai's wife.

Nickolai straightened his tie. The business suit gave his six-foot, 190–pound frame an air of power. As much as he hated suits, he knew when to "dress up," when to use his physical assets to get across his message. This was one of those times.

Nickolai waited for traffic to clear, then stepped into the street, crossing as quickly as he could. When he reached the other side, he walked toward the door. It was time to drop in on Dimitri Bakatin.

Chapter Six

RUSTAM HAD CALLED RIKKI MOGILEV after he and Galya had decided it might be best to meet him in a public place away from the Hermitage. They were browsing through rows of watercolors, acrylics, and oil paintings hanging from displays in the square outside of Nevsky metro station. Most of the works were for sale to tourists who wanted a painting of one of Petersburg's famous sights. St. Isaac's Cathedral, St. Saviour's Church, and the Hermitage seemed to be the most widely represented, but Galya was more intrigued with the colorful paintings of Russian folk tales. The colors were bright, the characters clearly drawn. She wanted one badly, but at more than thirty thousand rubles—twenty dollars American—it was impossible.

As she and Rustam bent close to one such painting, a man of slight build sidled up to them, peering at the work.

"Brother Mogilev!" Rustam said with visible delight. "Thank you for coming. It is good to see you."

Mogilev lit up like a street lamp. "President, good to see you as well." They shook hands vigorously. Galya was mystified at the names but settled her mind that it must be some sort of code. "This is my cousin, Galya Starkova, from Novosibirsk. She has a piece of work for you." They started to walk away from the displays and toward the canal Griboedova by way of Nevsky Prospekt. Galya started to retrieve the diary, but Mogilev placed his hand gently on her arm.

"A better place. Wait a bit, all right?"

Galya nodded.

"While we walk there, I have another matter, Rikki. A Church matter," Rustam said.

Rikki nodded for Rustam to continue while Galya listened in, confused. What church? Why would Rustam be discussing church matters? He was no priest, not even a member of the Orthodox Church, that Galya knew of.

"The tithing report. Did it get delivered on time? President Hayes says that he never received it," Rustam said.

Rikki looked a little concerned. "I sent it with Brother Orbeli. I am sure he took it . . . No, wait. His car broke down. Yes. He called me. He probably still has it in his possession. I will go there as soon as I can and take the report to President Hayes."

"No, no, that isn't necessary. It is only a report. See that he brings it to meeting Sunday if he hasn't delivered it by then, and we can make arrangements."

Galya wasn't able to follow the rest of the discussion any better. Talk of a relief society, primary, firesides, branches! It was all a mystery! But her admiration for Rustam grew as she watched him make decisions and discuss issues important to both men. Rustam was a gifted leader and was doing his duty, his Komsomol training finally good for something.

As they reached St. Saviour's Church, they turned into Mikhaylovskiy Garden, where they sat on a bench and Galya showed him the diary.

"Many pages are stuck firmly together. I can separate them but not without some damage," Rikki said.

"You are the artisan, Rikki," Rustam said. "We leave you to decide."

Rikki put the rewrapped package into his own bag. "Tomorrow afternoon. I will do all I can and have recommendations." He said good-bye and left the garden. Galya and Rustam started back to where they had parked Rustam's small Zhiguili.

"Cousin, you are a mysterious man," Galya said. "What was all that about? What are these tithings, and what is a fireside? And why does he call you president?"

Rustam laughed lightly, blushing. "The title is most difficult for me. It still makes me uncomfortable."

"What does it mean?"

"It means that I am a branch president for my church. I have responsibility for a number of people, mostly Russians, who belong as well." Rustam tried to explain the terminology and answer Galya's questions. By the time they had returned to his car, Galya thought she had it straight.

"Why religion, Rustam?" She asked as they pulled away from the curb. "Why not politics or leadership in a youth organization or something?"

Rustam laughed again. "You act as if I had joined to lead, as if the Church is some sort of club. It is very different from that."

"Then my question is even more important? Why religion?"

"It isn't just religion, Galya. In fact, it is nothing like the religion you and I grew up with. There are no cathedrals, no priests, no icons. We don't light candles and pray to saints for help, and we don't worship through chants and songs, at least not like the old way."

Galya smiled. "With all these gone, what is left?"

Rustam laughed. "Yes, what. Just Christ and the Holy Spirit. Just God," he said in reverence. "And a prophet."

"Prophet?"

"Like in the Bible. Isaiah, Ezekiel. Peter, James, John. Prophets. Like those."

Galya laughed again, picturing men in white gowns and long beards who brought down fire from heaven and parted oceans. She had read the Bible, secretly. She had admired its teachings when she was young but was not a believer in its stories any more than she was in the fairy tales and folklore of the Russian past—especially since God had sat still while her family and so many others had suffered hardships worse than death—if there was a God.

She felt a ridiculing word on the end of her tongue but bit it off. They drove in silence until reaching the embassy.

Galya started to get out, then closed the door, staring at her cousin. "This is what you found to replace Pozhar?"

He nodded.

"And Natalya, Larissa? They are also religious?"

"Natalya is afraid. We are watched sometimes because of our beliefs. She thinks religion is dangerous. But Natalya thinks that reading newspapers and going to art displays in the park are dangerous. She does not believe we have freedoms. To her, all that is happening is a ruse, a deception, and the government is just lying in wait, ready to destroy us for our disloyalty to Lenin and socialism." There was an edge of disgust to his voice. He took a deep breath. "It will take a long time for Natalya to be anything but afraid. As much as I love her, it drives me crazy."

"But Larissa?"

"She joined first. In fact, she was one of the first converts to our church in this country." He shrugged, smiling. "What did she have to lose? They had already taken away everything but what was in her heart. Believing in an American religion certainly couldn't make matters worse."

"An American church?"

"It started in America, but it has members almost everywhere. There are already several thousand in our country."

Galya shook her head in disbelief. A taxi was pulling in behind them, waiting to empty its passengers in front of the American consulate. The driver jammed a fist against the horn. Galya opened the door and got out, then watched as Rustam waved good-bye and drove away. Religion! It was the last thing Galya would have suspected as a replacement for Pozhar. They were so . . . opposite!

She started toward the consulate's front entrance while glancing at her watch. Just after lunch. This shouldn't take long. She walked through the door, her mind diverted by what she considered her cousin's passing fantasy, as Pozhar had been. People were looking for solutions to their problems, ways of escape. And she supposed American religion was as good as anything— especially if it used American dollars to ease the economic burden that was ruining her country.

She presented her passport to the guards, shoving the thoughts aside. It was time to find out about Robert Kitrick.

Chapter Seven

Up CLOSE, NICKOLAI COULD SEE that the old place had been remodeled—new windows, new paint, probably a new roof. Entering through new glass doors, he found himself inside a modern foyer. The walls were freshly painted, the floor clean and polished. To his left, a waiting area was well furnished in heavy, plush furniture that sat on a thick rug of wine-red wool. The tables were glass, covered in the latest in Western magazines—*U.S. News, Time,* even *Vogue*—copies in English, German, and French, the languages of the entrepreneur.

Two chandeliers hung in the room, crystal and gold with not even a single light bulb unlit. Now there was a sign of wealth and progress. Dimitri Bakatin had more wealth in his lobby than the average Russian would see come through the front door in a lifetime. Nickolai wasn't sure if he was impressed or disgusted.

The security station was to his left. Two guards in suits, badges hanging from their handkerchief pockets, sat behind the desk. One had eyes only for the monitors before him; the other was following Nickolai's every move.

"Who is it you want to see?" asked the guard, an attitude of non-interest orchestrating his posture.

Reaching into his suit pocket, Nickolai removed his papers and handed them to the guard while registering an opinion about the man on the other side of the desk. Broad shoulders, hard head—typical muscle.

"Dimitri Bakatin."

The security guard's eyes came up. "Is he expecting you?"

"I think he will see me. If you will call him, please?" Nickolai pointed at the phone.

"I cannot disturb Mr. Bakatin unless you have an appointment."

Nickolai pointed at the papers in the guard's hand. "You'd better take a closer look at those."

The guard did, then picked up the phone and quickly dialed a number. Turning his back on Nickolai, he spoke softly into the phone.

The guard placed the phone back in its cradle, a look of relief on his face. He handed Nickolai his papers, the one with Yeltsin's presidential seal now on top. "Take the elevator to the second floor. His aide will be waiting for you."

Nickolai forced a smile, then moved through the security gate.

As the elevator doors closed and the machine began to rise, Nickolai thought about the last time he and Bakatin had seen each other.

1951. Dimitri Bakatin and Nickolai Poltav had been considered the two most talented members inducted into the KGB that year. Competitive and hardworking, with an insatiable desire to protect Russia from forces they were told were destroying her, they had graduated from the training school at the top of their group. Nickolai had been the better tactician and planner, Bakatin the best at firearms and interrogation. Both were equally good at political studies and Marxist/Leninist philosophy. And, they had been best friends.

Training. Challenging, hard, exciting. A man's world of adventure. Bakatin and Nickolai had thrived on it, both determined, both dreaming of the day they would earn the Star of Lenin for their single-handed heroics against the capitalist hordes from the West. Nickolai smiled at the memory. What glorious safety there was in the fantasyland created by Communist indoctrinators.

With the first case assignment, reality set in. Nickolai quickly realized that all their training made them no more than spies in the business of destroying the lives of their own people, using fragments of real information and gobs of the manufactured kind, turning friends against friends, neighbors into informants. He hated it even as he did it. The inner guilt and anger at what he was doing started to eat at his gut. He started to drink to avoid the mental anguish, sobering up just enough to keep his job but not enough to see the faces, the lives of the people he was destroying. Bakatin also drank. But he lifted the glass to celebrate. For Bakatin each arrest cleansed the system. "It is like being a surgeon, Nickolai," he said once as they met after work to drink. "There is a cancer that must be cut out to save the life of mother Russia. If it isn't, our country will be destroyed, its greatness nothing but a memory. *We* must cut it out, Nickolai. *We* must become its greatest surgeons!"

Nickolai tried to talk sense into his friend, make him understand what evil they were doing. But Dimitri refused to listen, then began avoiding Nickolai, even threatening him. Nickolai had known then that a time would come when he would have to face Dimitri—when their two different belief systems would conflict.

The elevator doors opened. A young man stood to one side dressed in the tailored suit of a business executive. The silk, handpainted tie was from France, and the shoes looked like handmade Italian. A heavy gold ring with a large diamond hung loosely on a thin, long, almost feminine finger. The black hair was slicked down and combed straight back, the eyes set far apart above high cheekbones, while thin lips and an aquiline nose that almost looked out of place finished his appearance. He seemed to be the culmination of too many races to count.

As Nickolai exited the elevator, the man stepped forward and extended his hand. It was a strong grip, the thin fingers hardened by exercise. The eyes were intelligent, cold, calculating. Nickolai immediately registered a warning. He had dealt with men like this before. Young, ambitious, raised in a system that schooled them in the art of winning at any cost, they usually ended up on top of the heap or under someone else's feet, trampled in the race for survival. These days few were ever in the middle. This was a man who would betray his own family to maintain his lifestyle.

"Mr. Poltav. I am Aleksei Shelepin, Mr. Bakatin's assistant.

This way please," he said mechanically. "He is anxious to see you."

I'll bet, Nickolai thought. Bakatin and he hadn't spoken for more than forty years. His old friend would be about as happy to see him as Yeltsin would be to see the return of Gorbachev.

The office was spacious and well furnished, with large windows that looked out across the Fontanka into the Summer Gardens created in 1704 by Peter the Great. The aide ushered Nickolai through heavy doors into the office of Dimitri Bakatin.

Bakatin removed his glasses and got to his feet. Dismissing the aide, he came around the desk and greeted Nickolai warmly, two kisses on each cheek.

"Nickolai. It is hard to believe you are here. It has been . . . "

"A long time, Dimitri. How are you?"

"Old, can't you see?" Bakatin laughed the loud boisterous laugh that had been so familiar to Nickolai in their younger days, one that still made Nickolai smile. Actually, his old friend seemed trim and fit. His silver hair was still full, his face a little rounder but hard, with no sagging jowls or double chin. His shoulders were still broad even though there did seem to be an extra bulge over his belt.

"Yes, well, time leaves no one behind," Nickolai said, moving his hand through his own thick but graying hair.

"Please, sit," Bakatin said, pointing to a plush leather chair. "What brings the president's special investigator to Petersburg?" Bakatin lifted two cigars from an expensive hand-painted and lacquered box on his desk, offering one to Nickolai. Nickolai waved it off. Bakatin shrugged, putting one back, then nipping off the end of the other with a pair of scissors before placing it in his lips and lighting it.

"No time for small talk? It's been nearly forty years," Nickolai said.

Bakatin's brows lifted, then lowered as he shrugged his shoulders. "We both know everything there is to know about the other. You kept track. I kept track. It's that way with old friends who have parted ways." He blew out a stream of smoke before going on. "Especially when the parting is under less than favorable circumstances."

"Less than favorable for whom?"

Bakatin smiled. "There was nothing personal back then, you know that."

Nickolai looked toward the window. "How is Marina?"

Bakatin eyed him carefully as he leaned back in his chair. "Very well. I will tell her you are in town, that you asked about her."

Nickolai smiled. "You have taken good care of her?"

Bakatin nodded, biting down hard on the cigar. "Nickolai, you didn't come to find out if your sister was still putting up with her husband, and I don't think you are here drumming up support for your new boss. You know how I think."

Nickolai smiled. "I *thought* I knew your thinking." He glanced around the room at the expensive furniture and artwork. "You have changed. The man who wanted to purge the country of every vestige of Western decadence seems to have rehabilitated his thinking."

Bakatin forced the tightness in his jaw to relax. "I am a realist. When the horse you are riding dies under you, you have two choices: to go down with it, breaking your own neck, or to get off at the right moment and find a new horse."

Nickolai laughed. "You always were a chameleon, Dimitri. When we were young I envied you that."

Bakatin waved his hands at the same artwork and furnishings Nickolai had pointed out a moment earlier. "A survivalist, Nickolai, who has discovered greater comfort in a new direction." He leaned forward. "Now, what is it you want from me?"

The eyes were cold, devoid of the friendship that once had shown there.

Nickolai removed the papers, leaned forward, and handed them to Bakatin, who glanced at them.

"What are these?"

"Papers impounding all assets associated with one of your companies, EuroRuss, for nonpayment of taxes and the illegal shipment of foreign goods into the country."

Bakatin looked more carefully, then back at Nickolai, his eyebrows lifted. "This comes within the authority Yeltsin has given you?"

"It does."

"Do I have any recourse?"

"The courts. At present levels of efficiency your case should be tried in about 1997."

Bakatin blew smoke across the desk toward Nickolai. The distance between them prevented its arrival.

"Your new office will be very busy, Nickolai. Everybody in Russia does these things. It is called cutting costs and profit incentive. Your boss is slashing off the very hand he created to save his new reforms."

"Cutting costs is legal as long as you don't try to circumvent the laws regarding what items can come into the country. You have disregarded those laws. Actual tax evaders are simple thieves. They steal from the system that gives them opportunity in the first place. Under such conditions, neither can survive. In addition to these, it is my job to investigate links between corporations like yours and the government—find out if kickbacks and favors are giving you unfair advantage in the marketplace. Things like that could ruin the new economy, don't you think?"

"In the past this was the place of the Ministry of Security."

Nickolai smiled. "Things change. They have to when the watch dog needs watching." He leaned back. "I will need copies of all of the books you keep on EuroRuss. Everything."

"My corporation is completely legal, Nickolai. You will find no such connections." Bakatin's smile disappeared. Nickolai could see beads of sweat gathering on his forehead. "If taxes weren't paid, if there is a misunderstanding about what we have brought into the country, I am sure we can come to some agreement."

"Maybe."

Bakatin leaned forward, realizing he was being given a thin rope with which to rescue his largest company. "Maybe? Nickolai, have you come here to make some sort of a deal? Has the man with morals finally lost them and now wishes to take advantage like everyone else? I am shocked."

"Under the tsars such a statement would have me slapping your face and demanding satisfaction. Right now all I am interested in is information, so I'll forget the insult and satisfaction."

"What information?" Bakatin said, wary.

"Don't worry, Dimitri, I won't force any confessions out of you, even if I do think you are as crooked as a silhouette of the Ural mountains. I want everything you can get on a man named Yezhov—Yuri Yezhov."

The movement in the eyes was slight but recognizable, and Nickolai noted it.

"What has he done?"

Nickolai began telling the story he had rehearsed before entering the building. "We think he may be part of a group who is selling precious archaeological artifacts to foreigners—millions of dollars' worth. I had him under surveillance and followed him here, to Petersburg. He was carrying a package that seems to have disappeared. I want to find it."

Bakatin looked away, exhaling a cloud of smoke. "I don't understand what that has to do with me."

"Two KGB, excuse me, Ministry of Security officers were waiting for Yezhov when he got off a bus yesterday. Their appearance caused Yezhov to panic. He ran into traffic and was hit by a late-night delivery truck. I understand the agents were on your payroll at the time. Moonlighting. Their names are Kulikov and Bondorenko."

Bakatin shook his head, a fake look of mystification across his face. "Kulikov. Bondorenko. I don't recognize the names. Your sources must be mistaken. If they are agents, why don't you take your case to the Minister of Security, Georgi Zhelin? President Yeltsin's authority—"

"We both know that the president's signature means nothing to the Ministry—especially not to Zhelin. My position threatens him because, frankly, he is a part of the problem I am supposed to resolve. Zhelin considers our president a temporary inconvenience and obeys him only when it will give him, and those to whom he sells his soul, advantage. He will do everything he can to stop my investigation, to tie me up in a thick wad of bureaucratic paper pushing." Nickolai paused. "If Kulikov and Bondorenko *weren't* working under you, I am sure your contacts in the agency could find out who they *were* working for—and much quicker than I can obtain the same information."

Bakatin leaned forward, gripping the cigar between his first two fingers. "Let us assume I can get what you want. What am I to receive in return?"

Nickolai returned the steady gaze. It was the way the system worked—a favor for a favor, tit for tat. It would take two generations to change it, if it could be changed at all. He did not intend to change it today.

"I will give you thirty days to correct the mistake with EuroRuss and pay the proper taxes. I will give you the chance to save your largest company."

Bakatin sat back, the cigar going back to his mouth, his eyes never leaving those of Nickolai, measuring. "And if I refuse your offer?"

"I believe you are a smarter businessman than that, Dimitri. I give you the opportunity to save EuroRuss and bring it within the law. It is a fair payment for the information I want, and fully within the discretionary powers of my office. Compared to what I think Yezhov's package may give me, EuroRuss is a very small thing, especially if you bring the company in line with present law."

Bakatin was biting hard on the cigar, cutting it nearly in half with his teeth.

"Your concern for the welfare of EuroRuss is heartwarming." He leaned forward. "All right, I'll get your information—this time. Where can I reach you?"

Nickolai handed him a piece of paper with several phone numbers on it. "The first is my office in Moscow. The second is my office here in Petersburg. The third is where I am staying." Nickolai stood and went to the door. Bakatin remained seated, turning his chair to face the window as his old friend closed the door behind him. The meeting was over.

Shelepin entered the room.

"Have him followed," Bakatin said.

Shelepin picked up the phone and gave the orders.

"Do you know who that was?" Bakatin asked when Shelepin had put down the phone.

"Nickolai Poltav, your brother-in-law."

Shelepin knew the rest as well. Poltav was a former member of the KGB who had been exiled with position by Beria, Stalin's personal executioner. The report Shelepin had pulled up on his direct link inside KGB files said Poltav needed rehabilitation. When Beria was executed by Krushchev, Poltav and others who had refused to follow Beria were made heroes. He was given the Star of Lenin and a job in the Moscow police department. Eventually he became its leader. Retired in 1989. Recently recalled by Yeltsin to head a new special investigations department responsible for ferreting out corporate crime and mafiosi involvement in the new economy. Yes, he knew who the man was. He was a formidable and determined enemy.

"We were brand new, still wet behind the ears and malleable. Beria wanted us to kill Krushchev. Nickolai and two others refused," Bakatin said.

"The report said the others were shot by Beria."

"Nickolai escaped because important people intervened for him. He should count his blessings."

"The plot to kill Krushchev?"

"Was never carried out. A leak. Krushchev imprisoned and then executed Beria. The rest of us scrambled to reposition. I was lucky—I had a friend in high places. Two of the others disappeared entirely. One was reassigned to hard labor in the mines of Magadan. I understand he died there." He took a deep breath. "The key to survival, Shelepin, is knowing when to jump ship."

The aide smiled. "What did he want?"

"Information."

"About what?"

"Yuri Yezhov." Bakatin told Shelepin about Nickolai's offer. "See that EuroRuss is cleaned up and the taxes paid. Prepare the paperwork so I can hand-deliver it to Nickolai. I want the company removed from his hit list. Although I think his office is bluster and we have enough power to circumvent him, I don't want to challenge his authority unless it becomes a forced issue."

The aide was pouring himself a drink and hesitated while receiving his instructions, then continued. "Yezhov. The man killed yesterday. The one we suspect to be the courier. We told Kulikov to keep the old man's death a secret."

"When Yezhov was killed, Nickolai was there. There wasn't much Kulikov could do about it."

"A coincidence?"

"Nickolai was following Yezhov. He says the old man is suspected of belonging to a group that is selling Russian artifacts to foreigners for private profit. It comes under his office's jurisdiction."

"From the sound of the mandate Yeltsin gave Poltav, everything *we* do could falls under his jurisdiction."

"Why didn't Kulikov tell us that Nickolai questioned him?"

Shelepin shrugged. "I'll ask him. Do you buy Poltav's story about the reason he followed Yezhov?"

Bakatin smiled. "Very well rehearsed, but a lie. He knows that Yuri Yezhov was clean. To Nickolai the old man was nothing more than bait. He hoped to use Yezhov to trap Vladimir Tupolev. For personal reasons Nickolai has been after Tupolev for years. Nickolai must have contacts in the KGB or in Tupolev's organization to have found out about Yezhov—looking for something to prosecute Tupolev on."

"He has nothing."

"Not exactly. He connected Yezhov to us or he wouldn't have been here. Now he pushes for an opening."

"Then he knows of our involvement—that it was us whom Tupolev asked to get the package."

"Yes, but he will not concern himself with us. It still remains Tupolev that Nickolai wants, and it is Tupolev that Yeltsin wants. We are no threat to either of them if we give Nickolai what he is after."

"You should let General Tupolev know."

Bakatin walked to the window and peered across the

Fontanka, watching the people in the gardens just beyond as they enjoyed the warm summer sun.

"What do you want me to do?" asked Shelepin.

Bakatin was silent, thinking. Nickolai was commissioner for the investigation of anti-Russian activity—a broad title with broad powers. It authorized him to investigate problems of conflict of interest, tax evasion by corporations, and illegal shipment by the same. Some believed it was Yeltsin's attempt to circumvent corruption in the Ministry of Security, the KGB—with good reason, in Bakatin's mind. Nickolai had a healthy budget and had already begun hiring investigators. With offices in Moscow, on Kalinin Prospekt, and now one in Petersburg, he was expanding. Authority, presidential. Few could challenge it. But, under present conditions in Russia, most cases Nickolai might bring to trial could be easily overcome. He laughed lightly to himself. Tupolev and his organization owned most of the judges.

Shelepin picked up a cigar and lit it, waiting for his boss to finish his meditation.

"If conditions change in Russia, Nickolai could do a lot of damage," Bakatin said.

"Yes. If he can show some progress, support will follow."

"Nickolai has influence. His position as Moscow police chief speaks well of how deep that influence goes. Our friends in both the ministries and at the KGB are worried that this might be the man to force change in enforcement." Bakatin went to his desk, a worried look on his face.

"Our business cannot afford to get caught up in intrigues between Tupolev and Nickolai's office. Especially when Yeltsin wants Tupolev unable to influence the KGB—his new MB. Our president has other plans for his new ministry, and Tupolev must be eliminated to accomplish them."

Shelepin knew they didn't have a choice. Their business revolved around KGB/MB connections both inside and outside of the country. The purchase, shipment, and distribution of goods from Germany, Norway, and Japan were all arranged by agents inside that organization and at Tupolev's request. With the KGB's help, they avoided taxes on foreign goods that companies like

Sony and IBM had to pay. The tax savings alone amounted to millions of dollars while giving their companies the ability to undercut the prices of legitimate organizations, thus giving EuroRuss and their other companies the lion's share of the market.

"We still need Tupolev's connections," Shelepin said. "The KGB—"

"I am not so sure, Aleksei. We have connections of our own now, and we are so close to becoming legitimate, to no longer needing the influence of Tupolev and Zhelin . . . "

"We will still need their protection." Shelepin set his glass on the counter. "And it is foolish to think we can ever become independent of Tupolev."

Shelepin knew the problems. Russia wasn't a democracy, would never be a democracy. Russia's new system was nothing but a free market operating within the empty shell of a command economy gone bankrupt but still struggling to keep control. It was inefficient and controlled by different people at every point. Access was everything. Contacts, money, influence, the ability to intimidate and force—all were essential tools in making the kind of profits their companies were making.

Then there was the Mafia. They had been approached on three occasions by members of Mafia organizations trying to extort money and product from Bakatin companies. Each time, connections to Tupolev and Zhelin's people in the KGB had gotten rid of the threat. There was no getting around the fact that Tupolev had definitive influence among the new Mafia that kept them at bay. Tupolev's power was needed to survive the transition taking place in Russia for at least the next ten years.

Bakatin sat back. Tupolev! How he hated the man! And Zhelin! The weasel! Bakatin couldn't stand him. He hated the idea that his future rested on the shoulders of Vladimir Tupolev and Georgi Zhelin! "Tupolev and Zhelin extort more from us for their protection than the Mafia bosses have ever suggested," he said.

"That is because Tupolev and Zhelin are the more powerful, and everyone knows it," Shelepin said. "And don't forget that

Tupolev also gives us access. We would be nothing without his connections, his influence."

"We have our own people now—people allied to us because of the business we give them!"

Shelepin laughed. "How long do you think they would last if you withdrew from Tupolev's protection? They work with us, but they are allied to him."

"We could buy their allegiance. We have the money now."

Shelepin paused, staring at his boss. "You aren't seriously thinking of leaving Tupolev? Dimitri—"

Bakatin waved at his assistant, backtracking. "It is tempting to try, but, no, I understand the problems—not the least of which is that the old man would kill me."

"He would kill us both. He is crazy."

"More crazy than you know." Bakatin knew how crazy. He had known Lavrenti Beria and Stalin himself. Compared to Tupolev, they were candidates for sainthood.

"You must be patient. Tupolev is old. Death may free us from him," Shelepin said.

"Not if he passes his baton to Zhelin."

The men were silent a moment.

"What is in that package? What was Yezhov carrying?" Shelepin asked aloud. "Why does Vladimir Tupolev want it so badly?"

"He never told me," Bakatin replied. "Zhelin instructed me that I must have someone meet Yezhov at the bus and bring the package directly to Tupolev, that it wasn't to be opened by any-one but Tupolev. He said to use Kulikov and Bonderenko; he trusted them."

"Meaning he didn't trust you. If he did, he would have let us use our own people. Those two survive on kissing Zhelin's boots." He paused. "I do not like this, Dimitri. I have never liked it. We know that Zhelin wants to take away what we have gained, that he has other plans for it. The slightest excuse—"

"I don't intend to give him any excuse, Aleksei," Bakatin said with an edge of impatience in his voice. "Relax."

There was a silence between them. Bakatin knew the package was something awfully important to the old general. It seemed almost like an obsession with him. But why use them to find the package? Zhelin controlled the KGB. He had the power to accomplish the task without ever involving Bakatin. Why not just use that power and be done with it?

He could think of only one reason. The package belonged to someone the general didn't want knowing he was involved, and everyone knew Zhelin was connected body and soul to Tupolev. So he farmed it out to someone like Bakatin to insulate himself from the enemy he sought to steal from. This was not an uncommon approach with Tupolev; he did it all the time—a way of maintaining anonymity while asserting control over those who "owed" him allegiance.

Bakatin relit his cigar, then blew a ring of smoke into the air. "Yeltsin has organized Nickolai's office for a single purpose, to bring down Vladimir Tupolev. Nickolai insulates Yeltsin from direct involvement should Nickolai fail. That also puts our president in the position to claim credit if Nickolai succeeds. My guess is that Yeltsin wants a final end to Tupolev's power."

Shelepin sat back in his chair. "No one is stronger than Tupolev, not now, not in the past ten years. Such action by the president will lead to bloody politics."

Bakatin knew that his assistant was only partly right. Tupolev's power was very strong, but recently the old general had suffered a number of defeats at Yeltsin's hand. Tupolev had backed the coup against Gorbachev and was one of those who wanted Yeltsin out as well. Yeltsin's support at the grass roots had put Tupolev in his place. Then, just last year, Tupolev had been behind the attempt of the legislature to overthrow Yeltsin. The battle at the Russian White House was a resounding defeat for the old general. Even elements within Tupolev's old domain, the army, supported the president's position then. Tupolev was weakening. Yeltsin was trying to take advantage.

"Tupolev is as weak as he has been in years, and Yeltsin knows it. And another thing, dear Aleksei, something you do not know: Yeltsin uses Nickolai Poltav for a good reason. Tupolev is a part of Nickolai's past, a part Nickolai wants to destroy. On top of that, Nickolai is a moral man, if such a person exists in Russia today. He has an overdeveloped sense of right and wrong, good and evil. He doesn't care about money, except so he can eat and keep warm in the winter, which means he can't be bought. Yeltsin appeals to everything in Nickolai that is good, and to his belief that men like Tupolev will ultimately destroy Russia or force her back into the dark ages. To some Russians, Hitler was the great Satan. To Nickolai Poltav, the great Satan is Tupolev." Bakatin stood and went to the window. "He has come to me for help."

"But to help him would be suicide."

"Contact Simonov in the records department of the KGB. Have him put together a file on Yezhov for us—everything he can get."

"For Poltav?"

"Of course. Nickolai knows most of it anyway. Do not believe for a moment that he has no contacts within the KGB, Aleksei. How do you think he discovered Tupolev's interest in Yezhov in the first place? The man wasn't a success out of mere luck. Just as we have our people, he has his. He could get the information himself, but Nickolai is testing the waters to see if he has allies. We can use that to our advantage." He squashed the smoking ash of the cigar in the large crystal ashtray atop his desk, deciding to quell the anxiety he could see rising in his young assistant. Shelepin was a genius with business and figures, but when it came to playing the games of power he still had a lot to learn.

"For us, at present, Nickolai Poltav is not the problem, Aleksei. The package is the problem. Tupolev asked us to get it. So far we have failed. You know how Tupolev deals with failure. We have Kulikov, Bondorenko, and the others looking for it. Now we have Nickolai Poltav, a better man than all the rest together. We will let him search, even help him a little, while keeping an eye on him. If he finds what we want, we will take it from him, then get rid of him. Tupolev will be pleased. And that is what you fear, isn't it—Tupolev's displeasure?" He said it with a degree of disgust that made Shelepin's face redden.

He stood to leave. "I wish only to protect our position, Dimitri."

"Yes, yes, I know." Dimitri forced a smile. "Forgive my frustration, Aleksei. This creates a lot of problems for me, and a lot of pressure."

Shelepin gave a forced smile of his own as Bakatin turned, facing the window, his large hands clasped behind his back, the cigar now in the ashtray on his desk.

"Is there anything else?" Shelepin asked.

"Did Kulikov check the bus thoroughly?"

"Yes. The package wasn't there."

"And the passengers?"

Shelepin had almost forgotten. "According to Kulikov, the last one to be in contact with Yezhov was a woman."

"Who?" Bakatin asked, facing his aide.

"Fingerprints on the luggage she left behind tell us she is Galya Starkova, the author. Kulikov considers her their most promising suspect, and they are trying to locate her."

Bakatin turned back to the window. "One caution, Aleksei. Do not underestimate Nickolai Poltav. I have never met anyone in our intelligence organizations as good as he is. I want the report on Yezhov to be complete."

Shelepin left the office.

Bakatin went to the bar and poured himself a drink. Tupolev had told him to remove Yezhov from the bus and get the package he carried. He had said it was an old document about the war and had something to do with the White Guard, an organization with which Tupolev was obsessed. The only important facts Tupolev gave Bakatin was that someone had called, someone close to Yezhov, and told him about the package. There was something in that package that had Tupolev on the edge of insanity. Bakatin might be able to use something like that to get the old man off his case and force him into a partnership more amenable to Dimitri Bakatin than it had been in the past.

He placed the empty glass in the small sink. That wouldn't work. Blackmailing Vladimir Tupolev was asking to have your bullet-riddled body fed to wild dogs on the Siberian Steppe. The man had to be eliminated, his power base and property confiscated and put to work in better ways. Or he had to be obeyed. There was no in-between.

His mind worked on the problem for an hour, figuring the pros and cons, the chances of success. At the very least, he could use Nickolai to help him find the package. At best, Nickolai could rid Bakatin and the world of Vladimir Tupolev. He liked the feel of the second, the challenge. And most of all, the freedom.

It would be tricky business, a game of playing both sides against the middle, a game that could get him killed. But if he had learned one thing as head of the KGB's international intelligence arm for twenty years, it was how to play the game.

He went to the bar and poured himself another drink. Shelepin had been only partly right. What they needed was Tupolev's organization, intact, ready to attach to their own. They did not need Tupolev. Possibly now was the time, Nickolai the catalyst, for a dangerous game that entailed getting rid of both Tupolev and Zhelin, the two most dangerous men still breathing polluted Russian air.

He stopped at the window and stared into space, his mind focused on his nemesis, the man he feared most—and hated most. He had never dared question Tupolev, let alone try to overthrow him. There was something about Tupolev—a hatred for humanity that bordered on the insane—that left Bakatin weak in the stomach.

It wasn't that Bakatin hadn't thought about killing the old man. In fact, he had dreamed about it for years. The way the old general treated him, had treated the people Bakatin loved most, especially his wife . . . More than once he had choked the life out of Tupolev in his dreams. More than once he had stood him against a wall and had him shot so full of holes that even his favorite, Georgi Zhelin, couldn't recognize him. He faced the mirror behind the bar. "It is a brave new world, Dimitri," he said to the image in the glass. "Time to stop dreaming. The question is"—he sipped the drink—"do you have the guts to act?"

Chapter Eight

GALYA HAD BEEN WAITING for nearly four hours. She was hot, tired, and frustrated, at the very end of her patience. Standing, she picked up her papers and walked past a dozen other people, all of whom had been waiting less than an hour, to the receptionist's desk. "Enough," she said in the accented English she had learned as a part of her schooling in Tomsk. "I have waited four hours. You have sent twenty people, who arrived later than I, before me. I am tired of it. I demand to see someone this minute. Your highest official, what is his name?"

"Mr. King, Rand King. But he doesn't see people like you . . . I mean, your business isn't important enough to bother—"

"You are going to lead, I will follow. To Mr. King's office. Now, please." Out of the corner of her eye Galya saw several soldiers, marines she thought, approaching at a fast pace down the hall. They had been alerted to her actions, probably by one of the secretaries sitting dumbfounded before her. She didn't have time to force the secretary further. Her eyes darted to the nameplates on the doors behind the reception area. King's was the office at the end with the double doors. Quickly she grabbed her papers, pushed through the half-door separating her from the inner sanctum of secretaries, and hurried across the thick carpet toward King's office. A man sitting at a desk near the office door, his mouth half open and his glasses sitting precariously close to the end of his nose, started to stand to block her way. She straight-armed him, knocking him toward his chair. The chair, on rollers, scooted away, and he lost his balance, tumbling to the floor, his glasses bouncing on the soft carpet unharmed.

Galya sensed the presence of the onrushing soldiers and grabbed for the knob, thrust open the door, entered, and slammed the door behind her. She grabbed the dead-bolt lock and rammed it into place, then turned to face the man at the desk. He was watching her with a half-smile across his square jaw. Tossing his pencil to the pad in front of him, he sat back in his chair, his arms folded across his chest. "Don't tell me, let me guess. A secretary who wants a raise."

Galya noted the suit coat flung over a nearby chair. His white shirt was rolled up at the sleeves, and a silk tie hung from under a loosened collar.

She cleared her throat. "Mr. King," she said, "I have been trying to see someone for more than four hours. I cannot wait any longer."

King didn't move, just stared at her. She felt as if she were being measured for a body bag. The marines pounding on the door were a sure sign she might be right.

"Open it," King said.

"Will you listen to me?" she asked adamantly.

"Do you have your paperwork?"

She lifted her hand in which the papers were gripped so tightly they were nearly bent in half.

"Doors are expensive, and getting them fixed is nearly impossible. Open it and I'll listen," King said.

The door was bulging inward as the men on the outside slammed their shoulders into it. Galya turned and quickly flipped the lock and turned the knob. The door sprang inward, depositing a marine at her feet. Two others were behind him, automatics pointed at her heart. The first scrambled to get his legs back under him, then grabbed her by the arm.

"Take it easy, soldier," King said calmly. "She doesn't have a weapon." He waved at the others, who lowered their rifles. Galya jerked her arm free.

King reached across the desk with an open hand. "The papers."

She took several steps and thrust them at him. "You Americans do everything in triplicate. You are worse than Russians. And your office manners are archaic! Is this the way you treat anyone who is not American?" she challenged.

King's head came up and his eyes flashed, then cooled. He stared back at the papers. "It says here you want us to find a Robert Kitrick for you. Why?"

"He was in my country during the war. He may have known someone I am writing an article about, a Norwegian woman. Possibly they fought in the underground together."

King gave her a tight, indulgent smile. "Everything seems in order. Thank you, Miss . . . " He glanced back at the papers, looking for her name.

"Starkova. Galya Starkova."

"The author. I read your book." He motioned to the soldiers, who took her by the arm and started to move toward the door.

"Do you treat all Russians like animals?" she said harshly while trying to jerk her arm away.

"Only the ones that don't knock before entering," King said flatly. "We'll let you know if we find Mr. Kitrick." He glanced at the paper. "You can be reached at this phone number and address?"

She nodded.

"And the picture?"

"Of the man I am looking for—with the woman. I thought you could use it to verify you were getting information on the right Robert Kitrick."

"How thoughtful. The research will take us a few days. That leaves us nothing else to discuss." He lay the papers down and leaned on the desk. "Our security is stiff here for a reason, Miss Starkova. People in this building have been threatened with bodily harm by some of your more fanatic fringe groups, and we do not intend to let them carry out their fantasies using us as guinea pigs. Keep that in mind the next time you come to visit."

Galya knew she had been wrong and that an apology was in order, but she couldn't force the words out, her pride tying her tongue. She only stared at him, then turned on her heel and left the office. The marines closed the door behind her.

Chapter Nine

BAKATIN REMOVED HIS HANDKERCHIEF and wiped his sweating palms. What did Tupolev want? Hadn't the report over the phone been enough? The promises? Or had the old general found out about his private feelings? He had said an awful lot to Shelepin. If he knew . . .

Bakatin wiped his hands again. It had really only been more dreaming, nothing for Tupolev to fear. If that was why he was being summoned, he could put the old man's concerns to rest. He wiped his brow, cursing under his breath for his cowardice. But it wasn't the first time the old general had challenged his dedication. There had been so many times. Challenges, accusations, punishments, forced begging, ridicule, humiliation.

The hatred boiled. If he did survive this meeting, he had to do something! He had to quit being such a coward!

How he hated the way Tupolev treated him, as if he were a bug to be squashed one miserable millimeter at a time! He was tired of waiting for a bullet that was always threatened but never came. Tired of the fear. Tired of the intimidation and acting the slave and beggar. He couldn't go on living like this! It was eating his gut into shreds. He had to escape the old man. At least he had to try.

The black Chaika limousine pulled through the gates of Smolny. Smolny was dear to the heart of the old general. In 1917 Smolny had housed the Revolutionary Military Committee, which supervised the preparations for the armed uprising that October. In the forties and fifties, the early years of Tupolev's climb up the Communist ladder, his blood seemed to run Communist red. His speeches on Communism were infamous. Under Stalin he had sworn hatred for the West and everything democratic; under Krushchev everything changed. He was a practiced, perfect chameleon, blending in so well that even his closest associates didn't know where he stood. The only thing that never seemed to change was his lust for blood.

Dimitri knew firsthand that Tupolev and Lavrenti Beria, the butcher of the KGB, had been allies and that Tupolev had helped plan Krushchev's assassination. Bakatin was the only man alive who knew it was Tupolev who had turned on Beria at the last minute, turning him over to Krushchev for execution. Tupolev had found out that Krushchev knew what was going on and planned to send them all to the executioner. His betrayal of Beria was an act of self-preservation even Stalin would have admired. In the process he had saved Dimitri Bakatin from Siberia or the firing squad, knowing that Dimitri would owe him for the rest of his life. Dimitri had been paying ever since.

The Chaika came to a stop at a door near the end of the left wing of the building. Lenin, the first leader of the Soviet Union, had lived at Smolny for 124 days. The rooms in which Lenin had stayed and passed judgment upon so many in those early days were made into a memorial museum and carefully preserved. It was to those rooms that Bakatin was going. In a way he hoped it would be his last trip there. A bullet would be more welcome than additional humiliation.

Bakatin took a deep breath, then left the comfort of the Chaika and walked to the door where Georgi Zhelin, dressed in his usual business suit and accompanied by a guard carrying a semiautomatic rifle, let him in.

"Nice to see you," said Zhelin in a flat tone. Zhelin was fifty-two years old. Dimitri had sent him a birthday gift only two days before. He was putting on weight but still had the broad chest of a bull ox. His face was filled with large pores, and puffy cheeks sat beneath eyes that were set so deep in his skull that their color couldn't be seen except in a bright light. The moustache that hung over his upper lip was untrimmed so that longer hairs got caught between his lips. His appearance gave the impression of a brawler, an undisciplined slob, but he was shrewd, smart, and played the political games with brutal mastery. Tupolev had been his teacher. His intelligence coupled with his natural inclination toward sadism made Zhelin a man to fear.

Bakatin accompanied Zhelin and the guard through the halls and stairways to Lenin's old rooms. Fifty feet away from entering, Bakatin used the wet handkerchief to wipe his brow and face again, then stuffed it in his back pocket, applying the phony macho facade like a woman putting on a fresh coat of makeup.

Tupolev sat at the small writing desk at which Lenin was purported to have written the Decree on Land, which announced the immediate confiscation without compensation of landed estates, the abolition of private ownership, and the establishment of public and state ownership—a decree that had changed the face of the Soviet state for more than seventy years but was now unraveling.

The Luger lay on the table. It was a tool of intimidation, German, carried constantly and fondled like a piece of rare ivory. Bakatin had seen the Luger do its work, had seen the cold-blooded look in Tupolev's eyes as he had dispatched belligerents and failures through death's door. Bakatin often wondered if Tupolev wasn't Ivan the Terrible or Peter the Great reincarnate. Or possibly Stalin's spirit had just changed bodies.

Bakatin stood near the door. Zhelin waited for Tupolev's dismissal, then backed himself and the guard out of the room and took a position Bakatin knew was only inches away, on the other side of the door. That was the unnerving thing about Georgi Zhelin—he loved to hurt people, would relish the idea of hurting Bakatin if given the chance. It was another reason Bakatin even considered getting rid of Tupolev before the old man turned everything over to his crazy son-in-law. Zhelin had plans for Bakatin's domain, a brother whom he wanted to move into Dimitri's offices overlooking the Fontanka. The day Vladimir Tupolev died, Bakatin thought, would be the last day of his own life.

Only the raspy breathing of the old general broke the oppressive quiet. Finally, Tupolev lifted his cane and pointed at the single bed against the wall. Bakatin went to it and carefully lowered himself onto the quilted cover, afraid it might collapse. Tupolev would shoot him for such a desecration of Lenin's bed, he was sure of it. The bed held.

The light from the late afternoon sun flowed through the window and fell on Tupolev. He looked worse. Bakatin knew the old man was fighting old age but hadn't seen him for a while. He looked worse than Lenin lying in state in his mausoleum. They should both be buried.

He hoped the old man couldn't read thoughts.

Tupolev's hair was thin, nearly gone, and brown liver marks stained the gray flesh of his head and hands. Bony fingers encircled the cane's brass handle, a lion's head protruding out of one side.

"You have failed," Tupolev said in an even voice, the strength of which surprised Dimitri.

Dimitri had learned how to cover his fear. It was a matter of survival. Although he was a bundle of nerves inside, his exterior seemed unruffled, even confident. The trick was keeping his eyes from acting as a window to his inner turmoil while forcing his voice to be even, strong, and controlled.

"You told us to pick up Yezhov, to get the package. There was no package."

"You searched the bus thoroughly?" Tupolev asked.

"They questioned the driver. Yezhov never left his seat, never left the bus. We found nothing in a complete search. We are checking out the rest of the passengers." He inhaled as invisibly as he could. "If it was there, he may have given it to a woman. Galya Starkova, the author."

Tupolev smiled for the first time, his dentures shining between thin, cracked lips. "I have read her book. Very accurate account of what the KGB is about. Her only transgression is failure to recognize the need for such an organization. The socialist system cannot work without it. We have proven that. Stalin proved it. Fear is necessary to motivate the work force that produces the goods, the equipment, everything that gives their lives meaning. Fear is the lifeblood of the Communist system." There was a long pause, as if he had lost concentration. "We could have destroyed her without a second thought only a few years ago." He laughed coldly. "Now, in the new Russia, we are forced to play games with such people." He coughed. "Find her, Bakatin. Find that package. I must have it, and soon." He hesitated. "The past . . . it can be deadly. I must have it. I can be rid of them then—the only ones who have ever hurt me, ever controlled . . . " He bit his lip hard enough that Bakatin thought he would bring blood.

They. The White Guard. After receiving the original assignment from Tupolev, Bakatin had done some research on them. They were a pro-tsarist nationalist group with little written history. Stalin had hunted them for years, paranoid that they were out to kill him and send the country back into tsarist rule. Rumor had it that they claimed to protect the heir of the Romanov family that the revolutionaries had butchered in Ekaterinburg. Fanatics. Deluded, powerless. Like so many in the country, they were trying to find a way to power. He could never figure out why Tupolev was so concerned with them. The temptation to ask for an explanation was nearly overwhelming. He controlled it.

Tupolev coughed a second time. As the cough continued, he removed his own handkerchief and put it over his mouth. The sound of the old man's sickness was deep in the lungs, and when he pulled the white cloth away from his lips it was covered with pink mucus. He glanced at it, then stuffed it angrily into his right-hand pocket.

"Death is a strange foe, Dimitri, the only one I haven't been able to outmaneuver. He stalks me even now. I fight, but I know that I will lose." He paused, a cold stare replacing the desperate fear in his sunken eyes. "Consider me death, Dimitri. I will bury you before I go if you fail me."

Bakatin forced himself to remain unruffled. "I need more information, Vladimir. I need to know what I am looking for, why, whom I am up against."

The old man catapulted from his chair, his six-foot frame crossing the space between them so quickly that Bakatin didn't even see him cover the distance. Raised from his usually slumping stature, he towered over Dimitri like some hungry animal, forcing him backward toward the wall.

"You need to know nothing but what I tell you! Nothing!" He shouted, his eyes flashing and bulging with hate. "None of the rest matters! Only the package! With it I can control them, I know it! Their dark secret I suspect. But I must prove it! With it I can finally be free of them! And him, I can destroy him! He used me! No man has ever used me and lived!" He grabbed Bakatin's tie with his bony hand and jerked up on it with such strength that Dimitri felt his Adam's apple would be crushed. His eyes started to bug out as the old man placed a bony knee in the middle of his chest and pushed, tightening the silk noose around Bakatin's neck and shutting off the air to his lungs. He felt the darkness creep into his vision but knew if he resisted, the old man would kill him in an instant.

With a throaty growl, Tupolev released the tie with a disdainful flick of his hand and stepped back, returning to the chair across the room. He picked up the Luger and fondled it in shaking fingers while Bakatin gasped to refill his lungs and clear the cotton from his mind. He noticed Zhelin standing near the door, watched as the man grinned at his discomfort and then left the room again.

The cane lay on the floor between them, the brass lion's head staring up at Dimitri. The anger was flowing in his veins, overwhelming his good sense. He reached for the wooden shaft, a picture of the lion's open mouth and brass mane planted in the side of Tupolev's decrepit head vivid in his hate-filled mind.

The laugh was evil, the cackle of a witch, shrill, filling the room like a pit in the netherworld. Bakatin backed away from the cane.

"Wise, Dimitri. Very wise." Tupolev put the safety on the Luger back in the off firing position. "Now, is there anything else?"

Bakatin straightened his tie. "Nickolai Poltav is involved. He is Yeltsin's new Commissioner for the Investigation of Anti-Russian Activity. He was following Yezhov." He told Tupolev about Nickolai's visit.

Tupolev's face grew concerned. "Poltav. Our old friend. The one man Beria should have killed. I intervened on his behalf after your encouragement." Tupolev grinned. "Such a gallant thing you did then, Dimitri, purchasing his freedom with your own soul." He laughed a wicked chuckle. "How could Nickolai know about Yezhov?"

"He didn't say, but I am having him followed. I had my assistant build Nickolai a file on Yezhov."

"You included everything?"

"Yes."

"Good, good. Nickolai could help us, unknowingly of course, but to do so he will need information."

"In reality there isn't much information on Yezhov."

"Enough for Poltav. Stay very close to him, Dimitri. You know what you must do if he interferes with business. I don't want him too close." He smiled a fatherly smile, the one Bakatin always received after being disciplined. "Your wife is well?"

"Yes, fine," Bakatin replied. Tupolev always asked, not out of concern but more as a veiled threat. It had always been that way.

"Nickolai is her brother, as I remember."

Bakatin nodded.

"She has never stopped loving him," Tupolev said.

"They haven't spoken for more than forty years."

"Ah, yes, I remember. The one necessity I placed upon his survival. It is nice to know she has been true to her promise. Never once even wrote him a letter, eh? An honorable lady."

Bakatin felt the hate boiling up in his stomach again as he remembered the day Marina had insisted they go to Tupolev and beg for his help in saving Nickolai. They had both lost their dignity that day. And their freedom.

"Keep Nickolai under close observation, Dimitri. You have twenty-four hours to find that package."

Bakatin got to his feet, knowing he had been dismissed. He went to the door, turned the knob, then turned around and faced the devil behind him. They glared into each others' souls for long seconds before Bakatin opened the door and left the room.

Zhelin entered the room and tossed the gun on the bed. "I don't trust him."

"That is nothing new, Georgi. You have never trusted Dimitri. You fear he may be the one man who can keep you from inheriting all my property." Tupolev laughed. "Where is Shelepin?"

Zhelin walked to the door and opened it. The guard stood side to side with Aleksei Shelepin. "Come in, Aleksei," said Zhelin.

Shelepin was nervous but under control. He walked to a position ten feet from the old man, then stopped.

"Tell us once again about your conversation with Dimitri," Tupolev said. His smile encouraged Aleksei, who told them about the conversation he and Bakatin had had earlier in the day. When he was finished, he removed a handkerchief from his pocket and rubbed it across his forehead.

Tupolev went to the window, thinking. He had dealt with Dimitri's foolishness before but had never killed him. He wasn't sure why—possibly because the man was so gifted, and so obedient in most things. He knew Dimitri hated him. It had to be that way, it really was the only way of controlling people. But what to do now?

Dimitri was not brave enough to kill him. The conversation was suggestive of betrayal, but such action wasn't actually planned, only talk. But too much was at stake here.

"Georgi, call in Bondorenko and Kulikov. Tell them they are no longer under Dimitri's orders, even though they must make him think they are. You take full command of finding the Starkova woman."

"What about Dimitri?"

"Shelepin will watch him." He smiled at Aleksei, the smile of confidants in a great moment. He sat at the table again. "Mr. Shelepin, how much do you know about Mr. Bakatin's operation?"

Aleksei's ears perked up. "Everything."

"Could you help us transfer his assets to our companies?"

"Yes, but—"

"Of course, you will be taken in as partner, be responsible for running many of them." Tupolev smiled.

"We would need some signatures from Dimi—from Mr. Bakatin in order to transfer title of companies he owns," Shelepin said.

"We will see that you get them. Would there be any other problems?"

Shelepin shook his head. "No sir. Everything else would be rather simple. There are so few laws in Russia . . . "

"Good. Can I depend on your full cooperation—and your allegiance?"

"Of course, sir. Completely."

"Keep Georgi apprised of Dimitri's every move, understood?"

Shelepin wiped his brow again, nodding his head. "I understand."

"Thank you. Your coming here was the right thing. You will not regret it. Do you have a car?"

"Yes sir, A Volga."

"Get another car, Aleksei. Go to the American Ford company. Buy the one of your choosing. Tell them it is my gift."

Aleksei looked shocked, elated, and a bit frightened all at once. "Thank you . . . sir. I . . . will be your greatest help in this. I . . . "

"It is all right, Aleksei. Coming here is much appreciated."

Zhelin moved the younger man toward the door. When he was gone, he returned to stand in front of his boss.

"If you believe Dimitri will use this opportunity to kill you, we should do something about him now."

"He doesn't have the will for such action," Tupolev said in disgust. "What he intends is even more dangerous."

"What . . . ? I don't understand, Vladimir."

"He will use Nickolai. It is he who is much more dangerous to us. It is Nickolai who serves Boris Yeltsin, and Yeltsin is the one who wants my hide. We must be very careful. I don't want either of them forewarned that we are onto them. They might do something that could prevent us from getting the package, or find a way to ruin us altogether. We have the element of knowledge on our side, and that gives us the advantage. We will eliminate both of them—at the right time."

"Can we trust Shelepin?"

"He is greedy. Greedy men can never be trusted, just used. But Bakatin's businesses are very successful. Just our percentage of his interests brings us a lot of money. Taking them over will take a good deal of preparation, and Shelepin's knowledge. Once that is accomplished, his use to us is finished and we will get rid of him. For now, have him watched. And put men on Bakatin as well. Shelepin might miss something."

Zhelin went to the window and watched as Shelepin got in the cream-colored Volga parked below. Tupolev was right, the man could be used.

Georgi Zhelin had never liked Dimitri Bakatin and considered him a threat to the old man's empire, an empire Georgi Zhelin intended to inherit. Now Bakatin had given him the opportunity to be rid of that threat, and, possibly, inherit the empire at the same time, along with Bakatin's own holdings. It could all prove very profitable.

"I will take care of it, Vladimir." Zhelin moved to the door.

"Find that package, Georgi. More depends on it than you know."

Zhelin glanced back at the old man, sitting at the table, slumped with age, one foot in the grave. Old, too old to run everything anymore. In fact, Zhelin did most of it now, except when the old man's personal brand of intimidation was needed. But Tupolev still kept the records, still controlled the money. No one touched that part of the empire except the old general. Zhelin had seen his ledger, which contained code words for names, coded numbers for amounts received and paid for services rendered. Tupolev was a meticulous bookkeeper using an antiquated method. Soon Zhelin would update all that. There was so much growth potential in the old man's domain, so much more to be done.

"I won't fail you, Father," he said.

Tupolev didn't look up; he seemed far away. Zhelin closed the door. Too old, he thought. Vladimir Tupolev was just too old.

Chapter Ten

GALYA SAT ON THE OLD COUCH, a blanket covering her legs, staring into the late night through the window. Larissa came from the kitchen with two steaming cups of mint tea, sugar, and cream on a tray. Half a dozen square cookies were neatly arranged on a small plate. Larissa put the tray on the coffee table and sat in the chair across from Galya.

Neither had been able to sleep. Galya had been sleeping in the same narrow room she had slept in the night before, but for some reason she had felt claustrophobic and had come into the small living area to select a book from Larissa's tiny, well-used library. There were several works by Dostoyevsky and Pushkin, but she had selected a Russian translation of an Agatha Christie novel. Sitting on the couch, she had tried reading. That was when Larissa had joined her and suggested some mint tea. Maybe it would help them both sleep.

Galya added a pinch of sugar and a little cream. She knew that her hostess was sharing a rare treat and partook respectfully. They sat back, nibbling at a cookie, sipping the tea, both silent, content to be in one another's company. Finally Galya got up the courage to voice a thought that had been festering in the back of her mind ever since the confusing encounter with Rikki and Rustam.

"It is a strange leap from the fanatic anti-Jewish rhetoric of Pozhar to the philosophy of Jesus of Nazareth."

Larissa smiled. "Monumental." She set her cup of tea on the table. "But I was finished with Pozhar long before I converted to

Christianity. Actually, I was finished with about everything Russia had to offer. None of it worked, not for me. And there was no comfort in any of it. All it gave me was hate and hopelessness." She paused. "I tried to take my own life. There was nothing more to live for."

Galya remembered her mother—how she had quit living. Another form of suicide. She understood why Larissa had decided to stop the pain that seemed to have no end. Why live when dying was so much better?

"I was taken to a hospital—a mental hospital. I don't remember much about those first two months; they kept me sedated most of the time. In the third month they cleaned us all up, made us scrub the place down, gave us all showers and new clothes. Visitors from America, a team of doctors who came to work with our doctors for a week. One of them was a psychologist by the name of Romney. He took a personal interest in my case because he recognized who I was. He didn't tell them he knew. He was afraid they might keep us away from each other and he wouldn't be able to help me. We talked a lot."

She stood and went to the bookcase, pulling a blue, hardbound book from the shelf. "He left that with me the day he went back to America."

"Book of Mormon." Galya read the Russian title on the front cover. She thumbed through the pages, then closed it, laying it on the coffee table. Larissa had gone to the window. Pulling the lace curtain aside, she stared into the street.

"What is it? A medical book of some kind?"

Larissa laughed lightly. "Scripture, like the Bible but different. I read it in about two days. It changed me so visibly that within the month I was out of the hospital, willing to give life another try. Dr. Romney sent me a letter and included the address of a leader of his church who had just come to Petersburg to open a Church mission. A week later I was a member."

Galya glanced at the book but picked up her cup of tea instead. "Are you telling me this book made you well?"

"Yes, I guess I am, but you won't believe it, and you won't know why, or how, until you read it," Larissa said. She turned and walked to the table and put her cup on the tray there. "After that we will talk. Until then you will never understand how I feel." She smiled. "Good night, Galya. The tea seems to have helped. I can hardly keep my eyes open."

Galya placed her own cup on the tray, stood, picked it up, and deposited the dishes in the small kitchen sink. She washed and dried them, then went to the narrow bedroom, closing the door behind her.

She was feeling sleepy now. The herb tea was a different kind—a kind that made her drowsy. Larissa drank only herb teas, never Russian tea, never real tea. She wondered if this new religion had some sort of dietary approach to wellness. She had heard of such things. Actually she enjoyed the herb teas Larissa gave her. They were pleasant tasting with none of the side effects of other teas she had used.

She remade the bed, then slipped beneath the sheets, thinking about Larissa's challenge. That was what it was—a challenge to read this mysterious blue book from America.

She threw off the covers and went to the window, pulling the heavy curtains from different directions until the yellow haze of Petersburg's white night was shut out, the room dark. Then she went back to bed and closed her eyes.

They opened again a moment later and stared at the dark book a few feet away on the table. Turning her face to the wall, she closed her eyes again. There was nothing in religion for her. If she thought Marx's teachings had any validity, it was on that one point. Religion was the opiate of the people. It kept them from accepting responsibility for their problems, from working out their lives. She wanted nothing to do with such artificial crutches.

Five minutes later she was sound asleep.

Nickolai shoved aside the bottle next to the phone, and it fell to the floor. He groped further until he found the phone and lifted it from its armature.

"Hello," he said, his voice slurred with sleep.

"Nickolai?"

He lifted himself onto one arm, forcing the cobwebs out of his mind. "Yes, is this . . . "

"Never mind. Your phone is probably tapped. You must meet me. Eleven o'clock tomorrow. Do you remember the name of the place where you used to drink yourself into oblivion after work? In Moscow."

"Yes, I remember."

"There is also one here. The same name. Tomorrow. Eleven o'clock. I will give you more than you want." The phone clicked.

Nickolai hung up his receiver and plopped his head back onto the pillow and closed his eyes. Things were looking up.

———————

Galya felt someone shaking her, heard a voice. Her eyes popped open, and she sat straight up, moving away from the dark form coming toward her in the darkness.

"Galya. It is all right. It is me, Larissa." Larissa touched Galya's arm and spoke soothingly as she became fully awake.

Galya ran her fingers through her hair, her body weak.

"What . . . what is wrong, Larissa? Why did you wake me?"

"Get dressed. We have to leave. Quickly!" Larissa was already at the window. "I think they have found us!"

Galya felt the adrenalin rush and quickly began dressing, fumbling with her clothes in the darkness. "Can you see who it is? How did they find us?!"

"No, they are in the shadows, but they are talking, waiting for someone, I think. One of them keeps looking at his watch."

Galya finished the last button on her blouse and pulled on her skirt, then her shoes.

"Come on. There is a way out of the building through the basement." Larissa grabbed a flashlight and her bag, and Galya grabbed hers. Unlocking the inner door, Larissa peered through the peephole. All looked clear. Slowly, so as to be quiet, she turned the lock on the outer door. Galya could feel her heart thumping against her chest as Larissa pushed the door lightly and it swung outward into the empty hallway.

Larissa used her keys to lock the outer door; then they started down the stairs. As they reached the bottom, they could hear someone fiddling with the lock on the outer door that led to the street.

"Quickly! This way!" Larissa lowered herself through an opening in the floor to the side of the stairs. Galya handed down her bag as Larissa flipped on the flashlight and illuminated the dank, smelly tunnel that burrowed under the foundation. Galya held her breath and lowered her body into the hole. Stooping over, she followed Larissa as she made her way toward the back of the building. When they reached the far wall, she flashed the light along it until she found a small door fastened with wire. Undoing it, they eased the panel away, letting in both fresh air and the yellow haze of the night. Larissa slithered through, Galya handed her the bags, then followed. She found herself in a narrow alley between their building and the next. It was closed off at both ends by gates of wood. They ran quickly to the far end, where Larissa opened a small door in the gate and let them out. As Galya was about to go through the door, she turned and looked over her shoulder and up at Larissa's kitchen window. A man stood there, his body silhouetted against the light coming through the far window of the living room. Galya felt the hair on the back of her neck stand on end as he quickly passed through the gate and out of sight.

"It . . . it was the man at the bus. One of the agents!"

Larissa handed Galya her bag. They kept close to the wall, in the shadows, worked their way toward the street, crossed it, and went through the square of an apartment complex. Five minutes later, they were at the metro station and descending into the tunnels. At such an early hour only a few trains ran, and it seemed like forever before they heard one rumbling toward them out of the bowels of the earth. Then the light flashed in the dark hole and the metallic monster leaped into the opening where they stood. The grating of the metal wheels echoed off the walls and made Galya grit her teeth. Then the door was in front of them. It opened and let them in. They sat in seats near the door. Larissa watched through the window, but no one followed, no one boarded the train. It was a good time to run.

Chapter Eleven

NICKOLAI GLANCED AT HIS WATCH. Nearly noon. Where was he?
Had he come to the wrong place after all?

He picked up the bottle of Fanta pop and finished it off. It had
taken him most of the morning to find the bar. Dimitri had been
only half right. The name of the old one was Big Moscow; this
one was Little Moscow. He could only hope he had found the
right one. The day hadn't started out all that favorably. Still nothing on the Starkova woman, although his office was chasing
down a couple of leads, including a cousin who was supposed to
live in Petersburg. The name hadn't been attached to an address,
and without KGB connections it would be harder to find Rustam
Starkov. But maybe they'd get lucky. They had to get something,
and soon.

He rolled the bottle under his palm and against the flat surface of the table. A day and a half since Yezhov had been killed,
and he seemed further away from the package than ever.

He glanced up, watching as Dimitri Bakatin came through the
door of the restaurant, stopping to let his eyes adjust to the darkness. Locating Nickolai, he moved through the scattered chairs
and took a seat at the table. He eyed his brother-in-law's casual
attire with a smirk. "Dressing down today, are we?"

"Dressing for the place. Look around you, Dimitri. This is a
worker's pub. You and your tailored suit are being sized up carefully. I would hang onto your wallet if I were you."

Dimitri adjusted his tie, then shoved the folder across the table.

Nickolai glanced at it. "American manila folder. How elitist."

Bakatin let it go. "The information on Yezhov is inside. There isn't much except in the way of biography. One interesting fact: he seems to have belonged to an underground group called the White Guard."

"Who are they?"

"They don't exist anymore, but at one time they were said to protect the heir of the Romanovs. Stalin knew about them and wanted them destroyed. In the early fifties, Tupolev was given a general's status in the army for his work against the last of them. He convinced Stalin he had crushed the guard." He shrugged, leaning back in his chair. "He is crazy."

"So I hear. Anything else?"

"I have Kulikov looking for a woman, Galya Starkova. She was on the bus and seems to be the one who last talked to Yezhov. The address of her cousin is in the manila folder. The man who is watching the place reports to me. I thought you might like to know."

"Who's watching the place? Kulikov?"

"Yes."

"Kulikov owes allegiance to Zhelin, thus Tupolev."

"Presently he reports to me," Bakatin said.

"Are you sure? When was the last . . . "

"Sure."

Nickolai didn't pursue it. "Why so cooperative?"

Bakatin sat back with a shrug. "You want the package. I want you to have it."

"Dangerous. It might be for nothing."

"Over the years I have heard Tupolev brag about atrocities he was involved in during the war and after. I have the impression from him that this package may prove his guilt. If he is tried and found guilty, everything he owns will be stripped from him, and he will be executed. That is beneficial to me." He paused. "The man needs killing."

Nickolai didn't believe the package dealt with atrocities,

although that was a possibility, and good enough to have Tupolev's hide. At this point he'd take anything.

"You come out smelling like roses no matter how this turns out, don't you. If I get Tupolev, you can expand without having to give him the high percentage he now demands. If I lose, and Kulikov finds the package, you can deliver it to Tupolev and get a pat on the head for a job well done."

"I'm at risk here, Nickolai, and if you believe otherwise you have forgotten how evil Vladimir Tupolev can be."

"I haven't forgotten." Nickolai sensed something in Bakatin's voice that wasn't there yesterday. Hate. For some reason it had become personal. "Will you pull Kulikov off surveillance long enough for me to get to the woman?"

Bakatin shook his head. "I am a shrewd businessman, Nickolai, and not stupid. If you fail, my betrayal could be easily seen in such an action. You will have to work against Kulikov. A man of your talents should have no problem." Bakatin smiled.

"Thanks for the confidence."

"Also in the file, you will find paperwork showing that the taxes on the EuroRuss shipments have been paid. We expect that we will have no further problem on that count."

"Very efficient. It takes most corporations weeks to accomplish such a task."

"We have our connections," Bakatin said. "Can we trust that you will take no further steps against EuroRuss?"

"Not about this problem, but if I were you I would run a tight ship from now on. Big Brother is still watching." Nickolai smiled as he started to get up from the table. Then he leaned across, getting his face close to Bakatin's. "Two things. If I smell a rat, Bakatin, if you deal me over to Tupolev, my people will tie you up in so much paperwork your head will spin, and they will take away from you every last cent of your new-found fortune. Second, you have had me followed since I left your office yesterday. Call off your dog or I will be forced to break both his legs."

Bakatin didn't smile. Looking at a man sitting at a table near the front, he caught his eye and gave a signal. The man left the restaurant.

"Don't mess up, Nickolai. It could get us all killed."

"All?"

"Even Marina. I've crossed the line. I know what Tupolev does to people who cross the line," Bakatin said.

"I'll be in touch." Nickolai worked his way to the door satisfied but empty inside. Dimitri Bakatin's greed had proven to be very predictable, but he hadn't thought about Marina. Dimitri was right—they must be careful. This could get them all killed.

Chapter Twelve

RAND STRETCHED, WAITING FOR THE COMPUTER to complete its search. He glanced at his watch. It had been a busy day, but he had decided to do his own follow-up on Galya Starkova's request just so he could hand it to her personally, an answer to her challenge about American efficiency.

It was a lie. He just wanted to meet her again; something about her intrigued him. Her beauty was classical Russian—tall, lithe, and elegant. She had bearing and determination. He could still see her standing amid the consulate's burly marine guards, her head back, challenging the world to take a swing at her beautiful chin. A rose among the thorns. Galya Starkova was a woman of earthy elegance that made Rand's skin tingle.

He glanced at the set of contemporary clocks stuck to the wall. The one giving Washington time showed five minutes past seven. It usually took five minutes to dig something out of the mainframe in Washington and get it here by satellite link-up. Another two minutes.

He glanced at the open book on his desk. Galya Starkova was a talented, passionate writer. He had stayed up late into the night reviewing her work. It was even better the second time around, even though he still found himself arguing with some of her findings, especially those that pointed fingers at collusion between the CIA and the KGB. Not that it was out of the question—the CIA had done worse in its short history—but her evidence seemed a little thin, and he wanted to question her further about her sources and research.

He turned to the short biography on the inside back cover. Short, concise. A brief description of a woman who had lived the things she wrote about. Rand wanted to know more.

The screen started to fill, and Rand put on the wire-framed glasses he wore for reading. There was the usual biographical information then:

"WORLD WAR II ARMY AIR FORCE. FILE CODE NAME *ALLIANCE*. CLASSIFIED TOP SECRET."

He punched the keys on the computer.

"RECHECK. KITRICK, ROBERT. ARMY AIR FORCE. WORLD WAR II."

Rand waited, rereading the material on the screen, then finally having the computer spit him out a copy on the laser printer. Then he cleared the monitor and waited a few minutes before the information filled the screen again.

"KITRICK, ROBERT. CONFIRM: WORLD WAR II ARMY AIR FORCE. KILLED IN ACTION. FILE CODE NAME *ALLIANCE*. CLASSIFIED TOP SECRET. NO ADDITIONAL INFORMATION AVAILABLE. CONTACT OFFICE, GENERAL OF THE ARMY."

Rand sat back, his eyes glued to the screen. Whoever Kitrick was, he was involved in something heavy during Hitler's holocaust. Something very heavy.

Rand picked up the government directory and began looking for a number. After a minute he found what he wanted and closed the book, picking up the scrambled phone on his desk.

His position at the consulate had been preceded by a tour of duty as director of the counter-terrorism group for the United States Army Criminal Investigative Command, or CID. During the last two years of his tour, there had been an increase in terrorist activities on American soil and a number of threats on the lives of personnel his office was sworn to protect, particularly on the life of the Secretary of Defense. A terrorist using a high-powered sniper's rifle was nearly successful on one occasion, and only Rand's fast thinking had kept the Secretary's name out of the obituaries, but the assailant had gotten away. From evidence Rand had gathered once the weapon and hiding place were discovered, he suspected that the man was American military and asked for unusual access to the army's files on special operations personnel to find the sniper's identity. It had worked. Rand had personally made the arrest. A former member of a seal team group who had fought in Nam but had turned his skills and training to personal gain, the sniper would spend the rest of his life in a federal prison.

More important to his present situation, the method used to access the files of the General of the Army was now known to him.

He punched in the phone number for Colonel Ellen Langston and waited, glancing at the clock that showed Washington time. Seven o'clock. The early crew should be on duty, and knowing Ellen, she would be in the office.

Ellen was an old friend who worked as special assistant to the General of the Army. In fact, Rand and Ellen had met each other when he was searching for the terrorist who was trying to kill the Secretary of Defense. She had shown him the system, how the files were arranged, what code words to use. She could get what he wanted. Whether or not she would was a question he was about to get answered.

On the third ring, the operator at the Pentagon answered.

"Colonel Ellen Langston please. Rand King of the Petersburg Consulate calling." The operator left the line, and the phone rang in Ellen's domain.

It had been an on-again, off-again relationship, but he had finally asked Ellen to marry him. She had said no.

Actually, she had put him off. It was a religious thing he was just beginning to understand now but certainly didn't understand then. That was nearly two years ago.

After the terrorist incident, he was tired of the high-pressure, militaristic world of the CID. The Petersburg consulate job was a challenge but less pressured. It was also one of the most sought-after jobs in the civil service. Russia in general, Petersburg in particular was considered a plum in many circles. One of Russia's most beautiful cities, Petersburg presented coveted cultural and political amenities. It was also a hotbed of change offering anything but boredom.

Rand's training at Harvard had been in international law with an emphasis on the Soviet Union. As professional military, he was outside the civil sector and didn't have the credentials of his competition, but he did have an impeccable record, along with the undying gratitude of the Secretary of Defense—a powerful man with important connections.

His greatest asset was, however, his knowledge of the language. Rand spoke Russian, German, and French as well as or better than he did English. It gave him the edge he needed.

After getting settled in Petersburg, Rand had flown back to Washington once every two weeks so he and Ellen could spend time together. But, gradually, they had grown apart. She had expected a commitment he hadn't wanted to give. Not then.

Now they talked on the phone, about every two weeks. When people asked how things were, about all he could say was that they had a good friendship.

"Colonel Langston's office," a man said.

"Hello, Maldridge, this is Rand King."

"Hey, Colonel, I mean, Mr. King. Good to hear your voice. How are things in the netherworld?"

"Not bad. How about Washington?"

"Usual stuff. Crime is out of control, corruption is on the upswing, and scandal is keeping us all busy at lunchtime."

"And we want to give it all to the Russians."

"Hey, share and share alike."

"Is your boss around?"

"Walking in as we speak. Hold on."

Rand waited a few minutes. It would be nice to hear her voice.

"Hello, Rand King."

"Hi, El. How are you?"

"Nervous."

"Why's that?"

"Because you're calling me in the middle of the afternoon Russian time, after a six-week blackout without a single word."

"That long, huh?" The military made people sticklers for detail.

"Yes, that long." A pause. "Your apology is accepted. What have you been up to?" The smile returned to her voice.

"About six inches over my eyeballs."

"Oh, and they were so pretty," she said. "You're after something, Colonel. What is it?"

"Access to the General's files."

The phone was silent.

"Did you hang up yet, or are you just thinking about it?"

"Good-bye, Rand. Nice talking to you."

"Wait! It's an old file, El. Fifty years old. It probably shouldn't even be in there anymore. I just need some information on a guy who came to Russia in 1941 and who is probably dead now. I computer-checked the archives and was sent here."

"Who is this guy?" Ellen asked.

"His name is Kitrick, Robert Kitrick."

"Who is looking for him?"

"A writer."

"Why?"

"El, what is this? Twenty questions?"

"Why, Rand?"

Rand looked at the paperwork. "She's doing a story on World War II and thinks this guy may have been here then."

"We weren't in the war then."

"So I hear. Makes you curious, doesn't it."

"Umm. What is the file name?"

"ALLIANCE."

Rand could hear her typing, probably taking a look at the cover sheet on the file.

"Interesting," Ellen said.

"What?"

"ALLIANCE still carries a priority-one classification. That's unusual for a file this old."

Rand smiled. Ellen had the same insatiable curiosity as he did. It was what had made their relationship click in the first place.

"Oh, oh."

"I don't like the sound of that," Rand said.

"This file has an outside caretaker."

"Who?"

"Samuel Andrews. Former director of the CIA."

"He was General of the Army once, wasn't he?"

"Yes, but he is retired from public office now, even though he is still a very powerful man."

"What's a retired public servant doing as caretaker of a top-secret file? That's a bit unusual, isn't it?"

"Very. By special permission only."

"Your boss?"

"No. Permission was granted directly from the president on this one—Franklin Delano Roosevelt. If I let you access this file, both of them will receive a report by the end of the day."

"Roosevelt is dead, El."

"No kidding. The report goes to the White House, smart aleck. Clinton will have the report on his desk before he goes to bed."

"And he'll want to ask me questions."

"If you don't have the answers, you will regret it."

"Will it foul up your career?"

El laughed. "I'm too valuable to the general. He doesn't like Andrews and would love the chance to tell him where to get off. You, on the other hand . . . getting information for an author doesn't seem worth your career."

"Umm." He thought for a long moment. Something wasn't right, but El had a point. It wasn't worth his career. "Give me the access codes. I'll talk to this author, see if I can find out more. Then I'll decide."

There was a pause. "Do you still have Priority Clearance?"

No answer.

"I thought not. Rand . . . "

"Check, El. *Foxtrot.* Nobody ever told me I wasn't on the list anymore." El punched the code name *Foxtrot* into the computer. "Well, look there."

"Still cleared, I take it."

"Your lucky day. I'll have it removed in thirty-six hours." She gave him the codes.

"Okay, Rand, it's done. Your funeral. Are you on a scrambled phone?"

"Yup."

"There is some biographical information here. Nothing unusual or that would compromise the nature of the ALLIANCE operation itself. Do you want it?"

"You're an angel."

She gave him the information. He jotted it down in a sort of coded shorthand on the back of a business card and shoved it in his shirt pocket.

"Dinner when I come to town?" Rand asked.

"Yeah. We need to talk anyway," she said in a serious tone. "See ya, cowboy. Good luck."

Rand hung up. She was finally breaking it off. He didn't think it would hurt, but it did. And just when the only issue wasn't really an issue anymore.

After a few minutes Rand stood, put on his suit coat, tightened his tie, then shoved his glasses into his handkerchief pocket. He couldn't help but wonder what Ellen's future husband was like. One thing was sure, though: the guy was a member of El's church. He couldn't see her making the same mistake twice. He kicked himself mentally. That wasn't fair. El simply felt strong about religion, always had. Even now, unless it was an emergency, she refused to work on Sunday, even to go sightseeing. Sunday was for church and family.

It was Rand's lack of religion that had been the problem, and his refusal to take hers seriously. He had nobody to blame but himself if El found someone else.

At least she had made him think about things he had always dismissed with nothing more than a shrug. God, religion. It had given him an added dimension when dealing with people. He felt it helped him understand them better and gave him an edge when discussing issues of importance to them.

Then there was the personal side. In that arena he was a changed man as well. For that he owed El. It was not a small debt.

Referring to the paperwork Galya Starkova had left behind, he started to dial the number, then decided against it. The address on Vasilevsky Island was only a short distance. It would be better to talk to her in person. If she wanted his help, he needed more information.

He left the office, checking out with his secretary. He said good afternoon to the three marines at the front entrance and left the building. Climbing into the Mercedes, he started it and drove from the parking lot, his mind jumping between his relationship with El and the ALLIANCE file, finally settling on the most painful. A love relationship between them had really ended months ago. They were friends. Good friends. No, he was kidding himself. He still had feelings for El. Strong ones. But it was over. He could feel it, and it hurt.

He decided to focus on something less painful.

Why would Sam Andrews be watching the ALLIANCE file the way a mother hen watches her newly hatching eggs? Was he afraid of some sort of political backlash? What had operation ALLIANCE been involved in? The indication was that it had been a mission to Russia. But for what purpose? With a priority-one classification still intact, it must have been something important—something Andrews was afraid of.

He passed over Dvortsovaya Bridge, his brow wrinkled in thought. Galya Starkova was onto something. He had to find out what it was.

Chapter Thirteen

RUSTAM WATCHED FROM HIS DESK in the drafting room as the two men visited with his supervisor. He knew they were KGB, and he was prepared for their visit. From the look of them, they were probably the same men who had been present when the old man Galya had told him about was killed at the bus stop.

The supervisor pointed his direction. All eyes shifted to him. It was always the same—the fear, the curiosity, the check one did of one's life. All of these people were asking themselves what he had done. Then they would ask how it would affect them. Had they been too friendly with him? Would they be pulled into whatever trouble he was in? Rustam knew—he had asked himself the same questions many times.

The two men disappeared into a small office, and the supervisor came quickly to his desk.

"You are wanted, Starkov." He jerked a thumb toward the office. Rustam could see the unfavorable look in the man's eyes, the anger mixed with an attempt to hide his own concern. It had been the same when Rustam had told him about his return to religion. They had been good friends before that; now the supervisor's attitude bordered on aloofness. And now this. Rustam wondered if he would still have a job at the end of the day.

Natalya would throw a fit. She was constantly saying that his unwillingness to follow the norm would get him into trouble, get them both into trouble. She was paranoid about it. It made him weary.

He shoved his pencils into his desk, then locked it. Things

disappeared when they weren't locked up—sometimes even when they were.

He couldn't really blame Natalya. Both her parents had been destroyed by their obstinate refusal to bend to the party. Because of it, Natalya and her brother had been raised in virtual poverty in a communal apartment where four families shared the living space. It was a horrible way for a young woman to grow up. No privacy, married men who looked at her constantly, even invaded her privacy to get a better look. When she was seventeen, one had tried to rape her. That was the day she left home, vowing she would never go back. Her greatest fear was that Rustam's conduct might put them into such a place. She had nightmares about it.

Rustam walked to the door and went inside. The large man sat on the heavy wooden table, the smaller, stocky man with the short haircut stood looking at a picture on the wall—a cheap copy of a painting by Gerasimov. He faced Rustam.

"Comrade Starkov. Please, sit." His eyes went back to the picture.

Rustam stayed where he was, near the still-open door.

"Who are you? What do you want?" Rustam said, trying to hide the disgust in his voice. Rustam was not a member of the party, and the use of *comrade* as a title for him was inappropriate, especially in these days when the party was disreputable but still grasping for power. The title was now a tool used to ingratiate or anger—subtle manipulation that made Rustam sick to his stomach.

"I am Colonel Kulikov of the Ministry of Security," Kulikov said, still staring at the picture. "This man is Comrade Bondorenko." He faced Rustam. "I asked you to sit down."

"I prefer to stand," Rustam said.

Kulikov shrugged, but Rustam could see the red rising in the heavy flesh of his broad neck. Men like Kulikov had always been able to intimidate. Rustam wasn't about to be intimidated, not anymore.

"We want you to tell us where your cousin is."

"Which one, and for what reason?"

Bondorenko slid from the table and closed the door, then went back to the table. Rustam stayed put.

"Galya Starkova. She has stolen state property."

"Galya isn't supposed to arrive for three more days," Rustam said, avoiding the lie. That was the hard thing about his new religion. It taught honesty. In Russia it was hard to be honest. Communism's "new man" was forced to be just the opposite. Survival depended on it. You left work early or came late so you could buy groceries before they disappeared from the shelves of state stores and didn't have to purchase them at a higher price on the black market. You stole things, tools, pencils, paper, anything you could sell for a few rubles to make up for the lousy wages you were paid. You bought degrees from universities without ever attending them so you could be considered for better jobs. It was all a part of the system, and until it changed, people like him, people trying to be honest, had to play word games to survive *and* be religious.

"She arrived two evenings ago," Kulikov said.

"The newspaper provided an apartment. Check with them." Rustam reached for the doorknob. "Is that all?"

"A neighbor says your cousin came to your apartment."

"She isn't *in* my apartment, Colonel Kulikov," Rustam said calmly while opening the door. "If you wish, you can go and look. Now, if you will excuse me . . . "

The second man was quick for being so large. He was pushing the door shut before Rustam even knew he had left the table. His hand remained against it.

Rustam looked up at him, then turned and faced Kulikov. "New name, same tactics," he said flatly, referring to the "new" title for the KGB and its agents.

Kulikov smiled, facing Rustam for the first time. "With the same ability to either ruin your life or make it better."

Rustam felt the sweat trickle down his side but found that his face was unusually dry.

"Where is the woman?" Kulikov asked.

"I told you, I don't know." That wasn't a lie either, he told himself. He didn't know. Not anymore. Larissa had called early this morning and told him about their escape during the night, but she hadn't told him where she and Galya were. They had decided that the KGB were watching him, would visit him. It would be better if he could tell the truth.

"We think you do."

Rustam didn't reply.

"You know Larissa Vavilova, correct?"

Rustam's mouth felt dry.

"Yes. Larissa was married to a friend of mine."

"Konstantin Nogin. Larissa Vavilova is your mistress?"

Rustam felt the anger start deep in his belly. He fought to control it.

"Friends, that is all."

"How does your wife feel about your mistress?"

"Your tactics won't work, Kulikov."

"I think we will visit your wife, and your mistress. Maybe they know where this woman is."

"You can always ask my wife, *and* Miss Vavilova," Rustam said stiffly. He turned to leave, glaring up at Bondorenko. "I think your trainer is finished."

Bondorenko lost his smile, then glanced over at Kulikov.

"You belong to a new religion, an American religion," Kulikov said.

"Yes." Rustam turned to face Kulikov again. "Under laws established in 1989 and 1991 I have every right—"

"I know the law, Starkov," Kulikov said coldly. "I also know my powers. I can have your meetings shut down simply by taking away your meeting place. I can harass the members of your church and have their jobs taken away. Some may lose their housing."

Rustam kept his face blank even though his stomach was churning. He knew that Kulikov was right. He could do all those things. Such intimidation was still the KGB's greatest tool. They didn't threaten with personal harm now; they threatened the people their targets loved most—family, friends, fellow church members. That was the reason the Russian people were so unfriendly to one another, so reclusive. They were afraid that someone else's actions might affect them. Or that what they did might hurt others. People got hurt either way. The worst part was that you were powerless to stop it.

"I do not know where she is," Rustam said. It was the truth, but he also knew Kulikov wouldn't take the time to find out who the members of his church were and take action against them to bring him around. Individual members didn't have to register anymore, and it would take too much time to find out in other ways. Rustam knew Kulikov was bluffing, but it still gave him ulcers. He wondered if, under the old system, he would have been so brave, so willing to challenge a man like Kulikov. But then, under the old system he had been a different man as well.

Kulikov's frustration was written in the firm set of his jaw and the cold stare of his dark eyes. "We have people watching your apartment, and Miss Vavilova's. If we discover that you have been helping this criminal, we will see that you pay your debt to society. In the meantime, I would start looking for another job. I have a cousin who can use this one."

There it was, the real pressure, the final intimidation. To Rustam the job didn't matter. The Church had already offered him a position translating literature from English into Russian. The thought brought a smile.

"You do not believe me?" Kulikov said, irritated.

"I believe you, Kulikov, because I believe you are a fool. Only a fool would want this job for his cousin." Rustam turned to leave. Bondorenko let go of the door, and Rustam left. Going to his desk, he sat down and returned to his work. His legs started to shake, and his stomach felt nervous—not from fear this time, but from satisfaction. He had always wanted to stand up to a man like Kulikov. It had felt better than he had ever thought it would.

The two KGB agents hesitated at the office door, glaring at Rustam. The department manager, pale and fearful, joined them. The words weren't clear, but Rustam knew what was being said. He watched, hoping his manager and old friend would take a stand. It wasn't to be. As the two men stormed from the office, the manager turned toward Rustam. Their eyes met for only a moment; then the manager looked away and disappeared into his office, shutting the door. Rustam removed a small box from under his desk and began filling it with his few personal possessions. It was time to move on.

Volodya Vilechenko watched as the two agents left the office building where Rustam Starkov worked. From the looks on their faces, their call hadn't been productive. But then, *he* hadn't found the woman either.

He watched as they got into their car and drove away.

"Vasily," he said to his driver, "tell Leonid to stay here and follow Starkov."

Vasily picked up a small hand radio on the seat and gave the orders. A man in a car across the street, a tan Zhiguili, looked their way as he received the message.

"Did you plant the homing device on Kulikov's car?" Vilechenko asked.

Vasily nodded, opening a compartment in the dash and revealing a small screen. He turned it on. The ten-by-ten box was a small map of the city. A red dot flashed, showing the location of Kulikov's car. A contact within the military had sold them the device for a very reasonable price and guaranteed its performance. Now they would see.

Volodya smiled at Vasily, his head pressing against the top of the car because of the pillow he sat on to ease the pain of his confrontation with the dog. "Give them a minute to get out of sight."

Two minutes later Vilechenko's car pulled into the street and took a course parallel to that of the MB agent's Volga, keeping a block of buildings between them.

Nearly two days, and still the woman was missing. Rustam Starkov was involved but not likely to lead them to the diary. If Kulikov couldn't intimidate him, no one could. Even if he had, it would be best to stick with Kulikov. Eventually the security ministry agent would find the woman. It was just a matter of time. Then they must be ready.

He glanced at his watch—nearly three in the afternoon.

Another fruitless day. They turned right on Lomonosova.
Kulikov's car was now two blocks over, moving north on Nevsky
Prospect and increasing the distance. They seemed to be in a
hurry. Volodya got a knot in his stomach. Possibly Kulikov had
been successful with Rustam Starkov after all.

Chapter Fourteen

RAND PUSHED THE BUTTON AGAIN. If the apartment was on the top floor, it might take some time for Galya to get down to the entrance. He waited. Nothing. Then there was a woman's voice, muffled, on the other side of the door.

"Who is it?"

"Rand King, American Consulate. I have some information for Miss Starkova."

The door opened. A woman of about Rand's age and size stood in the opening. "I am her cousin's wife. I can give it to her."

"It isn't something I can give you. I must talk to Miss Starkova. Is she here?"

The woman look frightened, unhappy. Her eyes darted from side to side as if looking for someone. It made Rand nervous.

"No," she said.

"Then when will she come here? When can I meet with her?" He wished he had called.

"She will not come here." The woman turned to go back into the building.

"She gave me this address." He took the papers out of his pocket. "Rustam Starkov. This is his apartment building?"

"I told you, I am his wife."

"How can I reach him?"

"He is at work!"

"Can you give me a number?"

She hesitated. "All right. 78–87–64." She shut the door.

Rand unlocked the Mercedes. Seating himself and starting the motor, he removed the small cellular phone from under the seat and dialed the number. A year-old contract between America's AT&T and the Russian government had provided such Western technology and was quick to take hold among those who could afford it. After a few minutes he finally had Rustam on the line.

"Mr. Starkov, this is Rand King with the American Consulate. I need to get in touch with your cousin. It is important. She left me your address and phone number."

There was hesitation. He waited.

"You're lucky you caught me. I was just on my way out of this place. Where can she call you?"

He gave the number of the cellular. The sudden click and dial tone didn't surprise him. It was the Russian way.

He started the car and headed home. The phone rang as he crossed Dvortsovaya Bridge four minutes later.

"Mr. King?"

"Miss Starkova. I recognize your voice."

"Do you have my information?"

Rand thought the ice might freeze the phone in his hand. His brow wrinkled.

"Not exactly. We need to talk."

"We have nothing to discuss, Mr. King. I wish only to identify Robert Kitrick."

"I am trying. But there are some rather interesting complications."

"Complications?"

"Not over the phone, Miss Starkova."

There was a pause. "Where are you?"

"Near the Hermitage, just passing the square."

"Go to the Summer Garden. The fountain at the south end." She hung up.

Rand put the phone away. When he went after the consulate job, his direct dealings with the Russian masses had been through an occasional trip, and he hadn't realized how difficult they could be. Years of a system that had bred mistrust often left them cold and unfriendly, afraid to reveal themselves or their feelings, unwilling to let outsiders in. That made an American's life in Russia more difficult.

There was a sizable foreign community in Petersburg, a tight community within the community. Usually a Westerner's social life revolved around the events planned in that inner circle, simply because most of them had given up trying to break through the hardened exterior Russians put up to protect themselves from being hurt or betrayed.

But Rand kept trying. Although he had contact with the Western community, he refused to let himself be drawn totally within its boundaries. He didn't shop at the dollar stores or rely on privilege to get him a better apartment or tickets to the Kirov, now called the Marinsky Theater. He knew Russian but had continued taking some training, working on dialect and the language's nuances. For this purpose he had hired a Russian tutor, a professor from one of the universities who had lived down the hall from Rand.

Most of all, he was up front with the Russians he did come in contact with, letting them know that he would give them a straight answer and trying to earn the trust they needed to do the same. It had been a long road, but over the past few months it had begun paying dividends professionally. He had contacts now, in Petersburg and Moscow, people willing to keep him informed about political events and to help him work the system so that the consulate wasn't always banging its head against a bureaucratic brick wall.

The social arena had opened up as well. The professor, his wife, and two children had become Rand's close friends, introducing him to a wider circle of people who gave him a bigger window through which to see Russian society. Most of the people in his apartment building talked to him now, and the two grandmothers who lived together across the hall had taken him under their wing. They ate together at least once a week, and he took them to do their daily shopping when he could. He was beginning to feel at home but still felt that all the barriers hadn't come down.

All his life he had been told that Russians were set upon controlling the world, taking away other's freedoms and destroying democracy. He had found that most Russians were concerned about the same things he was—having a good life, raising a good family, enjoying good friends. He had discovered that the Russians had seen him in a similar light. He was a part of the great Satan, the government bent on ruling the world and taking away their right to live as they wanted. It had been hard for them to see him as human, a person with the same goals as they had.

Of course, there was a bad element—on both sides. Rand had been forced to fire several professionals from the consulate because they had refused to rid themselves of their biases, and he had run into hard-nosed Russians as well, people so full of hate for everything he stood for that he had wanted to throttle them. There were enough of them to give anyone who didn't really know the people the impression that all Russians were angry, hateful, and to be avoided. Unfortunately, the hateful ones were those he had to deal with most often in consulate business. Most of them were in official positions, the crooked backbone of the bureaucratic system, old party members still wearing the clothing of Soviet indoctrination. The worst were found among the hard-liners of the KGB and the public ministries where they had become entrenched.

He turned left, driving in front of the former general staff headquarters of the tsars, the Triumphal Arch in the center separating the left and right sections of the building. The place was huge, and Rand found himself wondering how the tsar had ever found enough work to keep so many people busy. Of course, executing revolutionaries probably occupied at least half of them. The others were kept busy pounding down the rest of the populace. He had never before lived in a place with such a violent history. When you came right down to it, the Communist system was little different than the system the tsars had used to keep themselves in power. Both had used violent means to deny the Russian people their right to freedom. Both had killed millions to hold onto the thin thread of power.

Rand's thoughts continued to wander. Consulate business. History. Galya Starkova. Ellen. He didn't see the black Zhiguili shadow his turn into Khalturina Street. Traffic was heavy. He had no reason to be looking.

Chapter Fifteen

GALYA STARED OUT THE WINDOW. The apartment was on Volnova
street. Across the Neva she could see Finland Station, the statue
of Lenin in the square out front. She was beginning to wonder if
the people would ever take it down, ever realize that the evil
hadn't started only with Stalin.

It was only a ten-minute walk to the Summer Garden from
Volnova. Turning, she looked at the clock on the wall. Nearly
seven. Larissa was already half an hour late. She hoped Mr. King
would wait.

She felt tired. The sudden move in the night, riding on the
metro until they were sure they weren't being followed, then
coming to this new place that belonged to another of Larissa's
friends, a dancer with the Marinsky Ballet, now on tour in the
United States, had taken its toll. Even when she had finally gotten
back to bed, she couldn't sleep. The adrenaline flow, the fear, was
just too strong.

Galya glanced at her watch again. Larissa had gone for food.
Where was she?

Another five minutes passed.

From the window she saw Larissa coming up the walk.
Relieved, she went to the door, prepared to open it. As the buzzer
sounded, she unlocked the first door. Looking through the peephole, she could see Larissa was there and quickly unlocked the
second. Larissa stepped inside. Galya took half the packages, and
they went into the kitchen and started putting things away.
Potatoes, flour, cheese, eggs, sugar, mint tea, all of Russian ori-

gin. Four oranges from Finland and a sausage from Germany, along with a plastic bag of cookies from Norway. Foreign goods were plentiful in Russia now—expensive but plentiful. Galya was glad that Larissa had balked when she had offered to pay for the groceries they needed. A pleasant side effect of her book— American dollars.

Galya told Larissa about the call from Rand King.

"Does he have what you asked for?"

"He said there were interesting complications. He has to talk to me."

"Have you heard from Rikki?" Larissa asked.

"Nothing. He did tell Rustam and me that the diary was in very bad shape and he would need at least a full day." She put the half-dozen eggs Larissa had purchased into the small refrigerator. "Possibly it will be ready later today."

"It cannot hurt to meet with Mr. King unless you think he is helping the people who are after you," Larissa said.

"I don't know how they found out I was in your apartment, but I don't think it was through Rand King. He isn't the type."

Larissa smiled. "I didn't know collaborators came in types. Be careful, Galya. Some of my worst moments came because I trusted the wrong people."

"Mine also, but Mr. King seems like a person who would hinder the KGB, or his own CIA, if given the chance." She smiled, then shrugged. "A feeling. It is all I have ever relied on, and it is my best guide."

They finished putting the groceries away. Five minutes later, they were turning the corner onto Naberezhnaya, the Fontanka River on their right, the Summer Gardens just beyond, where Galya hoped Rand King was waiting.

"Have you thought any more about who might be after this precious diary?" Larissa asked.

"Constantly, and I am sure of only one thing: It is related to the KGB. Other than that, I have no solutions, no answers."

"While I was out, I met with a friend of mine. He used to work for the Ministry of Security. Now he is a bodyguard for an important American businessman."

"A pleasant change for him."

"And better money." She paused. "He says he thinks he knows who it was you described to me."

"Who?"

"The shorter man is called Ivan, Ivan Kulikov. His partner is named Bondorenko. They work directly for Georgi Zhelin."

"The head of the KGB?"

"Yes, but all of us know that Zhelin works for Vladimir Tupolev. Zhelin is Tupolev's son-in-law."

"And his lackey."

"For now, but my friend says that Zhelin is worse than Tupolev. A butcher."

"They seem to run in packs, don't they."

They walked in silence, moving toward the bridge that would take them across the Fontanka and into the Summer Gardens.

Larissa continued. "My friend . . . he says we should give Tupolev what he wants. If he wants it bad enough, he will kill us for it."

Galya stopped in her tracks. Larissa turned to face her.

"Do you think we should?" Galya asked.

Larissa took her friend's arm and pulled her along. "I think that if Tupolev wants it so badly, it must be important, even dangerous to him. It would be a wonderful thing to help destroy such a man, don't you agree?"

Larissa laughed and Galya joined in, but her heart wasn't in it. She would never forgive herself if someone like Larissa got hurt over Galya's stubbornness.

As they reached the other side of the bridge, Larissa stopped. "Don't worry, Galya, it will be all right. We can always make a deal later." She paused. "I will go first, to make sure King is alone."

When they neared the pond, Galya slipped off to one side and took a seat on a rundown bench. She could see the area that Larissa approached through the trees, but King didn't seem to be around. Larissa sat on the grass and waited. Galya glanced at her watch, keeping an eye on her friend. Where was King? They were late. Possibly he was already gone.

"Hello, Miss Starkova."

Galya turned with a jerk, her face taut with apprehension. It was King.

The fear was visible to Rand. "Sorry. Were you expecting someone else?" Rand said evenly.

"No. You just frightened me. You were supposed to be—"

"Over where your friend is. I know. I saw you cross the bridge. What is going on, Miss Starkova? What are you afraid of?"

Galya's eyes searched for others.

"I'm alone."

Galya looked at him, then away. "Did you find out anything?"

"That depends on whether I get answers or not."

Galya started to stand. "It is not that important. There are other ways to find out what I want to know. I shouldn't have wasted your time, or mine."

"Still chafing from yesterday, Miss Starkova?"

"Are you going to give me what you found out or not?" Galya asked stiffly.

"In 1941 a top-secret operation was put together that involved Robert Kitrick. It has been under wraps for more than fifty years, which is highly unusual, and carries a priority-one classification, also highly unusual, but which indicates an operation of an extremely sensitive nature."

"Nothing on Kitrick himself?"

"His family was of Russian descent, emigrés from the revolutionary period. His father died broke, his mother shortly followed. He was an only child. He was a leader of an anti-Communist movement in New York when still in high school. He joined the army in 1939. He spoke excellent Russian and was immediately involved in intelligence work. He received some sort of special training in 1940." Rand started walking away. "Nice talking to you, Miss Starkova. Have a nice day."

Galya watched him move down the sidewalk. "Wait."

Rand turned but stayed where he was.

"Your country wasn't involved in the war in 1941," Galya said.

"Exactly. So I have a lot of questions. If you are willing to be a little more cooperative, maybe we can both get some answers."

Galya folded her arms, thinking.

Rand smiled. "It is a nice afternoon. The garden is uncrowded and pleasant and gives one a lot to see. Would you like to take a walk?"

Galya returned the smile and joined him as he walked toward the far end of the park.

"Miss Vavilova. Will she be all right?" Rand asked in Russian.

Galya looked at King. "You know her?"

"The Kirov Ballet. In the seventies she left dancing. Rumors were that she had become ill."

"Sick of telling her boss she was not interested in being his mistress." She kept her eyes on the walk. "It would take someone who is familiar with the ballet's history to remember Larissa."

Rand laughed. His voice was masculine but not harsh. Galya liked it. It helped her relax.

"A hobby I acquired when I first came to Petersburg," Rand said. "I hated ballet until I attended the Kirov—excuse me—Marinsky Theater." They both smiled at the change of the name back to the prerevolutionary title. "She and I have met." He shrugged. "Although I doubt she would remember. Why didn't she return after things began to change in Russia? A teacher, an administrative position or something?"

"By the time Gorbachev started his reforms, she had been away from ballet for nearly twenty years. Things change, but even if she had wanted to return to the ballet, perestroika has not broken down all barriers."

She turned to the right, taking a narrow walk that led toward the main walkway passing down the center of the garden.

"Meaning that even after reforms, she is still blackballed?"

Galya glanced at him, then looked ahead at nothing in particular. "You said you have read my book. Do you remember the chapter on punishments?"

Rand nodded while removing his suit coat and putting it over one shoulder, a finger wrapped in the collar. "Execution, gulags, economic sanctions, denial of privileges. You state that all four have been used since Lenin first came to power but that Stalin made the first two a fine art. Krushchev wanted the West to believe those had been stopped, but you state that to make that happen, he had to increase the use of economic sanctions and denial of privileges. You called it blacklisting."

"Very good, Mr. King. I am impressed."

"I had read your work, but after your visit yesterday I decided to brush up."

"Totalitarianism with its oppression of the people runs on fear. There is no other motivation for the masses to do their part. Under Stalin, our system was most productive because of the degree of fear he put into our hearts. Nearly every family lost someone to the NKVD or KGB purges ordered by Stalin. Twenty million people were butchered or sent into slavery in the gulags. The remaining population became pliant, obedient, subservient. It was the destruction of our humanity." She paused.

"When Krushchev came to power, mass executions were stopped, although the people in the camps still numbered in the millions. The size of the gulags began to dwindle through the seventies simply because we no longer needed as much slave labor to mine gypsum and precious metals out of the Siberian plain, or to build dams, railways, and highways. Machinery was better and required more than uneducated slave workers to operate it. Instead, Krushchev bribed our people to go to Siberia and work there. Higher pay, better housing, better food were all offered. Of course, this didn't work as well as originally hoped, so there was still need for political conscription. My father and mother were among these. But Krushchev was confronted with a new problem: His bribes and limited conscription not only did not fill the quotas needed, but without the fear factor, people were no longer motivated to produce for so little money and do as they were told. So he, and those that came to power after him, learned a new method—more subtle but just as effective: blacklisting."

"Deny them privilege."

"Deny them everything, if necessary—home, food, family, friends. You isolate them. Nothing is more demoralizing. They take away your self-respect."

They stopped to look at the statue of the Swedish Queen Christina between the first and second clearings of the main walkway. Because of its detail, Rand considered it one of the finest pieces in the garden.

"When Larissa refused the approach of the minister, she gained an enemy. He used his influence to get even. First he took away her position at the Kirov. That cost her a beautiful apartment and many other privileges. Then she was told she must dance with a small theater group in Murmansk—a humiliation for one of her talent, but she had no choice. Then she was hurt, and her career ended. She no longer had privilege, and she earned a pension that gave her so little she nearly starved. Friends, neighbors, everyone was contacted about her supposed disloyalty to Russia. They were warned off, and she became isolated. When she married, her husband lost all chance of further promotion.

"Larissa fought and refused to bend. That is to her credit. But the greatest lesson was to others. Few, seeing the result of her unwillingness, would follow the same path. More to the point: Few welcome her with open arms, even today. She is still tainted, still an outcast. The KGB, the party, the government win. Their intimidation keeps people in line. Even now, though many of us refuse to be intimidated anymore, even though the party is severely weakened and the KGB has lost at least some of its fangs, it still attempts to use such methods to control people.

"The sad thing is that even though the power of the KGB and the party are waning, people are still afraid—they still bend to the intimidation instead of fighting to be completely free."

Rand could feel Galya's frustration and anger—had felt it in others. There wasn't much he could say.

"Will she join us? I feel like I am being tailed," Rand said.

Galya began walking again. "You are. Larissa indicates that you were followed."

Rand stared at her. "You're joking. How . . . ?"

She started to walk toward the north gate, her expression and demeanor unchanged. Rand moved to her side casually, keeping his exterior unruffled. "What do you suggest?"

She smiled. "As I said, some things have changed. They do not kidnap people off the streets anymore, especially when one of them is an American of consulate stature. For now I think we are in no danger, and Larissa will warn us if that changes."

"Then they are from the Ministry of Security," Rand said.

"It is nice of you to use the new title. So politically correct, but to us they are still the KGB."

Rand knew that she was right about all of it. The new MB was really still active, still using many of the old methods of the KGB. The consulate, he knew, was bugged, and he had been followed more than once. He hadn't been able to prove it, but he was sure a few people inside the consulate were providing information to the Russians for money. For that reason he had always had his assistant, Ted Powell, maintain tight security. But he still suspected leaks.

There was still "spying" by both sides. Witherston, a man in a fairly minor role at the consulate, was CIA, Rand knew that. He didn't like it, but there wasn't a lot he could do about it. And Witherston was pretty easy-going about the whole thing, seemed to be touring a lot and spying a little. That was fine by Rand.

"A point well made. Why are they after you, Miss Starkova? What does Robert Kitrick have to do with it?"

She stopped, facing him. He could see she was making a decision about him. Should she or shouldn't she trust him? He had seen it often. The two babushkas he took shopping, his other neighbors, it was all the same—a period of testing to see if your desire for friendship was sincere or if you were just another person looking for someone to use. Sometimes friendship happened very quickly. Most of the time it took weeks, months, or even years. She seemed to make up her mind and began walking again, but she said nothing.

"Will you answer some questions or not?" Rand asked.

"I do not know that much, but if I feel your questions endanger myself or others, I will not answer."

"Fair enough."

They turned right and walked toward Peter the Great's summer palace, tucked away in the northeast corner of the gardens.

"Where did you get the picture of Kitrick? And who is the woman with him?"

"As I told you, the woman is Norwegian. Her name is Nora Larsen. It is inscribed in the front cover of a book, a diary. Her diary."

"Where did you get the diary?"

Galya thought a moment, then answered. "A few days ago I was on a bus with an old man. I don't know his name, but he was killed. An accident. Before he died, he gave me the diary." Galya told Rand what had happened. They sat on a bench located in the trees between the palace and the tea house. As she spoke, she felt more comfortable. There was something about Rand King that gave her confidence in him and made her feel safe. The feeling was something she hadn't experienced except with close friends like Larissa, but it was always the same. It always felt good. She finished by describing Nora's diary.

"Robert Kitrick is in the diary," Rand said.

Galya nodded. "Yes."

"Then it probably tells us more about the ALLIANCE operation I found in our files in Washington." Rand's brow wrinkled. He didn't like the smell of this. "If the MB is involved, there are two possibilities. Either we are dealing with government secrets, in which case you should give them the diary, or the two men who came for the old man are moonlighting—using their talents in behalf of a private interest. I lean toward the first," Rand said.

"Why?" Galya asked.

"Because of the ALLIANCE file. If Kitrick was involved in some top-secret mission between elements in this country and mine, and it is still under wraps after fifty years, your government and mine both have to consider it important, and we shouldn't be messing with it."

"What would our governments be doing together in 1941?" Galya asked.

Rand shrugged, thinking. "A joint operation against Hitler is one possibility."

"Not in 1941. Stalin was in love with Hitler—so in love he wasn't even willing to accept the overwhelming evidence indicating Hitler's betrayal. He wouldn't have planned to assassinate Hitler."

Rand shrugged. "I am not a student of the period, but other options must exist."

"I don't believe they are working for the government. I believe they are working for Vladimir Tupolev."

Rand's head jerked around to face her straight on. "What?"

Rand knew about Tupolev. The man was a parasite. As head of the consulate, Rand had run into Tupolev's crooked business dealings and powerful connections more than once. But what would he want with a World War II diary written in Norwegian?

"As you are an unsullied, highly qualified journalist who would always back up such a statement with proof, I wait with great anticipation for yours," Rand said with a smirk.

Galya laughed lightly. "A contact with the KGB. He has informed us that Georgi Zhelin hired the two men who came after the old man. Zhelin is controlled by Tupolev."

"Zhelin has interests of his own."

"Either way, one of them is after this diary. I don't think it is for government purposes."

"Zhelin is head of the Ministry of Security. It could still be government," Rand said.

Galya shook her head. "There are few cases in which the KGB has legitimate government interests to protect. When they do, they have no need to sneak about as they do now. A direct approach is warranted."

Rand took a deep breath. "All right, let's suppose you are correct. Tupolev is a powerful adversary, Miss Starkova. He doesn't like people interfering in his affairs. Are you sure you want to mess with him?"

"Tupolev is a cancer. If I can find something that will cut him out of my country's struggle, it will be a good thing."

"Now I understand why you are being so cautious. Has he threatened you?"

"No, but he is looking for me. He isn't sure I have the diary, but he knows I was on that bus." She paused. "I am not afraid of him."

"It is foolish not to be afraid, Miss Starkova, especially of a man like Vladimir Tupolev. He hurts people for fun. What makes you think you are exempt?"

"Not exempt, Mr. King, just hardened. The only thing that Vladimir Tupolev could do to me that others haven't done is take my life. Is it such a big thing?"

Rand didn't answer. All he could do was look at this beautiful, talented woman and know that it would be a loss.

"Do not misunderstand. I have no death wish, but I think that some things are more important than death. More lives would be made pleasurable by ridding my people of men like Tupolev than my life is worth."

Rand would have thought the comment insincere had he not seen the look on her face. Galya Starkova was a determined woman who believed the good of the whole was more important than the life of the one. Pure Marxist dogma—probably one of the few statements Marx had made that made any sense in the long run.

"What does Tupolev want with this diary?"

"I still don't know, but with your help possibly I can find out," Galya said. "Can you tell me anything else about Kitrick?"

"Only that he died in action, so talking to him would be a little difficult." Rand smiled. "I know someone who can take a look at that diary. He is a professor of linguistics at Petersburg University. His specialty is Nordic languages."

"He is a Russian friend?"

Rand nodded.

"He undoubtedly has a family and a good job. We cannot endanger him. Besides, I do not have the diary now. It is being repaired."

"When will you have it back?"

"Possibly this afternoon."

Rand heard a movement behind him and turned to look. Larissa smiled at him as she came to the bench. "May I join you?"

Galya and Rand stood. Rand had made note of Larissa Vavilova's classic good looks the first time he had met her. Then, knowing her past, he had done some quick adding and figured she was better than fifty years of age. But even now her lean, well-proportioned form was that of a much younger woman who paid religious attention to exercise and proper diet—as proper as you could get in Russia. Gray at the temples, her long, brown hair was silky, and her large eyes sparkled even though they showed a depth of experience and hardship he would probably never understand. It was to be expected that there were signs of a hard life—premature creases in her face, her delicate hands hardened with the toil the system had handed her, the elbow slightly bent in a permanent way. But her shoulders were pulled back in the carriage of a dancer, and she had a strong, determined air that called for instant respect.

It suddenly struck him, and he glanced at Galya. The two women were close to the same height and build, their eyes the same shape and color. Except for their difference in age and the fact that Galya's hair had no gray, they could have passed for sisters.

"Larissa, this is Mr. King."

Rand took her hand in both of his and pressed gently. "Nice to see you again," he said.

Larissa thought a moment; then the recognition shone in her eyes. "The church meeting. I remember."

Galya was confused again. "You are a member of Larissa's church?"

"I went to one of the meetings where she spoke. A fireside, I believe they called it. Miss Vavilova is a powerful speaker. Her story was mesmerizing." Rand smiled. "Unfortunately, I haven't been back since."

They started walking toward the main walkway again.

"There are two men watching us. The man in the suit near the tea house and the one behind us and to the left of the sidewalk. He wears knee-length tan shorts with a cream-colored short-sleeve sport shirt. He has a camera and has taken several pictures."

"The one in the suit is one of the men who was after the man on the bus," Galya said, looking at Rand. "They are Tupolev's men. I am afraid you *are* involved now. I am sorry," she said.

"Not to worry." He smiled. "Diplomatic immunity."

"The KGB do not care much for such immunities, believe me," Galya said. She turned to Larissa. "It will be easier to lose them if they think we have given Mr. King the diary."

Larissa nodded.

Galya opened her purse and handed Rand a package wrapped in brown paper, like the one she had said the diary was wrapped in. He put on his suit coat, then placed the package in the pocket.

"You were prepared," he said.

"If they stop you and take the package, let them have it. It is a copy of my book. They should read it, don't you think?" Her eyes smiled at him, and the touch of her hand lingered on his fingers as he took the book.

"Miss Starkova . . . "

"Galya, please," she said evenly.

"Galya, meet me at the consulate. I only have knowledge of the cover sheet of the ALLIANCE file. Now that we have met, I intend to see if I can look at it more carefully."

"When?"

"Unless these delightful gentlemen detain me for consorting with their enemy, I'll be there all evening. Come to the side entrance. I'll leave word to let you in."

Galya smiled. "Thank you, Rand King. We will try to keep this appointment," she said in broken English. Rand smiled his approval at her show of friendship. "Good-bye," Galya finished.

Larissa left, walking south toward the tea house. Galya turned on her heel and walked back the way she and Rand had come. He watched after them. Two very individualistic, stubborn women who could get into a lot of trouble trying to stop a man like Vladimir Tupolev. He admired their determination but feared for their lives. But he could see he wouldn't be able to talk them out of the course they were on.

Rand walked toward Peter's summer palace, one of the few tourist attractions he had never been inside. Now was a good

time. Maybe he could divert at least some of the women's ene-
mies away from them. He smiled at his chauvinistic concern.
Larissa and Galya had survived the KGB most of their lives.
Compared to them, he was the novice.

And the most likely to be found in the enemy's net when the
fishing was over.

Rand moved toward the museum housed in Peter the Great's
summer home. He had never been there before; this was as good
a time as any to see it.

Chapter Sixteen

NICKOLAI POLTAV WATCHED THE AMERICAN enter the palace. Kulikov followed, along with another agent Nickolai had never seen before—medium height, wavy brown hair, the look of a young tourist from the West. His clothes were Western as well, and he carried a camera. Nickolai ignored them and fell in behind the one following Galya Starkova.

He had seen Starkova give the package to King but, unlike Kulikov, he didn't think it was the package he was looking for. It had to be a phony. She was a journalist, and she wasn't about to hand over the diary to an American she hardly knew.

As he left the garden and came onto the sidewalk bordering Kutazova Street, Nickolai was alarmed to see Kulikov's partner, Bondorenko, getting out of a car at the curb with two others just like him in tow. He was even more concerned to see Georgi Zhelin sitting in the car behind Bondorenko's. That could only mean one thing: Bakatin was no longer in charge of finding the package. That meant his betrayal had been discovered and they were all in trouble. It was no longer a game of cat and mouse with the Starkova woman. Now that she was alone, shed of the American, they would pick her up. The thought was unpleasant.

Nickolai watched, keeping himself in the crowd. They wouldn't recognize him. Shortly after leaving Bakatin at the restaurant, Nickolai had changed his appearance in order to follow Kulikov and catch up with the Starkova woman. He had the look of a World War II veteran on a pauper's pension who had lost an eye and had a limp. The suit with the medals attached to the lapel and coat pocket was two sizes too small, and the old Lenin hat was greasy and full of holes from years of use. The shoes were beat-up boots with hobnail soles, and the cane was nothing more than a tree branch wiped clean of its bark. The moustache was bushy, like Stalin's, but gray, with a few bread crumbs. The smell he had added to the coat made people look, then turn away.

The only trouble was the eye patch. A man his age had a hard enough time seeing without losing half his vision to a greasy piece of leather.

The woman moved along the walk to the bus stop, her step picking up. She had recognized the danger. Nickolai hobbled along at a quicker pace. He had to stay close. If Starkova was foolish enough to bring the package along, these men would have her, and it, hustled away before he could get to her. That would put his chances of finding out what was going on at next to nothing.

The men were moving in as the bus doors opened to reveal an overflowing load of people. The Starkova woman pushed her way through the crowd surrounding the door as Bondorenko reached for her, grabbing an elbow. She jerked it free and injected herself into the bus by squeezing through a dozen people. Bondorenko started shoving people aside, trying to follow, but the crowd erupted with anger, calling him names and shoving him back, blind to who he was, their sights set only on getting aboard the late afternoon bus.

Nickolai suddenly realized he would lose the woman himself unless he got on the trolley. Quickly he limped to the front door, the one near the driver, rapping on it with his cane. Drivers usually opened only the back and middle doors of the bus, leaving the front one shut to protect their own little domain from becoming crowded. The driver saw him—and the hundred-ruble note in his hand—and opened the door. Nickolai hustled on as the bus started away. He opened the small door to the driver's compartment and shoved the rubles inside. Using the driver's-side mirror, he could see Bondorenko still trying to shove his way onto the bus as it pulled into traffic. The doors were slapping at the back-

sides of half a dozen people still pushing themselves inside, and
Bondorenko and his men couldn't get past them. As the doors
closed, the agent cursed, then moved quickly to the cars.

As the bus slipped in behind a car and a delivery truck,
Nickolai sought the woman with his unpatched eye. He found her
squashed between two men who both looked pleased. One said
something, and she shoved away, pushing through the crowd with
a disgusted look on her face. She tried to position herself so as to
see out a window but had no luck. Nickolai could see the wheels
turning inside her head as she sought desperately for a solution to
her problem.

A young woman saw Nickolai and stood, offering him the
chair she had been using. At least the disguise was still working.
He took it, his mind working on the problem he knew would confront them at the next stop. Unless he did something, Bondorenko
would be waiting.

Rand stood in front of the glass cases in which some of Peter
the Great's clothing was displayed. The man in the suit was
behind and to his left, the tourist type leaning over the barrier and
squinting at the display.

"Old stuff," The tourist said in English.

"Umm, 1700s. Are you from the states?" Rand asked.

"Just got here."

"What city?"

"San Diego, California."

"It has been cloudy there lately then?"

The man looked at him curiously.

"San Diegans are people with eternal tans, but your skin is as
white as the backside of a newborn infant." Rand faced the suit,
speaking in Russian. "I'm with the American consulate. You boys
have a problem?"

Kulikov didn't smile but nodded for the tourist to keep people
out of the room. The younger man pushed an incoming tourist
harshly through the double doors and closed them, five feet away
from Rand.

"The woman gave you something that belongs to the Russian people. We are here to get it," Kulikov said.

"Do you have some identification?" Rand asked.

The suit didn't move.

"I thought not. If you will excuse me . . . " Rand started for the door. The tourist blocked his way.

"Sorry. Just let him have the package. No sense having a war over so little a thing," the man said in perfect English.

"Maybe this will help," the suit said.

Rand turned to see the Makarov in the agent's hand.

"Ah, KGB, what a revelation. Oh. Sorry. It's MB now, isn't it. I get so confused anymore." He removed the package from his pocket and tossed it at the suit, breaking his concentration as he tried to juggle it and the gun. Rand grabbed the tourist by the camera strap around his neck and jerked, throwing the weight of the man into the suit's midsection. The gun and the book fell to the floor as both men crashed against the wall, then went down in a tangle. Rand picked up the gun first, aiming it at the suit's head, then retrieved the package.

The room fell quiet, the men staring at the gun, rigid, unmoving. Rand unwrapped the brown paper, revealing the copy of Galya's book. He waved it at the two men. "Buy your own copy."

He walked to the suit and removed the wallet from inside his coat, opening it to reveal the man's identity papers. He read them.

"Colonel Kulikov, who sent you?"

No reply. Rand stuck the gun barrel in Kulikov's ear and pushed, making him wince.

"I didn't hear you."

"Dimitri Bakatin."

"Don't lie." He pushed harder.

"Zhelin. Ministry of Security."

Galya was right.

"Colonel Kulikov, I will register an official complaint with the better part of your government about you and Mr. Zhelin. Our countries are friends now, and they won't like some half-wit like you giving them bad press. I don't want to see your ugly face any-

where close to me, the consulate, or my personal quarters. If I do,
I might get real nasty."

Rand slid both the wallet and the Makarov across the floor.
They came to rest under the glass cabinets housing Peter's clothing. Standing, he walked to the door and opened it. The crowd
gathered there must have alerted the matron, because she and a
security guard were hustling down the hall toward him. They
looked upset.

"There are two men in there trying to steal Peter's clothes,"
he said in Russian. "Stalin would have shot people like that. You
really ought to be more careful who you let in here."

The guard pulled his gun as he approached the door. Rand
had moved a comfortable distance down the hall when the yelling
started.

Nickolai stood and rapped on the door to the driver's compartment with his cane. The door opened, and he slipped the
upper portion of his body inside as he pulled his identification
from his pocket and showed it.

"I don't want you stopping until you get to Finland Station,
understand?"

The driver gulped, then nodded. Nickolai went back to his
seat. It wasn't uncommon for a loaded bus to skip a few stops,
unless there were passengers who wanted off. Then they'd raise a
stink, but that couldn't be helped.

As they approached the first stop, the Chaika came to the curb
and started disgorging Bondorenko and the others. By the time
they realized the bus wasn't going to pull in, it was already passing through the light and turning to cross Liteyny Bridge. Traffic
was heavy, and the Chaika got caught in a jam. It might give them
enough time.

Half a dozen people were cursing the driver for missing their
stop and crossing the bridge, but Nickolai could see that Galya
Starkova was relieved. The bus turned right, then ran along the
Neva for another five hundred yards before coming to a stop in
Lenin Square, directly in front of Finland Station.

Finland Station is the railway station where Lenin arrived to take command of the revolutionary forces after the revolution had already begun. There was a huge statue of the leader in the square and the station was one of the city's busiest. A metro station was inside the main building. Nickolai watched as the woman pushed herself free of the bus and ran toward the station. He followed, neglecting to hobble as he should but sure the woman was too busy staring at the Chaika coming over the bridge to notice. She pushed through the outer doors. He followed. When he shoved his way through the crowd to the gates, she was already rummaging for a token but couldn't find one. Pulling rubles from her purse, she went to the teller and bought half a dozen. Nickolai was already through when she dropped her token into the slot and headed for the escalator. Nickolai allowed a few people to separate them, glancing over his shoulder to see Bondorenko coming through the crowd, then knocking people aside as he pushed for the gate. The alarm sounded, indicating he and the two with him hadn't paid. Seeing the red identification booklet in his hand, the guard ignored them while the rest of the people moved to clear a path. They shoved their way through and moved onto the escalator. Nickolai watched as the woman pushed her way feverishly through the mass of bodies being carried into the earth. He followed, still doing his best to act the part of the old man he appeared to be. He felt a heavy hand on his shoulder as he was shoved aside, Bondorenko focusing only on the woman.

Nickolai saw her eject herself from the bottom of the escalator and begin running down the tunnel, looking over her shoulder. She disappeared under the arches to the left where the boarding area was. Bondorenko would have her before the train arrived unless something was done.

Fearful, Nickolai entered the boarding area on the heels of Bondorenko and his two henchmen. He was relieved to find that Galya Starkova had disappeared. The KGB thug sent the two other men back into the main hallway and across it to the loading ramp for the train going the opposite direction, then began his search for the woman in the mass of humanity waiting for the train on his side of the tunnel. Nickolai kept close to the archway, moving silently behind Bondorenko while watching for Galya Starkova. The sound of the train rumbled in the tunnel, then discharged itself from the darkness into the light. The scream of metal on metal filled the cavity in the earth as the train braked from nearly fifty miles an hour to a standstill.

Nickolai watched the doors, waited. Bondorenko seemed to spot her, then shoved people aside in a desperate attempt to reach her before the doors closed. Nickolai slipped close to him, shoving the cane between the man's legs and jerking backward. Bondorenko stumbled and started to fall, a mountain collapsing onto the people around him. His desperate grab to right himself frightened the woman on whose shoulder his grip closed, and she screamed. Men and women reacted, pushing, shoving, their desire to get on the train forgotten as they tried to keep upright, tried to keep their packages from being crushed.

Nickolai stepped back from the crowd and entered the first door of the car. Galya had entered at the far end. As the doors closed, Nickolai chuckled at the sight of Bondorenko struggling to stand over the people who had fallen around him, his fists clenched, his eyes on the train as it disappeared into the tunnel.

Volodya Vilechenko watched from a distance as Zhelin and his people moved in on the Starkova woman boarding the trolley bus. He was too late but elated when Galya made the bus, leaving Zhelin's people behind.

They had followed Kulikov back to Vasilevsky Island, to the apartment of the cousin, and had watched the agents hassle the man's wife at the entrance door until she was in tears. Once they were through with their intimidation tactics, they had returned to the car and waited for an hour before the American's Mercedes had pulled up in front and a man Volodya had recognized as Rand King, head of the American consulate, had approached the door. Volodya had watched as Kulikov's car fell in behind King. Vasily, his driver, had waited until they were sure the other vehicles were crossing the bridge off the island before he had turned on the tracking device, only to discover it had stopped working.

Quickly they had tried to catch up, but neither the American's Mercedes nor Kulikov's Volga were anywhere to be seen. They began searching for the vehicles from street to street. After nearly thirty minutes, the tracking device decided to work, and the red blip led them to the Summer Gardens.

Volodya had begun a search of the gardens, starting at the end by the fountain. He had found King and the Starkova woman at the other end, near the palace, another woman with them. As he had been about to approach, they had broken away from each other and headed off in different directions. He had started to follow Starkova when he saw Zehlin and his men at the curb and was forced to retreat.

As he returned to his car, Volodya saw the other woman standing at the street, waiting to cross into the Field of Mars war memorial. As she started to cross, he told his driver what to do.

"Vasily, follow her. Stop her on the far side of the street. I'll meet you with the car. Be careful, I don't want her hurt."

Vasily quickly dodged through traffic as Vilechenko started the car. If the Starkov woman escaped, this one would know where he could find her. It was his only hope.

Larissa walked across the street into the Field of Mars, a large park whose central feature was a monument to the fighters of the revolution. The evening air was pleasant, and dozens of people were sitting on the benches and grass enjoying a few minutes of relaxation. It was a five-minute stroll across the field to the Marble Palace, a branch of the Central Lenin Museum. Larissa had friends who worked there and who would usher her out through the employees' exit, giving her a chance to escape from the man she knew had crossed the street after her.

When Larissa reached the monument in the center of the field, she stopped to look at the eternal flame burning there, then turned casually to look at a parent picking up a child who had scraped a knee; actually she was checking on the location of her pursuer. The agent was nowhere to be seen.

Larissa moved on, the composed look on her face refusing to

reveal the anxiety in her stomach. There was nothing worse than not knowing where they were, what they had planned. She hadn't thought they would be so brazen as to try to pick them up in broad daylight. It made her think they were in more danger than she had allowed herself to believe.

The old fear of being hunted crept into her stomach. Her breathing became rushed and erratic. The old dreads, the interrogations, the damp cells and endless faces came back like a bad dream. She thought she had controlled all those old fears, that this time things would be different, but the fear was back, staring at her, making her cringe before it again.

She strode down the walk, the statue of Suvorov directly ahead across the square. Her muscles cried out to run, her eyes wanting to search right and left, locate the enemy, know where they were, but she kept her feet and eyes moving only toward Suvorov. She had done this before, too many times to count. She prayed silently for calm—for escape.

Then he was to the side of her, a car pulling up in front of them. He grabbed her arm before she could wrestle her way free.

"Don't be alarmed, Miss Vavilova. We are not KGB. We only wish to talk to you."

The door opened and the first man tried to push her through the door. The driver turned, a smile on his face. He said something but it didn't register. She could think only of getting away. She was afraid, afraid that if she got into that car it would be the beginning of more pain. Like before—so many times before! She prayed harder.

Leaning forward a little, relaxing the tension between their two arms, she jerked back, pulling herself away. Swinging her free hand, she hit the man in the nose, then raked his shins with the low, pointed heel of one shoe. He let go, cursing, but then tried to grab her again.

She ducked his reach and catapulted herself past him. She ran into the wide street, avoiding traffic, dashing for the other side. The man was after her now, darting, dodging, horns honking, people cursing. She glanced over her shoulder. Her ankle gave way, and she went down as her heel caught on the edge of one of the millions of potholes in the Petersburg streets. As she picked herself up, the assailant came around the only car that separated them. The man in the white suit, the one who had been driving, joined the first, grinning as he stepped forward, a hand extended. "Please . . . "

He looked up. The car was bearing down on him so fast that all he could do was step back or get hit. The Mercedes braked to a skidding stop between him and Larissa. She scrambled to her feet as the car door swung open and Rand King's face appeared.

"Get in," he said, already putting the car in motion. She swung into the seat and slammed the door closed, slugging the lock with the open palm of her hand. Through the rear-view mirror, Rand stared at the man in white who was left behind, motionless, frustrated.

The muscleman stepped to the man's side, and Rand pushed on the gas feed, the Mercedes skidding to greater speed, leaving both standing in the middle of the street.

"Who were they?" Rand asked.

"I . . . I don't know," Larissa said, trying to catch her breath while she rubbed her sore ankle. "At first I thought they were KGB, even when they said they weren't, but . . . but somehow it was wrong. They aren't KGB. They aren't Tupolev's people."

Rand saw the men hustling back to their own car. They'd be after them. "You're right. They're not KGB. KGB agents don't drive Mercedes." He took a deep breath. "I think we have another player."

Chapter Seventeen

GALYA FELT EXHAUSTED as the escalator carried her to the surface at Vosstaniya Station. Her pursuers would be on the next train but wouldn't know where she had gotten off. From here she could walk back to the apartment.

She felt the hand on her elbow as she came through the doors into the sunlight. The touch took her breath away.

"Keep moving, Miss Starkova. We do not know when they might have people here. I suggest a taxi." The pressure on her elbow directed her to the street. A cab was at the curb half a block away.

"Who are you?"

"You do not recognize me?" Nickolai asked with a smile.

"No . . . " She looked at him directly. He lifted the patch. "I still . . . "

"It doesn't matter. I saved your life back there. That should be a good enough recommendation."

"You caused all that?"

"Mr. Bondorenko was very cooperative. Without him . . . well, things could have gotten rather messy for you." He paused. "You know, you aren't very popular with them right now. First, you write nasty books about their operations, then you steal their property. Tut, tut, Miss Starkova, you have been a bad girl."

She glanced at him but didn't reply.

The cab driver took one look at Nickolai's clothes and started shaking his head in the negative. A beggar had no money for taxis. Nickolai pulled the rubles from his pocket as a sign of his sincerity.

"Where to, Miss Starkova?" Nickolai asked as they slid into the back seat.

No answer.

He leaned forward, speaking to the driver. "St. Isaac's Cathedral." He smiled at Galya. "As good a place as any for the moment, don't you think? Very public, a good place to talk, and the last place they would expect you to be—not to mention it is one of my favorite places to see in Petersburg."

"Why are you following me?"

"A simple thing. I want the package."

He started removing the makeup. Galya was amazed at the transformation. "Nickolai . . . the man on the bus. You . . . you were after the old man. You *are* KGB then. Tupolev . . . "

"I have no connection to the KGB, or Tupolev, but we'll talk about my credentials later. What do you know about the package?"

"We discuss your credentials now," she said firmly.

He removed his papers and handed them to her. "I'm after an organization, Miss Starkova. A very dangerous one. The same one that is after you."

Galya read the paper. "Nickolai Poltav. I remember now. You were once with the Moscow police. I tried to get an interview with you several years ago when you were in Novosibirsk, but you were never available."

"You didn't try that hard. One call."

"I was running out of time, and I had enough material. The KGB was suspicious, starting to make inquiries about my work. I thought it might be dangerous."

"You were right. They were watching me that trip. I was after one of their agents for murder."

"Did you catch him?"

"Two days later. I read your book. Well-done research, accurate, but you offer no solutions, only tell us what we all knew anyway."

Galya winced at the attack on the one sore spot she had about her work.

"So far you have been lucky, Miss Starkova. Tupolev's people have not found you, but obviously they are moving closer. They will find you again." He paused, glancing out the window as they passed over the Fontanka. "You are in over your head, Miss Starkova. Tupolev wants that package, and he will do anything to have it."

No answer. Galya only stared out the window.

———————

Agent Ivan Kulikov jerked on the wheel, whipping the Volga into Dvortsvaya Square and aiming it toward the bridge that led to Vasilevsky Island.

Rustam Starkov was a mouse, a vermin, who had let recent political changes affect his thinking, given him a false sense of bravery. Kulikov intended to teach the vermin a lesson—one that would make Starkov wish he had never been born.

He slammed on the brakes and jerked the wheel again, then pushed on the horn and yelled a curse at the driver of the trolley bus he had barely missed. He glanced at Bondorenko. The big man was sweating, fear in his eyes. Kulikov smiled, pushing on the gas and running the light, narrowly escaping a collision with two vehicles entering the intersection. Bondorenko's knuckles went white, his grip hardening on the dashboard, but he said nothing. He knew Kulikov's moods, knew when to keep his mouth shut. They sped across the bridge and turned left.

"Where are we going?" Bondorenko asked.

"To visit a lady," Kulikov said, an evil grin filling the lower third of his face. "Starkov said to ask his wife. So we ask his wife."

———————

The taxi pulled up to the cathedral. Nickolai paid the driver, and they got out. They didn't talk until they had climbed the steps and Nickolai had purchased a ticket for each of them to go inside the church. They charged for everything nowadays—more for tourists. That was one thing about the old system Nickolai hated to see change. But money had to be raised to keep everything up. The government was just too broke to do it all. They went inside.

"I want you to trust me, Miss Starkova, so I will tell you something I wouldn't otherwise." He proceeded to tell her about Dimitri Bakatin's involvement and betrayal of Tupolev. "Bakatin believes the diary might document atrocities Tupolev may have committed at the end of the war," he said.

They were looking at the beautiful art overhead. St. Isaac's contained more than 150 murals and pictures in oils, the largest collection of Russian monumental painting of the nineteenth century.

"Trust me, Miss Starkova. Help me end Tupolev's abuse of Russia's laws and people."

Galya found herself in the same predicament for the second time in less than an hour, but the fear engendered by Tupolev's men and the fact that Nickolai had saved her life made up her mind. She was in over her head and needed help. But she wasn't about to turn it all over to someone else, either. She was in, she would stay in. After a moment she spoke. "Postwar atrocities are not possible. The diary is of an earlier period, 1941." She told him about the package. "I have information that there was a joint operation between Russians and Americans in 1941. Do you know of any such plan?"

Nickolai was relieved at the show of trust. "None, but I am not a student of the war. Even if I were, I doubt that I would know of such a thing. Our government is not in the habit of revealing clandestine operations for public criticism."

They were in the west end of the cathedral where the paintings were of Old Testament scenes. In the central section of the vault was *The Vision of the Prophet Ezekiel.*

They continued walking toward the sculpted doors, where a guide was pointing out how Vitali had carved the figures so that they were almost in the round. It was a beautiful piece of work. Several tourists noticed the odor coming from Nickolai's clothes. He smiled at them, then took Galya by the arm and moved her away. "The hazards of effective disguise," he said.

"If you are after Tupolev, you must know something of his past. Where was he in 1941?" Galya asked.

"Tupolev's records are inconclusive, even misleading. But we do know that at the beginning of the war, when you say this diary was being written, he was a soldier stationed in Talinn. When the Nazis took the city, the troops were forced to retreat into Leningrad. He was with them."

"Even though I cannot read the diary as a whole, I noticed that the word Leningrad appears several times there."

"There was a lot of looting, theft, black-market crimes, and even the selling of human flesh for food. Possibly Tupolev was involved and the diary documents it," Nickolai said.

"It is possible, and enough to destroy him, I suppose, but I don't think this is about such things."

They walked to the right, looking at the icons there.

"Nickolai, could you even prosecute for war crimes from fifty years ago? It has been a long time."

Nickolai shrugged. "I am not a prosecutor, but Tupolev's actions are those of someone in danger. Possibly he fears prosecution. Whatever it is, he is acting out of self-preservation. When a man like that acts to save himself, everyone around him is in mortal danger.

"Why is Yeltsin after Tupolev now? For years they have made their deals and endured or ignored one another."

"Tupolev was one of the movers behind the overthrow of Gorbachev, and the more recent attempt to oust Yeltsin."

"There is proof?"

"None that was made public. But let me continue. These failures have diminished his power. He does not like it and works to get it back. We think he is trying to set up a parallel economy and establish a new power structure from which to work, a criminal hierarchy through which he can manipulate or even create competing economic conditions. We think he believes that he can defeat Yeltsin's reforms this way, thus defeating Yeltsin. In the chaos, his organization can regain control of power."

"And return it to Communism."

"Not necessarily. Tupolev doesn't care what form the government takes as long as his people have the control. He would support a king or a president as long as they were willing to do as they were told."

They were standing under the vault of the dome staring up at the paintings but not really seeing them.

Nickolai continued. "Over the years Tupolev has built a wall of protection around himself that law enforcement has never been able to breach. It is my job to find a weakness."

"Tupolev is old; his death will end his empire."

"Georgi Zhelin will take over. He is worse. By stopping Tupolev now, I stop them both."

He took her arm gently and pulled her toward the main iconostasis with the holy doors to the sanctuary at its center. "I have never been a religious man, but the artwork, it is magnificent," he said peering at the pictures in front of them.

"I assume you weren't foolish enough to take the package into the gardens."

Galya shook her head. "No."

"Where is it?"

"It was in bad need of repair. A man who does such things for the Hermitage has it."

"How did you contact this man?"

"He is a friend of my cousin's. We took it to him yesterday."

"When? What time?"

"About five in the afternoon. Why?"

"Tupolev's people were watching your cousin's house then."

"I wasn't at my cousin's at the time, and we made sure we weren't being watched before we made contact with the restorationist."

She became alarmed as she figured out what he was getting at. "You don't think . . . "

"I think they have lost you. They will return and talk to him. They are frustrated, tired of this game you are playing with them. They are dangerous."

"I should warn him." She started toward the entrance.

Nickolai was by her side. "A telephone." He showed his papers to the woman at the front desk, and she directed them to a room off the main chapel. Galya dialed. It rang five, six, seven times.

"Hello?" Galya breathed a sigh of relief. "Rustam! Are you all right?"

"Yes, of course. What is wrong, Galya?"

"You must leave immediately. Take Natalya. Go somewhere, where they can't . . . "

"Natalya isn't here."

Galya's heart stopped. "Where is she?"

"I don't know. Usually she . . . She never leaves the apartment alone. Possibly she has gone shopping with friends."

"Rustam, did she know about Rikki?"

The phone was silent.

"Rustam! Did she—"

Rustam's voice was hardly audible. "She knew that Rikki worked on documents. I told her I had seen him—that you were with me."

Galya felt faint and had to sit down. Nickolai took the phone and quickly explained who he was.

"Now listen carefully. We will go to your friend's apartment. You can meet us there. Don't panic. She might just be—"

Rustam interrupted Nickolai and told him about the confrontation at the office, about losing his job. Nickolai told him to go to Rikki's apartment. Then he hung up.

Galya forced the fear out of her mind, grasped to get control. Now was no time for weakness. She stood and walked stiffly to the door. Nickolai followed.

"They have Natalya."

"Come on. Do you know the address?" Nickolai asked.

"Yes."

They were already out of the entrance and moving down the stairs.

They ran along the walk, crossing the street to catch a cab parked in front of the Astoria. Galya glanced at the place where the bus had unloaded a few hundred feet away. There was nothing to indicate that all of this had started there, that one man had already given his life for the diary.

Galya felt the knot in her stomach. Natalya, an innocent, frightened woman she hardly knew, might already be the second. And it would be her fault.

"How did you know I was in trouble?" Larissa asked as they made yet another turn, making sure they weren't being followed.

"I didn't. Blame your good fortune on Petersburg's traffic plan. I went that way because I was on a one-way street. When I saw you and saw what was happening, I just pointed the car."

"What happened to you? How did you get away?" Larissa asked.

"I showed them the book Galya gave me. They lost interest."

She glanced at him, knowing there was more to it, but decided against another question.

"They probably went after Galya," Rand said.

She glanced over her shoulder. "Do you think we have lost them?"

"We've been chasing around this city for fifteen minutes. That car would stand out as badly as this one. I haven't seen a sign of them."

Larissa thought a moment, her eyes searching Rand's. "If they did not catch Galya, she will return to the apartment I found for her."

"And if they did catch her?"

"They will make her tell where the diary is."

"Then we should go after the diary first. If nothing else, it can be used to bargain for her freedom."

Larissa considered that. "Your position—you cannot be involved in this."

"As Galya said, I am already involved."

"Not enough to do you harm. You must let me off where I tell you. I will retrieve the diary and—"

"I am in, Larissa; no more arguments. When I saw you two in the park, I thought you looked enough alike to be sisters. Now that I've seen you have the same stubborn streak, I'm sure of it," Rand said with a smile. "Does the restorationist have a phone?"

She nodded in the affirmative without looking his direction. He picked up the cellular and handed it to her.

She smiled, relieved. Pushing the numbers, she put the phone to her ear.

"Rikki?" She hung up, her face pale. "It . . . it was someone else—a voice I don't recognize." She turned to Rand, giving him the address. "Please hurry."

Rustam felt his stomach turn over again, felt the hard sickness of fear shove bile into his throat. He struggled with the apartment keys, trying to lock the doors and get on his way. He dropped them for the second time, stooped, took a deep breath, and said a quick prayer in an attempt to get his nerves under control. He had never felt this way before—not even in the military when he lived in danger as a normal course of events.

Standing, he shoved the key into the keyhole, pulled on the door, and slid the lock into the slot. He yanked once to be sure, then turned and took the stairs two at a time.

Natalya was all right. She had to be all right. He couldn't live with himself if they had hurt her—or worse.

Closing the outside door, he looked up and down the street while moving toward where his car was parked. Nothing. Unlocking the door, he slid behind the wheel, fumbled the keys again, picked them up, and jabbed them into the hole, finally ramming the key into place.

The car wouldn't start. He turned the key again, the anxiety overflowing into his stomach and making him choke. The starter turned, but no ignition.

"Please, dear Lord. Please!" He turned the key again. Nothing.

Opening the door, he went to the front of the car, popped open the hood, and peered inside. He knew the motor like the back of his hand—a necessity in Russia, where parts and auto mechanics were as scarce as the hair on a bald man's pate. What he saw made the blood sink to his toes. His distributor cap was missing. That meant agent Kulikov had taken more than his job. He had also taken his wife.

———————

Nickolai took Galya's arm and together they moved across the street from where they had been standing for nearly five minutes. Nickolai was being cautious, but they hadn't seen anything out of the ordinary, and both were anxious about Natalya.

Galya retrieved the numbers for the door lock from her memory as they approached the scarred and run-down entrance. Rustam had given her the numbers in case both of them couldn't go after the diary when Rikki finished it. Rustam had repeated them several times, but now she was struggling to remember. After a brief hesitation, she pushed the numbers and heard the latch slip free. Nickolai opened the door, and they entered.

Galya cringed at the dark, hot, smelly hallway, the thought of the man with the knife still fresh in her mind. Nickolai sensed her anxiety and gripped her arm tighter. They moved toward the lighter outline that must be the stairs.

"No one replaces light bulbs anymore," Nickolai said.

They went up the stairs, the musty smell heavy in Galya's nostrils.

Rikki's apartment was on the third floor behind a fake leather door with buttons fastened through it. Nickolai stiffened as a streak of light cascaded from the crack in the opening. Galya felt her hands get clammy, felt sweat trickle down the side of her face. Pushing the door lightly, Nickolai peered into the hallway.

"What is it?" Galya asked. She glanced over Nickolai's shoulder and saw the body in the hall. Natalya lay on the floor.

Galya fell to Natalya's side and ran her fingers through the woman's hair. Nickolai knelt by the body and felt for a pulse.

"Natalya?" she said quietly. "Oh, Natalya, please, say something! You have to be all right!"

"She is breathing," Nickolai said.

Galya's lungs filled with air as the tension in her chest relaxed.

"Help me turn her over."

Galya felt the scream jump into her throat and slapped a hand over her mouth to keep it from escaping. Tears sprang into her eyes as she choked off the curses flooding her mind. Natalya's face was battered and bloody, her eyes so badly swollen that they were nothing but slits of bloated flesh. Nickolai felt down the arms, then unbuttoned her shirt and felt the rib cage.

"They always break the ribs. The danger is a punctured lung." He felt Natalya's ribs gingerly, probing. At the third rib, he felt the bone give. Two more were broken as well.

"She's in bad shape," Nickolai said through clenched teeth. "Probably a concussion." He stood and went to a desk near the living area window. Selecting a bottle from among work things scattered about the desk, he brought it back and removed the lid. A strong chemical odor filled the room. Nickolai stuck the jar under Natalya's nose. Her head jerked, her cut and swollen lips emitting a moan. Nickolai gave her another dose, then leaned down near the injured woman's ear and spoke. Natalya's lips moved slightly. Nickolai placed his ear near the swollen mouth. Bending down, Nickolai spoke softly again, then stood up, moved back to the desk, and dialed the phone.

"This is Poltav. Get Vostya." A pause. "Vostya, I am at apartment 13, 52 Baskov Street. A woman has been badly beaten. Get an ambulance here." Another pause. Nickolai answered several questions about Natalya's condition, then hung up.

"Vostya works for me. He will have help here as quickly as he can. We will cover her and take precautions against shock. If there are any badly bleeding wounds, we should try to bandage them tightly."

Nickolai looked more closely at Natalya while Galya tore a blanket from the bed and covered the unconscious woman from chin to foot. It was then she noticed that the apartment was a shambles. They had ransacked the place.

"No visible blood," Nickolai said. "But that worries me. She could be bleeding internally. I don't know what Vostya will be able to arrange, what kind of medical help we will get. Our contacts aren't as strong here as in Moscow. We are just beginning to locate in Petersburg." He paused as he pushed gently but firmly on the abdomen. "Rikki is the restorationist?"

Galya nodded, suddenly realizing that Rikki was not in his own apartment.

"Where could he be?" she asked.

Nickolai didn't answer.

Galya sat on the couch, her head bowed. She wanted to die. How could she face Rustam? How would he deal with this? After all this and they had the diary anyway. It had been foolish to try to evade them. Foolish! Just as Natalya had said. And now she had paid for Galya's haughty pride. To think she could somehow defeat Tupolev, his power, his control. So stupid! Stupid!

Nickolai went to the bathroom, returned with some rubbing alcohol, knelt, and began cleaning Natalya's wounds. Galya got to her knees, took the alcohol, and did the cleaning.

"What will they do to Rikki?" She asked, remembering the frail man Rustam had called counselor—remembering the kindness.

"I don't know. It is you I worry about now—you and this woman. For them to do this . . . " His voice was hard, cold. "They are animals! They will kill you. This is their message to all of us. We must get you to a safe place as soon as we can."

Galya finished cleaning the wounds and put down the alcohol. She rubbed her hand over Natalya's forehead and then through her hair.

Nickolai began bandaging Natalya's wounds.

"They will pay for this." The ice in his voice gave Galya a chill, and she knew it was more than an empty promise.

After they had finished bandaging, Nickolai walked to the window and moved the lace curtain just enough to peer into the street. It had been ten minutes since the phone call, but ambulance service in Russia was horrible. Nickolai wondered if Vostya would be able to find anything at all. Possibly they should try to call a cab—take her that way. He would wait another five minutes.

"There is more, Mr. Poltav," Galya said. "You are not telling me everything. You have something against Tupolev, don't you."

Nickolai faced her. "You are too young to remember Lavrenti

Beria, Stalin's executioner, a soulless man. He and Tupolev con-
spired to take power after Stalin's death. There were three men in
their way, Malenkov, Molotov, and Krushchev. Krushchev was
the unknown entity, the one Tupolev and Beria felt could be the
most dangerous. The other two could be pressured out."

He sat in the chair opposite Galya. Nickolai hadn't looked old
enough to be involved in the intrigues of the early 1950s, but as
he sat there, the weight of the past slumping his shoulders, he
seemed suddenly older.

"I was to plan and carry out the assassination; Dimitri
Bakatin was the gunman. I refused."

Galya kept running her hand over Natalya's forehead. Using
her free hand, she felt for a pulse. It was weak. Where was
Rustam? Where was the ambulance?

"They pressured you," she said.

He nodded. "My wife disappeared—only for a few hours, but
the message was clear. Like this one. I packed a suitcase for her
and sent her where I thought no one could find her. I was over-
confident."

"They killed her?"

"She never arrived at her destination. An accident. The bus
left the road after losing a wheel. There were only two survivors."

"It could have been an accident."

He nodded. "But because I knew them, because I knew what
they were capable of, I could not believe it. I refused to plan the
killing. Beria had me reassigned."

"Siberia for rehabilitation? You were lucky."

"Dimitri Bakatin and my sister intervened with Tupolev, who
convinced Beria to let my sins be paid for with something other
than my blood."

"I don't understand. If they saved you . . . "

"I owe Dimitri, but I found out later that Tupolev had ordered
my wife's death as a lesson to a wayward member of the inner
circle."

"How did you find out?"

Nickolai returned to the window. An ambulance was turning
the corner near the doors to the apartment building. It disappeared

out of Nickolai's view. Vostya had moved quickly, a positive sign that the young man was gaining ground on the Petersburg system.

"Secretly my sister, Dimitri's wife, informed Krushchev of what had happened. He already knew about the assassination attempt, and Beria had been imprisoned, then executed. But he didn't know Tupolev had been involved. By this time, five years later, Tupolev was too firmly entrenched as head of the army for Krushchev to do anything to him. He did the next best thing: He pardoned me, gave me the Star of Lenin, and gave me a job in the police department in Moscow. At that time, I investigated the accident reports. The driver was one of the survivors, didn't even get a scratch. I interrogated him. He told me he had been paid by one of Tupolev's people. I had him put in prison, but I couldn't get at Tupolev. I've been trying ever since."

"Tupolev must have been livid when Krushchev honored you."

"He exacted his revenge by lending support to Krushchev's replacement."

"But he couldn't get to you."

"It took him some time, but in 1984 he finally manufactured some evidence that I had been taking bribes from drug dealers who were trying to get established in Moscow. I could have fought it and proven his evidence false, but I was tired of fighting the system. Even in those days, I was arresting people and they would use their connections to get free. All the crooks were connected to someone like Tupolev, or Brezhnev himself. His son was one of the men I wanted most. He was a thief and a murderer. But I couldn't get it done. I was just tired. I resigned."

"Yeltsin brought you back."

"He and I know one another. We don't always agree, especially on politics, but we both hate Tupolev. We both know what bringing him down could do to the level of crime in Russia."

There was a knock at the door. Nickolai checked through the peephole, then opened the door, grateful help had arrived for Natalya.

Vostya stood there, rigid. An angry look filled his face. Then Kulikov stepped from the shadows, pointing a Makarov at Nickolai's heart.

Chapter Eighteen

RAND WATCHED THE ACTIVITIES OUTSIDE the apartment from his parking place behind a cannibalized old Volga. The car was sitting on blocks and had been stripped of its tires, windows, and interior. It had undoubtedly been picked clean by its owner or by one of the gangs now roaming the streets. Selling used car parts was a booming business in the black market.

"There's another car," Larissa said. A dark brown German Jetta braked to a stop just behind the ambulance that had arrived earlier. Another car was parked against the ambulance's front bumper. Two men got out of the Jetta and quickly entered the apartment stairwell. "That makes four men, plus the ambulance driver," Larissa said.

"Four we've seen," Rand corrected.

They had nearly been caught up in the events transpiring down the street while trying to find a parking place. None had been available at the time, so they had circled the block. When they returned, the ambulance was double parked in the street, leaving only a narrow traffic lane, and the driver was at the rear door removing a bag. It was then that a man Rand recognized as Kulikov had come out of nowhere and yanked the poor driver inside, a gun at his back. Luckily the space behind the beat-up Volga had been empty, and Rand had jerked the Mercedes in behind it. He could only hope his half-hidden car wouldn't be noticed.

"I do not like this," Larissa said through tight lips. "Rikki must be hurt. We must do something."

Rand touched her arm to calm her as Galya and an older man, badly dressed, were being escorted out of the apartment by Kulikov. Larissa jumped with shock. How did Galya get here? I . . . I don't understand."

"Who is the man?" Rand asked.

Larissa was out of the car before Rand could stop her.

"Larissa! You can't help them! Larissa! Get back here!"

She kept going, moving across the street then down the sidewalk as if she were out for a late evening stroll. Rand couldn't believe it. The woman would get them all killed!

He started the Mercedes and put it in reverse. The bumper bumped the car behind him, and he cringed. Now was no time to be noticed.

He shoved the gearshift forward. The Mercedes moved gently out of the slot and into the street. With one eye on Larissa, he guided the car toward the brown Jetta. Kulikov stood with his back to them. Rand glanced over at Larissa. Her jaw was set, and she strode forward, each step firmly placing her in more danger. Rand pushed the down button for the passenger-side window as Kulikov opened the back door of the Jetta. He glanced up. Saw the Mercedes. Hesitated. Then his hand went inside his jacket, and he yelled at the other two men. Rand punched the gas feed. Now it was their only chance.

Kulikov swore as the Mercedes bore down on him. Ripping the Makarov from its holster, he aimed and fired as the oncoming car sideswiped his Jetta and knocked it toward him. He jumped onto the hood of a Zhiguili, the hood sinking under his two hundred pounds. The Makarov flew out of his hand and onto the sidewalk, slamming into the wall of the building. The Mercedes backed up and burned rubber, repositioned for another onslaught as he tried to roll off the car. His suit-coat button caught in the crack between fender and hood, holding him for the briefest of moments and giving the madman in the Mercedes a clear target. Kulikov jerked on his jacket, ripping it free as the car rammed the Zhiguili, driving it against him and slamming him across the walk and against the building. The force of the Mercedes drove the Zhiguili after him, the scream of tires filling him with petrifying fear. He pushed against the wall, sucking in his gut, his brain telling his body he was about to be crushed. He closed his eyes and waited to die.

The crushing blow of the Mercedes against the Zhiguili threw everyone into motion, running, ducking, jumping for cover. Rand watched the Zhiguili slide toward Kulikov, saw him close his eyes, saw the car pin him down but stop within inches of crushing him altogether. With sweat running down his face, Rand threw the gearshift into reverse. The powerful engine screamed for mercy, and the gray smoke of burned rubber filled his nostrils. He glanced over at Kulikov. The man was already working his way free. Larissa had grabbed Galya's arm, and the two women were running down the sidewalk. One of Kulikov's men gave chase. He heard Kulikov scream to kill them, watched as the chaser raised a gun, saw the old man who had been with Galya show startling agility, grabbing the enemy's hand with a force that sent the pistol flying across the cars and into the street. A solid right to the chin drove the chaser against the ambulance, where he melted to the street. Rand could see that the old man wasn't so old after all.

He headed the Mercedes down the street and shoved the gearshift forward to go after the others. The Mercedes stalled, steam pouring out from under the hood in wet clouds that obstructed his view. He pulled on the door handle and thrust the door open. Keeping low, he moved down the side of the cars in the direction the others had gone, his eyes peering over the array of vehicles, scanning the scene, finding the women, counting the enemy. It was the first time in his life Rand wished for a gun, for anything to even the odds.

Kulikov had worked his way free and was on his hands and knees, searching frantically for his gun, cursing, yelling. One of his men came near him. Kulikov grabbed his weapon and aimed it, screaming at the two women to stop. The hair on the back of

Rand's neck stood on end as he prayed the idiot wouldn't shoot. He glanced over the hood of one of the cars and saw the old man, his arms in the air, turning to face Kulikov, trying to use his body to block the view of the women, give them time. Rand kept moving after them, keeping low, his body hidden from Kulikov's view.

He glanced over the hood of a car. They were standing there, facing Kulikov's direction, a man pressing a gun into Galya's back, making her wince. He must have been behind the building, must have come around when Kulikov filled the air with his unholy epithets. Rand now wished the Zhiguili had finished him off.

Rand heard the sound of gunfire, felt the projectile hit the car mirror near his shoulder and shatter the glass. Instantly he was over the car, rushing the man with the gun in Galya's back. The surprise and quickness of his movement startled the man—his eyes showed confusion, hesitation. Rand drove his shoulder into his side, throwing him across the walk and into the building. He grabbed Galya's hand and pulled her away, expecting Larissa to follow.

As they turned the corner, Galya held back, and Rand glanced over his shoulder. Larissa had picked up the man's gun, holding it on him, then pointed it at Kulikov as he came down the walk, his own Makarov aimed at her head. As he reached the old man, he smiled and began squeezing the trigger. Rand had never seen anyone move as quickly as the man in the too-small suit. He grabbed Kulikov's hand and drove it upward, the pistol firing into thin air. Suddenly there were three other agents running through the cars, moving in, surrounding Larissa and the man holding Kulikov's arm like a vise. Rand pulled, running, forcing Galya to follow.

"You can't help them! Come on!"

Galya stared at him, unsure, her eyes afraid. She pulled back. "I have to help them. I can't . . . "

"You can't help them, Galya! Come on!" He pulled again, this time with more force. She moved after him, running down the side street.

As Rand darted across the street and into an archway that led

into the center park-playground of an apartment complex, two
pursuers appeared around the corner from which they had just
come. The complex was overgrown with trees and bushes, and
piles of garbage were stacked in the middle. Any lawn had long
ago been crushed into oblivion or burned out for lack of water
and care. They ran through the center, using the trees and scrub
brush to mask their escape, to keep the pursuers from using their
weapons. Out of the corner of his eye, Rand saw several women
stop hanging clothes and stare at them. Their heads turned to
watch the ones who followed. Then they disappeared.

Rand thanked his good luck as they found and passed through
the small arched walkway on the far side of the complex. They
were suddenly in the middle of Liteyny Prospekt, a busy thoroughfare. A Volga closed in on them, then swerved at the last second, horn blaring, the driver's curses coming through the open
window as the car whipped passed them within inches. Rand
looked back again as they reached the center of the street. The
men still hadn't come out of the complex. He glanced around for
a way to go, a place to hide, while Galya took deep breaths, trying
to fill her overworked lungs. An old truck braked, then swerved to
miss them, passing close by at a slow speed. Rand grabbed Galya
by the waist and threw her onto the back of the beat-up vehicle,
then took half a dozen steps and launched himself after her. They
moved forward into the depths of the truck's covered backside as
the men appeared through the archway. Rand watched them from
the semi-darkness as they looked first right, then left, then across
the street. One of the men's eyes seemed to catch the back of the
truck and peer in, searching the darkness for the slight movement
that would reveal those he sought. Rand held Galya's hand
tightly, holding his breath until the truck turned the corner into a
side street and out of the way of the agent's prying eyes.

Quickly he pulled Galya to her feet and went to the back of
the truck. They sat down, then jumped to the ground, going for
the sidewalk. Half walking, half running, they entered the first
store they came to. Rand stayed close to the window, watching
the corner, waiting. A minute later the two men appeared, staring

after the truck. Then one waved down the street in the direction Rand couldn't see. The brown Jetta appeared.

The two climbed inside as a second car, a Volga, joined it. The cars turned into the street and followed the truck. As the Volga passed, Galya caught her breath. Larissa and Nickolai were in the back seat, Kulikov's gun only inches away from their faces.

Rand pulled Galya deeper into the store where customers were examining a few goods on otherwise empty shelves. He saw a door that led into the back. Grabbing Galya by the hand, he went that way, passing a startled woman who started cackling at them about rules, her finger wagging nearly as violently as her tongue. He reached the back door and thrust it open. They entered an alley where garbage cluttered the pockmarked pavement. He crossed it, knocking on another door. Nothing. He knocked again, louder. A woman came to the door, cursing. He shoved inward, making his apologies but driving her back as he and Galya walked down the dark hallway and into the main part of a dress shop. There was a chair against the wall, and he took Galya to it, sitting her down. When the woman protested, he pulled his money clip from his suit pocket and handed her two five-hundred ruble notes.

"The lady needs a dress. Find her one you think she might like," he said in fluent Russian.

Another clerk, sitting idle at the other end of the counter, saw the rubles and suddenly moved toward them as if she were in charge. She pulled a chair from behind the counter and offered it to Rand. He waved it off and moved closer to the window. As the clerks brought several dresses, Galya stared at him, then at them, incredulous.

Rand spoke in English. "We need a rest and a little time to get ourselves together. Play along, will you?"

Galya forced a smile and pointed to a dress behind the counter. After it was retrieved by a clerk, Galya went into a small cubicle and tried it on while the two clerks fussed and silently argued about who should get the profits Rand had already handed out. The bad economy was making beggars out of everyone.

The storefront faced Fontanka Avenue, the river itself just on the other side of the street. To his right, Rand could see the summer gardens he and Galya had walked in just hours before. Was it hours? So much had happened. To his left was the Belinskogo street bridge. He watched the traffic but saw no sign of the Jetta.

He turned to see Galya facing a mirror, a new red dress draped over her thin but well-proportioned figure. Her dark hair curled around her forehead, where it clung from the sweat of the run. Her cheeks were crimson and made her look even more beautiful, but the dark eyes, filled with concern, reminded him of their predicament.

He asked the price in dollars, then removed the amount from his wallet and handed it to one of the clerks.

"No! It is I who will pay for my clothing, not you, Mr. King. I do not need this dress and do not wish to purchase it," she said in English.

"They won't be looking for a woman in red. Besides, you do wonders for mediocre Russian workmanship. It is beautiful on you. Please, let me buy it. We can settle the problem of funds and personal pride later. We need to get moving."

Galya hesitated, then turned to the clerk. "Do you have a sack that I can put the old one in?"

The clerk nodded, then took the money Rand held out to her for the second time, pleased that the slight argument between her two customers had ended with her the winner.

Five minutes later, Galya had her old dress wrapped in gray paper and they were moving toward Nevksy Prospekt. Rand saw another clothing store and quickly pulled Galya inside. When they came back onto the street, he was wearing a sport shirt, slacks, and straw hat that to him all looked very Russian. The suit had been taken on trade.

"Let's get a cab," Rand said as they came to Nevksy. "I feel vulnerable, like I'm being watched."

Galya smiled. "It is the hat. Such things are for old men."

Once settled in the back seat, Galya lay her head back and closed her eyes.

"What happened back there?" Rand asked.

She told him about Nickolai, then about finding Natalya in Rikki's apartment.

Rand put his arm around her as she burst into tears, blaming herself for everything, afraid Natalya would die before help could get to her now, fearful for Larissa and Nickolai. He tried to say the right thing but wasn't sure what it might be. He believed in the Russian people; they kept fighting the system that still threatened to smother them. But when something like this happened, when the people were crushed like ants, it was hard to tell them to keeping walking under the feet of the oppressors. The real pain of it was that the system was still crushing people and getting away with it.

He tapped on the shoulder of the driver and asked him to pull over near a phone booth. A minute later, as Galya watched from the car, he phoned in a report to the police about an accident on Baskov Street. Then he climbed back in the cab and they were on the move again, hoping such help would be quick in responding this time.

They reached their destination. Rand paid the driver in rubles and helped Galya out of the car. They stood in front of an old apartment building as she finished drying her eyes.

"Who lives here?" Galya asked.

"I haven't the slightest idea. You?" He smiled, hoping she would return it. She did, barely. He took her arm and moved her along the walk. "I didn't want the driver to know our actual destination. It's another block." They started, both sets of legs tired, even cramped.

"What will they do with Larissa and Poltav?" Rand asked.

"Hurt them. Make them tell what they know." Galya paused. "Possibly kill them," she said, the pain evident in her voice. She was falling apart. He needed to get her to a place where she could rest and they could think things through.

"Possibly I should go to the police, tell them—"

Galya laughed. "They will be no help in a matter like this— not when they discover Tupolev is involved. They know what he does to people who get in his way. Oh, they will pretend for us, but if we want anything to happen, we must find other ways."

"What do you suggest?" Rand asked.

"Nickolai has an office here and in Moscow. We must try to contact them. They will know what to do. Possibly they can make a deal for Nickolai and Larissa by contacting Tupolev."

"If Tupolev has the diary, he won't feel compelled to make deals," Rand said.

"I don't think he has it."

"Why not? They were at the restorationist's. He is missing; so is the diary. You said so yourself."

"Why would Kulikov stick around and kidnap us if he already had what he wanted?" Galya asked.

"Maybe he was afraid you knew its contents."

"Maybe, but I noticed other things. Why take Rikki?"

"To finish the restoration."

His tools were still on the desk. He would need them, wouldn't you think? And the door locks were blown away with bullets. Why? Kulikov had Natalya as a hostage. Rikki would have opened the door. He wouldn't have let them hurt her if he had been there." Galya knew it sounded circumstantial, but there was something else. "Rikki's place was a shambles."

"A search?"

She nodded. "If they have Rikki, even if they break the door in and they have Natalya to force him to give them the diary, why a search?"

"I don't think Rikki was there," she finished.

"They tried to get more out of Natalya, thus the beating."

"And because they were upset with Rustam for his uncooperative attitude earlier in the day."

"Where would Rikki go?"

"I don't know, but Rustam will."

"Then we must contact him."

"He was supposed to meet us at Rikki's. He never came."

Rand was silent. The conclusions were obvious. Rustam would have come unless he was detained by the KGB.

"It is another reason to contact Nickolai's people. They can contact Tupolev, put him off until we can find Rikki."

They turned into the back gate of the consulate, both anxious to get to the phone.

Rustam jumped from the cab, his stomach in knots, working at controlling the anger. Finding a taxi had been nearly impossible in the late afternoon rush—the traffic had been bumper to bumper, mass chaos. Twice he had changed cabs, once he had walked two blocks to get around jams backed up at intersections and accidents.

His breath caught as he saw the crowd of people at Rikki's apartment. An ambulance stood in the street, a tan Zhiguili, battered and driven against the wall. No police had arrived yet, and half a dozen hooligans were removing items from a Mercedes with its front end smashed, the radiator still giving off a small cloud of steam.

Rustam ran to Rikki's doorway, pushed the buttons, and was quickly inside. Two children stood on tiptoe, straining to see through a small crack in the boarded-up window.

He lengthened his stride, taking three steps at a time. Rikki's door was open, the hallway dimly lit. His breathing was erratic from the climb and the fear, but he stopped altogether when he saw Natalya on the floor, her bruised and swollen face turned his direction, her eyes puffed shut.

He fell to the floor by her side before he realized there was another person nearby, inside the living area. His hands were tied and a gag was in his mouth. He was working frantically to free himself when he saw Rustam and began screaming muffled sounds, his eyes wide with anger. A wide gash that bled down the side of his face and onto his shirt creased the skin of his forehead clear to the bone.

Rustam untied the gag, then started on the knot on the ropes.

"Who are you?" Rustam asked, trying to stay in control.

"Vostya Dubenky. I work for Nickolai Poltav." He explained quickly about Nickolai and Galya as the two of them checked Natalya's vital signs.

"There is an ambulance out front. It's mine—well, a friend's.

We have to get her to a doctor. She is in bad shape," Vostya said. He fell back, feeling dizzy, disoriented. Pulling a hanky from his pocket, he pushed it against his wound. "Can you carry her?"

Rustam was already gathering his wife into his arms, his face set in concrete, both the bitterness and the anger visible in his eyes. Vostya stumbled after Rustam, and they were quickly out of the building. Vostya was stunned by the sign of mayhem but glad to see there were no bodies. Possibly Nickolai and the woman had escaped.

The crowd was getting larger, and they had to shove their way through to the ambulance. Thank goodness Vostya had thought to lock it. Several men were working the doors, trying to break in. When two blocked Rustam's way, belligerent, claiming the vehicle, Vostya pushed them aside like children. When one retaliated, the man found himself on his back trying to catch his breath. The crowd moved away.

Seconds later they were moving the ambulance through the crowd, meeting a police car at the far end of the street. It passed with hardly a glance from its occupants.

"Did you see who did this?" Rustam asked, his eyes on his wife's battered face.

"No, but I know who was there—who boasted of doing it." Vostya described Kulikov.

The rest of the ride was made in silence.

Chapter Nineteen

LARISSA, HER FEET FASTENED TOGETHER with tightly knotted rags and her hands bound with a length of curtain cord, rolled over on the bed and nudged the stranger who had saved her life.

He moved, but barely. Kulikov had started taking pleasure in beating the man until the phone call had come. He wasn't happy with the order to lay off, but after two additional jabs to the stranger's face Kulikov had stopped.

The call had been from Georgi Zhelin. Kulikov had used the name openly, taunting the stranger he called Nickolai with it.

At Rikki's apartment, Nickolai's actions had saved Larissa's life. Kulikov had taken offense then, but in the rush to catch Galya and Rand King, he hadn't the time to do anything about it. After it was evident that Galya and King had escaped, Kulikov had started spewing threats. The beating had followed as the KGB agent's psychotic behavior burst upon them. He had even hit Larissa twice.

Larissa found it ironic that a man like Georgi Zhelin, a sadist in his own right, had kept them from being beaten to a pulp. She could only wonder for how long. Only moments earlier, Kulikov had left the room after throwing several chairs against walls, leaving them in pieces. He would be back as soon as he decided his pleasure was worth more than a dressing-down by Georgi Zhelin.

Using her tied hands, she rolled Nickolai gently toward her. His face was slightly swollen, the lips cracked in two places. He opened his eyes and tried to move the lips into a smile.

"An angel. I've died and gone to heaven. Did they hurt you?" he asked, noticing a bruise already growing on her right cheek.

She shook her head. "Not badly." She glanced at the door through which muffled sounds of arguing no longer escaped. The quiet was frightening. "But I do not think we have much time."

"We have to get out of here." He moved his tied hands, testing the ropes. They cut into his flesh, and he realized for the first time that he couldn't feel his fingers. The circulation was cut off. "Any idea where we are?"

"A house near Baltic Station."

"You were foolish to try to help us. It accomplished only your capture," Nickolai said.

"But Galya is free."

"You must think a lot of her."

"She reminds me of someone I knew once."

"Who?"

"Me. I don't want to see her life ruined by these animals. They have ruined enough of us already."

Nickolai watched her, seeing her for the first time. "You . . . you are Larissa Vavilova." Many years ago he had seen her dance in the ballet, admired her classic beauty from the tenth row in the Bolshoi Theater in Moscow when the Kirov dancers had performed there. Like him, she was older now, heavier, but firm and still handsome. People were hardened by years of work in jobs left for those blacklisted by the government. But there was something different about Larissa. The hardness wasn't reflected in her eyes and face.

"Who are you, and what happened at Rikki's?" Larissa asked as she picked at the knots holding her feet together.

Nickolai told her what happened. By the time he was finished, she had her feet free. There was a bucket of water on the floor near the chair where they had sat Nickolai to punish him. Using the fingers of her tied hands, she ripped a piece of her blouse off and dipped it in the water. Returning to Nickolai, she cleaned the dried blood from his lips.

"How bad is Natalya?" she asked, concern evident in her voice.

"Broken ribs. Her face . . . the flesh is badly bruised. She may have brain damage. Hopefully her husband found her or some of my people showed up at the apartment when the ambulance didn't get to the hospital," he said, working at keeping his anger under control.

"Poor Natalya. She always feared this would happen to Rustam. She was afraid for him more than for herself, although some people always looked at her over-protective fits as selfish. I have talked to her for many long hours. She had some horrible things happen to the people she loved. It frightened her beyond reason that it might happen to Rustam. Now this. Even if she survives physically, I wonder if she will emotionally. What happened to the ambulance driver?"

"One of my people. The last I saw, he was tied up next to Natalya. How did you get with the American?"

"Like you, he saved my life." She told him about the man in the white suit.

"Not KGB. King is right. Another player. The ones Yezhov worked for. They are finally in the game."

"Who can it be?"

"Tupolev has many enemies, but possibly the diary is valuable in other ways. It may be wanted by a philanthropist, a museum, a relative of the woman you say was the writer. There are many possibilities."

She pushed him onto his side and started picking at the knots on his hands. They were very tight, and her fingers grew raw without sign of progress.

"You and Galya are in a lot of danger, especially Galya. We have to get you both out of Petersburg." He rubbed his tongue against the swollen lip, then winced as it brushed against a loosened tooth. The pain was that of something cold on a deep cavity.

"They will kill you as well. They have to now," Larissa said.

"Have you loosened the knots?" Nickolai asked.

"Not yet."

I can't lie this way. Bruised solar plexus."

She rolled him onto his back, then gently probed his midsection with the fingers of her tied hands. Nickolai thought it ironic that only a few hours earlier he had been doing the same for Natalya Starkov. He jumped when she touched the left side of his lower stomach. She probed more but found nothing as tender.

"They beat you pretty soundly. If the phone call from Zhelin hadn't come, he would have killed you."

Nickolai smiled. "Probably wants to save me for himself and Tupolev. We go back a long way."

She started pulling at the ropes with her fingertips again.

Nickolai forced his feet over the edge of the bed and with her help lifted himself into a sitting position. His midsection was sore but not badly damaged.

"Keep trying."

She slid close enough to work at the knots again.

"You were a wonderful dancer," Nickolai said. "When you danced at the Bolshoi, I never missed. How many years has it been?"

"Twenty-two."

"It doesn't seem that long ago."

"From your perspective or mine?" she asked.

He didn't answer, embarrassed at his own thoughtlessness. Blacklisting was a living death.

She laughed lightly. "Do not worry. I have very thick skin."

"I used to work for the people who hurt you," he said.

There was a slight hesitation in her fingers, but she continued to work at the knots.

"KGB? Few who served them have lived so long."

"I was thrown out at an early age."

"Then what?"

"Rehabilitation and the Moscow Police."

"Was it much different? The police?"

"For the most part the criminals didn't come to the office to start their day."

She laughed. It was a pleasant sound to Nickolai, very much like the laughter of his wife.

Finally she released the knots and freed his hands. He threw the rope against the wall, bent down, and untied his own feet.

Taking her hands in his, he began working on her knots. They were tight, and her hands were purple.

"You have seen our country at its very worst," Larissa said.

"And you. I know part of your story—how they forced you out of the ballet. I'm sorry."

Larissa was pleased at his sincerity. At first sight, Nickolai Poltav seemed rough, a brawler. But his touch was gentle and his behavior that of a gentleman. She admired that, especially from one who had been forced to face so much violence, corruption, and hypocrisy.

"How have you done it?"

It was his turn to be surprised. "Done what?"

"Kept yourself from being hardened by it all."

He had asked himself the same question many times. He finished untying the last knot and tossed the rope aside. "I haven't. Come on. We have to get out of here." He went to the window. Three floors up, no fire escape. "Lie down, put your arms behind you, your feet together." He wrapped the cords around her feet without tying them. Going to the door, he lightly scratched its surface several times, then ran to the bed and placed himself next to her, tossing a blanket over his feet.

"Tell them you think I'm dead—a heart attack from the beating. Heaven knows I look old enough." As he closed his eyes, the door opened slightly and a man looked in.

"He's cold. I think you killed him. You cannot beat an old man like that," Larissa said.

The man came into the room with a revolver in his right hand. He walked to Nickolai's side, wary.

"He's okay. We hardly touched him," he said, worried.

"He's dead! Feel him!" she said angrily. "I don't like lying here with a dead man. Get him away from me."

The man extended his hand toward Nickolai, his eyes on Larissa. He didn't see the hand that grabbed his wrist and twisted it so hard it snapped, didn't sense the fist that knocked his jaw into his upper teeth. Nor did he feel his body hit the floor next to the bed. He was already unconscious.

Nickolai took the pistol and went to the door. "You didn't

have to pour it on quite so thick. You can't beat an *old man* like that? I'm not that old." He smiled.

"Sorry. You didn't give me much time to come up with something less shattering to your ego," she kidded.

He could hear someone using the toilet and went into the hall. Opening the bathroom door with a jerk, he stared into the startled face of Kulikov, whose pants were around his ankles. Nickolai drove his fist into the man's nose until he was unconscious, his head against the left wall. He wanted to do more, inflict pain until the agent quit breathing, but he controlled his anger. Besides, more than his life was at stake if they lingered too long. He went through Kulikov's pockets and found the keys to the Volga, then removed the unconscious agent's pistol. Going through the drawers in the kitchen, he found several nails and a hammer. He drove them through the door and into the casing, sealing the bathroom shut.

Five minutes later the still-unconscious guard was tied and gagged, and Nickolai began a quick search of the apartment.

"What are you looking for?" Larissa asked.

"When we arrived here, Kulikov had some papers that looked like they might be copies of pages of the diary. Maybe he had the diary as well."

They searched together. Nothing.

"He must have already had them delivered to Tupolev," Larissa said.

"Tupolev is in Moscow. A meeting with a group opposing Yeltsin. He shouldn't be back until late tonight."

"You keep track of him?"

"Since yesterday. It is always best to know where your enemy is."

They left the apartment, working their way carefully down the stairwell toward the street. The Volga was parked in front of an American-style photo shop that advertised Kodak color prints. Two minutes later, they were turning into a side street.

"Where are we going?"

"A taxi stand. I think this car is marked, probably even

bugged. They do it so that if someone steals it, they can track it down. A new policy in the KGB. They are losing too many cars."

They drove several blocks, left the car, and started walking toward a main street looking for a taxi. Coming to a phone booth first, Nickolai dialed a number.

"Who are you calling?" Larissa asked.

"Dimitri Bakatin." He told her about his brother-in-law's betrayal of Tupolev. "Tupolev knows. I should have called Dimitri earlier." He cringed. He had thought of calling Dimitri but had decided he didn't care. Dimitri needed a lesson in humility. But now, after seeing what Kulikov would do, his conscience had gotten to him.

Shelepin answered, and Nickolai handed Larissa the phone. He didn't want the informer to know he was free.

"Ask him where Dimitri is."

She did. "When do you expect him?" Pause. "Thank you." She hung up.

"He says he left the city on vacation, leaving Shelepin in charge."

Nickolai felt weak. He had waited too long. "They have him." He picked up the phone and dialed another number.

"Marina? This is Nickolai." A pause. "Marina, just listen. Have you seen Dimitri?"

"Nickolai," his sister answered, "what is wrong? Where are you? Dimitri called but was cut off. I don't know . . . "

"I want you to leave your place and go to the address I will give you. My people will take care of you. Do you understand?"

"Yes, but Dimitri." She caught her breath. "Tupolev?"

"Yes. Here is the address." He gave it to her. "Leave now, Marina. Don't even take time to pack."

"Nickolai, Dimitri said something curious. He said . . . he said that if I saw you, to tell you to remember Tupolev's record book."

Nickolai thought a moment, unsure. Then it hit him.

"I understand. Marina, go. I love you. I will find Dimitri. Don't worry."

He hung up the phone, then picked it up again, calling his office, trying to reach Vostya. He wasn't there but had called from the hospital where he had taken Natalya Starkova, who was in critical condition. He hung up and they caught a cab. Five minutes later, they turned into an alley, the taxi stopped, and they were standing at a beat-up door that entered a building Larissa thought she recognized.

Nickolai knocked. A man answered the door. When he saw Nickolai, he was all smiles. He stepped aside and asked them in, and Nickolai made the introductions.

"Grisha Stachek, Larissa Vavilova." Grisha took Larissa's hand and kissed it lightly, snapping his heels together.

"Miss Vavilova, it is an honor to have you as our guest."

Grisha was short with pitch-black hair and the face of a Mongol. The eyes were large, almond shaped, the nose flat and the lips heavy. There was kindness there. He turned and led them through a short hallway into a large kitchen area. As they crossed it, Larissa asked a question.

"Are we where I think we are?"

Nickolai nodded. "The Astoria, dear lady. The Waldorf Astoria, and the home of one Vladimir Tupolev. I intend to pay him a visit."

Larissa gave him an unbelieving look, her eyes scanning for a sign of humor in his eyes. She found none. Nickolai wasn't kidding.

Chapter Twenty

VOLODYA VILECHENKO PACED. IT WAS after midnight and still no word. People had disappeared like flies on a frigid night. He had missed the Starkova woman at the Summer Gardens, along with her friend, a woman that Vilechenko now knew was Larissa Vavilova, the former ballerina. He hadn't realized it until he had seen her up close. She had changed from the tall, thin beauty who had performed like an angel on the stage of the Kirov Theater. But then, years under the system had changed them all.

Galya Starkova had disappeared. And the American, Bakatin, Kulikov, and Zhelin weren't to be found. After the American had whisked Larissa Vavilova out of his grasp, they had gone back to using the homing device, shadowing what they thought was Kulikov, only to find that the agent had given the black Volga to one of his men to take back to MB headquarters. Their efforts had been a complete disaster, making Volodya question his own ability and the strength of their intelligence operation. One thing was certain—no more of this technology. The old ways had always served him. He would use them again.

He pulled back the curtains, giving the bed a side glance as he did so. He turned away. It had been nearly ten years, but he still checked, still expected to see her lying there.

Damina Vilechenko was an artist, a tender soul who loved beauty more than life. It had turned him inside out to see her suffer so, then die. At first he had drunk himself into a stupor, refusing to face the empty apartment, the empty bed, an empty life.

His realization that he was about to lose his job as curator and his position in the White Guard had finally snapped him out of it, forcing him to dry out.

He glanced at his watch again, the amber haze of the Russian summer night through the bedroom window fully illuminating the dial. It had been ten hours since events at the park.

He had someone watching Tupolev's apartment at the Astoria, a night clerk at the front desk. She said Tupolev was in Moscow but was expected back about two in the morning. Zhelin wasn't at home; neither was Bakatin. They were probably together somewhere, possibly even with the Starkova woman. If they had captured her, that would be the likely scenario.

And where was the American? What did he have to do with this? Had Galya Starkova read the diary? Had she contacted the consulate about Robert Kitrick? It was a likely possibility.

He went to the bathroom and washed up, then shaved, thinking about his options. At present levels of success, a report to Alexander Bychevsky would not be well received. He had to do something.

Going to the phone, he dialed Vasily's number and got the driver out of bed, instructing him to bring the car around in half an hour.

Dressing in one of his four white suits, he placed his white fedora onto his silver hair and picked up his walking stick. He sat in the chair in the living room, his hands on top of the walking stick, his eyes fastened on the glint of the multicolored domes and golden crosses of St. Saviour's Church. His mind wandered over the past, back to Damina and their marriage, back to the years with Alexander and the changes they were forced to make with the failure of ALLIANCE. Back to the day of betrayal and Nora Larsen.

The team had arrived in Leningrad from Tromso, Norway, in March 1941, after two months of crossing the Norwegian/Finnish territory, arriving at Pechanga on Russia's northern coast. From there they had gone to Murmansk and caught a train to Leningrad. Volodya had been proud of the accomplishment. It was he who had made arrangements for papers, uniforms, tickets, everything needed. It was his connections in the Communist-controlled military that had cleared the way for the safe trip of the ALLIANCE team once they were inside his homeland.

After their arrival in Leningrad, Volodya had arranged for them to hide in an old warehouse in the northern part of Vasilevsky Island, where they carefully prepared for the death of Stalin and the overthrow of Communism.

The date to carry out their mission came and went without Stalin's arrival at the workers' meeting being held in his honor at the vaunted Kirov factory.

The people in high places who supported a Romanov return to power were afraid that Stalin had discovered the plot and that they were all doomed—he was playing with them, biding his time, arranging to gather them all into the same net and kill them personally. Word was sent to Alexander Bychevsky from Moscow that they had started jumping ship, putting the entire coup in danger. Alexander left the warehouse and went to Moscow to meet with the weak-stomached politicos, easing the strain and recommitting them to the overthrow of Stalin before he turned the whole country over to Hitler. As a seeming sign that all was well, Alexander pointed out to his political jellyfish that Stalin had set a new date for his visit to Leningrad. The timely coincidence eased a lot of fear among their well-positioned collaborators, and soon they had grown enough backbone to stand against Stalin again.

But the long wait had taken its toll among members of the assassination team. They became nervous, on edge, out of sorts with one another as they waited the long days for another chance. All but one held together. He decided to protect himself through betrayal.

Alexander returned on the 5th of June with word that Stalin would come on the 10th. They were betrayed on the 9th.

The Mercedes pulled up in the street below his window. Volodya rose from the chair, his shoulder slumped as if carrying a heavy weight.

Only five of the ALLIANCE team had remained alive, two of whom would suffer terribly, then die as well. Purges by Stalin followed, and the Romanov centers of power in Moscow were destroyed, setting their movement back fifty years. Soldiers had come to their enclave in the north, the place of gathering in which their movement had lived since 1919, the place where Volodya had been born and raised. Of ten thousand, only five hundred had survived.

It was all because of a traitor that still lived, still thrived, because he had become useful, essential to the survival of what remained of the White Guard. Awful. The man who had nearly destroyed them—but who had been forced to give them new life—was now trying to destroy them again.

But Volodya had no intention of allowing such a thing. Yes, the emergence of the diary was a threat if discovered by Tupolev, but Vladimir Tupolev would never live to use it. Volodya would kill him first. It might be difficult but not impossible. Volodya had planned it for years—dreamed of it. Only Tupolev's usefulness to the White Guard had kept it from becoming a reality.

He unlocked the door, then exited and relocked it. His usual exuberance gone, he took the steps gingerly, left the building, and entered the Mercedes.

"Where to, sir?" Vasily said.

Volodya stared at his driver a second before pulling himself out of his thoughts.

"Oh, Vasily, good morning."

"Good morning, sir. Where to?"

"The American Consulate, Vasily."

Vasily looked at him, bewildered. "They won't be open, sir. Not at this hour."

"I know, Vasily. I know." He sat back in his seat as Vasily started the engine and put the car in gear.

In Volodya's mind, Tupolev was a solvable problem, and he shoved it aside, concentrating on a greater worry. What he wanted was the diary and the chance for truth it offered. Things had begun that long-ago June 9 that had never made sense to Volodya. That had always left the empty feeling of doubt gnawing at his vitals. If he didn't find that diary, he would never know the whole truth about the traitor. He couldn't live with the uncertainty.

Nickolai Poltav loved white nights. He stood at the window
of the hotel room staring across the square at the Dome of St.
Isaac's, where the yellowish haze of the sun lay low on the horizon, sparkling on the dome's golden surface. The calm was wonderful. He loved the absence of city noise, the beauty of having
enough sunlight to see the city at its best hours, its quiet hours
when peace reigned for at least a few moments in his country.

He glanced at his watch. Nearly two o'clock in the morning.
Going to his dresser, he unpackaged a new black turtleneck and a
pair of black slacks he had purchased in the small shop near the
hotel, then began to pull them on. It had been risky to go out, but
he had had no choice. For what he intended, the old veteran's suit
and clothes were out of place. He grimaced a little at the pain in
his stomach. Stiffness had set in. He remembered a day when taking a small beating like Kulikov's would have meant little, the
soreness gone in a few hours. Now it took days.

Grisha Stachek had sneaked them into the Waldorf Astoria
through the kitchen, where, in the past, Nickolai had eaten a few
meals, discussing politics and the future with Grisha and his
friends. Grisha was a revolutionary, or at least he had been ever
since the coup attempt in Moscow. Knowing what might happen
and being fed up to his eyebrows with party leadership, he had
taken a train to Moscow and joined ranks with Yeltsin's group
against the party. It had been a decision of finality, and Grisha had
never looked back. Now he was head of one the branches of
Yeltsin's democratic party and a man with a purpose.

He was also the head waiter at the Astoria's dining room, and
its most influential worker. Grisha had finagled one of the
Astoria's nicer suites for Nickolai and Larissa without their ever
having to show their faces at the front desk. The assistant manager had a weakness for the wine in the Astoria's cellars—wine
Grisha had access to. The deal had been easy to make.

Nickolai had met Grisha in the early eighties. At the time,
Nickolai was investigating a car-theft ring in Moscow, and Grisha
had been caught red-handed trying to steal a Chaika belonging to
the Minister of Foreign Affairs. When Grisha was brought in for

interrogation, Nickolai happened to be in the office and decided to talk to the young man, then age seventeen, himself. Grisha had been pretty uncooperative until Nickolai had hit on the problem: The young man had felt it was a double standard to arrest him for stealing a Chaika that was crammed full of stolen liquor.

Further investigation implicated the minister in a plot to steal products from the government's specialized shops, shops where only the elite could buy products of all kinds and sell them on the black market.

The minister finagled his way out of prosecution but was replaced in his post. Nickolai got Grisha off with a year's probation. Then, through his sister Marina, he had found him the job at the Astoria. They had been friends every since.

Marina. He had lied to Bakatin about never hearing from her. In reality, they had corresponded often, even had lunch together a few times when Nickolai could get to Leningrad from Moscow. He knew about the requirement Tupolev had placed upon his sister in order for Nickolai to stay alive, and they had been careful. But they had never stopped helping one another.

At first Nickolai had despised his brother-in-law for what had happened, but over the years he had watched Dimitri Bakatin pay a heavy price in slavery to Tupolev—a fate worse than Nickolai's, and another important reason to be rid of the old man.

He glanced at one of the doors, the bedroom where Larissa was sleeping. They were safely tucked away in a suite big enough for Grisha's young family of four. It had two bedrooms, two baths, a telephone, a well-stocked refrigerator—everything they needed.

Nickolai had used the phone a half a dozen times, checking on Vostya Dubenky, on Natalya Starkov, making arrangements for his private visit to Tupolev's quarters. Natalya was in a coma. Her brain tissue was swelling, bruised to a pulp. She had less than a 50 percent chance of living. Nickolai had put out the word to his people that Kulikov was to be found and arrested. If Nickolai could arrange it, the man wouldn't get out of prison except to be buried.

He sent men to the apartment where he had left the psychopath locked in the bathroom. The door was lying in the hall-way, and Kulikov was gone. They would get another chance.

Galya Starkova and Rand King had made contact. They were safe for now, and he had elected not to make contact with them personally, not yet—not until he had paid his visit to their mutual enemy. He had his people pass along the word that he and Larissa were safe and that they would be in touch tomorrow.

He continued staring at the closed bedroom door. Larissa Vavilova was becoming a temptation. After they had settled into their rooms and Nickolai had purchased a few overnight things from the shop, they had talked while reducing a good meal Grisha had brought them to scraps. When Larissa had walked into the sitting room and taken a chair at the table set by room service, he had been afraid she would notice his inordinate interest in her. For a woman of fifty, Larissa had uncommon beauty and presence, an air of confidence that left Nickolai's stomach in knots and his eyes unable to turn away. With other women Nickolai had always felt uncomfortable, a real klutz. With Larissa he felt like a blub-bering idiot.

She didn't seem to notice, or if she did, she didn't seem to care. Status didn't seem to matter to Larissa Vavilova. He won-dered if it had always been that way. She had concentrated on her food and her story as she filled in some details about her past—the dismissal from the Kirov, the injury, then her marriage. She hadn't said much about the child, only that he had died.

He had felt something with Larissa he hadn't felt in a long time. Peace. Contentment. Larissa was a lot like his deceased wife, a woman with a cultured background, a kind heart, and a love of others. He wanted that feeling again, wanted a chance to rebuild his life on something other than loneliness.

Nickolai tied his shoes, a pair of soft, leather Italian models he had purchased in the store in the hotel lobby. Such shoes were hard to find in a Russian shop. Some old-fashioned saddle soap had taken the stiffness out of them. Now they felt soft, pliable, comfortable. Quiet.

He was ready—broke, but well clothed.

He went to the door and let himself out, making sure it locked behind him. He didn't like leaving Larissa alone, but from what he had seen, she could handle herself and wouldn't appreciate his thinking otherwise. Besides, he couldn't wait.

Dimitri Bakatin had disappeared, and Tupolev would be passing judgment on him as soon as he returned from Moscow.

Then there was Kulikov. Georgi Zhelin would protect the hit man, but if the record book held what Nickolai thought it did, he could keep Bakatin alive and get Kulikov's head in a basket as well. The question was, did the record book still exist?

Nickolai and Dimitri had seen the book a long time ago, when Tupolev and Beria were planning Krushchev's assassination and wanted the two young rookies involved. Tupolev had removed it from his desk and referred to it when discussing payment for the task they were to perform. Nickolai had caught a glimpse of it and realized it contained all of Tupolev's transactions, all his payments, his receipts. But over the years Nickolai had completely forgotten about it. If it still existed . . . the possibilities were endless, and whatever the diary Galya had been given might say would be insignificant in comparison—at least to Nickolai. The trick was getting his hands on it.

He took the elevator, ending up in the basement.

Bakatin must have seen the record book recently or he wouldn't have mentioned it. Of course, it had been Bakatin's original intent to inherit the book and its account numbers. If the old man was still using the antiquated accounting system, whoever controlled the record book would control the empire. When Bakatin knew Tupolev had discovered his betrayal, he had passed to Nickolai the only information he felt might save him.

Grisha greeted Nickolai with the usual smile, then led him deeper into the hotel's storage, heat, and air-conditioning rooms. When they came to a stop, it was in front of a table on which Grisha had laid the hotel's architectural plans for its last remodeling. The date in the corner read 1972. The plans were usually kept in the city planning department. Grisha was full of surprises.

Vostya Dubenky, Nickolai's assistant, was looking them over. He glanced up, giving his boss a grin.

Vostya was young, twenty-eight, unmarried, handsome, and a

dedicated criminologist. He liked the idea of putting crooks of all makes and models behind bars, but he was particularly fond of throwing the key away on people in high places who thought they were untouchable. It was the reason Nickolai had brought him on board.

A former member of the country's elite special forces, Vostya had fought in Afghanistan. He had come home wounded and disillusioned about his country's role there. He had left the service and started a vocal rebellion against central government leadership and the military's handling of the war. For his efforts he had gone to jail but was never tried. Under Yeltsin's government, he, along with others, had been set free. He had returned to the streets, an agitator for change. Nickolai had heard him talk at a rally held at the foot of Pushkin's statue a block from the American McDonald's restaurant, two days after Yeltsin had hired Nickolai in his present position. They had talked. When they had finished, Vostya had a new job. That had been six months ago.

"Hello, Papa," Vostya said.

"Keep calling me that, and I'll do what all good papas do to disrespectful children."

Vostya laughed. "You look like you were run over by a car, *Papa*."

Nickolai touched his puffy lips. "Your baby carriage," he said. He noticed the bandage taped to the younger man's forehead. "It doesn't look like you escaped undamaged."

"Kulikov is a nasty fellow. He clipped me with his pistol handle on his way out of the apartment. Being tied up at the time, I had no chance to respond."

"Maybe your time will come," Nickolai said.

How is Natalya Starkova . . . " Vostya began to ask. "Her husband . . . " He paused, thinking. "He is a priest or something. He gave her a blessing."

Nickolai was intrigued more by the reverence in Vostya's voice than by the fact Rustam Starkov might be a priest. More men were returning to the Orthodox Church priesthood all the time. But Vostya Dubenky had never shown any inclination toward religion or a belief in a supreme being. He pushed aside the urge to question his assistant's reaction.

"I am sure she is no better."

"What do the doctors say?" Vostya asked.

"Rustam Starkov was right to pray to his God. It may be her only chance."

"Possibly we can make her pain count for something, Nickolai."

"Yes. I think we can. Did you bring the items I asked for?"

Vostya pointed to several packages on the floor. "My connections in the army are still good. Be thankful." Vostya smiled.

"Why are the plans dated 1972?" Nickolai asked Grisha, looking at the blueprints.

"Tupolev wanted to be housed here. The top floor of the main wing was changed to accommodate his needs. It is a decadent penthouse with some of the finest furnishings I have ever seen. There must be twenty million dollars' worth of artwork alone— artwork that I know belongs to the people of Russia. The pieces used to be in the Hermitage and the Museum of Russian Art. Now you don't see them anymore.

"Tupolev's friends had them removed from the walls and brought here. It is for this man and others like him that we have been called to sacrifice all these years. I have thought of poisoning his food many times."

"Why didn't you?" Vostya asked.

"They would kill me, and that would be okay. But what they would do to my family, the miseries they would force them to suffer, even today—Tupolev is not worth such suffering."

The work of intimidation. The fear it created was better than imprisoning an adversary. Less costly as well.

"How do I get in?" Nickolai asked.

"The return-air vents are all connected to the main duct that leads back to the air-conditioning unit here, in the basement. We can get you inside that duct, and you can climb upward until you reach the very top of the building. There you will see two ducts that return the air from Tupolev's rooms. By taking the one on the left, you can go to the kitchen, living room, den, dining room, and half a dozen other rooms." Grisha shook his head disgustedly. "The man lives like the tsar. He has more room when he dines than I have in my whole house." He sighed. "The duct on the right leads to the bathrooms and bedrooms."

"Where is the safe?"

Vostya pointed. "I contacted the man in charge of remodeling. He says it is here, in the den, hidden by a panel of cherry wood behind Tupolev's desk."

"I don't suppose he knows the combination."

Vostya smiled. "Your talents will be tested, I am sure."

"All right. Grisha, I want you well away from here, in a public place, with witnesses who will verify your noninvolvement."

"But . . ."

"Vostya and I can handle it from here." He paused. "You have a family."

Grisha pulled a set of keys from his pocket and handed them to Vostya. "These unlock the elevator that goes from the lobby to Tupolev's suite. You will need them if Nickolai gets into trouble."

Vostya took them, thanked Grisha, and watched as he disappeared through the darkness of the basement.

"I still think it should be me who goes into the ducts."

"Because I am too old?"

"When we used to work out, when you boxed my ears regularly, I learned you are not too old. No, but because you are hurt."

"No more than you. I know what I am looking for."

They picked up the bags, and Nickolai followed his friend through the maze of plumbing, heating pipes, and ductwork until they came to the central heating/air-conditioning machinery. Vostya pulled aside a part of the ductwork as Nickolai removed a healthy length of rope from the backpack along with several other items. When the hole was big enough, he nodded at Vostya, then stepped into the windy opening.

"Should we turn off the air?" Vostya asked.

"No. I don't want anyone to come down here investigating because of tourist complaints. It will be all right." He braced himself against the strong current while attaching the rope to the spring-loaded grappling hook. Then he stuck the hook into the slot of the gas-powered launching pistol.

Aiming the high-powered flashlight up the duct, he pointed the gun at the top and fired. The explosion that sent the hook into the rays of his light was like a dull thud, but it was powerful enough to drive the hook and rope the six stories with enough force to split the aluminum casing of the duct's ceiling, then hook into the timbers beyond. Nickolai jerked on the rope until it held, then started strapping himself into a climber's harness.

"According to the plans, the room has sensors near the windows and doors, and a pressure plate below the safe. Both set off silent alarms. You will not know you have been discovered until it is too late."

Nickolai glanced up but kept buckling the harness. "Maybe you *should* go."

"The wires for the sensors run next to the ductwork. At the corner where you turn toward the den, you can cut through the duct and snip the wires. Red and yellow. Don't snip the others."

"Red and yellow."

"Yes. You will just have to watch your step around the pressure plate." Vostya showed him a small flashlight, a pair of wire cutters and tin snips, and the equipment he would need to break the combination to the safe.

"The safe is German—a very good brand. If you can't open it after thirty minutes, you will never open it." He placed everything into the padded backpack and helped Nickolai work it onto his shoulders, adjusting the straps for a comfortable fit. He handed Nickolai a two-way radio. "As soon as you are in the den, I will position myself in the lobby, near Tupolev's elevator, in case you need artillery support." He grinned. "Tupolev's plane is expected in about fifteen minutes. It will take some time to get from the airport. I estimate you have an hour."

"I hope you are right."

Vostya gave him an incredulous look. "Have I failed you yet?"

Nickolai gave him a snide look.

"Oh. We can't count at the apartment. I thought you had things covered. Kulikov . . . You didn't warn me. He . . . "

"Goodbye, Vostya. I'll keep in touch."

Nickolai put the small radio into his pants pocket, then hooked up the battery-powered winch that would hoist him to the top of the tunnel. Putting the rope through the carabiner, he pushed the button on the small motorized machine and began the ascent. In the old days, he would have had to climb the distance by hand. He was grateful for new technology.

When he reached the top of the shaft, he slid himself into the duct that ran to his right, grateful to be rid of the harness pressing against his sore abdomen.

When the ductwork had been added at Tupolev's request, the rooms on the top floor had had ceilings that were twelve to fifteen feet high. Now the ducts, electrical work, and other changes were housed in the top three feet with a false ceiling, just below the ductwork and Nickolai's feet.

As he had come up the main duct, the force of the breeze he was fighting had lessened. Comparatively, at the top the wind was hardly noticeable.

He came to the branch in the ductwork that would take him over Tupolev's office. It was smaller and gave him claustrophobia just looking at it. He took off his pack and removed the snips and wire cutters. Putting the small flashlight into his mouth, he worked the snips under a joint in the duct and began cutting a hole. A minute later, he removed the piece of metal to reveal the darkness outside the duct. He shined the light through the opening.

At first he didn't see the wires and had to cut a bigger hole to reveal them. They were bound together by strands of copper wire. Using the wire cutters, he snipped the copper and loosened the tangle of twenty-five to thirty multicolored, plastic-covered conduits. He found the yellow one, but there were two red. Turning them over in his fingers, he discovered that one had a black strip running down its center. Taking Vostya's word as absolute, he snipped the yellow, then the plain red. Putting everything back into his pack, he started working his way along the duct. He wore no metal, and his soft leather shoes made little sound as he pushed himself forward. His only problem was the pack. It took great effort to carry it without dragging it. Finally he found himself looking through a vent cover directly into Tupolev's office.

Catching his breath, he listened. Nothing. Removing the cover, he lowered his head to the eyes, scanning the room.

It was dimly lit and well furnished, the lair of a man who still felt he had fangs.

Nickolai removed the radio and pushed the button. "Vostya, I am leaving the ductwork and entering Tupolev's office. Do you hear me?"

"Loud and clear."

Nickolai flinched as the tinny sound of Vostya's voice echoed in the duct. Wishing he had an earphone, he turned down the radio, then put it back into his pocket. Lowering himself into the office, landing atop Tupolev's large desk, he waited for long seconds but heard nothing. Apparently he had cut the right wires.

He did a quick search of the desk, hoping Tupolev had left the record book lying around. No such luck. He was beginning to sweat.

Removing his pack, he gave the floor in front of the safe a once-over, wondering where the pressure plate was. He couldn't tell. He removed a sharp utility knife from the backpack and inserted it into the wall-to-wall carpet. Too bad. Such luxurious carpet was rare in Russia. His cut was three feet away from the wall, making a large hole. Removing the carpet square, he revealed the pressure plate. Now it could be avoided.

Placing the piece of carpet on the desk, he began searching for the secret to moving the cherry-wood panel that covered the safe. He felt along the wall for a button or switch, checked the desk drawers for the same thing. Nothing. Getting onto his back, he checked the underside of the desk. Still nothing. As he pushed himself to his feet, he looked carefully at the picture in the middle of the panel. Vincent Van Gogh's *Ladies from Arles*. It had disappeared from the Hermitage walls less than six months ago. Repairs, the people were told.

Nickolai squinted at the masterpiece. A small light had been hung on the top of the frame for better viewing, and he flipped it on. The panel, painting still firmly attached, slipped to one side, revealing the safe.

He removed his tools from the pack. He had never broken into any safe, let alone a German one, but he had been trained in the technique by specialists in the police department of Moscow. Then it had been to understand the principles used by safe-crackers and other notable citizens he was trying to apprehend. He never intended to use the lessons except to apprehend crooks. Now he wished he had listened better.

Ten minutes passed. He had the first click and its corresponding number. Twenty. He was sweating. The second click sounded in the stethoscope. The odds were getting worse; someone was bound to check the office.

There it was, the third click. He dialed the numbers, pushed on the handle, and opened the door. Stacks of American twenty-dollar bills lay underneath several documents, but there was no record book. Removing the papers, he gave them a quick once-over, then shoved them into the pack for more careful scrutiny later.

He removed the new money. Behind the twenties were tens and fives—altogether about fifty thousand dollars' worth. He started to shove them back inside when he saw the inch-thick, leather-bound book placed between the last row of bills and the wall of the safe. He pulled it out and quickly glanced through it. Inside the front cover were bank names, a series of letters and numbers by each. Coded, but poorly. He thumbed through the entries. Tupolev had never broken his meticulous habit. Nickolai had hit pay dirt.

He shut the safe, slid the panel back into place, put his equipment and the account book into his bag, replaced the carpet as best as he could, then went to the door. After catching his breath, he cracked it open. The hall was empty but well lit. Expensive paintings hung on the walls between two sets of doors on each side. These were by Russian artists. All of them were paintings of the revolutionary period. *Death of a Commissar,* by Petrov-Vodkin, and his *1919. On the Alert* hung close enough to the door that Nickolai could see the detail. Farther down he could see what he thought to be *The Vow of the Siberian Guerrillas,* by Sergei Gerasimov. Tupolev stole only the very best from the Russian people.

Four doors. Four rooms. The remodeling plans for the building indicated that the first on the left was a bedroom with a large, attached bath. Probably Tupolev's. Second room, same side, another bedroom, with a door leading to the first through the bath. Probably Mrs. Tupolev's until her death. Who used it now was anyone's guess.

First room on the right. The plans showed a lot of electrical outlets and wiring. It was probably full of computers now—maybe some communications equipment.

Second room on the right—file room. Tupolev probably had something on everyone he considered an enemy. Considering that Tupolev had been a student of Stalin and Beria, the files would be as complete as humanly possible. He opened the door and moved along the hall. The file-room door was locked. Removing a large screwdriver from his pack, he wedged it into the door frame and shoved, popping the door open. Then, entering the room, he closed the door behind him.

The cabinets were metal, four drawers each, each drawer marked by a letter or two of the Russian alphabet. He went to the one marked with a Russian B. Opening it, he looked for the word *belii,* or *white.* The file he found on the White Guard was thick, stuffed full of papers to overflowing. He pulled it from the cabinet, shut the door, and let himself back into the hall. Someday he'd come back to this room; it would prove interesting reading.

As he reached the door into Tupolev's den, he heard voices down the hall, beyond the door at the other end. He stepped into the den and closed the door. Had he set off an alarm? No, they were talking normally, without excitement.

He shoved the folder into the backpack, zipped it shut, and put the straps over his arms. Switching off the desk lamp, he launched himself upward, grabbing the edges of the iron ribs of the duct and hoisting himself in. Quickly putting the vent cover into place, he held his breath, then moved back farther into the duct as a switched-on light filled the office below.

Tupolev's head, topped with thinning gray hair, came into view. He lowered his aging body into the leather chair and placed a pistol on the desk. His Luger. Nickolai knew about the Luger—a World War II trophy taken from the body of a German soldier, supposedly a general Tupolev had killed with his bare hands.

"You searched the restorationist's apartment completely?" Tupolev asked.

"Every inch."

"And these papers were all that you found?"

"What you have are photocopies of a few pages of the diary. They were shoved under some other things on the desk. The restorationist must have missed them in his rush to leave the building."

"Norwegian. Have you had anyone interpret them yet?" Tupolev asked, thumbing through the half-dozen pages in his withered hands.

"We made copies of these, and they are with an expert linguist now."

"A man who can be trusted to keep his mouth shut, I would hope."

"Of course. One of the papers is a picture—a line drawing of Peter and Paul Cathedral."

Tupolev shuffled the papers, finding the picture. He seemed to visibly brighten when he saw it.

"It is here . . . " He jammed his finger at one of the pages, the picture of the cathedral. "Here their secret is kept. I know it! The woman hid here during the war. When I discovered it, she had already escaped the city. I searched this place then but found nothing. That diary contains the instructions to their secret! It must!"

Nickolai was surprised at the reaction. Tupolev's voice contained the shrill, high-pitched sound of excitement.

"I have fifty men working on it, Father. We will find the diary. It is only a matter of time," Zhelin said.

"We do not have time! If the people . . . if the White Guard find it first, I lose my chance to unmask their charade. I have a better way. The woman . . . "

Nickolai heard the door open; it was Bondorenko.

"What is it?" Tupolev asked impatiently.

"I must report, Comrade Tupolev. The . . . the two prisoners we held have escaped. Nickolai Poltav . . . "

Nickolai couldn't believe his ears. Kulikov had convinced this poor sap to take the heat even though it was Kulikov's responsibility, Kulikov's failure.

Tupolev came to his feet, walked to the side of the desk, and began pacing, the Luger in one hand which was clasped by the other behind his back.

"I am surrounded by incompetence! All of you have failed me!" Tupolev said. "The woman and the American escape, the diary is still unfound!" He faced Bondorenko, who was pale and sweating profusely. "And now you tell me the one man who could ruin everything has escaped as well! You are a fool, Bondorenko!"

"Yes . . . yes, comrade," the big man said sheepishly.

Nickolai was amazed. Bondorenko had strength enough to break Tupolev in half, and yet he cowered before this balding, frail piece of human flesh as if he were supernatural—a god like Thor or Zeus!

Tupolev waved a hand of dismissal at Bondorenko and spoke words that reduced the hulk of a man to nothing more than dust: "You have always been a fool. Your brain is the size of a pea! But then, you cannot be accountable for your weaknesses, your stupidity. These came from your mother, your father. Uneducated, unworthy even to live. It is my fault as well. I did not hire you for your brains, only because you are an animal. I cannot expect an animal to think. Why didn't you kill him when you had him? It is what you do best. Why?"

"Georgi told us not to kill him," Bondorenko responded weakly.

Tupolev turned to Zhelin. A cold quiet filled the room.

Nickolai was surprised at Zhelin's calm, unruffled form before his master—even more surprised at his answer as he threw responsibility at the man who could snuff out his life like the light of candle.

"I would have the woman here now, and the diary, if you had let me take care of it in the usual manner. Instead, you stick me with incompetents like Bondorenko and Kulikov! And traitors like Dimitri Bakatin! The blame rests with you if I have failed, Father, and with no one else."

Nickolai realized he was dealing with more than one man with ice in his veins. Zhelin was as cold hearted and calculating as his master.

Tupolev's hand tightened on the Luger, and he glared at his son-in-law. "You dare to challenge me?"

Nickolai slipped his forty-five from the backpack and pushed the safety into the firing position.

Zhelin, his voice still calm, forged ahead, ignoring the old man's behavior as if it were a common occurrence. "I state only the truth. You put me in charge, but you must allow me full use of my power and honor my decisions. Nickolai Poltav would be worse for us dead. Yeltsin would demand an investigation, and even if we could circumvent prosecution, it would cause unneeded stress on our organization." He glared at Bondorenko. "Letting him escape, however, was incompetent and creates a serious problem—one I am sure Mr. Kulikov and Mr. Bondorenko here will rectify quickly."

Tupolev seemed to relax, turning his back on the two as he spoke. "It is I who will rectify, Georgi. Not Bondorenko. Not you. It is evident that only my direct involvement in this matter will get things done as I want them. Nickolai Poltav is to be found and killed. I don't care what Yeltsin thinks. He cannot touch me! Your soft-bellied approach to this is inexcusable. As for the woman, she contacted me by phone. She is willing to give us the diary."

Nickolai nearly dropped his weapon.

"What? How could she . . . ? Why . . . ?" Georgi Zhelin said, confused.

Tupolev turned, a belligerent attitude in his stance.

"How? Why? You fool! Because she wanted to free her two

friends! Now they are free, our chances are next to nothing! Now we must hunt her again instead of having her come to us!"

Zhelin stammered. "But . . . but my . . . my decision was even more correct. By keeping them alive . . . "

"Your decision was wrong. Why do you think she is afraid for them? Because she saw what I am willing to do. The only good thing Kulikov did was beat the woman. It sent Miss Starkova a message. She is not stupid! And now what do we have for leverage? Even if Bondorenko had killed Poltav, we would still have had the woman to bargain with."

Nickolai shook his head in amazement at the rationalizing of a killer to whom death was always the solution.

"Now we must hunt them both!" Tupolev said. "But we will find them—and the diary! Because I am in charge! Because I know how to hunt and what to do with the prey once they are cornered!" He turned to the desk and sat down.

"But first, some restructuring."

Before Nickolai could blink, Tupolev had flipped off the safety on the Luger and fired. Nickolai's head jerked upward with the sound, and when he realized what had happened, it was over.

Bondorenko lay on the floor, his head resting in a pool of blood. Zhelin stood stiff, cold, staring at Tupolev, refusing to look down at the body, refusing to let the shock of it turn his eyes from the old man. The hair on the back of Nickolai's neck stood on end as the evil of these two men passed up through the vent so thickly it nearly took the air away. He felt cold, unable to move or even take his eyes from the duel of wills taking place below him. After long seconds that seemed like hours, Tupolev directed the gun away from Bondorenko's lifeless body.

"The man has died for both your sins, Georgi," Tupolev said through clenched teeth. "Even if I leave my daughter a widow, no one else will die for another of your mistakes."

Zhelin didn't answer. Nickolai was awed at his cold stare and rigid body. In the face of death, most people were reduced to begging. Nickolai found himself wondering which man had the coldest heart.

Tupolev turned away, toward a window. Now Nickolai

couldn't see his face, but the old man seemed to be thinking. For Nickolai, the fact that Zhelin spoke the next words was a surprise.

"You are not finished with your restructuring. Dimitri Bakatin has proven himself a traitor." Zhelin proceeded to tell Tupolev about Dimitri's meeting with Nickolai and that they had a witness—the owner of the bar.

Nickolai found himself sickened as the two men discussed Dimitri's death as if he were just another animal to be taken to the slaughterhouse for disposal.

"Where is Dimitri?"

Nickolai's heart stopped.

"Waiting in the outer hall."

"And Shelepin?"

"Also waiting, but in another room."

"Bring Dimitri in here." Tupolev returned to his desk chair, placing the Luger on its top, his hand still wrapped around the handle.

Zhelin stepped to the desk and pushed the button on an intercom to give orders. He was directly below the vent now, and Nickolai could see the nervous shake in his hand, the sweat dripping down the side of his face. Not so calm after all, Nickolai thought. A survivor, cold, calculating, devoid of human decency, but human—a man who knew fear. Nickolai noticed then that Zhelin had his other hand in his coat pocket, probably tightly gripping a revolver of his own. He couldn't help but wonder who would have won if the old man had decided to aim his Luger.

There was a knock at the door, and Zhelin left Nickolai's view to go to the door.

When he returned, Dimitri Bakatin, dressed in a business suit and tie, was with him. Dimitri was pale, ashen, but his features were set in concrete, a sign of resignation to his fate flooding over his face as his eyes fixed on Bondorenko's body.

Tupolev began fondling the Luger. The silence was deafening. Nickolai kept his eyes focused on the Luger, watching the safety as the old man's finger rubbed it. He wondered how many times this debate had taken place in the old man's mind.

Nickolai knew what was going to happen even before the old

general aimed the Luger at Bakatin. His decision to save his former friend was made before Tupolev had a chance to bring up the
gun. Using the butt of the Makarov, he pummeled the vent cover,
knocking it into the room below. It landed with a bang in the
middle of Tupolev's desk, giving all three men a start that made
them jump back. Nickolai shoved the pistol into the opening,
pointing it at Tupolev while lowering his head into the room.
Bakatin was pale, having just seen both his death and his resurrection take place in the bat of an eyelash.

"General, I'll kill you."

Tupolev stopped the motion of the gun.

"Remove the bullets—carefully and slowly. Place them and
the gun on the desk."

The old man complied.

Nickolai redirected the pistol barrel at Zhelin, who was slipping his hand free of his suit-coat pocket.

"Uh-uh. Put it on the floor, Georgi. Now!"

Zhelin dropped the pistol. Nickolai pointed the pistol at
Tupolev's wrinkled forehead.

"Dimitri, pick up the guns and throw them over there, toward
the window." Even now he didn't trust Bakatin. Some habits were
hard to break.

"You can't get out of this alive, Poltav," Tupolev said through
clenched teeth.

"I would argue the point, but I'm pressed for time. Dimitri,
these two have only one plan in mind for you, and it ends next to
Bondorenko. You had better get out of here."

"There are guards at the entrance to the elevators. I won't get
past them without Zhelin."

Nickolai thought a moment.

"You can trust me, Nickolai. I cannot survive with Tupolev,
that is obvious, and I wish to survive," Bakatin said.

"Get Zhelin's gun. Hold it on these two while I get down."

When Nickolai had joined Dimitri, he removed the small
revolver from his one-time friend's hand.

"Sorry, one gun in this crowd is enough." He removed the
bullets and shoved them into his pocket, then threw the gun

across the room to the window, near the Luger. "Get up there. When you reach the end of the small duct, turn left. Go to the vent that comes from the basement. There is a rope; take it."

"No elevator?" Dimitri said as he climbed onto the desk.

"We'll have one put in next week," Nickolai responded. It always astounded him how people reacted after they had survived a near-death experience. A joke at such a time showed that Dimitri was still in control of his sanity—a necessity if he intended to successfully escape.

"I'll have someone meet you. Go with him. I'll catch up with you later," Nickolai said.

Dimitri looked down at Tupolev. Nickolai could see there was still fear in his eyes, an inability to break the hold the old man had on him.

"Go, Dimitri. He knows you've been cooperating with me. This butcher will kill you if you don't get out of here."

"I will kill you anyway, Dimitri. I will find you and enjoy putting my Luger to your head."

Dimitri looked at Nickolai, then back at Tupolev. The old man's cold eyes tried to hold him, but Bakatin looked up, grabbed the edges of the duct, and hoisted himself in, his large frame barely fitting through the hole. Nickolai could hear him moving down the duct toward the main line. He removed the radio from his pocket. "Vostya, Dimitri Bakatin is headed down. Detain him."

"Loud and clear," came the reply.

"Give me the papers," Nickolai said, extending his arm toward Tupolev. "The copies of the diary pages."

Tupolev pulled them from his pocket.

"You won't get out of here alive," Zhelin said, a nasty look in his eyes. "My guards will cut you in half if you try going that way, and if you follow Dimitri, you will never get out before we—"

"I've always wanted a chance like this," Nickolai said.

"What do you mean?" asked Zhelin, suddenly wary.

"Look at the possibilities. No witnesses. Two dead bodies,

each with his own weapon missing bullets that are found in the other's body. A violent end to two violent men. Few would care."

"They'd discover—"

"Would they? Who? Who would take the time? Your office, Zhelin? That's a laugh. Your associates would be scrambling for power, each trying to occupy your chair before the other could. Yeltsin certainly wouldn't mind. With Tupolev out of the picture, he could appoint anyone he liked to fill your vacancy. The whole country would be better off."

"The police—" Zhelin said firmly.

"They will be glad to see you gone, and we both know it."

"He's just buying time, Georgi," Tupolev said with a challenge in his voice. "Nickolai's weakness was always his inability to make such a decisive move."

Nickolai smiled. "Shall we see?" He raised the pistol to the side of the old man's head. Tupolev didn't even flinch, and Zhelin only seemed curious, as if waiting to see who was right.

"Vladimir Tupolev, I sentence you to death for the murder of my wife, Svetlana Poltava, and thirty-three others, all innocent of any wrongdoing to you or to the Russian people. Sentence to be carried out immediately."

The sudden revelation of his past evil made Tupolev stiffen, his eyes suddenly filling with fear.

"I did not . . . you cannot prove . . . "

Nickolai grabbed the old man's coat, pulling as Tupolev tried to move away from the gun. Zhelin was both amazed and expectant, his tongue wetting his lips like that of a lion about to devour his dinner.

Nickolai shoved the old man away, lifting the gun. "But I have other ways to carry out the sentence." He looked up at Zhelin. "Sorry to disappoint you, but you'll have to do your own killing." He looked back at Tupolev, who was leaning over the arm of the chair, gasping for air. "General, you think you know this man, but he will kill you for what you did to him today."

Tupolev looked up at Zhelin, fear mixed with anger etched in the lines of his face.

Nickolai motioned toward the floor. "Both of you, down."

Once they were settled, he climbed back onto the desk and spoke into the radio. "Vostya, turn off the power to the elevators—all of them. But make sure the one to this suite is more than temporarily shut down."

Zhelin raised his head, saw the gun come his way, and put it down again. Nickolai launched himself upward through the hole and began scampering to the end, his paper-laden backpack in tow. The race was on.

Zhelin looked up and saw Nickolai's feet disappear. He scrambled to his feet and ran to the Luger as the old man struggled to get up. Rushing to the desk, he picked up the bullets and started loading. As Zhelin finished, the old man came face to face with him. Zhelin glanced at the hole, then at Tupolev, as if making a decision.

"What are you waiting for, you fool? Go after him! Kill him!" Tupolev was livid with anger, his eyes bulging, his face pale as wheat flour, splashed with liver spots. Zhelin pointed the gun at Tupolev.

"What . . . ?"

"Sorry, Father, but Poltav was right. If I let you live, you will kill me next time. It is a matter of survival."

"But—" the fear and confusion registered in an instant as Zhelin pulled the trigger.

When the body had stopped moving, Zhelin went to the old general's side and checked for a pulse. The door opened behind him, and Aleksei Shelepin stood there, his mouth hanging open to his chest.

"Close the door." Zhelin knew the guards hadn't heard the shot. They were too far away, with half a dozen doors in between. He turned and faced Shelepin. "With your cooperation, I am about to make you a wealthy man. Are you interested?"

Shelepin looked at the body of Vladimir Tupolev, then back at Georgi Zhelin, who had the Luger at his side, his finger on the trigger. His choice seemed obvious. "What do you want me to do?"

"Do you have a gun?"

Shelepin removed his Makarov from a holster under his belt. "The assailant went through the ductwork. Go after him."

Shelepin hesitated, unsure. "Who . . . "

"Your boss and Nickolai Poltav. You are a witness to their mayhem. Do you understand?"

Shelepin nodded. Zhelin pointed at the open vent. "There are two men who can dispute our story. If you want Dimitri's wealth, you had better get him. Go!"

Shelepin climbed up on the desk and launched himself toward the vent. When he had disappeared, Zhelin looked the room over, the complete story of what happened forming in his mind. With Shelepin coached properly as witness, with his influence in high places, Bakatin and Poltav would be through. Poltav would regret having underestimated him.

He walked to the desk, then pushed the button on the intercom and called the guards at the elevator.

"Tupolev has been killed, along with Bondorenko. A conspiracy. Dimitri Bakatin is responsible. Nickolai Poltav is his accomplice. They are trying to escape through the ductwork. I have a man going into the ductwork from this end. Get to the basement and see if you can catch them." He released the button. Going around the desk but avoiding the pressure plate, he dialed the numbers of the combination. He had to remove Tupolev's ledger, had to have the account numbers. He flung the door open and began removing the packets of money. As the space was cleared, he became more anxious; when it was empty, he felt panic. He opened the drawers of the desk and searched each one, then went back to the safe and looked again, separating the stacks of money in hopes the ledger had been sandwiched in between. Nothing.

It was then he noticed the knife marks in the carpet below the safe. He bent down and removed the cut-away carpet. Poltav! He cursed even as he fell into Vladimir Tupolev's empty chair.

––––––––––

Nickolai heard the gunshot, then a pause that made the hair on the back of his neck stand on end. What was going on back there?

He didn't have time to think about it; someone was coming into the ductwork. He could hear the hard leather soles smacking the metal. Zhelin would have someone headed for the basement by now, and his time was short.

Nickolai grabbed the rope hanging in the main duct and started down. When his feet touched the floor of the basement, Vostya grabbed him, and they started out, Bakatin two steps in front.

"Take him to a safehouse," Nickolai said. "I have to get Larissa out of here."

He was already removing the gloves and shoving them into the backpack, handing it to Vostya as they came into open air. Turning left, Bakatin and Vostya got into a car and pulled away. Nickolai went through the kitchen door into the main lobby and over to the elevators. He punched the button. Nothing. He had forgotten that Vostya had shut off the elevators. He felt the sweat trickle down the sides of his face and was grateful no one else was in the lobby. He walked toward the stairwell, wary. Zhelin's men would come that way.

As he reached the center of the lobby, the doors to the stairs flew open, and two men exploded into the room. Nickolai plopped himself into a chair behind a tall plant.

The two men, focused only on getting to the kitchen door, didn't notice him and soon disappeared. His heart started beating again, and he moved quickly through the door and up the stairs.

He walked as quickly as he could down the hall, forcing himself not to run, not to panic. Jamming the key into the slot of his suite, he moved quickly inside. Then, placing his back against the wall, he took in deep breaths of air.

Larissa appeared at her bedroom door. The look she gave him was one of bewilderment.

He smiled. "I think it's time we checked out."

Chapter Twenty-one

RAND AWOKE WITH A JOLT. A pain was shooting up his back and into his neck. He sat up, throwing the blanket off and putting his feet on the floor. The small couch in his consulate office was cramping his legs, which explained the pain. He felt tired, but then, he hadn't slept most of the night. He looked at his watch—five in the morning. The curtains in his office were pulled, darkening the room, but light still crept through the cracks and lit the large space to a dim gray.

The last dream had done it. He was standing before the president, who was passing his sentence and sending him to a federal penitentiary. Boris Yeltsin was standing next to him, loving every word.

Rand knew what the dream stemmed from—his decision to stay away from the authorities. He still wasn't sure it was the right one, but it seemed to be the safe one.

He couldn't go to the Russians. Tupolev and Zhelin controlled them, and Galya would be in prison before he could prevent it—not to mention where he would be. Besides, Nickolai Poltav *was* Russian authority. As soon as they could hook up to him, they'd be in good shape.

Going to his own government was a little stickier. As much as he thought he should inform his superiors, it would all end up in the same place—back in Russia, probably with Zhelin, who would go after Rand's hide and have him on the next flight back to Washington if he could.

He wasn't sure the reasons were good enough, if he was

really justified. Maybe that was why he was having the night-mares.

Galya was asleep on the larger couch. He watched her. She was a beautiful woman.

Picking up his socks and shirt, he went into the bathroom, glad he had remodeled the place and had included a spacious bath with a shower.

Fifteen minutes later he was dressed in fresh Dockers, a golf shirt, dark blue socks, and leather slip-ons. The shower and shave had woken him up; the toothpaste and liberal amounts of mouthwash had cleared away the halitosis.

Switching off the bathroom light, he went to a small refrigerator in the corner of the office and removed a pitcher containing orange juice. Although the juice was made from powdered concentrate, it was cold and tasted wonderful. He went to his desk and turned on the computer.

"Good morning," came the voice from across the room.

"Good morning. Would you like to sleep longer, or can I fix you some breakfast?"

"Breakfast? At five-thirty in the morning?"

"Get a good start on your day. Actually, its just orange juice, and some muffins if you want them."

She sat up. She had slept in her slip, so he looked away while she pulled the blanket around her. "A shower." She moved toward the bathroom.

"I can't provide much in the way of women's clothing, but there are some shirts and tennis shorts . . . "

"Thank you," she said, disappearing behind the door. "Anything from Tupolev?"

Rand checked the answering machine, although the phone hadn't rung all night. "No, nothing."

"What do you suppose it means?"

They had decided to contact Tupolev even after they had learned that Nickolai and Larissa had escaped and that Rustam was safe. Galya simply wanted it to be over, wanted no one else hurt.

"It means one of two things: Either he has no interest, or he doesn't have anything to bargain with."

The door cracked open. He glanced up to see Galya's face in the opening, his terry-cloth robe amply covering the rest of her. He smiled. "Or he hasn't gotten our message yet," she said. She closed the door and the shower went on, then the sink.

"There are extra toothbrushes in the top left-hand drawer," Rand said loudly.

The computer screen was showing the main menu. Rand took the business card out of his pocket and began the process of breaking and entering. Ellen's instructions were perfect, and soon he was re-reading the cover sheet on the file. Hitting the keys, he moved inside.

There were several sheets of background reading. Andrews, then a colonel in army intelligence, had made initial contact with Alexander Bychevsky, young leader of the White Guard, a pro-tsarist group who were said to be protecting the remaining heirs of Nickolas II.

The noise of the shower bothered him, broke his concentration. He sat back, his hands behind his head, staring at the door. He knew very little about Galya except that she was beautiful, intelligent, feisty, and, yes, stubborn. Their lives were separated not only by nine time zones but also by background, politics, and future plans. He liked Russia, but he would go home someday. He couldn't see Galya ever leaving her country to take up residence on a farm in Idaho.

And there was still Ellen.

He shook his head. It was foolish even to think about.

He went back to his reading as the light sound of humming came through the door. Five minutes later, the water went off.

He read aloud from the 1940 record: "The White Guard is the leading opposition force in Russia at the present time. They have delivered signed statements of leaders within the Communist hierarchy who support their claim and will deliver the seat of government to the heir of the Romanov line when the assassination of Stalin is finished."

Rand whistled lightly. So that was what ALLIANCE was about.

Galya came to the door, peering out through a slight crack. "Do you have a blow dryer?"

"Sorry. It's in my apartment. Did you find some clothes?"

"Yes, thank you. I will need a belt."

He removed his from his Dockers, walked to the door, and put it into her outstretched hand.

"You will not need this?" she asked.

"I have one in my suit pants I can use. I've opened ALLIANCE. I think you'll find it interesting."

"One minute." She closed the door. He stayed next to it, his forearm leaning against the jamb.

"They were after Stalin. The White Guard must have been powerful in those days. They had a coup set up."

"Does it say anything about Kitrick?"

"Not yet, but from his background I'd say he was the trigger man."

The door opened, and she came out, holding the tennis shorts up with one hand, the belt in the other. "You mean assassin. There are not enough holes in this belt."

"I'll make some."

She went to the computer. He wondered how a woman could look so beautiful when her hair lay matted to her scalp and she hadn't applied makeup.

As she read, he used a letter opener to force a hole through the belt leather about eight inches closer to the buckle. He handed the belt to her, and she took it without removing her eyes from the screen. He pulled up a chair.

"Sit," he said.

She did, then stopped reading long enough to feed the belt through the keepers and pull it tight. "Just right," she said, pushing the extra length through the keepers a second time. The shorts were gathered in bunches, but when she pulled the shirt over them the bunches disappeared.

Rand noticed that she smelled like fresh lilacs. She had used his soap, but he never smelled like fresh lilacs—more like sage-brush.

He punched the page-down key and tried to concentrate on the reading. Five minutes later they both sat back. Neither spoke; both were thinking. Rand went to the refrigerator and poured her a glass of juice. He gave it to her, and she sipped it.

"We have an A-1, all-out attempt to assassinate Stalin here," Rand said.

"But it failed."

"Unfortunate."

She shrugged. "Depends on your viewpoint. Stalin's dictatorial methods forced us to fight. With his gun in our backs, we had no choice. Some credit him with winning the war and saving Russia."

"Others think that is hogwash," he said in English. It was the first time he had spoken a complete sentence in English since he had met Galya Starkova.

"Hogwash? What is this?" she asked in the same language.

"Baloney, a snow job." He could see she was still confused. "A lie," he said.

"Yes, it is hogwash then."

"I wonder how many people died when this plot was discovered," Rand said, returning to Russian.

"It would be many," she said, sticking to English. "I am wondering . . . what of this heir?"

He smiled at her heavily accented but clear enough English.

"It is your history. Fill me in."

"The White Guard is only one of many groups who wanted the tsar to remain in power. The first was called Pravy Tsentr—Right Center. One of the men who led it was also called Bychevsky, possibly this man, Alexander."

"Or his father."

"Yes." She continued in English. "Pravy Tsentr planned to free Nicholas II and his family from Ekaterinburg, where they were taken prisoners. This White Guard—it is maybe . . . descended from Right Center."

"Do they still exist?"

"According to Nickolai, they may be the ones after the diary."

Rand sat back. "Tupolev and the White Guard, both after the diary." It made for an interesting combination. "It as much as says here that the heir they were trying to put back on the throne was directly related to Nicholas II. I thought the whole family was killed."

Galya pulled her feet under her, Rand's big desk chair giving her plenty of room. "There were many lines of possible heirs to the throne, but the Bolsheviks made sure most of them never escaped. Of the ones who did, the Dowager Empress Marie Fedorovna, mother of Nicholas, who escaped to England, was one. Then there were his sisters, Xenia and Olga.

"Grand Duke Cyril, a cousin, survived as well, even tried to claim the throne. He declared himself tsar of all Russia. But none of the family who escaped ever recognized the title. Grand Duke Nicholas Nicolaievich was better suited to take charge, but for reasons unknown to the world, he refused to do so. He had a great following back in Russia among the leaders of the White Army, at least before they were beaten by the Communists. But he was adamant in his refusal to succeed Tsar Nicholas II."

She took a deep breath. "Then there is the mythology."

"About Nicholas and his children? I know a little."

She nodded, staring into the gray darkness of the room.

"The historical version accepted in my country today is taken from the report of Nicholas Sokolov, who was hired by the White Army, the ones opposing Lenin and the Reds, to investigate the tsar's disappearance. Many believe Sokolov concealed evidence and wrote a report the leaders of the army wanted published instead of the truth of what happened."

"The Whites were monarchists," Rand said. "Why would they report the death of the one man who could continue to lead, whom they were fighting for, if it didn't really occur?"

"They were not fighting for Nicholas, not at the end. They were fighting for a monarchy. Most no longer believed that Nicholas should be the tsar. In their view, his ineptness had caused their problems and the loss of power.

"Then there was Empress Alexandra, a German—married to

the tsar, but still a German. Russia was fighting Germany for its life in 1917, and many considered the empress a spy who wanted Germany to win. Some things she did, or counseled her husband to do, could have been perceived in such a light." She paused. "Some think the Whites, who controlled Sokolov and the official investigation into the family's disappearance, didn't want the truth known because they wanted another member of the extended family to take the throne."

"The truth? You mean that Nicholas had survived?"

"Yes. Or members of the family whom they also did not want on the throne. Some say the Whites may have found the family alive, then killed them so as to take leadership themselves. By inviting another, distant family member to fill the throne as figurehead, someone like Grand Duke Nicholas, they would control Russia. This school of thought says that when they were refused, they decided they would put one of their own at the head of the state, once the Reds were defeated. Of course the Reds won, and their machinations were gone in a puff of smoke from the end of an executioner's gun." She paused. "There are many things wrong with this version. It is ludicrous, but some believe it."

"And the Reds? Why would they lie about the tsar's death?"

"They didn't. They killed the tsar. Lenin and Trotsky announced it the day after it happened. But they announced the death of the tsar only, not of the rest of his family. It wasn't until some days later that they added the others to the list. It is a very curious thing and has given rise to much speculation about the family's death. That is what has led to the mythology."

Rand was thinking, trying to catch up mentally. "For the Reds to let the heirs live would give their enemies some hope to cling to," he said. "Lenin himself said that they were all killed so there would be no turning back by his own people. To murder the whole family put the Reds on a path of no return. That is where he wanted the people, so he killed the family."

"However," Galya said, "he didn't make the statement until months later. And couldn't a *statement* of their death do the same thing as actually killing them? If the Reds were careful, kept Empress Alexandra and the children hidden, a statement of their deaths would have been sufficient. Lenin needed only a few months, possibly a year, to get himself established. Once his new government was recognized by other governments, once he controlled the halls of power in the Kremlin, any claims made to the throne could simply be turned aside and the heirs exiled. A new government in Russia, one established by the people, could turn the old government away."

"And Lenin kept them alive, took a chance on their escape or their discovery during all that time?" Rand shook his head. "No, not Lenin. He would have butchered them—gotten rid of such possibilities. The revolution was everything to him. He killed many more for being less of a threat."

"But consider, Rand. From one perspective, to kill all the family *would* have put the revolution at stake. Lenin killed the tsar and the boy. From his viewpoint he had no choice—they were the rightful heirs, the ones who could keep the Whites fighting, a rallying point. He took that away from his enemies." She paused, sitting back. "But Alexandra was German, and the daughters were hers. Russia was in mortal conflict with the Germans; Lenin had to avoid further conflict with them in order to buy time and save his precious revolution. He could have done that by promising the return to Germany of Alexandra and her four daughters."

"I'll bet there's no proof of that, though," Rand said.

"But there is some evidence—letters, affidavits, reports, testimony of people who saw the women alive many days after the Whites took Ekaterinburg and declared the tsar dead." She paused. "For many years the Reds suppressed this evidence. It is only now being made public, and only a little at a time. There is much interest in it in Russia. Many people here believe the tsar's family survived.

"You have read in the West of the survival of Anastasia?" she asked.

"The woman named Anna who turned up in Germany without a memory, then later claimed she was Nicholas's daughter?"

"Yes. Many studies have been done, scientific studies that

compared her facial lines to those of pictures of the real Anastasia. They are similar on all major points."

Rand frowned. "But the rest of the extended family, the descendants who originally escaped, including the Dowager Empress—Anastasia's grandmother—never accepted her."

"She may not have been the heir," Galya replied, "but it had been many years since the Dowager Empress had seen Anastasia, and Anna had been through many hardships—including loss of memory. The empress could have been wrong." She smiled. "You see, it is around such events the mythology continues to revolve."

"ALLIANCE says there was an heir," Rand said. "It was an attempt to put that heir back on the throne. Sufficient numbers in high places supported the heir's claim. That indicates a brilliant deception, *or* it gives truth to your mythology. Someone in Nicholas's family survived Ekaterinburg."

"And the diary may enlighten us, may enlighten everyone," Galya said. "The White Guard wants it because it is part of their past. But why does Tupolev want it?"

"A good question." Rand hit the keys and erased the file, then closed off the link to Washington. It was time to break the bad news.

"While you were asleep, I called the hospital where Nickolai's people said Natalya was taken."

Galya's posture stiffened.

"She is still in a coma. It doesn't look good."

There was a silence. Rand waited.

"Was Rustam there?"

Rand nodded. "I talked to him. Rikki hadn't called."

"Did he want me to come, to be with him?"

"No, he wanted you here. He knows you are in danger, and he can't give you the protection you need. He thinks I can. Possibly we should go to Rustam's and wait for Rikki to call there. It is the likely place."

Galya thought a moment. "First we should try another place, the only place Rikki could hide. I only hope Tupolev has not figured it out as well." She stood and started for the door.

Chapter Twenty-two

ZHELIN PACED. Things were getting complicated, and he was having to involve more people. The chances were growing that word of Tupolev's death would get out before he could build his case and get rid of the two men who would dispute his version of what happened. Poltav and Bakatin had virtually disappeared.

And so had the record book.

He cursed. Everything was in that book! Everything! And Nickolai Poltav had it. Of course it was coded, but the old man's code was a simple one, easily broken. He had to get it back before Poltav could figure out what it was and use it to destroy Tupolev's empire—*his* empire. He needed leverage. Anything would do—anything!

The phone rang. It was Kulikov. Zhelin glanced at his watch. 6:00 A.M.

"Did you get rid of the body?"

"Cremated it. You want Tupolev's jar?" Kulikov asked.

"This is no time for levity, Kulikov. What about Bakatin's wife? She's Poltav's sister, and we can use her."

"Gone. I left men at the house, but it looks like Bakatin warned her."

Zhelin cursed again.

"Did you take Shelepin to Dimitri's office? Is he making the transfers?"

"I'm with him now. The funds have been transferred into new accounts. The rest is very complicated. It will take much more time."

"Your men, they are all trustworthy? They won't let news of what has happened out prematurely?"

"Your generosity will keep them quiet."

"How much will it take?"

"A thousand American dollars—each."

That meant his bill was nearly a hundred thousand dollars. Acceptable. There was a thousand times that much in Tupolev's accounts. If the old man had allowed him such funding in the beginning, all of this could have been avoided. The thought gave Zhelin mixed feelings. He was free of Tupolev—even felt cleansed—but the freedom hadn't come without complications that the old man could have settled very quickly. The record book, for example. Tupolev had the bank account numbers memorized. He could have shifted the funds to new banks before Nickolai could do anything about it. Now Zhelin would have to force Nickolai to cough them up or lose everything. It wouldn't be easy.

"What about Poltav?"

"We have people watching his office both here and in Moscow. Of course, the phones are tapped. We intercepted three calls this morning." He paused for affect. "One was from Poltav. We traced it to a public phone in Moscow Station. He was not there when our people arrived."

Ah, at last, Zhelin thought, some progress.

"Was he given our message?" Zhelin had called and informed Nickolai's office of his desire to meet in behalf of Tupolev. "Was there any indication he knows about what happened? That Tupolev is dead?"

"He was given the message. I have listened to the tape, and I heard nothing that would show he is aware of how things happened." Another pause. "I may have found Dimitri's hiding place."

Zhelin smiled. "Excellent!" Just the leverage he needed. Even better than trying to get Nickolai to accept his life as a bargaining chip for the record book would be the lives of his sister and brother-in-law. "Excellent," he repeated. "Can you get to Dimitri and Marina?"

"My people are watching. Once we are sure, we will take him."

"Good. Today then. Good."

"There is one other thing," Kulikov said.

"Yes?" Zhelin said, expecting more good news.

"The diary. The linguist you had us hire has completed a translation of the few papers we recovered at the restorationist's apartment. I think you should take a look at them."

Poltav had thought he had taken the only copies. Zhelin had been grateful he had ordered work on the pages immediately after receiving them.

"Bring them here," Zhelin said. "No, wait. Tupolev said that what he was looking for might be at Peter and Paul Fortress. Is there any indication of something hidden there?"

"Possibly. The wording is . . . mystifying. Possibly if we go there . . . "

"Yes, a good idea. This afternoon, at two. You have done well, friend Kulikov. But do not underestimate Nickolai Poltav. Keep me informed."

Zhelin hung up the phone. Things were going well. Even if Poltav decoded the record book and emptied Tupolev's accounts, he would be forced to give everything back. For his sister's life, for Dimitri, Nickolai would beg to restore the money. And then, Zhelin thought, I will take great pleasure in killing him.

He checked his watch. Only 9:00 A.M. It seemed like an eternity since he had slept last. He stood, then took off his coat and threw it across the desk. Leaving Tupolev's den, where the red stain was still partially visible in the rug before the desk, he went to the old man's bedroom. He liked the apartment. He intended to take it, along with everything else. He would move his wife into the room next door, and they'd get on with their lives, but living in a little deeper luxury.

He went to the Italian marble sink in the bathroom, turned on the water, and began to wash up.

Lydja Zhelin, Tupolev's daughter, was the one beautiful thing Tupolev had created. Tall, stately, with the figure and face of a goddess and a mind of her own, Lydja liked money. She had married Zhelin because, next to her father, he could provide for her needs better than anyone else—except Dimitri Bakatin, who was already married, although Lydja had tried at one time to break it up. Even if she and her husband didn't get along all that well, Marina Bakatin was no fool. She had seen what Lydja was up to and had a little talk with her. Zhelin didn't know what Marina had said, but rumor was that it had given Lydja sleepless nights. After that, the witch had set her sights on Georgi Zhelin—a much more willing target.

From the very beginning of their marriage, Lydja had made it clear what her purposes were, and he had agreed. They never slept together, seldom ate together, seldom even saw each other except at state dinners and other necessary times of appearance. It was a marriage of convenience in which both had things to gain and dreams to realize. She knew that her father would never turn the empire over to her; he was a chauvinist of the highest order who didn't think women had brains for anything but household chores. She needed someone with her ambition and drive and yet who was easily manipulated. Zhelin had led her to believe he was both. Now that everything was in his hands and her murderous father was out of the way, he would let her know the cost. She would fulfill her conjugal vows or find herself in the street.

He finished washing, went to the bed, and removed his shoes. Stretching out, he closed his eyes. Soon, even the beautiful Lydja would be his, but first a minor inconvenience—Nickolai Poltav and the recovery of the record book. Hopefully it would be finished by the end of the day.

Rustam stood back, watching, as the nurse placed the sheet over Natalya's face. All his pleading prayers had been for nothing, the blessing unanswered. Tupolev's power seemed even greater than God's. But it had always been that way. He had been a fool to believe otherwise. God. Priesthood. None of it could stand up to the likes of Vladimir Tupolev and his killer, Ivan Kulikov.

"President Starkov . . . Rustam, are you all right?"

Rustam turned to leave, ignoring the missionary and his companion. As he opened the door, his heart felt as cold as the Siberian ice in winter. President Hayes walked up.

"President Starkov, how is . . . " Hayes looked over Rustam's shoulder. His face clouded with anguish as the two missionaries gave a sign of what had happened. Rustam put a firm hand on the shoulder of his leader and moved him enough to get by. He started down the hall for the door.

"President," Hayes said without following. "Where are you going? The funeral arrangements . . . please let us help."

Rustam didn't answer. He didn't know what to do. All he wanted was to be away. Natalya had warned him: Nothing was stronger than the MB—not churches, not the Russian people, not God. If he had listened, Natalya would still be alive.

He pushed through the outside door into the freshness of early morning. There was only one thing men like Kulikov understood; for that, he would need a gun.

He hailed a cab. As he lowered himself into the seat, a wave of grief rolled over him. He took a deep breath and fought it off. Not now. Later. Now he had to think.

Vostya Dubenky and he had talked and decided Kulikov hadn't found the diary or Rikki. That meant Rikki was hiding. Rustam knew the place. He would get his weapon, then he would get the diary. When Kulikov came for it, the man would pay for his murder with his life.

He lay his head against the back of the seat. Rustam Starkov knew weapons. He had been in the army, in a special unit trained to hunt and kill. He had done it well for four years on the borders of China. On his return from those very private wars, he had opted out, his hands stained with enough blood that he still smelled of it. It was a part of his past Natalya had known little of, except for the nightmares he suffered and then hid from her with lies.

He had gone back to school, finished his degree, and found a good job, all the while seeking for a way to rid himself of the spiritual sickness the killing had given him.

Religion had never really occurred to him. He had been

taught that churches were just another oppressor of the masses, and from what he knew, from their collaboration with the Communists, he had believed it. It hadn't been until a much-waited-for trip to Helsinki, Finland, that the answer to Rustam's problem had come.

There he had met an East German—like Rustam, a drafts-man—and a Christian. In the two weeks they had been together on their special project, Heinrich Gottlieb had convinced Rustam Starkov that a unique form of Christianity known as Mormonism had answers. Rustam smuggled both a Bible and a Book of Mormon back to Petersburg. In them he had found peace. With them he had made a covenant.

Two years later he returned to Helsinki. Another meeting. Heinrich was there—a prearranged event. In 1988, December, they broke a hole in the ice along the Baltic Sea and Rustam was baptized—one of the first Russians to join the American church. If it had been discovered, Rustam would have lost everything and been given residence on a North Sea fishing trawler, the punish-ment for Petersburg men in those days.

He felt a twinge of conscience. There was the covenant. He shoved it aside. That was then, this was now. Natalya had been killed for no purpose, and Kulikov must pay. The system still did not punish such people, so someone must. There must be an accounting, a payment for taking the life of Natalya! There must be.

The wave of sorrow rushed at him again. He couldn't stop it. Gone! She was gone! How could it be? Why? If God cared, if God honored the blessings of his priesthood . . .

Tears rolled down his cheeks and dropped onto his shirt. His breath caught in his chest, then released in great sobs. He tight-ened the muscles in an attempt at control, but the anguish was too great, and the sobs bolted from his throat. He reached into his pocket and removed some rubles. Without counting, he tossed them into the front seat as the cab stopped at a stop sign. Jerking on the handle, he threw open the door and ejected himself onto the sidewalk. The tears blurred his vision, and he bumped into several people before wiping the water away and clearing his view. He walked aimlessly but in the general direction he wanted to go. The tears released the anguish but not the hardness he felt in his heart.

There was the door. He entered, climbing the stairs. His old unit leader lived here. He had a gun, a very special rifle—Rustam Starkov's rifle.

The Chinese who threatened the Soviet Union with their incessant attacks on Soviet citizens living in border towns had learned to fear Rustam's rifle. When they had come in the night to rape and pillage Soviet villages, Rustam and others in his talented unit had sent them home with their numbers considerably diminished.

Rustam knocked. The last time he had come to this door was on his return from Helsinki after joining the Church. He had brought the weapon. Before that he had kept it hidden because it was against the law for a civilian to have a Dragunov sniper's rifle. He had brought it because he was afraid of it—afraid he would use it to stain his life again.

Now he didn't care.

The door opened. For Rustam, it was time to kill again.

Chapter Twenty-three

DIMITRI BAKATIN'S NERVOUSNESS made his stomach churn. He checked traffic, then crossed into the middle of the street, glancing over his shoulder as he reached the other side. Nothing. He was sure there had been someone. It must have been his imagination. It seemed like everyone was watching him, everyone whispering as he passed by. He should never have crossed Tupolev.

At the door to the stairway he paused, shifting his packages from one hand to the other while he checked the street. He knew agents of the KGB, knew how they looked, how they worked. He had been among them, was one of them once. He saw no signs, no indication of their presence, and yet—a feeling. Just a feeling. He shook it off.

Pushing the buttons, he entered, closing the door firmly behind him. He leaned against the wall, the muggy stench of the rundown building filling his nostrils and making a thin layer of sweat break out on his forehead.

Turning toward the stairs, he moved up five flights to apartment number 10. Every muscle in his body seemed to ache with tension. He was too old for this sort of thing. His eyes focused on each apartment door as he passed them, as if he expected someone to suddenly jump out, bludgeon him, and drag his body into the street. As a member of the KGB, he had always been the pursuer, the one giving other people ulcers. He had never been forced into their position, to see things from their perspective. Now he was seeing all of it for the first time, and it wasn't pleasant. The beatings, his knuckles covered with other people's blood, the intimidations and threats! He had been, was, a monster—a Tupolev in miniature. The thought made him ache inside.

He rang the doorbell three times, paused, then rang it once again. The locks turned inside, and the door opened. He slipped in, trying to catch his breath as his wife took the packages. He hurriedly locked the door.

"Did you watch the street?" Dimitri asked.

Marina nodded, the fear evident in her eyes. "Nothing. You shouldn't have left. It is too dangerous. Vostya told you—"

"We had to have food, and I needed to make some calls. I couldn't do it from here; the place doesn't even have a phone. Have you heard anything from Vostya yet?"

She shook her head in the negative. "He said he would be back by ten. Nickolai will tell him what to do, how to get us to a safer place."

Dimitri went into the kitchen and began removing the food from the sack. Marina followed him. As he moved about the kitchen, he kept glancing out the windows. Nothing. He started to relax a little.

"Would you like some tea?" She asked.

"That would be nice." He smiled. She removed a cup from the cupboard and filled it with hot water already simmering on the stove. Removing a tea bag from a package, she slipped it into the cup and sat it on the table. He folded the sack and put it on the shelf over the sink, then sat down. After fixing her own cup, she joined him. There was a long silence between them. They hadn't been close for nearly twenty years—separate rooms, separate lives. She had remained with him because, even though she hated what he had become, she had never stopped loving the part of him strangled by his work and his essential loyalties to men like Tupolev.

"I called the house. Mikhail was frightened. I could tell that some of Zhelin's men were there. I hung up," Dimitri said.

"Will . . . will they hurt him?" Mikhail and Katja Astafyev were the people who worked for them—house and yard help. Dimitri had hired them a year ago when his business had deliv-

ered the first million dollars into their bank account and they had
built the large home on the outskirts of the city—at least large by
Russian standards. Marina had hired Mikhail and Katja and had
come to love them. Now Katja had gone to stay with her parents.

"No. They won't hurt him, but they are looking for us. I also
called the office. They are everywhere. I can't find Shelepin. I feel
completely cut off."

"Did you try his home?"

"Yes, but his wife says he hasn't been in all night. Business. I
will call again later." Dimitri's face remained passive even though
his stomach was churning. Had his assistant betrayed him? He
couldn't believe it. Nickolai had said so, had said he was at the
Astoria at the same time Tupolev was going to kill him, that he
was working with the old man. But it couldn't be. He had brought
the boy into the business, educated and trained him. He took
another sip of tea. He had to trust Shelepin, had to find him. His
whole future depended on how fast the boy could destroy their
records and prevent Tupolev from getting them, from taking
everything. If Shelepin was working for the old man now . . . No,
he refused to believe it! It would destroy everything. There were
other explanations for his disappearance. He was probably taking
care of things even now. Dimitri had to believe it; everything he
had worked for hinged on it.

Tupolev was right—he would find Dimitri eventually, and
Dimitri knew it. The least to be done was to protect his assets so
that Marina would not die in poverty. He owed her that. She had
put up with him all these years—he owed her even more.

They sipped their tea. After long moments, Marina bit her lip
and forced out the words. "I am frightened, Dimitri. Tupolev
knows what you have done, so he can't let you live."

He had told Marina what had happened. It was the first time
in twenty years he had told her anything about his world. As soon
as Vostya had driven them away from the house to safety, it had
all come out in a rush that was both embarrassing and cleansing.

"Everything will be all right once we are out of the country.
Nickolai will arrange it." He reached out and placed his large
hand on hers. It was a halting, clumsy, but genuine move. Marina

had aged well. Her face was still smooth even though her hair had gone from black to dark gray. Even though their physical relationship had deteriorated to the point of nonexistence, he had never stopped his quiet admiration of her physical good looks. It was the loss of those tender moments of being close, moments in which, when they were first married, they had shared not only themselves but also their innermost thoughts with one another, that he regretted losing most.

"I . . . I never stopped loving you, Marina," he said, a tight lump in his throat.

She looked into his eyes and saw the old Dimitri there, the one she thought had died so many deaths over the years. Nickolai had escaped the hell of the KGB and the Party; Dimitri had stayed and paid the heavy price survival demanded. She leaned across the table and kissed him lightly, then leaned back, her hand against his cheek.

"In the old days I used to fear the day you would fall into disfavor. It frightened me so much I . . . well, it is the reason I refused to have children. Now . . . " She bit her lip, the tears springing form the corners of her eyes. "Oh, Dimitri!" she said in anguished pain. "They have taken so much from us!"

He slid onto the stool next to her and took her in his arms, holding her close, feeling her warmth. It had been a long, long time.

When Nickolai saw Vostya coming toward them through the doors of the metro station, he felt both apprehension and relief. He didn't like leaving Marina and Dimitri alone, but this was the safest way to help them.

Vostya placed a token in the gate and headed down the tunnel to the boarding area. Nickolai followed with Larissa. When they were aboard the train and traveling toward the outskirts of the city, they gradually worked themselves closer together. By the time they reached Grazhdanskiy Prospekt, the car was sufficiently empty that Nickolai felt Vostya hadn't been followed and they could speak.

"How are our patients?" Nickolai asked.

"Frightened but safe. I just hope Bakatin will convince himself we are his best bet. Trust isn't his long suit," Vostya said.

"Years of habit for all of us. What is he telling you about Tupolev's operation?"

"I told him to write down everything he could think of that might help us break up the old man's business. He was more than willing."

"It is a matter of survival now. He knows that in order for him to live, Tupolev has to die."

"Then what I just found out will make his day—although I don't know that you will be very happy about it. I know how much you wanted to have a hand in it." Vostya smiled.

Nickolai looked at his young associate with bewilderment.

"Rumor has it Tupolev was killed last night. You and Bakatin are both being hunted in connection with an apparent double murder."

Nickolai tried not to look shocked, but Larissa could not help herself. Nickolai smiled at her. "Bondorenko was dead, but Tupolev was a very healthy man when I left last night, honest."

"Then either it's a smoke screen or Zhelin decided it was time to move into the driver's seat," Vostya said.

"I checked in at the office by phone. Zhelin wants to talk."

"Well then, Tupolev has gone to the hell he so richly deserves and is fighting with the devil instead of with us. What now?"

"I have a record book—coded, but it is Tupolev's operations book. It contains payoffs, receipts, account numbers for his funds, that sort of thing. Zhelin wants it."

"He will try to make a deal," Vostya said.

"My life, and Dimitri's, for Tupolev's empire."

"He has no proof you were there, does he?"

Nickolai shrugged. "One never knows what one might leave lying about when one is running for his life, does one." He paused. "I'll ask him."

"Then you intend to meet."

"Preliminary discussions, without the record book. If he kills me, we always have you to carry on."

"That isn't funny, Nickolai," Larissa said.

He glanced at her, flattered that she would even care.

"Just kidding."

Vostya saw the look and forced back a smile. His boss looked at Larissa Vavilova like a man in love. That was fine with him; Nickolai Poltav was just about the finest man Vostya knew, and the "Papa" moniker he had graced Nickolai with was more than a younger man's joke on a respected elder. To Vostya, Nickolai *was* Papa. His real father had died when Vostya was only two.

"One thing we'd best not forget is that Zhelin is an expert when it comes to manufacturing evidence," Vostya said. "If Tupolev is dead, he killed him, and he'll want to make sure someone else shoulders the guilt."

"Maybe. Tupolev is old. He could die of natural causes, have a funeral, and no one would know the difference. It wouldn't be the first time he or others in his position have died violently, then have the world told they died of natural causes. Krushchev, and Beria before him, disappeared under those conditions, remember. Zhelin wants the record book very badly. I can force him into a situation that allows Dimitri and Marina the chance of escape while protecting myself—all of us."

"That still leaves Zhelin in the catbird seat," Vostya said.

"Vostya, you are hanging around with your Western friends too much. You are starting to talk like them and make even less sense than they do. What is this catbird seat?"

Vostya grinned. "You know, he's in the driver's seat, the man, top dog." He laughed lightly. "The bottom line is that we are going to have to make a deal. And he'll get Tupolev's empire. He could be worse than the old general."

Nickolai remembered the cold calculation, the evil he had felt from Zhelin. "Worse, much worse," he said.

They stopped at a station, and several people boarded. They moved further into the corner.

"Did you bring the equipment?"

Vostya lifted a cellular phone out of his briefcase, then a bag with several other items.

"Your number is 99–11–36. Mine is 99–78–54. I have taped them to the base of the phone." Vostya pointed.

They pulled into Akademichskaya Station, and people loaded. They pushed their way free and got off at the last second. No one else rushed to the doors to join them.

"The address of the safe house is on the paper in the bag," Vostya said. He lifted some keys from his pocket. "These are to the apartment and a white Volga parked in the complex parking area. You will know it from the others because it has a streak of blue paint on the back fender."

"Customized paint job." Larissa smiled. "How decadent."

Nickolai laughed lightly. "Any problem getting all this?"

Vostya smiled. "Your budget is limited, but your power is not. Your call to Yeltsin worked miracles. Everyone I contacted was begging to be of help. Are you going to let our illustrious president know about Tupolev? It would make his day."

"Not if his special investigator ends up accused and convicted of the crime. I'll see what Zhelin has to say first." He took Larissa's arm and moved toward the escalators that would take them back to the surface. "Get back to Dimitri and Marina's apartment," he said to Vostya. "Take a van. I want them out of the city." He handed Vostya a piece of paper. "Instructions. A man in the village of Gryady. He knows you are coming. I have already made arrangements for train tickets to Kiev, Ukraine. From there we will fly them to Amsterdam. When I contact Rand King, I will make a deal for the Americans to take them to safety from there." He paused, glancing at Larissa. "I have bad news. Natalya Starkov died this morning."

Larissa grabbed her mouth, stopping the anguished cry. Her eyes filled with pain, then tears. She leaned against Nickolai.

"You can still reach the American through the consulate—his private phone. Leave a message if he doesn't answer. I think he already has the bad news about Galya's cousin's wife." He handed Nickolai the piece of paper with the number on it.

Nickolai nodded. They stopped short of the escalators. "I'll be in touch, Vostya," he said softly. "You are the chief of the Petersburg office; I expect you to have it functioning at its very best." They started up the elevator, leaving Vostya behind, with Larissa still leaning against Nickolai for support. Nickolai turned back. "And Vostya, tell Marina that her brother sends his love."

Vostya waved. Nickolai touched his lip where the cut was bleeding a little. His face felt stiff, sore. So did the muscles in his midsection, but not nearly as much as his inner stomach. Larissa put her arm through his, removed a hanky from her purse, and wiped at her tears.

"Where do we go now?" she asked.

"The apartment Vostya arranged for us is not far from here. We are both exhausted and need a couple of hours of sleep."

"I must try to reach Rustam. The burial . . . Natalya . . . " She choked on the words. "I should have been there last night."

They walked away before she was able to speak again. "What are you going to do about the record book? You can't be serious about meeting with Zhelin."

"Yes. I will meet with Georgi. It is time the man was told what lies in his future."

Chapter Twenty-four

SAMUEL J. ANDREWS HAD DECIDED TO FLY to St. Petersburg. Too much was at stake to do otherwise, even though his health was poor and the trip could kill him. He had been waiting with dread for nearly fifty years; he couldn't be anywhere else.

ALLIANCE had been his brainchild. His boss at the time, General Roderick Stevens, commander of intelligence with responsibility for the Soviet Bloc countries, was responsible for watching Stalin and keeping the president informed of the butcher's machinations. They had learned of the Soviet dictator's plan to sign on with Hitler more than five months before it actually happened, but they were powerless to stop it. Once the two warlords had struck a deal, Sam Andrews knew that the world was in trouble and that Europe was now Hitler's for the taking. That was when he began to think about the best way to get rid of both devils.

Andrews knew that Hitler's weakness was his insatiable hunger for more territory. Even in 1939 Andrews could see that the German dictator was spreading himself too thin, creating an Achilles' heel. Spreading his men and matèriel over so many fronts had weakened all of them, so it was no surprise when Hitler sued for peace with Stalin so that he could concentrate on Western Europe and England. It had been a black day for France when Stalin sold out to Adolf Hitler.

Stalin was a fool, but, as Hitler's forces gobbled up Europe, it became apparent that Russia was the key to stopping the Führer. Dozens of diplomatic attempts to convince the Russian leader failed. Stalin would not accept that his own country's time at the hands of the Germans was coming, that as soon as the Führer felt the western shores of Europe could be his, he would turn east. Everyone else seemed to recognize that Russia was in deep trouble, but nothing they did could convince Stalin.

Andrews figured they had until 1941 to change Russia's mind and stop Hitler by creating a second front on which he had to fight. With all diplomatic doors closed, British and American intelligence began casting about for other alternatives. The assassination of Stalin was just one of them.

Such a move by the United States government was dramatic in those days and considered by most as immoral and completely out of the question, especially since the United States was not at war with either Germany or the Soviet Union. But Andrews quietly began searching for a way to get the job done without the Western powers ever being accused of involvement. It was then he discovered the White Guard.

Few people knew of the existence of the White Guard. Lenin and Stalin had convinced everyone that such groups had all been crushed, that there was no heir to the tsar, that the entire royal family of Nicholas II had been killed by fanatics even Lenin hadn't been able to control.

But intelligence reports from inside Russia since 1917 told Andrews two things that contradicted all that. First, the fanatics were at least "encouraged" by the Communists under Lenin to butcher the tsar's family, then deserted as scapegoats when their trials came up. Second, the fanatics hadn't completed the job. There were survivors, spirited away from Russia by members of forces opposed to the Communists.

American intelligence had been unable to verify the reports, even though they saw signs that Lenin and Stalin both believed in at least one survivor of Nicholas II's family, maybe more. Stalin had been particularly paranoid, slaughtering anyone, even whole villages he suspected of collusion with forces who supported the return of the Romanovs.

For Samuel Andrews the truth came when members of the White Guard contacted American officials about recognition for a woman they claimed was Tatiana Romanov, daughter of Nicholas II. It was during talks with the White Guard leaders that Andrews found a way to be rid of Stalin.

Few people in the American government knew about Tatiana Romanov. Besides Andrews and General Stevens, both called on to try to verify the Guard's claim of her authenticity, only Roosevelt and two friends in Congress had any knowledge of the apparent heir's survival.

After Andrews and Stevens returned a report in which they stated the claim had credibility, Roosevelt decided the whole thing was too hot for the White House to handle, but he left the door open for one of his congressional friends to do some follow-up and create a plan for further action.

Andrews had worked the congressman, insisting that recognition should be given only on condition of a successful coup against Stalin. The congressman, anti-Communist to the core, had agreed, and ALLIANCE had come into being.

Andrews found the Guard to have determined leadership and substantial support inside the Soviet government, enough to pull off the assassination and at least the first stages of a coup. Their most critical and unstable support was in the army. Leaders willing to go after Stalin were not in high office there, and, because of Stalin's recent purges of their ranks, what support the Guard did have was soft, unwilling to fully commit until Stalin was known to be dead—a detail Andrews was determined to secure.

If Stalin were killed but the military was uncontrolled by the White Guard and its allies, it could throw Russia into a civil war, allowing Hitler the chance to waltz into Russia unopposed and giving him an industrial power base from which to control the entire continent. The Führer would be unstoppable.

If the coup was successful, with new, anti-German leadership firmly in place, the Russians could go on the offensive against Hitler before he could amass the forces necessary to repel them and deal the Führer a mortal blow. In an attack timed properly with England and France, Germany could be defeated. After the war, the Romanovs would be encouraged to make Democratic reforms, and Communism would be stopped in its tracks.

How it could have changed the world!

After careful planning, Andrews had presented the final analysis to his congressional friend. Together they had decided to proceed without direct presidential involvement, although Roosevelt's signatures mysteriously appeared on all the necessary documents. Andrews understood the position. If Stalin were killed and the coup failed, the repercussions could be devastating. If it became known that an American president had brought about the conditions by which Hitler was able to conquer the known world, the president would have suffered a fate worse than death. Better to keep it under wraps, with no American involvement that could be proven.

From that moment, Andrews found himself in a unique position, alone but with full authority to get what and whom he needed without consideration of cost. Funds were funneled through secret accounts, and supplies became limitless. His authority was never questioned; ALLIANCE became a reality.

Then things had gotten away from him.

Andrews was jolted out of his thoughts as the plane touched the runway at Pulkovo Airport outside Petersburg. It had been a long time since his last visit in 1953—his last delivery of many that had made him a rich man.

Now everything was threatened. The call had been brief, from a friend inside the office of the General of the Army, a man Andrews had hired to keep an eye on things. King had contacted the office of the General of the Army and requested permission to open ALLIANCE. He hadn't done it, at least not by the time Sam Andrews had left Washington, but he would.

Andrews wondered what King was up to, what secrets he had discovered, and how dangerous he was. He opened the personnel file on his lap. King was educated at Harvard, a rising star in CID, the United States Army Criminal Investigative Command. Why had he given it all up to accept charge of the Petersburg consulate? What future was there in that? Had the man discovered something even at that early point? He had been in the files during that terrorist thing, when the Secretary of Defense had been threatened. Maybe. When he found out didn't matter. He needed to be warned, told to back off, before he knew so much it would get him killed—and get Andrews put in prison.

He closed the file. He should have destroyed the ALLIANCE file long ago, but it had been all the leverage he had. His old ally wanted him dead. Only the file had proven a deterrent. Only as long as his enemy knew he would pay for murder could Sam Andrews sleep at night.

His enemies didn't know that the file was harmless to them, a snake without fangs. Andrews couldn't take a chance of putting too much into a file that, although classified, was still accessible. Such stupidity could be as deadly for him as were his enemies.

Destroying it would have led to his own death—Andrews had been sure of that. He hadn't wanted to chance it. Hiding the ALLIANCE file deep in the American files where his old friend, who was also his old nemesis, didn't have a prayer of ever reaching it had been a perfect solution. Until Rand King had broken in.

The plane taxied to the unloading area. Andrews put King's personnel file into his briefcase and snapped it shut, then lay his head against the back of the seat. He was tired, weak. What was he doing here? What could he do? He had no authority, at least nothing official. All he had was his influence, which was considerable; King was a strong personality and talent, not easily intimidated. But such men usually had large egos and big dreams. Andrews' hope lay in his ability to offer Rand King a sizable boost to his career—no small thing—and a commodity he could trade for King's silence.

And then there was his former partner. They were saint and sinner, held together by a traitor and a lustful need for money. Of course, the saint held that his purposes were lofty, the saving of mother Russia, while Andrews was serving only himself, serving his greed.

Andrews smiled. It was a point with which he couldn't argue, but he had held all the cards. The saint had no choice but to work with him. And Andrews considered himself a fair man. His 20 percent, although worth nearly four million dollars, was a pittance to what "mother Russia" received.

And most of the risk of selling and transporting was his.

Frankly, he could never understand the saint's hatred for him. Without his services, the saint's program would have floundered long ago.

People stood, plucking their carry-ons, packages, and other paraphernalia out of the overhead storage bays. Andrews stayed seated, deep in thought.

He hadn't been able to meet with leadership from the Guard until the summer of 1940, and by the time trusted people in the underground networks of four nations could be found who were supportive of their position, it had been Christmas. By then Hitler's plans had been obvious to everyone but Stalin, and Andrews had been desperate to get the job done. But he had found himself dragging his feet, unsure of one member of the team—Robert Kitrick.

He hadn't wanted to use Kitrick. There had been something about the man, his cavalier attitude, that had bothered Andrews. But under the circumstances, he hadn't had a lot of choices. Kitrick had known Russian better than English, even then, and his family had hated Communism since being forced to flee the country in 1917. They had emigrated to the United States, changed their name, and gotten on with their lives, never forgetting, never forgiving.

When Andrews had discovered Kitrick and interviewed him, the hate had been palpable enough. The man had relished the idea of killing Stalin. But there was the other, the concern for payment, the concern for self. Always the talk of money, then the return of his family's properties in Russia as a part of his payment should the coup succeed. They had argued about all of it, and Andrews had decided to find someone else. When Kitrick had been told he was out, he had done some quick backtracking—the money, the land were no longer important, he had said. The repentance had seemed sincere enough, and when another candidate as well qualified couldn't be found, and with the time element pressing in on him, Andrews had gone ahead.

It had been a mistake. Kitrick had betrayed him. Betrayed them all.

The last of the passengers passed his seat, and Andrews

stood. One of the flight attendants helped him with his suit coat, then handed him his briefcase from the seat. Going to the door, he began the descent to the tarmac on the heels of the last passenger. He stepped into the transport for the short ride to the customs area of Pulkovo.

There had been method to being the last passenger off; it made him among the first passengers to arrive at customs and passport control. He entered one of the slots and showed his papers. The soldier behind the glass screen looked at him, then back at the passport. Then he glanced at a list on the table. He picked up the phone.

Andrews knew the call was going directly to the saint. For now, he preferred that his old partner remain unaware of his arrival. Andrews removed his airline ticket cover from his suit-coat pocket and slid it under the glass partition. The soldier lifted the flap, saw the crisp stack of five-hundred-dollar bills, then glanced at Andrews, trying to decide if the old man with the liver spots was of any real danger to his people. He put the phone back on the hook, stamped the passport, filled out the temporary visa, and shoved them to Andrews. The five bills had disappeared.

Andrews walked through the crowds and exited the building. Locating a taxi, he asked to be taken to the Moskva Hotel. It was close to the consulate. From there he would phone King, make an appointment. He didn't want to look overly anxious or demanding. A delicate situation required delicate handling.

If there was no response? Well, Andrews might be old, but he was still shrewd, still knew how to get people to see things his way.

King would be no different.

Rand and Galya went through the front doors of the Hermitage museum. Galya walked directly to the ticket window across the main hall while Rand did a quick appraisal of the crowd.

Schoolchildren mostly, there to see the great art of one of the world's finest museums.

No one watched him, no one seemed to take any notice of Galya. She came back and handed him a ticket.

"Is he here?" Rand asked.

"I don't know. I asked only for an old friend. The ticket woman called her office. She will meet us. This way." She led him to the grand staircase and they went quickly to the second floor. Passing through several rooms, they came into the hall of tapestries. A dozen people stood about the long hall, admiring the old wall hangings but none of them was Galya's friend.

"I don't like this," Rand said. "What if the woman was told to watch for you?"

"Then visitors will come." She smiled. "You are in charge of escapes. You do it so well."

"Gee, thanks," he said, wiping his clammy hands on a handkerchief. They moved to some padded chairs and sat down, then waited for nearly an hour. The people in the room kept changing except for one, a young woman. Rand had decided she was KGB and was simply waiting for reinforcements to haul them away. For the first time, the hall emptied of everyone but the three of them. The woman quickly walked to them. She smiled at Galya, then gave her a quick hug. Galya seemed shocked. "It has been a long time. Come with me. Now. No questions. Just come!"

They stood and followed her from the room. She led them through several rooms, then to a locked door behind one of the displays in the Pavilion Hall. She locked it behind them, and they descended through a dark, narrow staircase past the first floor clear to the basement.

"It is so good to see you, Galya!" the woman said. "How long—"

"We were children when my family was sent away," Galya said.

"Yes, I remember. I cried for a week."

Exiting into a hallway with poor lighting, she led them to a locked room.

"Luda and I wrote to one another after my family was sent to Novosibirsk," Galya explained to Rand. "Neither of us received the other's letter until after my mother's death and I was no longer a threat to the state. I have looked forward to this day for ten years."

"Once the letters started getting through, we became friends again," Luda said.

Somone knocked at the door. Luda quickly opened it, and a worried Rikki Mogilev, the restorationist, stood before them. Luda hugged Galya again.

"Rikki and I are more than friends. We will soon marry. He has told me about your diary." The smile turned to a look of concern. "Be careful, if the KGB is after you, after Rikki—"

"Don't worry," Rand said. "They won't be after Rikki once we have the diary."

"I must go back to my office. From there I can watch the entrance. If I see anyone suspicious, I will let you know."

"The woman at the ticket counter, can she be trusted?" Rand asked.

"Even today it is hard to know who your friends are. Money is scarce, and people do awful things for it. I will watch." Luda left.

Rikki ushered them into a small workroom, then closed the door and locked it behind them. Rand's eyes adjusted slowly, the only light coming from a small lamp on the table. Mogilev was pale with worry but was relieved to see Galya and Rand.

"Thank goodness. After what happened at the apartment I was afraid you might also have been hurt," Rikki said.

Galya hugged him. "I am so glad you are safe, Rikki! How did you get away?"

"I was gone, returning only after you had come and gone. My neighbors told me what had happened, that people had been hurt. I came here immediately. I have been hiding ever since."

"This seems an obvious place for them to look," Rand said.

"Some did come, but there are many places to hide. That is why it took us so long to bring you down here. We wanted to be sure you weren't followed."

He went to the desk and retrieved the diary, handing it to Galya. "The work was difficult, and some pages are still sealed shut. I am sorry, but it is the best I can do."

She took the book, then kissed the younger man on the cheek. He blushed. "Thank you, Rikki. Thank you very much."

"Rikki, did you make copies of any of the book?" Rand asked.

"Yes, the pages I thought cleaning might blur or destroy. Six I think." He looked away. "They were left behind. I am sorry, but . . ."

"It is all right, Rikki. We're just grateful you are safe," Galya said. "But Natalya . . . Natalya has been hurt." As he sat down, she told him what had happened. "We haven't contacted the hospital since last night. We think she is still the same. A coma."

Rikki stood. "I must go there and find Rustam."

"Not yet, Rikki," Rand said. "They may be watching the hospital. It will be dangerous until we get in touch with Tupolev and get this whole matter cleared up."

Rikki thought for a moment. "All right, but call Luda when you think it is safe." He took a deep breath. "If I had stayed— given them the diary."

Galya understood the pain in his voice. What she felt was worse. The whole affair was her fault. How she wished she had never seen the horrible little book in her hand!

"A telephone?" Rand said.

"None here," Rikki said. "Upstairs in the cloak room. The area is under renovation, but the phone works."

Galya looked at Rand quizzically.

"I want to call Tupolev—warn him off now that we have his prized possession. Nobody else gets hurt."

Galya nodded. She gave Rikki's hand a last squeeze, stood, and went to the door as Rand opened it.

Rikki forced a smile. "If you ever find out what it says, let me know, will you?"

Galya nodded. Rand closed the door behind them, and they worked their way to the end of the long hall where there was an exit into the museum. It opened directly into the coat-check area Rikki had mentioned. There were counters on each side and checking areas behind the counters. The workers were gone, and tools, buckets, and paint-splattered tarps were strewn about. A thin layer of dust lay over everything. Empty coat racks had been shoved into the middle of each room. The phone was missing from the wall.

Rand went to a plastic tarp hung across the hall to the main entry and pulled it aside enough to look out. As they climbed the stairs, moving away from the cloak room toward the main entrance hall, Galya froze. She grabbed Rand's sleeve and pulled him back toward the lower level, through the plastic tarp, then into one of the coat-check booths.

"What?"

"KGB. The one who was in the garden with Kulikov."

Rand remembered—the one who had tried to pass himself off as a San Diegan. "Did he see us?"

"No, he was looking toward the grand staircase. But there may have been others. It was crowded with tourists."

Rand thought of just handing them the book but then thought better of it. Tupolev had to receive it personally. Anyone else might still take out personal frustrations on him and Galya.

Rand went to the small half-window and tried the latch. Sealed. He moved about the room like a caged lion. Leaning out over the booth's counter, he peered up the steps. He could see the outlines of two people coming down. He jerked himself back.

"Two people are coming this way." He moved her toward a small indentation in the panel and wedged her in, out of sight. Then he went to the counter and crouched in a small nook underneath, his head bent to his knees. The two agents came to the counter, peered into the booth, and were about to move on when Rand noticed his blurred reflection in the metal coat racks. One of the agents noticed at the same time and leaned over the counter to get a better look, unsure of what he was seeing. Rand grabbed him by the hair and jerked his head downward onto the counter. The body went limp, then started to slide to the floor. As Rand came up, the other agent was already pulling his gun. Rand placed a hand on the counter and swung the weight of his feet into the man's torso, knocking him across the room and against the far wall. The gun hit the floor with a clatter and slid into the booth on the opposite side of the hall, out of reach. Rand pushed a fist into the man's stomach, then slammed his hand across the back of his neck. As he dragged the body into the booth and retrieved the gun, Galya joined him. He grabbed the workers' gowns hanging on a hook to the side of the entrance to the booth and threw one to Galya. They each put on a gown. Rand shoved the pistol into a pocket, and they headed for the stairs. At the fifth step, Rand could see into the entrance hall. The San Diegan stood near the entrance, his attention on the hall that led to the main staircase.

"Talk to me about art," Rand said, removing his reading glasses and putting them on. They walked straight to the man, chattering. San Diego didn't see them until it was too late. Rand stuck the pistol into his ribs and pushed.

"Outside."

The man didn't refuse, and they were quickly through the entrance and onto the porch.

"Across the street."

Rand pushed until they were at the tourist boat dock. He handed his wallet to Galya.

"Purchase three tickets." He turned to the agent. "Nice to see you again. How did you know where we were?"

The agent looked away. No answer.

"You tell Tupolev that Rikki Mogilev doesn't have what he wants anymore. Tell him to leave all of us alone or he'll never see it. Tell him I have his precious package, and if he wants it he will have to talk to me."

"Tupolev didn't send me. He isn't sending anyone anymore."

Rand sensed a man willing to sell some information.

"Go on."

"You have a very heavy wallet." He looked at where Galya stood in line.

"If I like what I hear, I may lighten it."

"Tupolev is dead."

"Who killed him?"

"Georgi Zhelin. He is trying to keep it quiet—to place blame on Dimitri Bakatin and Nickolai Poltav."

It had been a busy night in Petersburg. Galya came back with the tickets and handed Rand his wallet. Rand retrieved twenty dollars and handed it to San Diego.

"Keep going. You're just starting to get interesting," Rand said.

"Zhelin sent us to look for the restorationist. Zhelin has copies of some of the pages of the diary, but he needs all of it."

Rand eyed the man. "Why?"

"It starts to get expensive from here," the man said.

Rand withdrew a fifty-dollar bill from his wallet.

"One page was a photocopy of a picture. Peter and Paul Cathedral. Zhelin is meeting Kulikov there at two this afternoon."

"For what reason?" Rand handed him another fifty.

"Kulikov said the diary mentions treasure—a hidden vault of some kind. Zhelin thinks the diary can give him the location."

The boat was preparing to leave.

"That's all I can tell you," the man said.

Rand kept the pistol in his ribs. "Sorry. We'll go for a boat ride first. Make sure your two friends don't catch up to us."

They boarded. Five long minutes later they were moving away from the dock.

"There is something else," the man said.

"Awfully cooperative, aren't we?"

"In this town, this day and age, it is important to have many friends—many contacts with heavy wallets. It is how we survive."

"What is your name?"

"Sasha Zagladin. Kulikov confides in me. He considers me a friend. But these are bad people. They kill their own as easily as they do their enemies. I stay only because I must feed my family. If I find something better . . . " He shrugged. "Are you interested?"

"Go on."

"As I told you, Zhelin killed Tupolev and now scrambles to get control of the business. He intends to stop at nothing and is after Nickolai Poltav." He told them what he knew about Tupolev and about Nickolai's rescue of Bakatin. "Two of my friends were on guard that night. They know what happened. Bondorenko's body was cremated along with Tupolev's. Zhelin is worried."

"Why is Zhelin worried?" Rand asked.

"Kulikov says that Nickolai Poltav stole Tupolev's record book. Without it Zhelin cannot run the business, and Poltav can empty the foreign bank accounts, leaving Zhelin with nothing."

Rand leaned forward. "You said Tupolev was going to kill Bakatin. Why?"

Zagladin shrugged. "Some say it is because Bakatin betrayed Tupolev to Nickolai Poltav."

"And what do you say?"

"It is because Tupolev and Zhelin wanted his businesses. This morning Bakatin's aide, Aleksei Shelepin, helped Kulikov and me clean out bank accounts belonging to Bakatin. Now Zhelin must kill Dimitri for two reasons: He knows Zhelin killed the old general, and Zhelin has stolen from him. If Bakatin is smart, he will leave the country and never return."

"Bakatin will fight him," Galya said.

"He can try, but Zhelin is powerful. Bakatin is ruined. In this country the word of Georgi Zhelin, as heir to Tupolev, carries much more weight than that of Dimitri Bakatin."

"How would you like to go to work for me?"

"Now?"

"Right now. Two hundred American dollars for the next week. After that we'll see about giving you permanent work through the consulate. I have some investigations that need to be done."

"You have both my talent and my soul. What do you want me to do?"

"A warning first. If you play both sides, if you betray me to Zhelin, I will use my power and connections to ruin you. I will make you look like a traitor to your own country. You will lose privilege and never work again."

Sasha Zagladin thought a moment. He didn't like Zhelin, didn't trust him. The man could turn on his own. It was a dangerous life. Sasha wanted to live to see his son grow up.

"It is a fair statement. You have my word, but you must

understand what you ask. By accepting your offer, I am through in the KGB. I will be unemployed if they learn of my allegiance to you. I cannot provide for my family without work."

"I understand. If things don't work out at the consulate, I will use my connections to find what you need. You have my word. But do not close the doors at the Ministry. Your connections may help keep us alive."

Sasha smiled. "For information of this kind, another hundred dollars a week."

"Fair enough," Rand said.

"Then I work for you," Sasha said.

"Good. Your first assignment, Sasha, is to get us a car."

They were nearing the dock, and Rand prepared to get off. "We will meet you at the south entrance to the Summer Gardens in an hour. Can you do it?"

"The car will cost you at least thirty dollars, maybe more, for a few hours of use."

Rand handed him another fifty dollars in tens. "Use that and what I have already given you. Keep track of expenses. I'll reimburse you for them weekly."

They left the dock. Sasha turned left toward Liteyny Bridge; Rand and Galya went right, the diary safely in hand.

Chapter Twenty-five

Volodya Vilechenko had followed them to the Hermitage but was forced to keep his distance for fear of being recognized by Rand King. King and Galya Starkova had disappeared for a time, and he thought he had lost them again—another failure. Then they had appeared in the main hall, dressed as workers. He had stayed clear, followed, and watched as they boarded the boat, noting that King had the diary.

He had thought about using the gun in his pocket and making a frontal approach, but after catching a glimpse of the half-hidden gun in King's hand, he decided against it.

Once the boat left the dock, Volodya had Vasily follow along the embankment with the Mercedes, saw King and Galya Starkova leave the boat and turn right along Robespera Street. He left the Mercedes and fell in behind them. At the trolley bus stop, he stepped to King's side and spoke.

"You are a hard man to catch up to, Mr. King."

Rand looked at the old gentleman and remembered the day before.

"The man in the Mercedes. Nice to see you again."

"I don't suppose I can talk you out of that diary without starting a war?" Volodya said.

"Not after what we have been through to get it. Blood will run in the streets."

"Well, shall we try and prevent that?"

Galya looked at both of them astonished, wondering what was happening.

Volodya tipped his hat, scanning her feminine good looks even in Rand's golf shirt and too-big tennis shorts. "Miss Starkova, I feel like I know you. My name is Volodya Vilechenko, chief intelligence officer for the White Guard."

Galya was stunned and didn't respond even when he kissed her hand.

"My car is just up the street."

"Uh, sorry, Vilechenko, but stupid is not my middle name."

"I promise no kidnapping, only a talk." He gave a disarming smile.

Rand glanced at Galya. She nodded lightly, curious but still in shock.

They walked the short distance to the car and climbed inside. Vilechenko leaned forward and gave instructions to the driver, who got out of the car and stood on the street a short distance away, then disappeared toward a row of shops.

"Just the three of us. Where shall we begin?" Volodya asked.

"Why are you after the diary?" Galya asked.

"It contains information important to my organization. It was carried by a member of our group on a mission we participated in more than fifty years ago."

"Nora Larsen was a member of the White Guard."

"She was. We had many members who were foreigners. They believed in our cause."

"Sam Andrews fell into that category?"

"Ah, you have been busy. No, Andrews had his own motives. He wanted Stalin dead strictly for political and military reasons. He believed that killing Stalin and putting the Romanovs back on the throne would free our country to fight Hitler."

"Was he right?" Rand asked.

"He was. Had we been successful, our first order of business would have been to push Hitler back to Berlin. Unfortunately, we failed to rid the world of the one butcher who put even Hitler to shame."

"What happened? Why did the mission fail?" Galya asked.

"A traitor. The night before we were to complete our task, the night before we could have gained control of Russia again, soldiers showed up at our place of hiding. We were nearly wiped out."

"Nora escaped," Galya said.

"Yes, but she was trapped in Leningrad during the siege. She didn't get out for six months. She worked her way to a village, Bologoye, northeast of Moscow, on her way to finding our enclave. She got no further before falling deathly ill. She sent a message to us, but by the time we arrived she was in a coma. Her body was emaciated by the starvation of the siege. Heart and other vital organs failed. She died the next day."

"Didn't she have the diary?"

"She knew she was near death. Before entrusting herself to strangers, she hid it. We never knew where until Yuri Yezhov went looking."

"How did he find it?"

"As I told you, Nora sent a message to me." He reached into his pocket and pulled out a yellowed sheet of paper. Opening it, he handed it gingerly to Rand.

"Escaped. Dying. Our lady has diary. Beware of traitor. Come for me."

Rand handed it back.

Vilechenko put the paper back into his pocket. "At the time, we didn't realize what "our lady" was. As you know, it is a term for Mary, the mother of Jesus, and there are many, many pictures and icons of her all over Russia. We looked in all the wrong places—mostly here, in Petersburg, where she had spent the last six months." He paused. "A few months ago, at my request, Yuri Yezhov began a search. But even he found the diary more by chance than intent." He told them about the church in Bologoye.

"Why is the diary so important?" Galya asked.

"That I cannot tell you," Vilechenko said, looking out the window. "It has many things to tell me—things that are not important for you."

Rand saw the car pass by—four men, all casually dressed. They looked toward the car but kept going. He felt jittery but relaxed when the car turned into a side street and disappeared.

"I can purchase it from you."

"What does it have to do with Vladimir Tupolev?" Rand asked.

"It doesn't matter; Tupolev is dead."

"You have people inside the hotel," Rand said.

"Yes. The word is that Zhelin killed him but intends to blame your friends. I can prevent this and promise to do so for the diary. It is a fair trade."

"Is the heir still living?" Galya asked.

Vilechencko looked surprised.

"It was in the ALLIANCE report Andrews made," Rand said.

"Mr. Andrews is no longer a friend of the movement," Vilechenko said. "In answer to your question, yes, the line of the Romanovs is still well established. With the diary's help, we intend to put an heir before the people."

It was Rand's turn to look shocked. "What?"

"We wish to present a new direction to the Russian people, a new leadership. It is nothing to be amazed at, Mr. King. Russia has been led by a monarchy much longer than she has not."

"In place of Yeltsin?" Rand asked.

"Yeltsin will be very much a part of our formula for success. We do not intend to overthrow him—just to offer him a lucrative partnership."

"You propose something like England has?" Galya asked.

"Very much like that. The royal family will be in place, offering stability, but the people will vote for other officials such as a prime minister. We believe that our royal family will take their responsibilities more seriously, set a better example than that of the English, and we know the family intends to use a large portion of their wealth to help the Russian way of life heal itself. We are willing to purchase properties, once stolen from us, for the family's use, and we will pay a fair price. It will amount to billions of dollars—a windfall to strengthen the Russian economy."

"How strong are you?" Galya asked.

"Although we could mount an army of considerable size from among our followers, that is not our intent. Only more Russians would die. Our solutions are diplomatic. We believe the people will support us once they come to know of our existence."

"Why so secretive?" Rand asked. "It seems to me that if you have the answer to the chaos your people are experiencing in this country, you would have made your presence known or at least presented yourselves as a party of choice."

"It is a matter of timing. We do not wish to be just another party among the many. Our purpose is to give the people a chance to see all that is offered, a chance to realize that for Russia none of the present political parties will work." He smiled at Rand. "Not even Yeltsin's. Then we will mount what you Americans call a media blitz."

"You're taking a horrible chance, aren't you?" Galya asked. "Someone, some party out there right now might become acceptable."

Volodya smiled. "Have you seen one thus far, Miss Starkova? Is there any of these that, over the long term, can make Russia great again, or that can really satisfy the people?"

"Given a chance, Yeltsin's reforms might work," Rand said.

"Yeltsin is losing ground. Already he is backpedaling on Western-style democracy and will have to reconsider many of his programs. The people have shown their disapproval of what he has offered in this last election by voting for the fascist Zhirinovsky."

"Then Zhirinovsky is the people's choice," Galya added.

"Hardly. He is another Stalin. Again, the vote wasn't for him but against Yeltsin's programs. The people like Yeltsin but not his Western style of change. That is why we will ally ourselves with him, if he is willing. We can help stabilize things and give his policies a chance to work. Our funds will give much-needed relief, and our partnership will allow the dismantling of a corrupt bureaucracy more quickly."

"The people will never buy it."

"We won't know that until they are given the chance to decide."

"Who is the heir?"

"Grand Duke Peter III, grandson of Nicholas II, heir of the Romanovs and to the throne of all Russia."

"His father?"

"That doesn't matter. The father was Prussian, of royal lineage. His mother was Tatiana, duchess of Russia, daughter of Nicholas II and Alexandra."

"You can prove this?"

"Yes." He was still looking out the window.

"How?" Galya asked. "Tatiana was killed at Ekaterinburg."

"When the Empress Alexandra and the daughters escaped, Marie and Anastasia both turned up in the West. Their stories are well documented, although contested by the part of the family who felt they would lose control of the family name and fortune if they did otherwise—members of Cyril's family, for instance. Olga and Tatiana, the two eldest girls, along with their mother, the Empress Alexandra, disappeared."

"Your organization set them free?" Galya said, her voice tinged with disbelief.

"Our organization came later, but it originated from the one that freed them."

"How? There is no proof, no record," Galya said.

"The Reds were moving Alexandra and the two eldest daughters by special train to Kiev, then to the Crimea. Our people intercepted them and were successful in bringing them to safety in Russia, north of where they were originally kept captive at Ekaterinburg. Later, both daughters left the country, secretly, and lived in Germany under our protection—and the protection of the German royal family until Hitler deposed them," Volodya said.

"Marriages were arranged, secretly, so that the royal line could continue, and an heir was prepared for return to power. Unfortunately, when Hitler took control of Germany, we were unable to get Olga, her husband, and her children out of the country before the Führer found them and slaughtered them. Actually, we think it was Stalin who discovered their whereabouts and requested Hitler's help," Volodya added. "They are buried in Germany.

"Lenin knew that the heirs had escaped, but he didn't reveal it to anyone but the inner circle. He did everything within his power to hunt down the family. He was afraid, with good cause, that they could mount an army to retake Russia. Anyone he considered part of this conspiracy was shot. Thousands died. Whole villages, suspected of harboring the women, were wiped out. He was unsuccessful, however. When Stalin took over in 1924, he kept up the search, intensified it. He was successful in finding the empress. She was executed by the butcher's henchmen at what we thought to be a safe haven in Vienna, where she had been taken the year before. She was secretly buried in Germany—an unmarked grave near those of her royal family, and next to Olga. We intend to bring them back to Russia one day."

"Then Tatiana alone remained," Galya said.

"In 1939 she was in England under another identity, and under our protection. She agreed to begin planning a return of the royal family to Russia. She felt it was all that could save the Russian people from destruction, either at the hands of the Germans or the hands of Stalin himself.

"Other governments wanted to be rid of Stalin. Some, when shown that a legitimate heir was still alive, were willing to grant us immediate recognition if we were successful."

"That led to ALLIANCE," Rand said.

Vilechenko nodded.

"How could such things be kept secret? Surely the escape of Alexandra, of the children, would be widely known."

"It was difficult but essential to their safety."

The car was coming back. A red flag went up in Rand's mind, and he pulled Galya down and yelled at Vilechencko. "Get down!"

The gunfire that erupted blew the windows out in the Mercedes. Vilechenko was hit in the shoulder as he flung open the door and dove for cover on the sidewalk side of the car. Galya was still screaming and covering her head as the firing stopped. Rand flung himself into the front seat and started the Mercedes. Ramming it into reverse, he poured on the gas. They were nearly to the corner as the assailants' vehicle passed the spot where Vilechenko lay in the street. Rand was grateful they didn't fire at the old man, but he dreaded the feeling of what that meant: Whoever it was, was after them.

He drove like a madman down Robespera until he reached

the first side street. He didn't even know the name. Jerking the
wheel right, he sped through the narrow thoroughfare, dodging
cars and people as he went. He drove street after street, mile after
mile, until he knew he had lost them. He pulled the Mercedes
over, exhausted. His forehead was lying on the steering wheel
when he heard the sobs coming from the back seat. He climbed
over and helped Galya from the floor. Her hands had been cut by
the glass, and she had several scratches on her face. She began
sobbing again, her face planted firmly against his shoulder. They
would be late to the appointment with Rand's new employee,
Sasha Zagladin.

––––––––––

Rustam pulled the blankets off the bed down to the sheets.
Laying the briefcase on the floor, he pulled up a chair and began
removing the parts to the Dragunov sniper's rifle. It had been
some time since he had held the rifle. It would need careful
scrutiny; then he would spend some time in the hills. There he
would center the rifle's scope at fifty yards, then begin expanding
the distance. He had hit targets perfectly at better than six hundred yards in the China border skirmishes. Twice he had been
given targets at better than eight hundred yards. One was through
a window, which altered the trajectory of the bullet. He had
worked it out carefully, finding out the kind of glass used, its
thickness and strength. He had made allowances for the change
in trajectory. The Chinese man hadn't walked away.

Rustam stared at the parts laid out before him. His hands and
face felt clammy, and he wiped them on the blanket. He knew
what picking up the pieces would mean. Killing was like any
other addiction—giving it up couldn't be done halfway, and if
you returned to it . . .

He sat back in the chair, staring at the weapon. He remembered the feel of the cold steel, the sound of the bolt mechanism
as it slipped smoothly into position, the click of the shells as they
were pushed into the chamber, the snap of the recoil against his
shoulder as he squeezed the trigger, and the smell of the powder
as the semiautomatic ejected the spent round. He remembered the

view of the kill through the scope after the bullet struck home exactly where he had sent it.

But it was the adrenaline rush that a sniper was addicted to. Sitting on a hill, in a tree, atop a building, hidden, waiting, your senses alive with the danger. All of it held you like the arms of a woman.

A woman. Natalya.

He reached for the smooth barrel with both hands, an unholy excitement filling him.

"You promised." His fingers jerked back from the rifle as if they had been burned as the thought jumped into his mind. Then the picture of Natalya's broken, swollen body shoved it away. With determination, he grasped the barrel.

The promise didn't matter. Not now. All that mattered was Kulikov's death. No one else would care, nothing would be done, unless he did it. It was the way the system worked. The innocent were driven, persecuted, killed, while the guilty walked away to commit their atrocities again. It was why he had killed in the first place. The Chinese had crossed the border, murdered even women and children. He had seen the bodies. It had given him reason, a sense of purpose, just as the view of his own wife's body now drove him back to his weapon.

On the border with China, Rustam's job had been only one of many necessary to teach the Chinese a lesson and to punish them for their heinous crimes. At first they were positioned for days at a time near villages considered potential Chinese targets. Then, when an enemy unit showed up, he and others like him would begin picking them off from deadly distances. But the Chinese kept sending their hate squads.

Next he was sent inside China to go after specific targets—commanders who thought they were safe, men who ordered the atrocities but never allowed themselves to be in a position where they could be called to account for their murders of the innocent. Rustam became their judge, jury, and executioner. He did his job well.

He held the barrel up to the light and carefully checked inside. Over a distance of more than five hundred yards, the slightest flaw could throw the trajectory of a bullet off by several feet. There were no flaws. He lay it back on the bed, a bit amazed at the pounding of his heart. The old feelings were coming back—the excitement of planning the hunt, of taking out an enemy who had been marked for death because of his crimes. The finality of his role as executioner.

His stomach churned, a part of him recoiling against his return to the old life, reminding him of the other side—the dreams, the horror, the dying inside each time he snuffed out the life of another. These were feelings that even psychological treatment and personal rationalization couldn't do away with—the self-hate, the wanting to die.

Only the promise had saved him. If he broke the promise . . . No!

He picked up each part in its turn, forcing himself to concentrate on the weapon, on his responsibility to Natalya. He had made some calls to old friends from the military. One was now in the KGB, another still in the army but climbing the ladder, able to supply materials and equipment to make his own bullets, to find his target. Both men knew Kulikov; neither was in love with the man, and both were willing to get Rustam what he needed.

He removed the sack from the case and opened it, revealing materials used to clean the weapon. He glanced at his watch. Both his friends would be calling in soon. It should be an easy kill. Kulikov would never suspect he had such a deadly enemy. Rustam's background as an army sniper was never put in any personnel file. He had been part of a military group that was never supposed to have existed. Even the best background search by Natalya's killer wouldn't have revealed Cobra, the army's top sniper.

He started cleaning. Mission president Hayes had called. Arrangements had been made for Natalya's body to be prepared for burial. A date for a funeral had been decided, a place where she would be interred. They had discussed it all. Rustam had felt like a man standing outside his own body, viewing the conversation but not participating, his mind and heart still unwilling to feel. When Kulikov was dead, then maybe he could feel something besides empty hatred.

He cleaned each part carefully, laying them back on the clean sheets where the oil residue created a series of stains. He started putting the cleaning materials back into their package.

He had asked to be released. President Hayes had wanted to talk. There was nothing to talk about. He had given up his old life, believing that God and religion offered a happier one. It had. But with Natalya's death, all that had changed. Now, in Rustam's mind, acceptance of God was partially responsible for Natalya's death. If he had left religion alone, she would have been less afraid, less miserable. He should have considered her feelings instead of following his own. He should have stayed with her, cared for her, instead running off to meetings and seeing to the needs of others. His wife should have come first.

But it hadn't been possible then. The feeling had been overpowering. He had never been a religious man, never belonged to a church. He had never even dreamed of becoming religious. But then, he had never dreamed of being an executioner, either—the very experience that had driven him to religion.

He could not deny that God had entered his life. The feelings had been overwhelming, the inner change making him want to live again, giving him the hope that he could be clean.

But the promise was a part of that.

He felt the anger. He wasn't the one who had broken the promise. God had failed to protect the one person Rustam had ever really loved. He owed God nothing now. He shoved the thoughts aside, the confusion. Now was no time for doubts. Doubt only prevented a clean kill—created a failure. He had failed Natalya, failed to protect her. He would not fail again.

He started assembling the rifle, each piece coming together quickly, easily, under his professional touch—the long, thin barrel with the combination flash suppressor/compensator; the open butt stock, fitted with a cheek pad for ease in sighting; and the PSO-1 optical sight with an integral, infrared detection aid and illuminated range-finder reticle mounted over the receiver. Each piece was so familiar to his hands that he could assemble and disassemble them in the dark. He removed ten standard 7.62 x 54R cartridges from a box, picked up the magazine, and loaded it. The magazine snapped easily into place in front of the trigger and under the receiver. He walked to the window and drew the curtains back. Standing a few feet back and in shadow, he placed the rifle against his shoulder and put his eye at the window of the scope. Making several adjustments, he focused the powerful lenses on a distant target—an old man dragging his small cart loaded with packages. Using a unique breathing technique he had developed, he felt his entire body prepare itself, felt his mind collapse inward, focused only on a small pin on the old man's chest. Physically he was still, but in his mind he squeezed the trigger, felt the snap of the butt stock against his shoulder, watched the target drop to the pavement. He lowered the rifle, sweat pouring off his forehead, his heart pounding so hard he thought it would explode.

He lay the rifle on the bed and eased himself next to it, closing his eyes, exhausted. Soon the killer of his wife would be dead.

They had come to the apartment Vostya had arranged. It was small but clean and comfortable. Nickolai was stretched out on the floor, Larissa on the couch, but she couldn't sleep. She had tried to reach Rustam, but he couldn't be found. She had talked to President Hayes, helped with the funeral arrangements as best she could by phone, but she was upset that present circumstances didn't allow her to be where she was needed. It hadn't been pleasant to put President Hayes off without giving reasons, but he had been patient, taking her mysterious answers in stride, willing to wait until she could discuss what was going on without reservation. She hoped that time would come soon.

She worried about Galya. Even though Larissa knew Galya was with the American, they were dealing with deadly forces, and all of them were in danger much worse than Natalya had suffered. She worried about how it would all end.

"Nickolai, are you asleep?"

"Uhh." His arm lay across his forehead; his eyes remained closed.

"Will Zhelin let us alone, all of us, if you give him the record book?"

Nickolai lifted his arm and turned his head enough to look at Larissa as she pulled herself into a sitting position on the couch. He put his head back down and closed his eyes again.

"Yes, he will leave us alone."

"How can you be sure?"

"He has no call to harm you. He has destroyed Bakatin's empire, and thus Bakatin is no threat to him, nor is Marina. To kill the American would only call for an investigation he doesn't want. Once he has the record book, why should he kill Galya?"

"And you?"

He lifted his arm again and looked her way, then put it back. "I will always be a threat to him. It will always be dangerous for me."

"And for many others."

"What are you saying, Larissa? That we shouldn't give the record book to Zhelin?"

She nodded. "Men like Georgi Zhelin must be stopped."

"The Zhelins of Russia are only a small part of our problem, Larissa," Nickolai said. "My office, the police, all of us who have to deal with crime are overwhelmed with it. Half the population, maybe more, steal—maybe not on the scale of Georgi Zhelin, but they steal, they lie, they keep us so busy we never see our families. It is becoming a national sickness."

"It is not the same," Larissa said. "Georgi Zhelin does not do it for survival. He lives in expensive homes, drives expensive cars, surrounds himself with expensive things. He is greedy. He is our Mafia. As to the people, many are trapped by the system and have no choice. They do not have enough money to feed themselves and their families. I understand why they steal. Men like Zhelin have a choice. Whenever one has the choice and chooses evil, then he is evil as well, and he must be stopped."

Nickolai sat up and leaned against the wall. "Everyone has a choice, Larissa. You were caught by the system, but you didn't choose to sell yourself to the bureaucrat who demanded your body as payment for leaving you in your position with the Kirov."

Larissa looked away, folding her arms across her midsection as if she were suddenly cold. "I am not so honorable, Nickolai. I have made other choices that have not been so good."

The anguish was evident in Larissa's posture, but Nickolai said nothing, waiting.

"I was married to a good man, a seaman. I told you about him. We had a son." She took a deep breath as if mustering courage. "When my husband died, the government refused to pay me his pension. I was still treated as an enemy of the state. Even though friends secretly brought us food, Dima, that was my son's name, became ill. I took him to a hospital but was refused treatment."

She spoke evenly, without emotion, as if talking about something that had happened to someone else. It was the usual way, necessary to keep from being consumed by the bitterness and hate—the loss. When Nickolai's wife died, he had learned to deal with it the same way. Always just under the surface was the pain.

"A friend, a chemist told me what medicine Dima needed, but I couldn't get any. It was an antibiotic distributed only through the hospitals, and I was not cleared to receive such medicines. I left the child alone that night and went to the hospital in Murmansk. Only a nurse was on duty, but she refused to give me the medicine. She went to a cabinet and brought it to the counter, just out of my reach. She told me that for the right price I could have it. She wanted two hundred rubles. In those days it was a lot of money, and I didn't have it. When I told her so, she laughed and started to take the medicine away. Something broke in me; my heart turned black as night. I grabbed her by the hair and pulled her back. She fell, banging her head against the side of the counter. Blood went everywhere as she collapsed to the floor. I didn't care. I was filled with hate, wanted only to have my child well. There were no other nurses. No one. Grabbing the medicine, I ran to the cabinet and took more, then ran from the hospital. No one had seen what I had done, but I knew it. I knew I had killed that woman, and I didn't care. I was only afraid that somehow I would get caught before I could get the medicine to my son."

She pulled her knees up to her chin, her arms around her legs. "When I got back to our apartment, Dima was already dead."

It was silent for a long time. Nickolai knew to say nothing, only to wait. Words always sounded trite, were never enough. Silence was always better. It conveyed understanding.

Larissa regained control, then spoke again. "Would you like some mint tea, Nickolai?" she asked, getting to her feet.

He nodded. She disappeared into the small kitchen.

Tea. The medicine for all that ailed a Russian.

He forced his stiff body to stand and move to the kitchen. Larissa stood near the wall, one arm against it and her head against the arm. She was sobbing. He wondered if she had ever let another see this wound, feel this pain.

He took her by the shoulder and turned her around, enfolding her with his big, clumsy arms.

Now he wished he hadn't said it. It was wrong. Not everyone had a choice. That had been the horror of the system. It took their choices away, made animals of them.

He pulled her to him, knowing he could never make the pain go away. You had to heal your own wounds. And if you couldn't, you buried them inside, deep inside, where they ate at you and left you empty. To some, healing never came. The only escape was death. That was why suicide was common in Russia—many had no one, nothing, to live for.

They stood like that for a long time—so long the teapot screamed at them and moved them apart. Larissa wiped away the tears and tried to smile. Nickolai sat at the table and watched her fix the cups of hot liquid. He didn't want to leave the apartment, the room, didn't want the spell between them broken. She placed the cups on the table and slid into the chair next to him. In silence they added their sugar and sipped at the hot liquid. The silence was warm between them

Nickolai felt a sudden lump in his throat, a sudden fear that clamped at his stomach like a vise. For the first time since the death of his wife, he was afraid he might die.

Samuel Andrews stood and walked to a picture on the wall—
Russian, recent work; probably an unknown artist, but a good
one. He glanced at his watch, his brow wrinkling. Powell had
kept him waiting for nearly five minutes.

He was livid with anger. King hadn't returned his calls.
Nothing had happened. He was being treated as if he didn't exist,
and he didn't like it. It was time to call King to accounting, time
to bring the upstart farmboy to his knees.

But first Andrews had to find him.

He walked stiffly to his chair and sat again. As the hot anger
grew in his stomach, a side door opened, and Ted Powell entered
the room. His suit was hand tailored, his shirt and tie expensive.
The shoes were Italian leather. He carried himself like a trained
bureaucrat. But then, as Rand King's assistant, that was exactly
what he was.

"Mr. Andrews, sorry to keep you waiting, but some important economic matters have my attention. I apologize."

The voice was out of place for a man who stood more than
six feet tall. It was almost nasal, but it carried a professional air.

Andrews bit off what he wanted to say. This wasn't the man
whose hide he wanted on his wall. He placed a false front on his
demeanor as easily as if dressing for a special occasion. "It's quite
all right," Andrews said, shaking Powell's offered hand. The
shake was firm but not crushing. Andrews quickly sized up his
man.

"I have been trying to get hold of your boss, Rand King, but
I can't seem to make the connection. Do you know where he is?"
Powell picked up a pencil and held each end in the fingers of sep-
arate hands, turning it slightly.

"I haven't seen him for nearly twenty-four hours. I am sorry,
but consulate business often takes him away from the office. Did
you leave a message with his secretary?"

"Several." Andrews felt the slight stiffness in his own voice.
He forced a disarming smile.

"Again, an apology is in order. I will check . . . "

"It's quite all right. Possibly he doesn't know who I am."

Powell smiled. "I doubt that, Mr. Andrews. Your name is a household word in Washington, and Rand lived there before this assignment."

Andrews forced himself to look flattered. "You're kind. Possibly you can reach Mr. King for me."

"I am afraid he hasn't left an itinerary, but I can let him know you want to see him when he calls in."

Andrews leaned forward as if to speak to a confidant. "I must see him, very soon. Mr. King is in a lot of trouble." He leaned back again, hesitating long enough to give the impression that he was making a decision about whether or not he should go on. "Mr. Powell, yesterday Rand King broke into top-secret files at the Pentagon, files that only I and people now dead have ever seen. I came here to find out why he took the liberty to breach security through clandestine means. Then I will make my recommendations concerning Mr. King's future to the president."

Andrews watched as Powell sat back in his chair, the wheels turning in his green eyes. This was a man replaced, a man who had expected to head a consulate but who had missed the chance because of power struggles in faraway Washington. But he was obviously a good bureaucrat as well, dependable, efficient, a man who kept his feelings hidden under layers of protocol. He was also a man who could see opportunity from the other side of the Neva. Now, Andrews thought, I am getting somewhere.

"A breach of security?" Powell asked.

Andrews drove forward. "Do *you* know anything about this? Did Mr. King confide in you? Are *you* involved?"

With each question Andrews could see Powell getting one shade paler.

"Absolutely not! I run this . . . I mean, this consulate is run by the rules." A little guilt showed. "Mr. King must have had a good reason. He is an excellent administrator."

Good boy, Powell. Protect both ends of the rope. That way if you lose your grip on one, you always have the other to pull you through.

"If he is such an excellent administrator, where is he?" Andrews said in his most intimidating voice.

Powell stood and went to the window. "I told you, I don't know. He left a note with his secretary saying he would be out of the office all day." He hesitated. Andrews could see beads of sweat forming on his forehead. The man was trapped. Andrews wondered which way he would go. "Excuse me for doubting your word, Mr. Andrews, but *that* is all I have as evidence that Mr. King is in trouble. As a private citizen . . ."

Andrews gave his most understanding smile. "I appreciate your position, Mr. Powell." He then pointed to the phone, a series of numbers rolling off his tongue. "The White House. My authority comes from there. You can call if you like."

Powell glanced at the phone, then at Andrews. Sam knew what was going on inside. A decision was being reached. Do you go by the book and offend this powerful man who can make or break careers, or do you bend the rules a little, and make a friend? Powell would reach the latter conclusion, Andrews was sure of it. Low-level bureaucrats wanting to reach the top always did. It was the only way up.

"I'm sure Rand will be checking in," Powell said.

"Would he be in his apartment?"

"I can call, sir."

Andrews smiled. Sir. The sure sign Ted Powell was now his. Things were going well. He could only hope that Rand King would be as easily manipulated.

"Please do."

Powell picked up the phone and dialed. He left a message on Rand's answering machine.

"Sorry, Mr. Andrews, he's not there."

Andrews stood. "Get in touch with him, please. As soon as possible. The man is in trouble unless he comes up with some very good excuses. His job is on the line."

Powell's eyes jumped with expectation.

Andrews continued. "Tell him I want to talk to him, and if he wants to save his career and his life, he'll do it. I am at the Moskva Hotel, not far from here. Let me know where and when. By messenger. No phone calls." He smiled. "I hear the KGB is still watching Americans—possible phone taps, that sort of thing."

"Yes, we even check ours—daily. I see that this place is kept clean—security tight. I'll send a man."

Andrews gave Powell that "you're a good man" look, then got to his feet and reached across the desk to shake hands. "I'll be waiting."

Powell was his.

———————

Ted Powell stared at the door, then pulled a bottle of vodka from the drawer. Removing the cap, he downed two swallows, letting the hot liquid burn his throat and stomach. Then he put the lid back on and returned it to its proper place. He had never seen the tossing of so much hogwash since leaving Washington. The man was a politician, through and through. But a powerful one. He would need to be treated with the utmost diplomacy. Which meant lots of tender, loving care but no substance. He rang his secretary.

"Judy, I want the head of state treatment for Sam Andrews, the man who just left my office. Contact Terry and have him get on it, will you? Car service, the works. See if he wants to visit a few palaces until Mr. King can see him. Thanks."

He put the phone down, then picked it up again, pushing another button. "Deidre, Ted. Where is your boss?"

"I'm not sure, Ted. He slept here last night." A pause. "A woman's clothes were in the bathroom."

Powell smirked. "Not a chance."

"I'm serious. But they left before I arrived."

"A first?" No answer. "No word left for us puny underlings?"

"Nothing. Sorry."

"Let me know if he calls, and see if you can find him. I have a message. Sam Andrews wants to see him."

"Gotcha."

They hung up. Powell sat back. Bases covered.

He stared at the phone, thinking, then picked it up and dialed an outside line.

"This is Powell. You told me to let you know if Samuel J. Andrews ever made contact with this office. He is here."

Chapter Twenty-six

WHEN VOSTYA DUBENKY REGAINED CONSCIOUSNESS, he was lying on the living-room floor, blood drenching the rug around his head. He blinked his eyes several times, trying to clear his vision, trying to remember. The door to the room was directly in front of him, and he could see into the hall and the kitchen beyond. There was no sound. He pushed upward with his hands, trying to lift himself, forcing his body to move to the chair a few feet away. He half fell, half stumbled in that direction, caught hold of the arms of the chair, and hoisted himself into it. Taking a handkerchief from his pocket, he pressed it against the cut in his scalp and immediately felt the blood ooze through it and against the palm of his hand. He glanced back at the rug and saw that the puddle was frighteningly thick. He had to get to a doctor. He reached into his pocket for the portable phone but found it was gone. He picked up the one on the table to his left and dialed the numbers as he remembered them. A woman answered.

"Larissa?"

"Vostya? What is it?"

"Get . . . get Nickolai."

Nickolai came on the line. "Vostya?"

"Nickolai, they have Dimitri and Marina. I am sorry. I don't know how—"

"Thank heaven you are all right. They already called using your portable phone, the number you put on it. They told me you were dead!"

"Nearly. Can you . . . can you get me to . . . " He felt the dizziness, the nausea, the blackness filling the edges of his vision.

"Vostya?"

"I . . . I am going to pass out."

"I am nearly there, friend Vostya. Hang on! Vostya?"

There was no reply.

Nickolai jammed the gearshift down and jerked the wheel to the left. The car slid around the corner, then righted itself, and he punched the gas again. Larissa sat in the passenger seat, hanging on for dear life.

They had found the safe house! How? Did he have a leak in his office already? Or was it Dimitri? Had he contacted Shelepin? Tried to protect his empire?

He came to a light. It was red. He honked the horn and dodged cars, working his way through to the other side of the intersection.

Kulikov had called. Nickolai could still hear the gloating, confident voice as Kulikov told him Dimitri and Marina were now in his care, that Vostya needed immediate attention. Then the laugh! Larissa was right. Men like Kulikov and Zhelin had to be stopped. Had to be!

He slammed on the brakes in front of the apartment house where Vostya was. He bolted from the vehicle, Larissa right behind him. Taking the stairs three at a time, he was in the apartment in less than a minute. Vostya lay on the floor, another pool of blood gathering on the rug where he had fallen from the chair.

Larissa ran for a towel while Nickolai turned his friend over and checked his pulse. It was weak.

"He has lost a lot of blood. We have to get him to the hospital," he told Larissa, who was applying pressure to the wounds. Zhelin's men had ripped the stitches loose from Vostya's earlier wound and widened it, then added another to the back of his scalp. Probably Kulikov. Nickolai had never wanted to get his hands on anyone so badly in all his life!

Old as he was, Nickolai Poltav was a strong man. He scooped

his young friend into his arms and carried him to the car as easily as he would have carried a small child. He put him into the back seat with Larissa, then got behind the wheel. The Volga jerked into the street.

When they reached the hospital, Vostya was rushed into surgery by the same doctor who had worked to save Natalya Starkov. When he returned, his expression was serious.

"He has lost blood, and we have no blood supply. Do either of you have type O blood?"

Larissa nodded. After running some quick tests, they put her on a gurney and wheeled her in next to Vostya for a direct transfusion. Nickolai stood between them, holding Larissa's hand. When it was nearly finished, he spoke to her.

"You know where the record book is if anything should happen to me. I want you to go back to the safe house as soon as you are strong enough to leave the hospital. Wait for me there. If the American or Galya call, make arrangements to go with them. Tell King what has happened and that I will contact him this evening at the consulate."

"No, Nickolai . . . you . . . you can't do this alone."

"Without the book they won't harm me. I have to meet with them, make the arrangements." Impulsively Nickolai bent over and kissed her lightly on the forehead. "Thank you for helping Vostya."

Larissa put her hand behind his neck and pulled him to her lips. Nickolai tingled clear to his toes.

"Be careful, Nickolai Poltav," she said almost gruffly. "I am just getting used to you."

With a smile Nickolai pulled away, kissed her hand, and left the room.

Larissa listened until the click of Nickolai's shoes quit sounding on the tiled floors. Fear tugged at her stomach. All her life things had been taken away from her by evil men. Now she was afraid it might be happening again.

A tear ran down her cheek as the doctor inserted the needle into her vein.

So much had gone wrong the past few days. Why was it that

fighting for the right things always had such a heavy price? She didn't know the old man whose death had started everything, but others did. Others ached because he wasn't here anymore. As Rustam's heart must be aching for Natalya. Poor Rustam! Where was he? What was he doing?

Only she and President Hayes knew about Rustam's former life. They both knew what Rustam was capable of, but they also knew of his promise to keep himself clean—never to kill again.

Her heart raced. He was out there, planning, preparing to kill again. She knew it, could feel it. And there was no way she could stop him.

Rustam removed the earphones. His friend with the KGB had provided a tap on Zhelin's business phone—a dangerous thing, and one that showed the man's friendship and allegiance to a former way of life.

The tap had finally paid off. He reversed the small tape recorder, then pushed *Play.*

"Zhelin, this is Kulikov. We have the bait."

"Excellent! You are working miracles. Excellent!"

"Where do you want them kept?"

There was a long pause.

"Make arrangements to house them in the old prison at the fortress." A slight laugh. "Nickolai will be calling. I will set the meeting up for that place, this afternoon at three o'clock. You and I will met there at two about the other matter."

A click, and the conversation was over. Rustam shut off the recorder. He glanced at his watch. Two hours to get into position. Soon it would be over. He picked up the items and shoved them into a leather satchel, which also held a portable device used to monitor conversations from a long distance. His friend had told him it was powerful enough to pick up conversations through nearly an inch of solid glass at more than five hundred feet. He would take it along; it might be useful.

He closed the satchel, then hung it from his shoulder with the attached strap. Picking up the case containing the rifle, he headed for the door, his mind already picturing the fortress. The cathedral tower was probably the best location, but there would be no escape.

But then, what was there to escape to?

Volodya Vilechenko took the pills handed him for pain and pushed them down with a healthy swig of water. The nurse helped him put his arm into the sling, then slipped his blood-stained coat onto his shoulders. He stood carefully, making sure the dizziness was gone, that he could stand without crumbling like a house of cards. He could.

He used his cane and helped himself through the door and into the hall. He had come on his own—a taxi, flagged down in front of a crowd of startled, frightened people, none of whom, thankfully, had been hurt.

Walking through the dimly lit halls, he came to the main entrance and into the midafternoon sun. It felt good. He hailed a taxi. As he approached, another car pulled up behind it, and Vasily got out. Volodya stiffened.

"Vasily." He took another step toward the taxi.

"Sir, you won't need the taxi. I am to pick you up."

Volodya looked at his driver and one-time friend. "You betrayed me, Vasily."

"I had my orders. I had no choice. Please, sir. Get in the car."

Volodya took another step toward the taxi.

Vasily displayed a small handgun. "Now, sir. Please, in the car."

Volodya hesitated, then moved to the car, opened the back door, and let himself in. Vasily got behind the wheel and quickly moved the car into the street.

Volodya kept his eyes looking out the window, feelings of anger mingled with disappointment and giving him indigestion.

"I am sorry," Vasily said. "You . . . you weren't supposed to get hurt."

Volodya didn't respond. He lay his head against the back of the seat and closed his eyes. He was too old to play this game anymore. His mind was too slow. It had all been right there in front of him, but he had refused to see it, and his carelessness had nearly gotten two innocent people killed. But then, that was the kind of thing that happened when a friend turned out to be the enemy.

"Where are we going?" he asked.

"I am only to keep you out of the way until they find the diary. We are going to an apartment where you will be comfortable. You can rest."

Volodya put his head against the seat and closed his eyes. He would need his strength. Vasily was a strong man.

Chapter Twenty-seven

THE CAR BELONGED TO A FRIEND of Sasha Zagladin, Rand's new employee—if you could call it a car. It had been an ambulance at one time. It was a station wagon with curtains and a panel between the front and back seats. The seats were shredded to the point that Rand could feel several springs pushing at his backside. The dash was covered with stickers, one X-rated photo (now disposed of), and a coffee cup that was stained dark brown. The Sony tape player stuck out of a hole that looked like it had been cut with tin snips, the wires falling to the floor beneath, then going under what was left of the carpet and disappearing under the seat. The player probably cost the owner more than the entire vehicle.

Rand shifted down, grinding the old gears and wondering if the shake and shudder of the car was from a flywheel's missing teeth or a motor out of tune and without half its mounts. The strange thing was, he was grateful. It wasn't exactly the kind of car Zhelin's people would be giving a second glance. The old clothes he, Galya, and Sasha were wearing would also help.

Rand glanced through the small opening in the partition. Sasha lay half asleep among empty cans, bottles, and old rags. Rand could only shake his head. He wondered how the man could sleep in all that trash—not to mention the fact that the car hammered his spine every time they crossed a pebble. It was beyond Rand's understanding.

Sasha's employment had already paid off, not just in the vehicle but in information. After leaving Vilechenko's bullet-riddled Mercedes and getting different clothes, Rand and Galya had wound their way back to the park and found Sasha asleep on the grass near the fountain. They had plenty of cuts and abrasions to give him pause, and Sasha had asked what had happened. After listening, he had grown still, then told Rand he was not surprised. "Zhelin is a violent man," he had said. "He would kill you both if he thought you had something he wanted."

Rand wasn't sure the attack had come from Zhelin, but other options hadn't presented themselves yet. There were many strange things about all this, too many characters, too many missing pieces in a confusing puzzle. What he did know was that as long as they had the diary, their lives were in danger.

Sasha had given them the bad news about Natalya Starkova. Galya had fainted. Using the ambulance for the first time, they had gone to Sasha's apartment. If he hadn't been worried about Galya, Rand would have found the ride a laugh a minute, but he had been preoccupied with worry.

When she had regained consciousness, Rand had seen the pain, the guilt in her eyes. The tears, the anger, the hate, had all flowed freely. She had cursed Yuri Yezhov for giving her the diary. Then she had cursed the diary itself. Finally she had cursed her own stupidity for involving her cousin.

Then she had broken down into body-shaking sobs.

Rand had wrapped her in his arms and worked at finding the right words to ease the guilt and make the pain go away, even though he knew the attempt was useless. The tears, the gut-wrenching cries would do more to cleanse than his words.

The sobs had finally stopped, the tears dried up. For a long time they had sat close to one another, her head resting on his shoulder. He hadn't known what she was feeling inside, had known he couldn't understand it, but she had seemed to be gathering strength. Finally she had lifted her head from his shoulder and kissed him lightly on the cheek. Then she had stood. The worst seemed to be over, the look of guilt replaced by one of determination.

They had tried to reach Rustam by phone without success. They had considered going to his apartment but knew it would be foolish and dangerous. There were still enemies to deal with, even if they weren't sure who they were.

It had been Galya who decided the best thing to do was find out the diary's secrets and use them against the people who had killed Natalya.

At first Rand had worried that Galya's drive for revenge might throw them all headlong into the snapping jaws of their enemies, but he had relaxed when she let him temper her heated feelings with common sense.

He had called an old friend, a Norwegian—someone who could read the diary.

Rand turned left on Kristovskiy Prospekt, one eye on the rearview mirror that was loose on its moorings and shaking like a leaf outside the driver's door. There was a Zhiguili back there, but was it following them? It turned into a side street. He let his muscles relax a little.

He gave Galya a once-over. The color in her cheeks was back to normal, and she seemed in control.

She saw the concern in his eyes and smiled while squeezing his hand where it lay atop the gearshift. "I am fine."

They entered Primorskiy Park. He could see the stadium at the far end. The mouth of the Malaya Neva was on the left, the Vostok restaurant coming up on their right. Parking the Volga, he turned and spoke to Sasha through the small hole.

"Stay here, but keep an eye open for trouble. If you see anything suspicious, come after us." Sasha sat up, alert. The windows were so dirty that Rand wondered how he could see anything.

Rand felt good about Sasha Zagladin. He seemed to be trying to upgrade his employment to take care of his family. He had already had plenty of opportunity to betray them, probably for a substantial amount of money, but he hadn't. Rand thought the key was the children they had met in Sasha's apartment. It was apparent that he loved them, wanted to be a good father to them, and wanted them to be proud of him. Working for the KGB these days carried a stigma, one Rand thought Sasha was glad to be rid of.

But Rand had been wrong about people before. He'd keep an eye on their new friend for a while.

Galya had added a white, floppy cap to her disguise and climbed out of the car. Rand lowered the straw cap onto his head and put his glasses on, then joined her. They walked to the path and started for the restaurant.

Elina Sorenson was standing near the door, looking calm as a summer's morn.

"You are sure about this woman?" Galya asked.

Rand nodded. "She hates your bureaucracy worse than you do. She has to shove papers through it on a daily basis. Elina has a linguistic background and knows more languages than I have fingers."

"How did you meet her?"

Rand smiled at the memory.

"A state affair. Black tie and all that stuff. I wore jeans and cowboy boots. She was amused."

"I'll bet, along with the rest of the crowd."

"All but the snobs—most of the Americans."

Elina walked toward them, smiling. So much for the disguise.

Galya noticed that the woman's blond hair bounced as she strutted down the path. A woman in her mid-thirties, Galya estimated, with designer clothes that fit like a hundred kilos of potatoes in a fifty-kilo sack.

Elina gave her biggest grin to Rand, hugged him, and gave him a peck on the cheek.

"Horrible disguise, Rand, and you smell like you fell into a vat of pickle juice."

Rand had noticed the smell as well but could only shrug. They had purchased the clothes at a second-hand shop, and the selection was either this one or one that smelled like a barnyard. He had given that one up when he left the farm in Idaho. "How are you, Elina?"

Elina seemed to pout. "You haven't called. How good could I be?"

Galya thought Rand blushed.

"This is Galya Starkova," Rand said.

Elina did a critical once-over. "You don't look like the type who would keep company with smelly old men."

She put her arm through Rand's and pulled it close. Galya didn't like it. "What can I do for you, cowboy?"

Rand reached for the diary. "Norwegian. Can you read us a few pages?"

Elina took the book, her professionalism suddenly evident. "An awful lot of damage, but I can read some of it." She kept her eyes focused on the pages while turning onto a path that bordered a small lake. "Come on. We'll find a place a little more private." She turned to Galya. "This is yours?"

"By default more than intent," Galya said.

Elina led them to a bench, her mind focused on the contents of the diary. Galya could see that her first judgment of Elina Sorensen had been a bit rash; the woman was a professional.

"Sit down," Elina said without taking her eyes off her work. She turned to Rand. "I see you've had someone work on this, clean it up. But there are still a lot of pages stuck together."

"Give us what you can, Elina," Rand said. "We'll take it in for further work later."

Elina turned to the first page and started reading. "'We leave tomorrow. The training has been hard, lasting two months, but we are prepared. I shoot well now, hitting the targets with nearly 100 percent regularity. I am ready if the Germans get in the way.'"

Elina stopped. "She sounds as if she belongs to the underground, during World War II."

Rand nodded. "Go to another entry. We'll come back if we need to."

Elina carefully turned to another page. "'We crossed Lyngen Fjord by boat during the night and began the climb to the plateau below Mt. Baeccegelhaldde. The load is heavy, but the dogs and men handled it well. The weather is bad, and we are forced to dig in until it passes. Robert worries that we will not make the train connections in Pechanga. The Russians say not to worry. They will get us through to Leningrad. They seem to have many connections inside the Soviet army. Alexander and Robert have had several disagreements. I am afraid that some of it is over me, although Alexander does not show his affection so openly as Robert. I sometimes feel that I have fallen in love with this

American, but I try to keep these feelings from interfering with our mission. Alexander doesn't think I should be put at risk like this. He is very protective, even when I tell him to stop. I am capable and it is my choice. My membership in his organization comes from my hatred of Stalin and Communism and what they have done to so many.' "

"That checks out with what Vilechenko told us," Rand said.

Elina continued reading. " 'My brother, Norstrum, came with us across the fjord. He is still unhappy that I go instead of him. He has a family and should take care of them. It is better this way.'

"The dates of the entries get farther apart from here," Elina said. "Here is another: 'We arrived at Pechanga. We lost two men coming across the mountains on the northern tip of Finland—not to Germans but to the weather. They became disoriented and wandered from the camp in a horrible blizzard. We waited and searched as long as we could. They are probably dead. Olaf had two children. Lod had one. My heart aches for their families. They came for the money. Fortunately, they were paid in advance. At least there is that consolation for their loved ones.

" 'Sometimes I am not sure why Robert came. He says it is because he knows that Stalin must die. His family are Russians, immigrants from before the revolution. They lost everything. He talks as if this will return it all to him, that he can reclaim his family's rights and property. He seems more interested in what was taken from him and his family and speaks of being Russian again and again. He wants his heritage back and says that the money and the change in government will do it. I can tell he wants very much to be rich.

" 'Alexander and Volodya came through for us. We have boarded the train and are moving southeast to Murmansk. The men have Russian uniforms. I am dressed as Volodya's wife.

" 'Alexander received word from his contacts in Leningrad that the target is going to be in the city on schedule. We will arrive in time to prepare. The other part of our mission concerns me. It is the timing. Is it right? How will the people respond? Do Volodya and Alexander's people have enough power? Does the heir to

Nicholas have enough support? The future of Russia, the future
of the royal line, could end here.'"

"Assassination and overthrow, as Vilechenko indicated,"
Galya said. "A return to the rule of the tsars."

Elina had an unbelieving look on her face. "An heir? Who?
What is this about, and who was the target, Rand?"

"Stalin. What is the date of that entry?"

"May 15, 1941."

"Go on."

Elina turned the page. "The period before Leningrad is easier
to read. From this point to the back it gets progressively worse.
Many pages are badly stuck together. I am afraid that if I try to
pull them apart . . . "

"Read what you can," Rand said.

"'May 20, 1941. It has been unsafe to write. In traveling south
I almost gave us away. Usually the men keep me safely tucked
away where they say I cannot be a temptation to the many Russian
soldiers going back and forth to the front. Some haven't seen a
woman for months, and they are anxious for female companion-
ship. But the constant rocking of the train made me sick, and I
went into the hallway late at night to walk it off. A soldier came
up to me and started getting friendly. I couldn't just ignore him for
fear that he might force his way into my room, where many of our
supplies are hidden. It was the wrong approach. He tried to kiss
me, and I had to slap him. He then became more forceful. Only
William saved me. He had to kill the soldier and toss him off the
train. Luckily no one was in the walkway but our own people. I
owe my life to him. He is so strong for one so young.'"

Elina turned the page. "Who is William?"

"We haven't identified all the men on the mission yet," Rand
said. "What's next?"

"'We are in Leningrad. Our hiding place is an old warehouse
on the outskirts of town. Volodya says it is never used, but I often
see soldiers close by. Leningrad is a big city, bustling, full of military people. We are in the part of the city closest to the Finnish
front lines. Leningrad is the city to which the soldiers come on
leave. One good thing: Our men are dressed in Russian uniforms

and have good papers. All of them know the language and have no difficulty moving about and making preparations. I am mostly responsible to find and prepare food but will play an important role when the proper time comes.

" 'There is a delay in the arrival of the others who are to meet us. Alexander said that everything in Moscow is ready. Now we must wait for the target. We must depend on God to get him here.' "

Elina perused several other pages. "Some of the words on this one are blurred and unreadable. I'll read what I can and leave the other places blank. You see if you can understand it: ' . . . hiding. All . . . lost. Soldiers . . . surprise . . . warehouse . . . captured or killed . . . I and . . . escaped.' "

Elina hesitated. "I think it says, 'What has Robert done?' "

"Anything else?" Galya asked.

Elina lay the book on her lap and concentrated, using her finger to follow the words. When she got to the end of the page, she leaned back and spoke.

"She watched the end from the roof of a nearby building. Volodya was captured, and there were many bodies.

"It happened as she was returning from going after food. She heard gunfire. She tried to help them get free. She was able to get to one of the men but doesn't give a name, although from what she says it must have been the boy. They escaped together. She didn't know what to do, where to go. The boy was wounded. She wondered if she should try to get them to Helsinki to get away, but she was afraid the boy had lost too much blood, that it might kill him."

Elina paused. "She saw Robert. He was alive. She says he had betrayed them."

Galya removed the group picture from her purse. "The young one with the moustache must be the boy," she said.

"William. Nora must have escaped with William," Rand added.

"Nora's message to Volodya—beware of the traitor. Kitrick?" Galya asked.

"Umm," Rand replied, deep in thought.

Elina glanced at the next entry. "She isn't writing as often. This entry is on the 18th of June, 1941. I think I can read most of it: 'On the 10th our secret was discovered. Anna found us in the basement of her building. She was afraid but did not go to the police. She says they are bad. They took away her husband before the war. He has never returned. She knows I am a foreigner, but she doesn't care because I am with William, and he is Russian. She asks few questions. She brings food when she can.

"'On the 16th there was a rumor that Stalin would come to Leningrad. William was too weak to carry out our orders. I went to the place with a revolver in my bag. I was going to finish what we came for, but it was a trap. Robert knew I would come. I escaped only because many others had heard the rumor and filled the square. I saw Robert waiting. He was in a Russian uniform. I wanted to kill him but could not get close enough.'

"This one is several days later," Elina said. "'The Germans invaded Russia today. My friend Anna told me so. The city is chaotic. Some people are already leaving, afraid. I don't know what to think. Should I hope the Germans will come? No, I know what they are, what they do. The Russian people are good people, but they have monsters for leaders.'

"That was June 22, 1941," Elina said. She continued reading. "'I worked on the code. William is feeling better and was able to help. We were able to decipher only a part of it. Anna spends a lot of time with William. I caution him. He only smiles. I am afraid his heart is lost to this poor peasant girl. What can I do? I am not his mother.

"'At least Robert's dream of riches will not come true. We have the instructions. Even if he obtains the code key from Volodya, it will do him no good. I am sure he is searching the city, frantic to find us so he can rob the vault and escape before the Germans completely surround the city. But with Anna's help we seldom leave the basement, and with the Germans surrounding the city, the Russians are kept busy with other matters. I wonder what happened to Volodya. They must have tortured him.'"

"Vilechenko never did tell us about his capture and escape," Galya said. "I hope he is all right. The attempt on our lives . . . he was the one who was hurt."

"Has it occurred to you that Volodya might be the enemy?" Rand asked.

"And have himself shot at? He was with us, Rand. That would be most foolish."

"But he wasn't seriously hurt and reacted rather quickly when the firing began. And they didn't stop to finish him off. Why?"

"You two have lost me," Elina said. "What are you talking about?" She closed the diary. "No more until I know what is going on."

Rand glanced at Galya, then told Elina what he could. She wasn't smiling when he finished.

"Sorry I asked. Running around with you two could lead to high doctor bills."

"We hope what you are reading will give us some clues to end all this," Rand said. "Go back to the last entry and read it again."

She did.

"What does Nora mean by working on the code?" Rand asked.

"What code? Volodya never mentioned any code, or a vault." Galya looked a little nervous.

Elina read on. " 'We must concentrate on escape now. We must find the enclave. But getting out of the city will not be easy. We may have waited too long.'

"Half a dozen pages are stuck together here. The next readable entry is July 1, 1941. I can't read all of it." She was silent a moment, leaning over the book, focused. "Listen: 'The city is under siege conditions already as the Germans surround it. We have tried several ways to get out, but security is tight. They check everyone's papers. We know they are looking for German spies, but they look for us as well. We have seen papers with our pictures on them warning the people, telling them they will be rewarded if we are turned in. Robert is responsible for the search. He must be. Only he had a picture of us. Someday I will kill him for what he has done.

" 'I have wondered about Anna, but her hate for the system seems stronger than the promise of a reward for our capture—as does her love for my young companion. As things get worse, I wonder if she will change her mind, if the promise of money or food will be too much of a temptation. Now I can only say I am happy she seems to be in love. Alexander won't be happy if William brings Anna to the enclave. In Alexander's mind, it would ruin everything.'"

"Kitrick wanted them very badly," Galya said.

"It was survival," Rand said. "His chances of escape got worse as the Germans tightened the siege. But he couldn't leave without finishing off any witnesses to his betrayal. They might have shown up later."

"Then there was the vault, the riches," Galya said. "That was why he really came, what he really wanted—the reason for his betrayal in the first place. He couldn't leave without them or the whole thing would have been pointless. Keep going, Elina."

Elina took a long time reading through the next few entries. The stains and water damage were getting worse.

"Three entries cover two months—mostly about survival. She seems very depressed. The young man is ill again—an infection to his wound. She and Anna are scrounging for food all the time. Anna has a five-year-old child, Yura."

"A child," Galya said softly. "It was worst for them, and old people."

"Next come a number of pages that are barely readable. This is in October. She has been ill." Elina bit her lip. "She was shot! While she was standing in a food line someone recognized her—the pictures placed around the city—and went for a soldier. Nora saw them coming and ran, escaping but losing a lot of blood. The man is still too weak to help much but tries when he can. Anna has a hard time getting food enough for all of them. She would go out all day with Yura, begging in the streets. They were able to get some potatoes and onions from a small garden plot behind a bombed-out house. No doctor, no sanitation.

"The next entry is in November." Elina looked up at Galya and Rand. "It gets worse. They have no heat, no wood for a fire. Nora is also sick and can't go out to help find what they need. Yura is sick and needs medicine. He won't eat. Nora is afraid for him. She reads from her Torah often. William is a little better and is searching daily for food and medicine. She sees herself in a piece of broken mirror. She cries."

Elina looked up again. "They have deciphered more of the code."

"Does she say what it is?" Rand asked.

"No," Elina said. "The next entry is in December. The bombing is horrible; houses all around them are destroyed. At least they have wood. They take it from the bombed houses. They live in the basement of Anna's apartment building. Much of the upper floors have been destroyed. There are bodies in the streets, emaciated, frozen. Wagons pick them up as soon as they can, but there are so many and everyone is so weak, it isn't often." She hesitated, taking a deep breath. "They are taking wallpaper off the walls and boiling it in water. The flour paste gives them nourishment. Yura has gotten very sick. His fever is high. He never cries, never plays. She is afraid for all of them. Anna's features are sunken. She is too weak even to get off her blankets. Now Nora and the man are scrounging for food, firewood, anything that will help them survive the winter."

Galya looked pale. Rand took her hand, squeezing it. "Are you all right?"

She nodded, forcing a smile while returning the squeeze.

Elina had been concentrating on the next entry. "I can't believe it. They bought food," she said.

"Bought? With what? And who was selling?" Rand asked.

"From the black market. History tells us there was hoarding in the city at first. When things got tough, people began to sell some of it at exorbitant prices—at least what they thought they wouldn't need. Some sold themselves right into starvation."

"There is proof that some were stealing the bodies of the dead, cutting them up and selling them." Galya shrugged. "When you are starving to death, you don't ask questions."

"But where did she get money?" Rand asked.

"I'll read it if you like."

They leaned forward.

"Robert would be angry. Thanks to William's work on the

code, the treasure Robert coveted has come into our hands. We have bread tonight. I have never tasted anything so sweet, so wonderful. Anna is feeling better tonight, but Yura, he will not eat, he has not the strength. His poor stomach is swollen, and he cries constantly. William is in anguish. He loves them both too deeply to stand by and watch them starve. With the help of the code, we obtained items to bargain with. The tsar may not have control of Russia, but today he has saved our lives.' "

"The tsar's treasure," Galya said. "It was rumored that Nicholas II put many things into hiding when he abdicated and lost the throne. Gold, silver, artwork, jewelry, diamonds and other precious gems—today it would be worth millions."

"They must have taken coded instructions of some kind telling them how to get into the tsar's vault. They broke the code and found the vault."

"They used some of the treasure to trade for food on the black market," Galya said.

Elina was reading further ahead. "Oh!" she moaned. She never lifted her eyes from the book. "Yura is dead. The food . . . it was too little too late. Anna and William mourn. I mourn. Just when hope had come. Just when surviving had become a possibility."

Elina stopped, wiped a tear, then read more. " 'We move tomorrow—a place close to the vault that is miraculously still in decent condition, although we did have to remove the frozen bodies of a family of four. The windows are not broken. The room is small, but it has a stove, a sink, two beds, and a marvelous view in two directions—a much better place than our basement. I wish Yura might have lived to see it. It would have made him happy.

" 'For the first time in many months I think of Tromso, of my brother, Norstrum, and his little family. I think of returning to my mountains and the cold, crisp air off the Norwegian Sea. It seems so far away, and yet I smell it.' "

Elina turned the book as if to get a better view, a quizzical look on her face. "This picture."

Galya looked at it. "I did not see it before." She touched the pages, then sniffed at them. "Rikki must have separated them."

"The Cathedral of St. Peter and St. Paul, inside the fortress. This must be one of the pages Sasha said Zhelin has copies of. Look, it is a war drawing. See how the artist drew the camouflaging that covered the spire?"

They were looking at a line drawing of intricate proportions. "Whoever drew it was a stickler for detail," Rand said. "Look at the trim around the windows, the columns at the entrance."

Galya nodded. "Underneath the picture. What does it say, Elina?"

"It isn't very clear, but the approximate translation would be, 'If when choosing between the Savior and the tsar you stand upon high ground, the kingdom shall not be lost and the true riches found.'"

"A religious riddle?"

Elina turned the page. "Another picture—of a key in the palm of a hand. It is a beautiful drawing." The key seemed so lifelike that she could lift it from the woman's palm in which it lay.

"Look at the lines of the hand. How detailed!" Galya remarked.

Rand stared at the drawing, then looked at the lines in his own hand. "They are all wrong. Look at the lines in my hand. They are curved more gently than those of the drawing. There is a pattern to the lines in Nora's hand, almost like . . . "

"A tattoo or something."

"Possibly scar tissue—as if a square portion of the lower palm had been ripped away, then resewn," Galya said. "A wound."

"The key must fit something," Elina said.

"There are letters on the key—Cyrillic writing," Galya said. "To enter the kingdom pay homage to the Christ child."

"A church key," Elina said, standing. "Many of the old churches had keys like that one. Possibly it was to the front door of St. Peter and St. Paul. Maybe she drew it because she had nothing better to do."

"Galya, where in the fortress would she have been in order to draw that picture?" Rand asked.

Galya looked at it a moment, then thought about it. She had

been inside the fortress many times, but it had been long ago. The entire place had been turned into a museum in 1921, and she and her parents had visited. Tsar Peter the Great had built the fortress in 1703 to defend the outlet of the Neva to the Baltic Sea, which Russia had taken from Sweden. Peter had located it well, and the guns along its bastions had prevented Russia's enemies from entering any of the branches of the great river. At first the walls had been made of wood, but over the next thirty-five years they were replaced with brick. Then, in 1780, the walls were faced with granite slabs, giving it its present dark and forbidding appearance as it brooded upon the banks of the Neva.

There were many buildings within the walls of the fortress— housing, arsenals, and the prisons in the walls themselves. These had been created in the 1800s as the Tsars began imprisoning their critics. But the picture had to have been drawn from a room in the Mint House. A tall building across the courtyard from the cathedral, it had been built in the 1800s and was still the only place that coined Russian money and commemorative medals.

"The Mint. Probably a room on the top floor."

"Were there people in the fortress during the siege?" Rand asked.

"As I remember, soldiers were housed there, and there was a limited arsenal. The weapons were probably all distributed to the army or the volunteers, and by December there was no heat, no food. But people lived there in the rooms of the old prison, in the barracks and houses. It was one of the safest places in the city."

"Could they have taken the fortune from the church?" Rand asked.

Elina spoke. "From my reading of history, by December people were so hungry, so weak, that most were like zombies, uncaring or unconcerned about what others did. It took all their strength just to place one foot in front of the other or to keep warm. Nora and the others could have removed the bodies and moved in with hardly a side glance. No one would have cared."

"Still," Galya remarked, "removing large amounts of the treasure would have been difficult."

"Then at least a portion of it may still be in the vault," Rand said.

"There are no more entries," Elina said. "The rest is missing. From the look of it, the diary was split into two sections."

"Why would she split it up?" Galya asked.

"We'll probably never know. The riddles are the key to finding the vault. William created them from the code, and we'll have to figure them out."

It was apparent to Rand that ALLIANCE had had two goals. First had been the assassination; second had been the coup. In order for the coup to succeed and to give the new government a chance of lasting, they had needed money to provide weapons, food, everything for the fighting of the Germans. That had made the treasure necessary, its removal critical to any coup attempt.

When the team had come to Leningrad, they had brought instructions on the location of the vault in coded form, probably located in the second half of the diary now missing. When things had fallen apart, Nora had taken the diary and escaped with it—a small glitch in Kitrick's well-laid betrayal plans. William had worked on the codes. William was the hero. But then, of the team members, who had a better chance?

"There is one thing I don't understand," Galya said. "If the riddle contains the instructions to open the vault, why would William and Nora write it out like this? If the diary fell into enemy hands, they would lose it all."

"Even though the pictures give us a clue as to the vault's approximate whereabouts, I think we'll find the riddle difficult to understand," Rand said.

"You mean all of what they knew we still don't have?"

"Oh, I think it's there, but it was clearer in its original form— clearer for them."

"Then this is a restructuring? But why?" Elina asked.

"Think about what the diary tells us. Kitrick knows about the diary and about the code. Volodya is being hauled away to prison for interrogation. Volodya was the one who was supposed to be carrying the key to the code. If Kitrick had the key and the diary came into his hands, he could enter the vault. I think they destroyed the coded instructions and left these new ones behind so that the man they hated most, but who was most likely to find them, could never enter the vault."

Galya thought a moment, her lips moving slowly as she spoke the words of the riddle quietly again.

"Most of the tsars are buried in the floor of the cathedral, and the church itself probably represents Christ, but what does it mean to stand upon high ground?"

"I think we need to visit the fortress."

"How can we search for the treasure in such a public place?"

"We use a camera first, take some pictures."

The two women stood, and the three of them walked back toward the car. Elina gave each of them a kiss on the cheek, then walked back toward her own car.

Galya put the diary into her purse while watching after her.

"I wouldn't worry about Elina," Rand said.

"Treasure can be very tempting."

"For some. Elina isn't one of them. She is the heiress to a fortune. Her father practically owns Oslo. She runs all his businesses here because she enjoys the challenge, not because she needs the money. Elina says it keeps her young. Someday she'll go back and live in the big mansion, run it all."

She glanced at Rand. "She likes you."

"The feeling is mutual. Elina is a good friend. I could trust her with my life."

"You have, Rand." She put her arm through his, and they moved to the side of the old car. Sasha smiled at them through the grimy windows.

"Do you think this thing can get us to the fortress?" Galya asked.

Rand opened the door for Galya. "I'll wind up the rubber band and we'll see."

Galya slid in, then waited for Rand to go around and get in on the driver's side. "We have one stop to make, Rand."

"Important?" Rand asked as he turned the key.

"Something I learned from Nickolai Poltav. It may save our lives."

Chapter Twenty-eight

ZHELIN STARED AT THE TRANSLATION of the diary. The photocopies of the pages had been unclear, their meaning full of blank spaces, question marks. Having just six pages, with none of them in sequence, created huge gaps in the narrative.

But the overall feeling was that Nora Larsen had found something of considerable value. The question was, where—and was it still there?

He stared at the copy of the line drawing of the cathedral, comparing it with the real thing several hundred yards away from his seat in the limousine. The cathedral was decorated in beautiful detail, in which he could see places where work by restorationists had been done since the war. He read the translation of the inscription again.

If when choosing between the Savior and the tsar you stand upon high ground, the kingdom shall not be lost and the true riches found.

A clue, but what did it mean?

Then there was the drawing of the key—a church key, in the palm of a woman's hand. The picture was blurred, the intricate details of the original running together, but the Russian words were still visible.

To enter the kingdom pay homage to the Christ child.

He slapped the papers in Kulikov's lap with a frustrated curse. "What does it mean, Kulikov?"

"Both sayings are concerned with religious subjects; the drawings are clues as well. Why else would she draw them?"

"Why indeed. Possibly because she had nothing else to do as she passed the long winter days beating starvation away from her door. Where do you think she was when she drew this picture?"

The limousine was parked at the mouth of the narrow street in front of the commandant's house. The mint building was to their left, the cathedral to the right. Directly ahead of them was the pavilion housing the ship that Peter the Great had made with his own hands. Kulikov pointed at a window on the nearest end of the top floor of the mint.

"There."

"You have checked it out?"

Kulikov squirmed a little. "We're still waiting to get inside the building. They still do work there and allow no visitors—at least during regular hours."

"When?"

"This evening, when we search the rest of the premises, including the cathedral. We have several points of leverage. The director of the mint is having an affair, the woman at the gate needs money for her daughter's education, we . . . "

Zhelin waved his hand in dismissal. "Spare me the details. Our people are here? With the diary still missing, I want this place well guarded. Whoever has it is going to end up here, sooner or later. I want that diary."

"There are twenty-four in all, seven women, seventeen men. They blend in well and will disappear into the woodwork at night. If anyone comes, they won't escape.

"It would help if we knew more about what we were looking for, Georgi. *Treasure* is a pretty broad term."

"You read the pages. The person keeping the diary called it the tsar's treasure—probably some of the things Nicholas II hid up when he saw things were out of control and he was losing power. Russian myth says it was worth millions."

"General Tupolev, then, knew of this story and thought it to be true. He was after this treasure?"

"Possibly, but it seemed more than that, more than greed for money. He has plenty of that. It was almost a desperation." He shrugged. "When we get the rest of the book, possibly it will tell us more. Right now we have more pressing matters that will bring greater returns."

Zhelin watched as several small groups of tourists milled about the courtyard and garden area of the cathedral, their guides directing their attention to points of interest. "Poltav knew to meet us here?"

"He should arrive at any time. I have instructed our people to let him come without interference."

"Dimitri and his wife?"

"Near at hand." Kulikov looked out the window. Nickolai was walking toward the Chaika. Kulikov got out while Zhelin stashed the papers in his briefcase and closed it. After being searched, Nickolai slid into the seat next to Zhelin, and Kulikov got in the front seat next to the driver.

Both men stared at the pavilion through the front window. An old couple stood there, reading the literature, admiring the architecture. To Nickolai the woman looked slightly familiar as the couple moved across the porch and entered the church. But they were just tourists, come to see the past greatness of Russia.

Zhelin pushed the button that closed the window between the front and back seat. It was time to do business.

Rand leaned toward Galya and spoke softly while keeping his eyes on the church ceiling. "You are beautiful, even at seventy."

She poked him lightly. They had gone to the house of a friend of Larissa whom Galya had met her second day in Petersburg. He worked at the Marinsky Ballet—a makeup specialist. Over an hour's time they had been transformed from young to old. For Rand it had been strange to see himself as he would be in another fifty years. If he lived that long.

"Thank goodness it is cool in here. This horrible plastic he used is so hot," Galya said in a low voice.

"Zhelin's people are all over the place. Do you know any German?" Rand asked.

"A little."

"Use it when speaking about the things tourists come to see.

It will add to the mystique of these two old people clinging to one another like young lovers."

Galya glanced at him. "Yes, we are, aren't we."

"Umm, kind of nice. I'm beginning to like the idea of sticking around long enough to see you grow a face like that all by yourself."

She grimaced. "I should hope not! I look awful."

They moved toward the iconostasis at the front of the church. Rand had purchased a Canon camera at one of the foreign shops and paid the extra rubles that allowed him to take pictures inside the cathedral. He began snapping shots from all angles, some with Galya posing, some of the ceiling, the iconostasis, the heavy ornate columns, and some of the marble monuments over the tombs of the tsars.

Peter's was in the corner of the church, on the right side, a bust of the Russian leader sitting atop the sarcophagus. Rand stood at its foot, realizing that the man who had built Petersburg was buried on that spot, a place he had personally selected. He stepped back and took several pictures. Possibly more was buried there than Peter's bones.

Galya took his arm. "We are being watched. Possibly you take too many pictures." She had a worried look on her face.

Rand chuckled like the old man he was playing, then hugged his aged wife, giving her a sturdy kiss on the lips. He spoke in German. "I will find out."

He walked to the woman who seemed to be watching them and spoke to her directly in broken Russian with a German accent. "Tylet? Mya Zhena . . . " He pointed at Galya, who could feel the heat rising in her cheeks. "Ty . . . let?"

The woman couldn't help but grin and point toward a side door.

"Spaceba," Rand said with a German accent, then went back to Galya. They giggled like an old couple on their second honeymoon as they moved to the door where they would find a restroom.

Rustam focused the scope, bringing the crosshairs to bear on Kulikov's forehead. At this distance the shooting would be child's

play. He flipped off the safety, the conversation from the car playing in his earphones. His friend had been right about the high-
powered listening device—the voices were clearer than over the
telephone.

He began the special breathing process, focused on shutting out
the world around him. His finger applied pressure to the trigger.

"Where are Dimitri and my sister?" Nickolai said stiffly.

"Safe. Where is the record book?"

"Zhelin, I'll make you a promise. Harm them, even in the
slightest, and I will personally . . . "

"You are in no position to make threats, Nickolai. I have both
you and Dimitri placed at the scene of a rather horrible crime in
which one of Russia's great war heroes was murdered. I even
have a witness who saw you do it."

"Shelepin."

"Most cooperative. He has already, single-handedly mind
you, dismantled Dimitri Bakatin's business interests and placed
them inside ours."

"He had better hope you win. Dimitri will kill him."

"He has nothing to fear. I *will* win." He paused. "In less than
twelve hours, I will be completely prepared to break the news of
the murder to the press, and you will be this country's most
wanted criminal."

"Unless you get the record book," Nickolai said.

"Of course. It is mine anyway."

"Why did you kill the old man?"

"You saw how close I came to leaving this world. It was too
close. I decided it would be best if he went first. And, I was tired
of waiting. His empire is just beginning to blossom and under my
guidance will be rivaled by none. Even Boris Yeltsin will be
forced to pay homage. My power will determine economic strat-
egy in this country. And in a democratic system, economics is
everything."

"Other businessmen, so called, may dispute your right to

leadership. Tupolev had a unique style and method for capturing their allegiance."

"He used me, and the security ministry I controlled. I still have those reins, will always have them. It is the basis of power right now."

"He gave you those reins and could have taken them from you at any time."

"Another reason to be rid of him." He paused. "You have deciphered the code in the record book?"

"Enough to know that I can stop your dreams from coming true."

"Yes, it is critical that I have access to Tupolev's accounts. Money is everything in business, everything. But you won't fail me, Nickolai, I know that. You are too much of a humanitarian. People's lives are at stake."

"What makes you think I won't come after you once I have Marina and Dimitri where I can protect them?"

"Because I will keep my files on Tupolev's murder. If you don't retire from law enforcement, I will use them."

"Your former boss forced me out of my job once. I don't like the idea of it happening again."

"Then you will be responsible for the death of your sister."

There was a long pause.

"You know that Dimitri intended to do the same thing by using you to get rid of Tupolev," Zhelin said. "I only changed the players a bit."

"Dimitri and I had the same goal in mind. He was motivated by greed; I was pushed by revenge. Both these emotions can be controlled. You, on the other hand, are like Tupolev. You are not just greedy for money and wealth but for power. Nothing is sacred to you, not even Russia. You use your influence to protect the Mafia while trying to overthrow reform and progress. And, worst of all, Georgi, you are a murderer in your heart."

"You flatter me."

"I intend to kill you."

The sweat poured into Rustam's eyes, and the muscles in his arms ached from holding the gun in position. His trigger finger was numb but he couldn't get it to finish the job. He grimaced, trying to force himself to do it. It was only one more kill. What was that to the hundred and four before this? Nothing.

And it was for Natalya.

He ignored the sweat, the ache, tried to get focused again, but now the conversation he had just heard reverberated inside his gray matter. Zhelin had hostages. Other lives were at stake. What was in the record book? One thing was obvious: It could stop Zhelin, end everything for him.

It had shocked him to hear that Vladimir Tupolev was dead. He knew of Tupolev. He was former military, a violent man. Had Zhelin killed him? Why?

He moved his eye away from the scope. Placing the barrel of the rifle on one of the louvres between which it sat, he used his free hand to wipe away the salty sweat flowing into his eyes and making it impossible to see. Then he went back to his shooting stance.

None of it mattered. Tupolev, Zhelin. Even Poltav. None of it. Only Kulikov mattered. Only his wife's murderer.

"Rand King, you are crazy!" Galya whispered as they passed into the hall.

"When I played sports, I was always taught that the best defense is a good offense." He pointed at the door marked "toilet." "Hurry, my love. We have so much more to see."

He played at the souvenir table as he waited. There was some good art work—lacquered boxes, well-done Matryoshka dolls, and even some embroidered blouses of intricate quality. Using rubles, he bought one for Galya, along with several other items the typical tourist might scarf up. When Galya returned, he handed her the blouse, exclaiming his love loudly in German. She played her part well, and they went out by the door to their left.

Georgi stiffened.

"Not now, not next week, maybe not for some time to come," Nickolai said. "I want you to look over your shoulder, to fear me as others have feared you and your personal army of corrupt agents within the KGB. Then, when you are happiest, I will take away what you love most, one item at a time."

"Then I must kill you first."

"It seems so, but first the innocent must be removed from the battlefield. I will give you your record book in exchange for my sister and Dimitri. After that, you are fair game."

Georgi was starting to sweat even though he knew he was safe, that Nickolai could never win such a war against him.

"You cannot win, Nickolai. I have hundreds who can protect me; you will be alone."

"Numbers, Georgi, do not concern me."

There was a long pause.

"Time and place," Nickolai said, watching as the old couple came out of the church to stand in the courtyard and take several pictures.

"Tonight at midnight. Here at the cathedral."

Nickolai pulled on the door handle and started to get out. "It is a place that favors numbers, Zhelin, but make note: I expect you to be standing in the middle of the square, unarmed, for the exchange. Don't send brainless automatons like Kulikov to do your work for you. Second, the book will not appear until Marina and Dimitri are safely away." He stepped out of the car, then turned back. "Let your plans take into consideration that I have forces of my own, and the fortress could turn into a bloodbath if you are not careful. In that case, there will be no winners. And both of us want a winner." He closed the door and started away, then turned back and opened the door next to Kulikov. "You killed an innocent woman for no reason."

Kulikov smiled but said nothing, staring straight ahead.

"No matter what happens to me tonight, or to Zhelin, you, Ivan Kulikov, will suffer a fate worse than death. You I will send to Magadan."

Kulikov's head jerked toward Nickolai, but the door was already shut, and Nickolai was walking away.

Rustam was sitting on the dusty floor, the rifle next to him. Tears made channels across his cheeks and dripped onto his shirt. A low, anguished sound came from between his lips.

He had tried. He had failed. Natalya was still unavenged.

He had changed. He wasn't a killer anymore. The promise was too strong, too ingrained into his system.

He had thought he could fight past it, throw it off like a bad dream, but it was stronger. It clutched his heart, like a man's fist!

He pulled his knees up to his chin and lay his head on them. The tears turned into sobs, the pain of losing Natalya hitting him in the gut like a sledgehammer. Then came the remorse, hard, relentless, making his head ache from the pit of his neck to the front of his forehead.

It would be long hours before the tears would stop and the pain subside. Then Rustam would roll onto his side, exhausted, his mind a blank. He would feel empty and alone, and he would want to sleep.

And he would sleep until midnight.

Galya and Rand moved along the south side of the cathedral toward Peter's Gate, stopping at one of the tourist kiosks so that Rand could check if anyone was following. He didn't think so, but the place must be riddled with Bakatin's men.

They passed through Peter's Gate, trying to act like old people out for a look at the sights, stopping to notice things of interest, take another picture, then move on. When they walked under John's Gate and down the bridge crossing the moat, Rand began to breath easier. As they crossed Kirovsky Prospekt, Rand saw the woman from the church a hundred yards behind them.

"We have a tail," he said. Galya stiffened. "Uh-uh, it's critical we don't panic. See the ice-cream stand? Let's get some, shall we?"

The ice cream was a square on a stick covered in chocolate

and topped with nuts. That was one thing about Russia—the place could be going to hades in a handbasket, but there would still be ice cream. Rand gave Galya one, then took her hand and walked into the park that bordered Kirovsky. The woman followed.

"Do we go to where Sasha waits with the car or head for the metro?" Galya asked.

"Neither. We are old, rich tourists. We take a cab." They meandered a bit farther, then started toward the street. As Rand watched for a cab, he lost track of the tail. Suddenly she was behind Galya, moving quickly, reaching for the gray wig that to Rand had looked so natural. Before he could yell, before he could make a move, Galya had swung around and jammed the ice cream into the woman's face and eyes, pushing, rubbing hard. Then an uppercut to the chin sent the woman reeling backward. She hit a bench and went down with a thud that made the dust rise. She didn't get up.

Two young people on the walk nearby stopped, their mouths open.

Galya looked at them, pulling up the sleeves of her sweater, then adjusted the purse that hung over her shoulder. Turning, she walked to Rand's side as a car pulled to the curb.

Galya was stunned. "Nickolai!"

"Get in, *Mother.*" Nickolai smiled.

Rand opened the door, stepped back, and let Galya slide in, then joined her. As they pulled away, all three waved at the two young people, who were still picking their chins up off the ground.

"They will have more respect for their grandmothers after that, don't you think?" Galya said, smiling.

Rand and Nickolai laughed lightly. Nickolai shifted and moved farther into traffic. Rand offered Galya a taste of his own treat. She licked it, then used her lips to bite off a corner.

"You are a lovely lady, Galya Starkova—especially well preserved for a woman of your age."

She slugged him in the arm, then pulled it close. "Nickolai, is Larissa all right?"

"Fine. We shall see her soon."

"And Rustam. Has anyone heard from him?"

"No, nothing. Possibly he is in the country. Larissa says he has a small place there, just a garden plot. He may have gone there to be alone."

"Nickolai Poltav. I've heard a lot about you," Rand said.

"And I about you, Mr. King, from the same source." He glanced at Galya through the rearview mirror. "What were you doing at the cathedral?"

Rand told him. Nickolai's brow wrinkled. Galya then enlightened him about their visit with the chief of intelligence for the White Guard, Volodya Vilechenko.

"A complicated web," Nickolai said. "I never would have suspected Vilechenko to be a part of such an organization. He is the curator for the Hermitage and other sights in Petrodvorets and Pushkin. The Palaces."

"Saving them for a future ruler," Rand said. "Let me make it worse for you. Samuel Andrews is in town. He wants to see me."

"The man who put together ALLIANCE?"

"One and the same. It seems he has a personal interest."

"When are you meeting with him?"

"According to the message I received the last time I checked in, he's fit to be tied, but he'll keep until tomorrow morning."

Nickolai filled them in on events with him and Larissa since parting ways with them at Rikki's apartment. Then he told them about his meeting with Zhelin and about the exchange that was to take place at the fortress.

"Why the fortress?" Galya asked.

"Zhelin wants to keep an eye on things," Rand said. "He has copies of the pictures and the riddles and will probably begin a search for the vault tonight."

"I saw many of his people while I was there," Nickolai said.

"Yeah, we got pictures," Rand said. "Drop us at our car, Nickolai. I want to get the photos developed. It will help in planning your return to meet Zhelin tonight while giving us a chance to figure out the diary's riddle. I'll give you the address, and you can meet us there later after picking up Larissa. We have work to do."

Chapter Twenty-nine

THE ROOM WAS A DUNGEON, tucked into the corner of a basement with no windows. The concrete was covered with mildew and smelled like sewage. Sasha sat on an old wooden chair, propped against the wall near the forty-watt light bulb. He was trying to read an American photography magazine.

Rand glanced at the door, which supposedly led to a dark-room. He was still wearing the makeup, and it was beginning to itch. If he scratched it, it peeled. If he didn't, it drove him crazy. He was nearly insane.

"You are sure about this guy?" he asked Sasha. "He won't ruin the film?"

Sasha nodded, still concentrating on the magazine. Finally he raised his eyebrows, sighed, and tossed the magazine to Rand.

"Busy yourself, my American friend. Entertain your worried mind. I can't read your horrible language very well anyway. He will be through shortly, and your photos will be perfect."

Rand glanced at some of the pictures as he thumbed through the magazine, but his mind wasn't on them. He lifted his arm so the light from the bulb hit the face of his watch. It was 5:30 P.M. What was taking Nickolai and Larissa so long?

Galya came through a low door to Rand's right, returning from a visit to the powder room in the apartment one floor up. She turned up her nose at the smell. Rand wondered how she could make old clothes, warts, and wrinkles look so good.

"Whew!" she said. "It is worse here than in his bathroom."

"Is that a surprise?" Rand asked.

"You should see his bathroom." She turned to Sasha. "Your friend lives like a pig, Sasha. How does he stand it?"

"He is seldom there. He is a freelance photographer, and he travels a lot—especially now that foreign magazines and travel agencies want pictures for their publications." He shrugged. "Feodor, or Freddy as we call him, isn't so bad—except when he is drunk."

The door across the room opened, and Freddy stepped out. He tossed the glossies into the middle of the beat-up table, then wiped his still-damp hands on his greasy pants. Rand removed his wallet and paid the agreed-upon price of thirty thousand rubles, about twenty-five dollars. Freddy wadded it up and shoved it into his pocket.

Galya and Rand picked up the photos and began exploring their content.

"Do you have a magnifying glass?" Rand asked Freddy.

The photographer went into his workroom and brought out a funny-looking table with a piece of glass suspended over it by means of an iron post.

"The glass is magnifying. Adjust with this." He twisted a handle on the post.

Rand put the first picture on the flat surface and adjusted the glass. Freddy, garlic breath and all, hovered over his right shoulder. Sasha and Galya leaned over the glass from each side.

"See anything?" Galya asked.

Rand shook his head. "Nothing revealing."

He handed Sasha a twenty. "Freddy's been working hard. Take him and find some dinner or something, will you?"

Sasha looked at a smiling Feodor. Then they left.

Rand rummaged through the pictures until he found the enlargements of the limousine. Shoving them under the glass, they looked carefully at the faces.

"Zhelin doesn't look too happy. Nor Kulikov," Rand said. He looked at the rest of the pictures without the glass, quickly picking out others he thought were Zhelin's people, pointing at them while counting.

"At least a dozen people. If we go back inside that place, it could be suicide," he said.

"He'll have many more there when he meets with Nickolai," Galya said.

They started a more careful investigation of the interior shots of the church, the riddles in the diary turning over in their minds. High ground. Between the Savior and the tsar. They looked until their eyes ached. Thirty minutes passed.

Galya walked away rubbing her forehead, then came back. "It is driving me crazy, Rand. Something is here, I know it, but I just can't put my finger on it!"

"I know what you mean." Rand took his reading glasses off and rubbed his eyes. Leaning forward, he took a last look at the photos, then placed them all in a neat stack and picked them up. "Let's leave it until morning. A fresh look."

"But Zhelin will search the cathedral tonight. If we delay . . . "

"The place has been remodeled, visited, cleaned for more than fifty years. No one has hit upon a treasure yet."

"But Zhelin has the clues."

"And at least a dozen people on the grounds just waiting for us to barge in. It isn't worth our lives, Galya." He pointed at her bag. She handed it to him, and he put the photos inside.

Galya was scratching lightly at her plastic nose. "Can we remove this? It is most annoying."

Rand reached out and plucked the nose out of its place to expose her own. Little by little he peeled away the old woman's face to reveal Galya's rose-smooth cheeks. Removing a handkerchief from his pocket, he wiped away the brown makeup that hung to the edges of her hair, his free hand holding her chin.

Her eyes fastened to his, and she used her soft fingers to peel away the plastic that gave his face wrinkles and changed the firm cheekbones and square jaw to the sagging flesh of a man twice his age. Taking the hanky, she cleaned the excess from around his nose and eyes.

He lifted the wig and mussed her brown hair. It fell to her shoulders and onto her forehead. His fingers gently held some of the silky strands and slipped downward, a finger rubbing gently against her ear, then a soft cheek. "This must be what it's like in the resurrection—the old for the new, the wrinkled and worn for the soft and smooth."

"You believe such things?"

He gripped her chin and lowered his lips onto hers. Her response was to press herself gently to him, her arms slipping around his waist and her fingers pulling gently into the muscles of his back.

Her lips were soft, inviting. He pulled her closer, the kiss lingering.

Gradually they pulled back, her head going to his shoulder. Her hair smelled of a light perfume, and his hands came onto her shoulders and then the back of her neck. He leaned back, kissing her forehead, the tip of her nose, then her lips again, his hands on the sides of her face. As their lips gently released, his eyes sought hers. The long lashes rose, and he could see the dark brown of her eyes. As she closed them again, he kissed first the right, then the left. She placed her head on his shoulder, pulling him to her.

The sound of the others coming down the stairs pushed them apart, her fingers lingering on his sides, then going to his hands. He held them tightly for the briefest of moments; then they busied themselves with gathering everything. Except for the blush in their cheeks and the look in their eyes, everything was back to normal when Sasha entered the room. Behind him were Nickolai and Larissa.

The two women hugged each other tightly, relieved, happy that the other was safe.

"Where is Freddy?" Rand asked.

"Eating away the rest of your money."

"You're trusting KGB now, Rand King?" Nickolai asked, eyeing Sasha.

"Only the smart ones," Rand replied.

The five of them climbed the stairs to Freddy's apartment. After throwing Freddy's stinking old clothes into the bedroom and clearing empty beer cans and vodka bottles away, they had a relatively decent environment in which to sit. Larissa and Galya placed the pictures on the floor and began going over them again as Galya told her friend about the revelations of the diary.

Before Sasha could seat himself, Rand handed him another twenty and told him to get groceries. Sasha was miffed until Nickolai glared him into submission.

"He doesn't feel that I trust him," Rand said as the door closed behind Sasha.

"Do you trust him?"

"Not completely."

"We can't take any chances. You did the right thing."

Nickolai lifted the record book from a waterproof case he had purchased—Rand didn't ask why.

Nickolai set it in front of them and opened it to the first page. "These are the banks." He pointed at a list on the inside cover. Rand looked. The bank names were clearly written by the actual account numbers, which were coded using symbols.

"Tupolev's ill-gotten gains?" Rand asked.

"Over fifty years of stealing from the Russian people—all in easily transferable American dollars."

They looked at the other pages.

The first column contained the date of each transaction, the second the place. The third and fourth columns were coded, but Rand could tell what they were.

"It looks to me like this column, the one with lots of symbols"—he pointed to the third—"details the transactions. The last column is the amount paid or received."

He turned page after page. The figure column was a series of symbols, each symbol representing a single number. Some of the lines were between five and seven figures long. There were a surprising number of these between the years 1941 and 1953.

"The man made millions from the war," Rand said.

"Probably selling Russian secrets, troop movements. Possibly he stole from the Russian military and sold weapons to foreign countries. It was a wide-open market in those days," Nickolai said.

"One of our computers at CID would pick this code apart in a few hours," Rand finished.

"CID. Impressive," Nickolai said.

Rand nodded. "I used to head its anti-terrorist section."

Nickolai smiled. "This is where you learned the ways of the spy."

Rand laughed. "If our spies were as ignorant in such things as I am, we would have lost the cold war."

"Did you win it?"

"A point well made. There were no winners, were there."

"Just arms dealers, warlords, politicians, and bankers," Nickolai said. "I have made copies of everything. Once we are through with Zhelin, we can send the information to CID."

"I intend to give this book to Zhelin tonight, but I want the accounts to be empty. Can your CID break them in the few hours we have left?"

Rand wasn't sure but reached for the phone. He could call in the information and at least give them a chance.

While Nickolai stooped down to take a look at the photographs, Rand gave the information CID needed to begin breaking the code. After this was finished, he joined Nickolai, who had gone out to the balcony while Rand was on the phone.

They stood watching the street through the thick trees.

"I don't think you came out here to get fresh air. What's wrong?" Rand asked.

"Larissa must be sent to safety, and Galya also."

"Galya won't go, and if they are as much alike as I think they are, Larissa won't either."

Nickolai smiled. "You're probably right. But they are not to come to the fortress."

Rand agreed but didn't answer.

"If we can decipher Tupolev's codes, I want all of the money put into an account in the United States," Nickolai said.

"You have one, I suppose."

"No, but you must."

"You are making me a happy man," Rand said.

"I am depending on your honesty to return the money to Russia when this is finished," Nickolai said.

"Poor deluded fool."

"But part I want retained and given to Larissa. I also want you to help her immigrate to your country and work in the ballet there, even if it is only to teach children. Because of her past, she will never have a chance to do it here. Such ability should be shared with the next generation."

"You talk like you won't be around to take care of this yourself. That's foolish, Nickolai."

Nickolai didn't answer.

"I understand your wishes. If anything happens to you, I will see that they are carried out. But nothing is going to happen," Rand said.

Nickolai shrugged. "Peace of mind, Rand King. In our line of work it is a very good thing."

"Have you worked out what you want to do tonight? Zhelin will try to kill us."

"I have. But I cannot ask you to go."

"I am not waiting for an invitation. Just be warned: If your plan stinks, I'll stay here with the ladies."

Nickolai laughed. They began a discussion. It was a bold plan, but Rand could see one important thing—Nickolai was placing himself in extreme, even fatal danger. He thought about it as Nickolai finished his run-through, then offered a couple of changes that would give their smaller numbers at least a fair chance. Nickolai agreed. They worked out the materials they needed and how to get them. By the time they were finished, Rand had a pretty good idea of why Nickolai was looking for insurance. Everyone had a reasonable degree of chance for survival but him.

"We need more people," Rand said. "Three isn't enough."

"An army would only start a war. This is between Zhelin and me. I do not want a bloodbath."

"Your chances aren't good."

"Better than Zhelin's."

They were finishing preparations and phone calls for equipment when Sasha came back with the food. The women started making some sausage and cheese open-faced sandwiches and preparing herb tea. Rand told Sasha the part of the plan he needed to know, then sent him away with a sandwich and some orders. He would meet them at a prearranged place at eleven o'clock.

They sat down to supper with the women and discussed everything from American and Russian literature to Western-style line dancing and ballet. They stayed clear of the diary, politics, and Georgi Zhelin, afraid such topics might ruin their digestion. Nobody wanted to think about dying.

After eating, Rand and Nickolai began reading Tupolev's file on the White Guard. It was well documented and helped Rand piece together more parts of the puzzle that were banging around in his head like loose rocks. Before he knew it, the clock was hitting ten.

It was time to go.

Chapter Thirty

RAND AND SASHA BALANCED THEMSELVES on the small walkway of the fishing ship Sasha had hired, waiting for the signal to enter the waters of the Neva. They would pass by the west end of Fortress Island any minute, enter the water in scuba gear, then swim to the island itself, invisible to Zhelin's men atop the fortress walls.

Rand pulled his mask into place and checked the breathing device. The signal came from the captain, and he grabbed Sasha's arm and pulled him off the walkway. When they hit the water, both used their fins to drive themselves deep into the Neva's blue-brown waters and begin the swim to shore. Rand was dragging a waterproof pack containing weapons and climbing gear; Sasha just worked hard to keep up. He had never been in scuba gear before, and their fifteen-minute crash course before leaving the docks had not consoled him much. Rand smiled at his new associate's bulging, frightened eyes behind the plastic shield of his mask as they searched for the rocky embankment ahead of them.

It had been some time since Rand had been underwater. His flesh was chilled even in the wet suit, and his muscles felt stiff. The current thickened as they neared the shore, and he had to push with his feet for all he was worth to cover the last twenty feet.

They came up a little north of their intended spot, but the trees still blocked any view Zhelin's men might have from the walls of the fortress.

In fact, they had selected this approach because a small park and the outer walls of Alexeyevsky Ravelin separated them from the fortress proper. It also gave them better access to Trubetskoi Bastion, where Marina and Dimitri Bakatin were being kept.

Sasha had met them at the appointed time with good news. He had called in to Kulikov to make his excuse for not being at the fortress with Zhelin's forces—his mother was sick and in the hospital. It was a truth of sorts. She had gone there at his request to cover his backside—Kulikov had told him he had prisoners housed in the Bastion and was very upset that his best man wasn't available to take care of things. Rand had decided Sasha's story might be a bit of an exaggeration, but it was evident that the Bakatins were inside the fortress at Trubetskoi Bastion, the old prison the tsars had used to put away revolutionaries.

Discarding their air tanks, Rand and Sasha threw their equipment onto shore, climbed from the cold water, and slipped into the cover of heavy shrubbery. Changing out of their wet suits and into camouflaged fatigues, they moved through the trees until they were against the fortress wall. Working their way toward the main branch of the Neva, they came to a point where Trubetskoi Bastion stood a hundred feet from its banks.

Rand looked west. He could see Dvortsovy Bridge, its mid-section lifted high in the air making way for late-night boat traffic, the amber glint of white nights cascading across the river's surface. It was a beautiful sight. In the trees Sasha positioned himself to watch the walls while Rand removed his equipment.

Rand put his rifle over his shoulder by use of the strap, then picked up the grappling hook attached to the rope. Except for the very tips, the hooks were heavily coated with plastic to reduce the clatter of metal against rock. The other end he tied firmly to a tree. Once it was ready, he started swinging the hook in a circular motion, watching Sasha for the signal to move into the open and throw it.

Sasha had removed the sniper's rifle and positioned it for firing. The crosshairs were on the forehead of one of Zhelin's guards as he stood on the top of the fortress wall a hundred yards to the left of where Rand was hidden in the trees. For the bullet to do its deadly job, Sasha had to allow for distance, wind, and the hindrance of the silencer attached to the barrel. He prayed the guard wouldn't turn and face them at the wrong moment. He knew the man by name. They had both worked for the KGB for five years. Their children went to the same schools.

Sasha raised a single finger as a signal, and Rand moved into the clearing and launched the hook over the wall. He heard the light sound of metal as it popped against the far wall and jerked on the rope. It held. Quickly he climbed the wall until he reached the top edge. Peering over, he made sure the guard was looking away. Then he scrambled across the top of the wall, pulling the rope with him. As it tightened against the tree, he threw himself over the opposite wall and lowered himself into the inner courtyard of the bastion. Firmly attaching the grappling hook, he threw a small stone back to where he had come from as a signal that Sasha should now count to fifty, then follow.

Rand moved to where he could see the guard along the wall, then removed his rifle. It was his turn to protect Sasha.

As he lifted the rifle to his shoulder, he noticed the dial on his watch. It was time for Nickolai to enter Peter's Gate.

Nickolai checked the time, waiting until the second hand was at the twelve. Then he got out of the car and began the walk through Peter's Gate and into the fortress proper. He was wishing Vostya was with him, but his best lieutenant was still in the hospital. He was better but incapacitated.

There were guards on both sides of the gate who stopped, then searched him. When they tried to take Nickolai's weapons, he refused. The man in charge had a radio and called Zhelin, then handed it to Nickolai.

"Leave your weapon, Poltav," Zhelin told him.

"When your people are off the walls and outside the fortress, Zhelin, not before."

"You have the record book."

"It is available but not in my possession."

There was a pause. "Come ahead."

Nickolai started down the road, passing first the old artillery arsenal, then striding alongside the south side of the cathedral. He glanced between the buildings at the outside walls of the fortress. Zhelin's men were strategically placed, but there weren't as many as Nickolai had thought there would be. Some wore street clothes, some were dressed in the camouflaged uniform of the military— probably members of the personal guard it was rumored Vladimir Tupolev had been training for his own protection. They would be tough, hardened killers, deadly.

He wondered where King was. He hardly knew the man, or his skills. And Sasha Zagladin—he knew him not at all. But the plan didn't rely on them. Even if King failed to get to Dimitri and Marina, Nickolai had no intention of giving Zhelin the record book until his brother-in-law and sister were free and clear, and Rand and Sasha had at least a chance of escape. After that, numbers would make no difference.

Nickolai had no delusions. His chances of surviving were slim to none. To free Dimitri and Marina, he would have to deliver the record book to Zhelin. Zhelin was a pragmatist. He knew his days were numbered if Nickolai Poltav lived to see breakfast. One of them would have to die. Three against thirty did not give Nickolai much of a chance. Nickolai's only wish was that Zhelin's blood would flow onto the cobblestones next to his. Then maybe his death would mean something.

As he came into the square, he thought about Larissa, and a sudden wave of regret washed over him. For longer than he could remember he had been alone, only his desire to avenge his wife's death keeping him from committing suicide. Now that Tupolev was dead, the victory seemed empty, the years wasted. But he could have a good life with Larissa Vavilova. They could be happy again, and he could make up for so many years of bitterness. But it wasn't to be. Georgi Zhelin stood in the way.

He saw the black Chaika parked in the square, with Zhelin by its side. He had a sudden desire to turn and run. Instead, he quickened his pace. Soon it would be over.

Rand kept the rifle's sights on the guard while Sasha removed the grappling hook and threw it back across the wall and into the far trees. They both gave a silent prayer of thanks that the young guard had been sleepy and unaware of their movements. It had kept them from killing him.

They kept themselves in the deep shadows next to the wall, moving toward the door that led from the courtyard into the main hall of the old prison. Just as they were ready to go for the opening and get inside, a man shoved the door open and came out, stretching, filling his lungs with fresh air. Rand shrank against the wall while Sasha tried to burrow into the ground behind a stand of weeds.

The guard was dressed in a military camouflage uniform with a matching duck-billed hat that shaded his eyes from view. This was a member of Tupolev's elite attack group, a man not to be trifled with. Rand worked on the problem: How to eliminate without being eliminated.

The soldier removed a pack of cigarettes from his pocket and searched it for a smoke. Removing the last one from the pack, he crumpled and tossed the remains into the weeds. Lighting the cigarette, he sat on an old piece of concrete fountain and puffed away. Rand looked at his watch. They were running out of time.

Without warning Sasha hopped up, crossed the twenty feet, and hammered the guard on the back of the skull, sending him immediately to la-la land. Rand joined him as Sasha stripped the unconscious man of his uniform.

"Him I didn't like. It was a pleasure to dent his hard skull."

Rand put on the coat and hat. Opening the door, they went inside.

The long hallway went both right and left. It was empty. Sasha believed that the Bakatins were being kept nearer the front of the Bastion. Quickly they ran down the dark hall to the corner. Peering left, he could see two guards near one of the cell doors.

"I know them both," Sasha said. "They will recognize me, and I can make excuses for my presence until we get close enough to use the pellets. You take the one on the right."

Rand nodded. They removed their handguns and loaded them with a single shot of special ammunition. Stun pellets, when fired at close range into the chest of a man, would knock the wind out of him sufficiently to incapacitate. The trouble was, the type of load they were using didn't allow for accuracy over long distance, nor could they be used in automatic weapons. But Rand and Sasha had decided to use them whenever possible because Sasha didn't like the idea of killing his friends and leaving their children without fathers. Neither did Rand.

Removing his rifle, Rand stowed it against the wall. He wouldn't need it now; only Sasha kept his second weapon.

Taking a deep breath, Rand lowered his head slightly, allowing the cap to shade his face. The handgun at his side, he stepped into the hall alongside Sasha. The two guards were busy having a laugh and didn't notice them at first, but they needed another ten steps to be in optimum position for the pellets to do their work.

"Sasha!" one of the guards said with apparent good feeling. "Where have you been? What are you doing here?"

It occurred to Rand that this was another time for Sasha to betray him—a perfect opportunity. He shoved it aside. Sasha had proven himself.

"Good morning, Alosha!" Sasha said. "Kulikov sent me for the prisoners. Zhelin wants them."

The two men looked at each other, confused, then back to Sasha. Five feet more. Just five.

"But Comrade Kulikov just left with . . . "

The man lifted his gun, suddenly wary. Rand aimed the pistol and fired. The pellet slammed into the startled guard's chest and knocked him across the table behind him. Sasha's pellet drove the other one into the wall. He melted to the floor, gasping for air.

"Forgive me, Alosha. You will be very sore for a few days, but be thankful. You are not dead." He turned to Rand. "You must try to catch Kulikov. I will tie them up, then go to my position. Go!"

Rand exited the front of the Bastion and peered around the corner into the street. He saw Kulikov fifty feet away, the

Bakatins ahead of him. Half a dozen guards lined the street toward the far end. He had to move quickly.

He stepped into the narrow street, his heart thundering in his chest. Above him on the wall he sensed motion. Another guard. Probably watching him. The disguise should hold. He kept walking, trying not to look in too big of a hurry but still closing the distance.

Fifty-five feet separated them. Fifty. A sudden thought occurred. He had not reloaded. His gun was empty. To load now would be dangerous, a sign of aggression that might reveal who he was. To leave it empty left him defenseless. He had never felt so naked in his life.

Nickolai stood two steps away from Zhelin.

"Nickolai," Zhelin said confidently. "The record book, where is it?"

"Coming. Where are my sister and Dimitri?"

Zhelin looked down the street that led to Trubetskoi Bastion. The street turned at a right angle to the west some two hundred feet away. A guard stood there, saw Zhelin's look, and glanced down the portion of the street he could see from his position. He waved.

"Also coming."

The sound of a chopper overhead forced Zhelin to look skyward. He raised his hand toward three of his men in uniform atop the south wall. One raised a ground-to-air missile pod and prepared to fire.

"If you want the record book in one piece, I suggest you allow the chopper free flight. It is a commercial bird, not armed," Nickolai said.

Zhelin raised his hand again and waved it. The soldier put the missile down. The chopper hovered high above, the sound of its blades filling the square. Nickolai and Zhelin both looked toward the street to the bastion at the same time. Marina and Dimitri were just turning the corner.

Sasha came into the street and went left, keeping to the shadows, watching for guards. The street here was narrow, the buildings tall. He was glad he had switched clothes with Alosha. Running, he soon came to the door he wanted. It was locked. He loaded his handgun, screwed on a silencer, and fired at the lock. The crack of the gun was muffled but in the narrow street sounded like a clap of thunder to Sasha. He jerked open the door and went inside, closing it, hoping he hadn't been noticed. The stairway was to his left. He started up, the gun ready.

He removed a small two-way radio from his pocket and turned it on to contact the chopper overhead. "Bluebird, this is Assault Two. I am about to exit onto the roof, northwest end of the mint. Will I have opposition?"

"Affirmative, Assault Two. Two men. Rifles aimed at us."

"Bluebird," Sasha said, "where is Assault One?"

"I'm not sure. From our position we can't see, but he didn't get to the Bakatins in time. They are approaching the square."

Sasha was sweating. He had no choice now. He had to get into position where he could protect Nickolai. Without King in place to protect the Bakatins, he was the only chance. What had he gotten himself into? Was he on the wrong side? Again? It didn't matter. He was committed. Zhelin would kill him for his betrayal or he would die in battle. He preferred battle.

He reached the door to the roof. Slowly he opened it, then slipped out. The first man was squatting behind a chimney, his gun on the chopper, eye in the scope. Sasha put the pistol against his skull and told him to drop the gun. The blades of the chopper were deafening. The wind, even though still a hundred feet above them, kept the words from reaching the young man's ears. He jerked around in an effort to put his gun on Sasha. Sasha slammed a fist to the side of his face and knocked him unconscious.

Sasha didn't hear the bullet, only felt it as it grazed his arm and knocked him off balance. He fell next to the other man, grabbing his wound as the second soldier ran to him and placed the silenced, automatic sniper rifle between his eyes.

For Sasha, the battle seemed to be over.

Rand shoved the pistol deeper into Kulikov's back, making the big man wince. They were approaching the square, had passed a dozen guards, and he was still alive. There had to be a supreme being.

"You have done well, Kulikov. Don't mess up now," he said in fluent Russian.

"You won't get away, King. I will personally break you in half," Kulikov said.

"Oh, and we've had such a good time these past few days. You just do as you're told or you'll be coughing up the remains of the bullets in this gun." Interesting thought, Rand said to himself, considering I haven't got any bullets in this gun.

Rand noticed that Zhelin's men were moving into the square after them, sealing it off from any visit by forces from the outside. He counted a dozen men but knew there were more on the walls and near the gates. Nickolai had been right—bringing more forces would have led to a bloodbath. The odds were miserable and getting worse. Getting to the Bastion late had thrown everything off.

Zhelin had no intention of letting the Bakatins or Nickolai leave the fortress alive. Rand and Nickolai both knew that. Zhelin had no choice. His trumped-up charges accusing the two of Tupolev's murder wouldn't stand up under scrutiny, especially if Nickolai got hold of Zhelin's chief witness to the event, Aleksei Shelepin. Of course, Zhelin could have coerced a signed paper from Shelepin stating he had seen the murder, then dispatched him beyond death's door where Nickolai couldn't get at him to discredit his story. But Rand figured Zhelin needed Shelepin alive, at least for a while. According to Nickolai, Shelepin still had to complete the transfer of Dimitri Bakatin's operations into Zhelin's newly inherited empire. Now was no time to kill him. As Nickolai and Rand saw it, that left Zhelin with only one option— elimination of the only other people who knew the truth, Dimitri Bakatin and Nickolai Poltav. From the looks of things, Zhelin might pull it off.

"Dimitri, Marina, stop at this end of the car," Rand said. "No closer. When I tell you, I want you to get into the vehicle and get out of here."

"But—"

"My assignment was to get you out of harm's way. I didn't get to you in time at the Bastion, so we have to improvise. Not only your survival but ours depends on it. No arguments!"

Bakatin nodded slightly, Marina's head turned a little so as to hear. They had been troopers. When Rand had stuck the gun into Kulikov's back and told them of his presence, they had kept their cool. It had been a critical moment.

Rand glanced up at the roof of the mint but saw nothing. Where was Sasha? They needed him on that roof now more than ever. Their chance of survival was dimming, and without him it would be nil.

Originally Sasha was to be there, the crosshairs of his scope on Zhelin's skull in case he took violent exception to Nickolai's renegotiation of terms once Zhelin discovered his hostages had been spirited away by Rand. Although Zhelin's death would bring a sudden, violent reaction from his little army, it would at least give Nickolai a chance to take cover and even escape by use of the chopper hovering above the square.

But that had all changed now. Now Sasha would need to protect them all. Rand felt the trickle of sweat drip down the side of his face.

They reached the end of the Chaika. The chopper was high enough off the ground that it didn't prevent communication but low enough to make them want to stoop. Rand overcame the impulse.

Bakatin did as Rand instructed and stopped when he reached the Chaika.

"Closer, Kulikov," Zhelin said, his eyes still on Nickolai.

"This is close enough," Rand said loud enough that he was sure he had been heard above the thunder of the chopper.

Zhelin's head jerked in Rand's direction. "You ... How ... ?"

"Hows take so long to explain. Let's just have a nice peaceful solution to this and all go home and get some sleep."

Nickolai seemed a bit relieved to see that the soldier he

thought was going to complicate his life was really a friend. He removed two radios from his pocket. "The chopper will deliver the package only when Dimitri and Marina are away from here," Nickolai shouted at Zhelin.

Zhelin's lips were drawn tightly across his teeth. Rand could tell he was angry, his mind working out a way to regain the upper hand. "Only Marina goes. Dimitri stays."

"Not a chance," Rand said quickly.

Dimitri spoke. "I'll stay. Just get Marina out of here."

Nickolai knew that was what Zhelin wanted; if they complied, they would all be dead. "You go, Dimitri." Nickolai handed his brother-in-law one of the radios. "Get into the Chaika with Marina and get her out of here. When you are safe, radio back to us. If you don't, he can kill all of us. Go."

Dimitri opened the door. Zhelin spoke. "If I raise my arm, my men will kill you now. Dimitri stays."

"If you raise your arm," Rand said, moving his pistol to the side of Kulikov so that it was pointed directly at Zhelin's lower midsection, "I'll kill you. And remember, Zhelin, I have nothing to lose."

Zhelin's cold eyes stared into Rand's, looking for some sign of weakness, but they found none.

"Get into the car, Dimitri," Rand said.

This time Zhelin didn't protest. Marina eased into the driver's seat, and Dimitri handed her the radio.

"Go, Marina. You know how to drive and can use the radio. Go!" He closed the door, cutting off her protest.

"What are you doing, Dimitri?" Nickolai protested. "Get into the car! With you gone we have a chance."

Bakatin waved harshly at Marina. With fear in her eyes, she started the car and put it into gear. The Chaika moved across the square, Zhelin's men opening their cordon to let it through.

"You are a fool, Dimitri Bakatin!" Nickolai said loud enough to be heard above the chopper. "You have killed us all."

"Leaving here will save only my life, not yours, Nickolai. Do you think for a moment that my being out there will change anything that happens here, to you? If you do, *you* are the fool. I stay." As inconspicuously as he could, he reached inside Kulikov's coat and removed his weapon, preparing it for firing by flicking off the safety. He pointed it at Zhelin. "You wear a bulletproof vest, but I will put my shot between your eyes if any part of you so much as twitches," he said firmly.

All of them watched as the Chaika disappeared through Peter's Gate. No one spoke. Nickolai put the small radio to his ear, waiting for word from Marina. It seemed like forever before the radio crackled to life.

"Marina?"

"Yes, brother. I am on Kirovsky Bridge."

"Are you being followed?"

"Yes, a white Volga, it . . . it has a blue cloth tied to the radio antenna. Two women."

"Pull over and go with them. They are friends and will make sure you get to safety." He changed frequencies. "Larissa, do you have Marina?"

"She is pulling over now."

"Are others following you?"

"No, no one."

Nickolai looked toward the chopper as he changed frequencies again. "Go. You are finished here." The chopper dipped, then moved away, disappearing on the far side of the cathedral. The square became quiet enough to hear the scuff of a boot on stone.

Nickolai put the radio away but left his hand in his jacket pocket. Rand knew it was wrapped around the butt of a pistol. Against the men and weapons that circled around them, the three pistols they held were like peashooters. Rand wondered how his mother would react when she received notice: "Dear Mr. and Mrs. King, we regret to inform you . . . "

He shook off the thought, his eyes wandering over the square. All eyes were on them, guns ready. One miscalculation and the whole place would erupt—not a happy thought when you couldn't shoot back. His mind went to the clip in his back pocket. He wondered if he could get it loaded, ready to fire before he was thoroughly dead.

Zhelin's face was shaped by a cruel grin. "I assume the chopper was here for other purposes, that the record book was not on board."

No one gave him an answer.

"Our lives for the record book," Nickolai said. "The deal hasn't changed."

"And if I refuse?"

"You have only one guarantee: The three of us will all shoot you. After that, you will not know if we live or die, or if your men really will die for you. The chances are they won't."

"Look, Zhelin," Rand said. "Everyone here wants to live to see another day. A little cooperation, and we all leave here under our own power. That will make everyone happy. Tell your men it's over. Then we can make a deal for the record book."

Zhelin's smile was not a picture of cooperation.

As the chopper moved away, Sasha smiled up at the man who had just put a bullet through the fleshy part of his arm. "Hello, Ivan."

"Sasha! What . . . " He looked at the unconscious man lying next to Sasha. "Why did you hit him? What is going on?"

Sasha tried to get up, and the gunman let him, still unsure.

"Give me the gun, Ivan."

"Why . . . I don't understand."

"You and I have known each other a long time. Zhelin is wrong in this. I work for Nickolai Poltav. Join us."

The man hesitated, anger, frustration, and instability all crossing his face in quick succession. "I work for Zhelin." He waved the gun toward the front of the building. "Move."

Sasha glanced at the gun. Ivan's hand rested firmly against the trigger. To grab it would be foolish, a quick death. He started walking. Nickolai was on his own.

Zhelin looked at Rand, then at the others. "Do not fool yourself, Nickolai. These men will kill you whether I am dead or not.

They will do it not because of love for me, but because they love to see another man's blood."

"Then no one wins," Nickolai said.

"You win if I let you leave," Zhelin said. "I would rather die here, now, than wait for you to come for me later. And you will come, won't you," Zhelin said.

Nickolai didn't answer, but Rand knew Zhelin was right. He didn't like what that meant. Zhelin was trapped with no future, no reason to live beyond the next few minutes. That did not bode well for the rest of them. Rand studied both their faces. Neither was about to back down.

Zhelin spoke. "I am not a fool, Nickolai. You know that. My background should have told you that I would plan for this contingency."

Rand felt his mouth go dry, his heartbeat move from fast to furious. What could the man do that would possibly save his life from three shots fired at the same time from three different individuals? Well, two shots—his gun was still unloaded.

"You will never get the record book," Nickolai said. Rand was amazed at how calm his new friend was. Not a single bead of sweat showed anywhere.

Zhelin shrugged. "A casualty of unfortunate circumstances. If I let you live, I lose everything, not just Tupolev's money. Which would you choose?"

"Don't do it, Zhelin. You will get us all killed," Rand said, realizing that the man was about to play out all their lives.

Zhelin ignored him.

Rand saw the slight smile crease his lips, felt Kulikov's muscles tighten, a rabbit about to spring for safety. Rand threw himself into Nickolai with all the force he could muster, knocking him to the ground as a sniper's bullet creased his left arm and ricocheted off the cobblestones. The two of them scrambled toward the front entrance of the mint as the place erupted. Arriving at the door side by side, they threw themselves into it and smashed it open, their bodies coming to rest next to one another on the concrete floor.

Rand pushed himself up and started running down the hall, going five steps before he realized Nickolai hadn't gotten up.

―――――――――

Rustam had been awakened by the chopper. Trapped in the tower, he had turned on the listening device and picked up the conversation between the men in the courtyard below.

The crack of the rifle had caught him off guard. He watched, stunned, as Nickolai and the one Zhelin called King, who was dressed in a Russian uniform, went down in a jumble. He watched as Dimitri Bakatin was shot through the back and knocked onto the cobblestones. From the look of the bloodstain, he would never move again.

Snipers.

His experience told him to look in high places. His position was the highest and gave him a clear view of the surrounding roofs. He quickly picked them out. He snapped the Dragunov to his shoulder. A second later he had the crosshairs focused on the first sniper's cranium. He moved the hairs slightly left and fired. The first bullet hit the sniper's rifle at the receiver and shattered it, driving shards of metal into the man's face. He dropped the useless weapon, screaming. Moments later the second bullet hit the next sniper in the leg, the third bullet ramming through the discarded rifle and leaving it useless.

Rustam pivoted. A man was on the roof with a prisoner. He fired. The man with the gun jumped as the shell exploded the masonry at his feet. The prisoner saw his chance and took it, slamming a fist into the other man's rib cage and ripping the weapon from his hands. A quick blow to the side of the head and the soldier went down.

Rustam did a quick once-over of the courtyard. The doors to the mint were shattered. The thought flashed in his mind that he had seen Poltav and King go through them. Kulikov was opening the door for Zhelin. Rustam snapped and fired, shattering the window to the vehicle, making both men dive for cover behind the vehicle. Several soldiers were firing at the doors to the mint. Rustam aimed, fired, aimed, fired, aimed, fired. The first shot hit a weapon, the second passed through a man's shoulder, the third went into a leg.

He reloaded. He had killed no one. It was all right. He had to help these men or they would die needlessly. He shoved the magazine into place and snapped the rifle to his shoulder again. In seconds he was on a new target.

Sasha didn't know who had fired, didn't care. It had given him the chance he had needed. He began firing, knowing that his bullets were not the only ones causing the panic below. Whoever was on the other end of the other rifle was good, exploding shards of cobblestone into legs, knocking weapons from hands, wounding, driving the enemy from the battlefield.

Sasha saw Kulikov moving toward the building. He injected another shell, aimed . . . too late! The man had passed out of view below. The Chaika was moving. Zhelin. He aimed, fired. The windshield shattered. A second later two wheels blew—probably punctured by the sniper who had saved his bacon. The car kept moving. Sasha reloaded and fired into the motor. Steam. He fired again. The vehicle came to a stop.

The square was empty. He could see men regrouping near the wall. Where were they all coming from? One of their number gave orders, then several groups broke off in different directions. Time to get off the roof.

He started scrambling back from the edge of the roof. Half a dozen men went to one knee, aimed, and fired. The bullets from the automatic weapons blew away a large part of the plaster along the roof's edge where Sasha had been, sending plaster shrapnel zinging in every direction. He knew he would have only a few minutes to get off the roof and find a safer place before his exit was cut off.

Rustam saw the man on the far roof disappear. He stopped firing. No incoming bullets. His position was still unknown. He removed the rifle and replaced the slats in the vent, then waited. He had done all he could.

He sat on the floor, his back against the wall. His hands started shaking. They always shook after a mission, violently. The steady calm he exhibited during battle would leave in a rush of overwhelming fear mixed with adrenaline. After a few minutes he'd be able to function again, but now he had to fight for control.

Sasha took the steps down from the roof two at a time, the sound of the boots taken from Alosha sounding like thunder in the narrow staircase.

As he came to the bottom and was about to burst through the outer door and into the street, something told him to stop. He jammed his boot into the door and knocked it open. It was immediately riddled with bullets. He turned left, aimed his rifle at the locked metal door leading inside the mint, and fired. The door didn't budge.

Charging back up the stairs, Sasha exited onto the roof. He looked in all directions, trying to find some way of escape. Nothing. He tossed the rifle over the edge of the roof with disgust. Removing his packet of cigarettes as the gun clattered onto the street below, he removed one and stuck it into his mouth. He struck a match. He had nothing to do but wait—and hope the first person up the stairs was someone he knew.

Rand knelt by Nickolai and rolled him over. Blood was draining from a wound in the upper right quadrant of his chest and from a deep cut on his head. He was unconscious but alive. Rand felt the sting in his upper arm. A graze, hardly bleeding. He had been the lucky one.

"Move and I'll kill you, King."

The sound came from the hole left when the doors had shattered. Rand looked down the hall in both directions. This was a mint; shouldn't there be guards or something?

"No help will be coming, King. We sent the guards away earlier. There weren't many to pay off because they don't keep much of value around here anymore—a little gold for medals doesn't warrant much protection."

Rand stared into the barrel of the gun, wondering if it was possible to see the bullet that would kill him.

"Is he dead?" Kulikov asked.

"Close," Rand said, looking down at Nickolai's ashen face. "He needs a doctor."

"None available." Two other men appeared at the door. The firing had stopped out in the square. Kulikov turned and ordered them away. "These two are mine. Check on Zhelin." The men disappeared.

"Did your snipers kill Bakatin?" Rand asked as he stood.

Kulikov laughed lightly. "I didn't take time to check, but I'd be willing to place money on it." He stepped to the window near the door and glanced out. Two of his men were helping Zhelin from the car. He didn't look good. "Your snipers did a job on Zhelin."

Rand had forgotten about Sasha, but he was curious at the use of the plural. He let it go, worried that Sasha hadn't survived, regretting he had ever let the man come. He had a wife and two kids.

"What now?"

"Do you know where the record book is?"

Rand nodded. "Zhelin won't like you making deals that don't include him."

Kulikov looked out the window again. The men were laying Zhelin onto the cobblestones.

"From the look of it, Zhelin won't care."

"I wish I could say I'm sorry."

"We go and find the record book. I want those account numbers."

Rand smiled. "Back to square one." He mumbled to himself—all of this over that miserable record book and its promised riches.

"What?"

"Nothing. I'll give you the record book, same terms as before. Nickolai gets a doctor. Any of the rest of us still living get free passage out of the fortress."

Kulikov smiled. "I agree, but the record book must come here before I let you go."

Rand pointed toward Kulikov. "The radio. I'll need it to send word."

Kulikov nodded. Rand removed the radio from Nickolai's pocket and checked it. Still working. He turned it on and spoke.

"Larissa, do you read me?" Nothing. "Larissa, this is Rand. Do you read me?"

"Yes. Rand, what is happening? Why didn't you come out with the chopper as planned?"

"Complications. I need that record book back here, and quickly. Send the chopper. Have him keep this channel open, and I'll give him instructions when he gets close." He paused. "And Larissa. We have wounded. The chopper will have to deliver them to the hospital. You and Galya go there, along with Marina Bakatin. Wait for us."

"Who?" Larissa said. Rand sensed the fear in her voice.

"Dimitri and Nickolai, maybe Sasha. Get the chopper on the way."

Rand busied himself with stanching the flow of blood from Nickolai's wounds, then requested that his friend be moved into the square so that he could be quickly transported to the hospital. Kulikov agreed and had several of his men help. They lay Nickolai next to Dimitri, who was lying in a small pool of his own blood, face down on the cobblestones. He was dead. Rand glanced over at Zhelin's lifeless body. An old Luger lay next to him. The man was such a fool.

Rand saw a group of men appear around the south end of the building. Sasha walked with his hands atop his head. Rand felt relief until he saw Kulikov's cold look at his old friend.

"Touch him, Kulikov, and we have no deal," Rand said.

Kulikov didn't answer, only shrugged. The group drew close,

and before Rand could prevent it, Kulikov had pistol-whipped Sasha across the side of the face, opening a wide cut and knocking him to the ground. Rand reached out and grabbed Kulikov's arm as he brought it back for another blow. Two soldiers grabbed Rand and tried to pull him away, but Rand held his ground.

"So help me, Kulikov. You touch him again and you'll die a poor man instead of a rich one."

Kulikov lowered his arm and signaled the others to back off. Rand helped Sasha stanch the bleeding. In the distance they could hear the sound of the approaching chopper. Rand put the radio to his mouth and spoke, telling the pilot to hover northwest of the cathedral.

"Look around you, Kulikov. People are dead because Zhelin refused to use good sense. I'll give you the record book, but I expect to be allowed to load my wounded and living on the chopper before I do."

Kulikov's brow wrinkled. "How do I know I can trust you?"

"Because I want to save Poltav's life, and each minute I delay, my chances get slimmer. I have nothing to win now by fighting you. I have only his life, our lives, to lose."

Kulikov thought a moment, then nodded. "Tell your chopper to land."

Rustam heard the chopper and went to the vent. Peering between slats, he saw Kulikov holding a gun on King. He picked up the Dragunov and ejected the magazine. He reloaded, then replaced the magazine. He flipped off the safety, then adjusted the scope, the crosshairs resting on Kulikov's thinning bald spot.

This time the anger was gone, the overflowing desire for vengeance nonexistent. If he had to kill the man, so be it, but now it would be justified.

Rustam felt calm.

He waited.

"Tell him to land, King," Kulikov said.

"Not until your men are down there, next to the commandant's old quarters. You and I wait here. I'll be your hostage until the loading is done. Then I deliver the book."

"Agreed."

"One man stays to help Sasha load Dimitri's body and Nickolai." Kulikov nodded.

Rand gave the new instructions to the pilot as Kulikov gave word for his troops to move to the far end of the square. When the chopper placed its skids on the ground, Sasha and Kulikov's man took Nickolai to the chopper while Rand waited in the square. Dimitri's body was quickly put aboard, and then Sasha climbed in. Rand looked at Kulikov, who told him to go ahead.

Rand went to the chopper. He brought the book back halfway, laid it on the ground, and returned. By the time he was aboard, Kulikov was anxiously thumbing through the pages of the book.

"Let's go," Rand said. The chopper lifted off. Kulikov looked up, then back at the book, then toward the far wall where two men appeared. They were holding a ground-to-air missile.

In the back of his mind Rustam knew the chopper was lifting off with all aboard, but he was completely focused, calm, the crosshairs still on the crown of Kulikov's head. Then he sensed Kulikov's change, his hand going up. A signal!

Rustam left off the trigger, his eye leaving the scope to look through the slats at the far-off wall. Two men—a missile.

He swung the Dragunov as the roar of the chopper lifting from the square only feet away sounded in his ears. He found the missile in the scope and fired. The shell hit the metal container housing the computer-aided tracking mechanism, shattering it and knocking the trajectory down. The missile launched.

Rand watched in horror, saw the missile, then saw the sudden jerk as something hit and shattered part of the metal container. The soldier firing it stumbled, the trajectory changed, the missile launched into the square.

Kulikov didn't have a chance.

As the courtyard erupted into a plume of dust and shards of cobblestone, the pilot dipped the chopper toward the Neva. Rand watched as the dust cleared, revealing nothing but a crater. The last of Tupolev's empire had just crumbled.

Rustam walked from the fortress, Dragunov case in hand. The place was quiet, empty. It had been two hours since the missile had misfired. Zhelin's car, the body, the wounded had all been removed. In terms the KGB would have understood, the place had been "sanitized." When workers arrived in the morning, they would have nothing to give them answers—if they were allowed access at all. The KGB would probably keep the place closed until the crater was filled in, the cobblestones replaced. The way things were in Russia, that might be a very long time.

He turned right when he reached Kirovsky Prospekt. It was three in the morning. The town was cool, quiet. His body was drained by the adrenaline rush of battle and the emotional release of discovery.

But his mind was clear for the first time since Natalya's death.

Natalya. His heart still ached, wishing it were all a bad dream, that he would go to their apartment and find her sleeping there, that she would welcome him into her arms and hold him close.

But it wasn't to be—not in this life.

He leaned against the rail of the bridge and stared through tears at the flowing surface below him. He stood there a long time, wondering when the pain would ever go away.

He reached down and picked up the gun case. It seemed unbearably heavy. He lay it on the wide concrete rail.

Had he broken his promise?

His mind settled on the story that had given him so much comfort years ago and led to his covenant with God. Lamanite warriors, men who had killed for their country so often that killing had become a part of them, had heard the sons of Mosiah.

They had converted, giving up their swords, refusing to take them up again. And more than a thousand of them had died because they had kept their promise.

When he had read the story, it had given him hope, a way to be free of his own past, his own killing. Now he understood what the people of Ammon had done, how hard such a promise was to keep.

And why they had buried their weapons.

When he had made his promise, he had pushed aside the feeling that he must destroy his weapon. Instead, he had given it to a friend. A gift, he had told himself. A valuable gift, not really his to destroy. Others could use it to protect his country.

Rationalization, all of it. His promise had been conditional, and it had come back to haunt him.

But hadn't he saved lives?

He rubbed the gun case. A man and his weapon—a unique form of addiction. He lifted the lid. There were the parts, the empty casings he had gathered at the tower, leaving no trace of his presence. Ever the professional.

He closed the case, then pushed it over the edge of the rail. It seemed like a long time before the case hit the water. It sank almost instantly. Gone. Buried.

Too late? Maybe. Others would have to decide.

He starting walking south across the bridge, glad to be rid of the weight in his hand—willing to deal with what remained in his heart. Church leaders must be told, must make decisions about his actions.

He shoved his hands into the pockets of his light jacket and walked toward the hospital where her body would be. It was time to care for his wife.

Volodya Vilechenko knew that a direct approach with Vasily, once his driver and now his captor, would get him nowhere. He decided that a flanking move was necessary and worked out a plan. Sliding under Vasily's bed, he removed all but a few of the straps that held the two inches of foam pad, blankets, and sheets in place. Then he slid into his own bed fully dressed.

He waited several hours, dozing from time to time, until Vasily slipped into the room. Volodya pretended to snore while watching the big man undress. As he was about to plop himself onto the mattress, Volodya prepared to move.

Vasily sat on the wooden side of the bed, taking off his socks. He stretched, then leaned back to ease himself onto the mattress. It all gave way, and he went clear to the floor, the blankets and mattress squeezing in around him. Volodya ejected himself from the bed and was at the door before Vasily could struggle free. Flinging it open, he went into the living room, then into the hall and to the outside door. It was locked.

He could hear Vasily struggling to free himself, hear his cursing. He went to the window. Three stories up, no fire escape. He took a chair and flung it through the glass, then eased himself out onto the thin ledge. Taking a deep breath, he leaped for the branches of a nearby tree.

The spring in his legs wasn't what it used to be, and he came up short of the strong branch he had aimed for. His hand clasped around a smaller limb, and he felt it start to rip free. Reaching with his free hand, he grabbed for another, felt the rough twigs and branches tear at the skin on his arms as he desperately tried to get a firm hold. As the one branch ripped loose, he caught the bigger one and hung on with renewed hope.

Vasily came to the window as Volodya swung himself into a fork in the tree and began scrambling down. He reached the bottom as Vasily ran down the stairs and rushed to collar him. Volodya picked up the branch that had torn away and swang it, catching Vasily across the face. The supple branch slapped Vasily with enough force to stun him. Volodya grabbed the big end of the branch and jammed it into Vasily's solar plexus, then whipped it across the back of his skull. The big man hit the ground and stayed there.

Volodya went to one knee, out of breath, gasping, wondering if he would have a heart attack and die right here.

He glanced up at the window, then at the tree, amazed that he had actually made it. He looked down at Vasily. It would have been easier to use a chair across his thick skull.

"Sorry, Vasily." He patted the unconscious man on the shoulder. "You were a good boy. Tell your uncle he should have trusted me."

He stood and started walking. Half a block later he caught a cab. It was 3:00 A.M.

Chapter Thirty-one

FOR THE SECOND NIGHT IN A ROW, Rand had slept on the consulate couch and had hardly closed his eyes. Marina Bakatin hadn't taken her husband's death well, and Galya was staying at their home, trying to give comfort.

Nickolai remained in critical condition at the hospital. His chest wound hadn't hit any vital organs, but the blow to his skull had given him a serious concussion. He was in a coma. The doctors weren't sure he'd ever come out of it. Larissa was there along with Rustam, who had showed up early this morning. He hadn't said much about where he'd been, but Rand was glad he was safe. He seemed prepared to get on with the hardship of being alone.

So many had been hurt. Vostya, Nickolai. And Yuri Yezhov the archaeologist, Natalya, Dimitri—all were dead. For what? A diary. Riches. He shook his head. So much for so little.

After taking Galya and Marina Bakatin to Bakatin's Dacha on the outskirts of town, and after delivering Sasha, his face now sewn back together, to the safety of his own home, Rand had decided to come to the office. Through most of the night, pieces of the puzzle had spun through his mind in an endless whirlpool of conflicting, topsy-turvy clues he couldn't quite put together. He felt that he had all the pieces; he just wasn't able to put them in the right places and come up with a picture. One thing was sure— there was more to this than Tupolev and Zhelin, more to it than just greed.

He focused on the dial of his watch. He had sent a message to Andrews for a 10:00 A.M. meeting in Decembrist Square—at the statue of Peter the Great. It was was now 8:00. Possibly Andrews could give him that last bit of information that would bring things together.

The intercom from the guard station filled the room.

"Mr. King, Miss Starkova is here, along with a gentleman by the name of Shelepin—Aleksei Shelepin. Should we accompany them to your office?"

Rand was surprised. He had known Galya would be coming, but what was Shelepin doing here? He pushed the button.

"Search Shelepin thoroughly; then bring them up."

Rand quickly straightened things up and put them away so that it wouldn't be obvious he had slept there instead of in his own bed.

As he tossed the still-damp towel from the previous night's shower into the bathroom, he felt the sting of the cut he had received but not noticed when he and Nickolai had crashed through the heavy doors of the mint building. He checked the bandage. It wasn't bleeding.

The door opened and Galya came in. Behind her was a man with ashen face and slumping shoulders. His eyes darted from side to side as if he expected to be pounced on within the moment. Rand felt no compassion for him. His betrayal of Bakatin had caused all this. Good people were dead, and he was still breathing. Rand didn't like that result.

"What's he doing here?" Rand said flatly.

Galya pointed at the couch, and Shelepin went there like an obedient dog. "The KGB is looking for him; so are friends of Dimitri. I think you will find him very cooperative."

Over the next twenty minutes, Rand found out the details of Zhelin's killing Tupolev and the orders from Zhelin to dismantle Bakatin's considerable empire.

Rand took the orange juice Galya offered. "What do you want, Shelepin?" He took a drink. "Asylum? Protection? What?"

"Protection. A visa out of the country. Asylum. Anything. I am a dead man if I stay here."

"It happens to people like you." He took another drink of the juice. To him, rats like Shelepin deserved nothing but to be thrown to the animals hunting them. But in this instance there was another consideration. "If I give you access to a computer, can you undo all the damage you've done to Bakatin's empire over the past few days?"

Shelepin looked down at the floor.

"Can you or can't you, Shelepin?"

"Uh, yes sir, most of it."

"Most of it?"

"Some of it is missing. A few hundred thousand. I—"

"You stole it. I want it back for Marina. All of it."

Shelepin seemed to sink further into the couch but didn't answer.

"I'll give you the protection you want when you return everything to Marina Bakatin—not before."

"Everything? I will need money to live. I—"

"Everything. If you want to live at all."

Over the next half hour, Rand typed a confession of sorts for Shelepin to sign, making sure that in the problem of Tupolev's death the right people got the blame. Then he took the weasel into another office, gave him a computer with a modem, and told him to get started remantling Bakatin's businesses. He locked him in with a promise of lunch and dinner and told him he wanted a printout of every transaction directly from the banks he was dealing with. There was a fax machine in the corner.

There would be nothing more for the thief until he accomplished his task. Even with that, the weasel seemed relieved.

Rand went to the bathroom to shave. He left the door open so he could hear Galya's conversation over the phone. She was at the desk talking with Larissa, who was at the hospital. There was no change in Nickolai. She talked to Rustam and seemed relieved that he was handling things. Rand was grateful that he had placed no blame on her already-sagging shoulders. He was amazed she hadn't had a nervous breakdown. She was blaming herself for all of it. That was why she felt obligated to Marina Bakatin. Galya felt it was her fault Dimitri had been killed, and Natalya. If Nickolai ended up on that list, it could put her over the edge.

He dried his face with a towel, put on a casual white golf

shirt, then closed the door slightly so as to remove a forty-five from the bottom drawer without being seen. He fed a clip into its handle before stuffing it into his belt, under the shirt, at the small of his back. He didn't expect Andrews to be dangerous, but one could never be sure how a man would react when his reputation was in danger of being destroyed. The past few days had proven that to Rand. He'd better be prepared.

After mulling things over half the night, Rand had made several phone calls to the States.

The first call had been to the archives at the *Washington Post*—to a reporter on the terrorist thing when Rand had been with the CID. He owed Rand a favor.

There was a long list of information on Andrews. It was all there—the awards, medals, accolades, honors. Family was listed, place of residence, job portfolio. In Washington the man had become one of the elite, the kind of person Rand King avoided like the plague. He was also filthy rich. And that was curious. Early on, Andrews had come up through the ranks of the army, the hard way. There had been no silver spoon in the man's mouth, no connections—just spit, polish, and hard work. But at the end of the war, things had changed.

But then, it had changed for lots of war heroes who had tapped into the system. He had married well, for one thing, in 1953—to a woman with a name that practically oozed money. But from the looks of it, Sam Andrews had boarded the train to wealth long before meeting his wife. His income-tax reports showed that he was a millionaire in 1949.

After finishing with his friend at the *Post,* Rand had called David Brannigan. Brannigan was a fellow graduate of Harvard who was now working for a think tank in Washington. Their specialty was the former Soviet Union.

After complaining about being awakened at such a ridiculous hour, Brannigan had fed him thirty-two pages on Vladimir Tupolev via fax.

There wasn't much on Tupolev prior to the war, but then there wasn't much on anybody. The American intelligence organizations had had little reach inside the Soviet Union then, and even after the war things had been very sketchy. What he did know was that the old warlord had apparently come from a peasant family turned Communist who had all died before the war and left him as the only surviving family member. Rand found it curious that his records included no apparent birth certificate, but that wasn't unusual for the period.

In the early years of the revolution, such things had been haphazard at best until everyone had been forced to get registered. Then during the war the system had fallen apart. Many records had been lost to fires and the wanton destruction of the Germans. Men and women alike had lost or found new identities during the period.

According to the information, Tupolev had joined the army in 1940, just in time to go up against Hitler. That was when he had really come into his own. He had gone all the way from inductee to general in four years. Stalin had seemed to like him, had decorated him with every medal ever made.

After the war Tupolev had become a dedicated Stalinist who had ridden Beria's coattails into the inner circle. For Rand that was a red flag in itself. Beria had been a butcher, a thug, like Stalin. It had been a day for celebration when he was put to rest by his own kind. According to David's file, Tupolev had been in on the kill.

Rand could see that Tupolev had been a survivor. The way he had worked himself out of Beria's camp and into Krushchev's, playing both ends against the middle, was a work of art. Then to be given charge of the army for his betrayal of Beria—yes indeed, the man had been shrewd. And dangerous. But now he was dead.

Just more pieces of the puzzle.

Andrews had gotten into the war early, assisting the British intelligence services from 1938 through late 1939. From there he had taken a few month's vacation, then entered OSI as a Russian expert. General Roderick Stevens had been his boss. Beginning in 1941, things had taken off for him. He had been responsible for information that had virtually told the United States when and where Stalin would act to contain the butcher, Hitler. Andrews had been good—too good.

After a thorough comparison, it had been clear to Rand. Tupolev and Andrews had been talking to each other in those

early years. Most of what Andrews had been able to reveal to
American intelligence in 1941 through 1945 was information
dealing with Russia's Northern Command—the place where
Vladimir Tupolev was playing soldier at the time.

Did that explain the receipts in Tupolev's record book?
Maybe. Some of them.

For Rand, the clincher had been the picture Brannigan had
faxed him of Tupolev in the early years, proving that all things
are not what they seem and showing just how far someone might
go for money. It was no wonder Tupolev had taken such a violent
approach to life. He had had everything to lose.

Rand took a deep breath. Getting away without Galya would
be difficult, but it had to be done. He had to meet with Andrews
alone.

He removed his jacket from the small bathroom closet,
switched off the light, and went into the office.

When Galya saw the jacket, a question came into her eyes.

"I have to meet Andrews," Rand said.

A knock came at the door, and Ted Powell, Rand's assistant,
came in.

"Who is the guy in the extra office?" he asked.

"A bad boy caught between a rock and a hard place. Have the
Marines keep a guard outside his door, Ted. No one in, no one
out—except when you deliver his meals. If he wants to sleep, get
him a cot. Understood?"

"Is he a prisoner?"

"Sort of."

Powell looked miffed at getting so little information, but he
moved to the next question like a good bureaucrat. "Any other
instructions this morning?"

Rand shook his head. "Miss Starkova will be staying here for
a few hours. See that she is made comfortable. Also, she'll give
you a list of patients at the hospital who need flowers sent to
them, along with cards. Have someone see that it's done."

"Yes sir. Anything else?"

"Anything earth shattering I need to know about?"

Powell shook his head. "There is the matter of your car. It

was found wrecked and stripped of everything important. It will take several days to get another. If you need transportation, we can make arrangements . . . "

"I won't need anything today. I have arranged my own."

"I'll get something for tomorrow, then."

"Thanks. I'll be back in the saddle tomorrow," Rand said. "Sorry about putting so much on you."

Powell seemed pleased at the apology. "What about Samuel Andrews? You really should call him, Rand."

"Already have, Ted. I meet with him at the statue of Peter in about an hour and a half."

Powell said how glad he was to meet Galya and left.

Rand picked up his half-empty glass of orange juice and downed it, then wiped his face with a handkerchief. "Gotta run. If you want to go to the hospital, tell Ted. He'll see that someone drives you."

Galya picked herself up off the couch and spoke, firmly. "I will come with you."

"No, Galya. You need to be here. Make sure Shelepin does what I told him, and keep in touch with Larissa. When I get done with Andrews, I think I'll have some answers. I'll come and get you." He smiled as disarmingly as he could, then started for the door. Galya stepped into his way.

"I will go," she said in English.

"Nope."

"But—"

"No arguments, Galya."

She didn't move. Instead, she kissed him.

"I'll be back before you know it." He slid past her and went to the door.

"Rand."

He turned back.

"I am in love with you. Please . . . " She was working at keeping herself from tears and forced a smile. "Please, be careful."

He smiled at her, then closed the door. She was on the edge. This had to be settled soon, or she would break into a thousand pieces.

Ted Powell went to his office and quickly picked up the phone, dialing the familiar number. "This is Powell." A pause. "Nothing. He is not in a talkative mood. I don't know what happened. What you heard could be true. His upper arm is wrapped in a bandage." He paused, listening. "He's meeting with Samuel Andrews. Decembrist Square, the statue of Peter the Great at ten o'clock." Another pause. "Andrews said King had been into some top-secret files back in the States. He had to talk to him about it." Another pause. "I saw the diary on the table in King's office, but the Starkova woman is there." He listened again. "How much?" The figure was repeated for him. "For a million dollars I will deliver it to you. Where?" He made note of the instructions, hung up, and went to his desk.

Powell was no novice with a revolver. Consulate personnel were well trained in firearms, and he had graduated from the courses with high honors. He placed the clip into the handle of the government-issue forty-five and stuck it into his pocket. The trouble was the woman. If he left her behind, he was through and would be prosecuted. She had to go. He'd deliver her along with the diary, let them get rid of her.

And they would have to get rid of her. She knew too much anyway, just like King.

Powell walked to the door and let himself out. The secretaries had all arrived and were busying themselves with the tasks of the day. He would have to use Rand's private exit. Walking across the secretaries' space, he paused at Rand's door. There was no noise. He opened it and went in, closing it behind him. Galya looked up from the couch, where she was thumbing through the diary. He took the forty-five from his pocket and pointed it, smiling his best diplomatic smile. "You, I, and that little book have an appointment with its rightful owner. Let's not keep the man waiting."

Chapter Thirty-two

RAND WALKED ACROSS THE STREET toward Decembrist Square. He had left the consulate forty-five minutes ago, picked up his car, gassed it up, and come to the square. By normal transportation, it would have taken an hour. This way, ten minutes.

He dodged a tourist bus just pulling to the curb and stepped onto the sidewalk. Four more buses lined the front side of the street, and small groups of sightseers strode about as their guides gave their spiel about the statue's symbolism.

"It was on this square in 1825 that the Russian revolutionary gentry first rose up in arms against the government. Tsar Nicholas I had ordered his troops to open fire on the rebels and filled the square with the dead. Later, five of the leaders were sentenced to death while more than five hundred others were sentenced to hard labor," one of the guides was saying.

In Rand's mind, this singular event had been the beginning of the end for the tsarist regime.

He sat on a bench in front of the statue. Peter the Great, on horseback, sword extended, a huge snake under his rearing steed. Symbolism at its best. Peter, holding back Russia and riding her to her destiny while stamping out the evils that dared face him. The Great Tsar of Russia, the builder of this city on the Neva. A high-handed dictator, not so different from Stalin but still honored by his people. Time had a way of dimming the truth, and Rand couldn't help but wonder if someday Stalin's statue wouldn't work its way back into the memory of the people as well.

"Mr. King."

Rand turned to face a gentleman with silver hair and aged skin. Dressed in a light summer suit, a white shirt with a collar two sizes too big, and a colorful silk tie, Andrews looked out of place among a flurry of brightly if scantily dressed tourists trying to get pictures.

"Andrews," Rand said evenly.

"Shall we walk?" Andrews said, pointing to the circular pavement that surrounded the statue with his cane.

Rand nodded. Andrews was smaller than he expected, but Rand respected anyone who carried a walking stick big enough to bludgeon a person to death.

"You came a long way. Enjoying the sights?" Rand asked.

"I haven't seen many yet," Andrews said. The irritation of the past two days of waiting quickly dissipated, and Andrews was glad to get on with the business of making King an ally. Belittling King for his treatment of him was no longer on Andrews' agenda. "I was here at the end of the war for a few weeks, but things have changed."

"It must have been horrible-looking then."

"Actually they had begun rebuilding in 1942 or 1943. The city was in pretty good shape by 1946. Clean at least. This statue had been uncovered, and the square looked very much like it does today. I didn't get to see the palaces and all. They had been destroyed. It took them many years to rebuild—a lot of dedicated work."

"You would be amazed at the result."

"One of the world's great cities, rebuilt on the hard labor and sacrifice of her people. I have often thought that is one thing wrong with our American young people today. They have never suffered such deprivation as the Russians have. In the end, our ease may be our downfall," Andrews said methodically.

They stood at the rear of the statue, gazing toward the Neva. A boat had docked—a sightseer that floated the river—and was letting off passengers.

"Why come all the way to Petersburg to see me?" Rand asked.

"Your inquiries about a file kept in the office of the General of the Army needed to be discussed. Unfortunately, according to a call I made this morning, you have now broken into that file. You had no clearance, and now your career is in jeopardy."

Rand didn't flinch at the apparent attempt at intimidation.

"Why is the ALLIANCE file still sealed, Mr. Andrews? And why do you still keep tabs on it? You haven't the proper clearances either."

"You have read it. Surely you understand its sensitivity. The attempted assassination of a world leader—"

"Poppycock. It stopped being sensitive the moment Stalin was revealed for what he was in 1956. The world would have applauded you for what you tried to do."

"You know that more than an assassination was involved. It was an attempt to overthrow their government and return the Romanovs to the throne. Knowing we participated in such an attempt could have strained relations beyond the breaking point. And then there was the Guard themselves to consider. The Communists never liked opposition groups running free in their country. They would have begun a hunt for the White Guard again. Revealing the ALLIANCE file could have cost thousands of lives."

Rand knew all of what Andrews said was true, but he also knew there was more to it than that.

"You didn't have permission, did you," Rand said.

Andrews smiled. "Roosevelt's signature is on the paper authorizing ALLIANCE."

"Forgery is a federal crime—another reason you didn't want that file introduced to the public eye, at least until your death."

"You're guessing."

"Only a thorough investigation will tell us for sure, but I think I am on pretty firm ground."

"I'll ruin you, King."

"Too late. I informed the General of the Army about ALLIANCE less than an hour ago. My transportation carries a phone."

Rand was surprised at Andrews' control.

"His reaction?"

"Guarded, but he intended to investigate."

"He won't find anything. I had the file removed."

Rand glanced at his adversary. "Files don't disappear, especially top-secret ones. Not without a paper trail. You will have to account for it."

"Mishaps happen. The point is, your evidence is gone."

They walked a short distance without speaking.

"I copied the file, and I have other evidence," Rand said.

Andrews grinned. "I thought you might. You want something; what is it?"

"The truth, Mr. Andrews. As difficult as that may be for you, that is what it will take if you want to die outside prison walls."

They walked on, Andrews' brow wrinkled in thought.

"I will tell you as much as I can, but there are some things even I don't know. You have to understand that. But I have a price. You have to keep my name out of all this. ALLIANCE is old, mistakes were made, but there is nothing to be done about them now—at least not about my role."

"I have no desire to put a man your age away for what years you might have left, but I will if you lie to me."

"Ask your questions," Andrews said.

"What went sour? Why did ALLIANCE fail?"

"If you have any evidence at all, you asked the obvious. Kitrick betrayed us—for money."

"The tsar's gold was too much for him," Rand said.

"It has been a long time since anyone uttered those words. How did you come to discover them?"

"Nora's diary."

"Did they find the vault?"

"Yes, they did. They used some of the items to buy food. Nora survived the siege but died later."

"Then you probably know more than I do about Kitrick and his betrayal."

"About the history, probably. What I want to know is when you discovered that Kitrick was still alive, that he had become Vladimir Tupolev."

Andrews flinched but kept moving. "Tupolev will kill you if he finds out you know."

"Tupolev is dead."

Andrews stopped. Rand turned to face him, repeating his question. "When did you find out Kitrick was Tupolev?"

"In 1945. Who killed him?"

"Georgi Zhelin."

"Twins, except Zhelin is worse. As head of the KGB and with Tupolev's empire . . ."

"Yeltsin is looking for a new director of his Ministry of Security."

Andrews laughed lightly. "You are a man of infinite surprise, Mr. King. Is this what you have been doing for the past few days? Restructuring the Russian hierarchy?"

Rand smiled. "Who contacted whom?"

"What?"

"Tupolev contacted you, didn't he. He wanted to trade information for money."

Andrews started walking again. "He became our number-one agent. Always has been. No one has ever equaled his value to our intelligence-gathering community. He helped destroy Lavrenti Beria, was instrumental in bringing down Krushchev, and created a network of agents within the Soviet system that fed us invaluable political and technological information."

"He wasn't a hero; don't make him sound like one. He was a butcher."

"All a matter of perspective. He killed only when he felt threatened from inside. His information was instrumental in bringing down the wall. You remember the wall, don't you Mr. King? He helped destroy Communism."

"And moved right in to grab up the spoils."

Andrews laughed. "Yes, Kitrick always was an opportunist. That was what got him into his mess in the first place—that and greed."

"His betrayal of the ALLIANCE team cost some good lives," Rand said.

"Yes, I never forgave him for that. If Stalin had been killed, if the coup had been successful, Communism would have been destroyed in Russia, and millions of lives would have been saved. I grant you that, Mr. King. But we took what we could get."

"There was a time when he wanted out, to be left alone."

"That is why I kept the ALLIANCE file, and other information. I made him pay for his treachery, Mr. King—for long, hard years."

"You ran him. You were his controller. I always wondered why you ended up as head of the CIA."

"My talents go beyond information received from Kitrick, but yes, that is the main reason. Nobody ever equaled my accomplishment in that arena."

Rand removed two sheets of copy paper from his back pocket and handed them to Andrews.

"What are these?" Andrews asked.

"Tupolev kept meticulous records dating back to 1941 when Kitrick stopped existing. The first is a copy of one page of the original ledger. You will notice that all of it is done in code. The second is a copy of the translation from code. I received it from a friend in CID this morning. At first I didn't understand. Thanks to you, I think I do now."

He let Andrews read it, watching as the man's pallor turned to that of chalk. He folded each page carefully and handed them back to Rand.

Rand continued. "I grant that Kitrick/Tupolev was probably one of the greatest spies ever to serve the free world against Communism, even if it was a forced issue most of the time and you had to pay him well. That explains at least a portion of the large amounts of money he recorded having received into four of the five foreign accounts he controlled. It doesn't explain the payments. Nor does it explain why your name is next to those payments."

Andrews looked unsteady and walked to a nearby bench. Rand sat next to him, watching the busses come and go in front of the statue area. The puzzle was finally turning into a picture.

"He emptied the vault, shipped the items to you, and you sold them," Rand said. "The funds were funneled through your regular payments for his work as mole. He then paid you for your work by depositing money in the fifth account—the only one that had a separate withdrawal code—the only one I couldn't get at. The two of you stole millions of dollars of the Romanov fortune."

The two men were silent for a long time.

"It . . . " Andrews drew a deep breath. "It worked very well, but Kitrick wasn't the one who stole . . . "

Rand saw the small red dot on the front of Andrews' white shirt blossom into scarlet in less time than it took to blink. The laser-directed bullet found the old man's heart and killed him instantly. Rand dove for the grass, the sudden revelation passing through his brain like an electric shock. There was a third party, a third partner.

Bullets chased Rand across the lawn as he rolled toward the statue. People scattered in all directions, screaming, the popping sound of an automatic weapon filling the air. Rand was up and running now, passing the statue and flying across the lawn, unsure of where the assassin was, where the stream of bullets originated.

A bullet grazed his arm; another passed through the flapping sleeve of his shirt, pushing his speed up a notch and beyond his previous best. He had only one chance.

He hit the paved walkway and poured on the steam, the hair on the back of his neck standing on end as he waited for a bullet to catch up to him.

As he ran between two busses, projectiles shattered the windows and planted themselves in metal around him. A car slammed to a halt in front of him, a gun aimed through its window. He dove to the ground and rolled under the bus to his left. He pulled his gun free and aimed, blowing out the tires of the vehicle that was after him, causing it to skid, turn on its side, and spin in half a circle. Another car jolted to a stop next to it. He was about to fire when another gun sounded and blew out the front windows of the vehicle, forcing the driver and the assassin in the back seat to the floor.

Someone was fighting on his side.

Rand saw the Italian shoes and white pants moving toward the assassin's car. Moving forward from under the bus, he was a bit surprised to see Volodya Vilechenko, one hand in bandages, the other enveloping a pistol.

"Mr. King."

"Vilechenko. You do turn up at unexpected times."

Volodya's gun swung in his direction. Rand followed it, then was relieved to have the man aim it back toward the men who were trying to free themselves from the wreckage.

Vilechneko smiled. "According to my sources, this has been happening to you a lot lately." He motioned toward the two men scrambling out of the wrecked car. "Disarm them. Leaving guns lying about is dangerous, don't you think?"

The driver had his hands raised, as did the shooter, his laser-guided rifle sprawled at his feet. Rand removed his handkerchief and took the weapon, then tossed it onto the grass.

Vilechenko stepped closer to the second vehicle and took the weapons as they were handed out. "Go," he said to the two men. They climbed into the second car with the others and were quickly gone.

"What in the . . . " Rand began to protest.

"Do not worry, Mr. King. I know who they are, and who sent them. The police have the weapon and enough eyewitnesses to find the killer. It is more important that we deal with who sent them than with his assassins. Do you have transportation? The police will be coming, and we don't have time to explain all this."

Rand smiled. "That depends on where you want to go."

"The vault, Mr. King. We must go to the vault. I assume that by now Nora has told you its approximate location."

"In that case, I have just the thing." Rand started across the street toward the river. Vilechenko gave him a curious look, then followed.

As they came to the dock, Vilechenko's curiosity was satiated. Tied at one end was a sleek blue-and-white speed boat with the words *Momma's Boy* painted in Russian across the back.

"I had it shipped from America—arrived several days ago. I picked it up at a private dock a couple of hours ago. My only toy. When I set up the meeting with Andrews, I selected the spot I knew I could reach by boat."

They went down the steps and were quickly aboard. Rand fired up the engines while Vilechenko unfastened the lines that held the vessel to the dock. A minute later they were skimming over the surface of the Neva toward Peter and Paul Fortress. Rand shivered at the thought, the events of the previous night still heavy in his mind.

"Why the vault?"

"Patience, Mr. King. You will see. What did Andrews tell you?" Vilechenko asked.

Rand glanced at him. "First you answer one for me."

"If I can," Vilechenko said.

"Who are you after?"

"A traitor, Mr. King. A traitor."

The cathedral lights were all on, the beautiful paintings and gold-painted architecture bright, mirroring Alexander's anticipation.

Alexander Bychevsky had the fortress to himself. The place was shut down after last night's fiasco between Zhelin and Nickolai Poltav. Workers had been ordered to repair the courtyard, and KGB guards watched the entrances. A few phone calls to the right people along with the right number of American dollars, and all of them had taken an early dinner. No tourists, no workers. The chapel area was devoid of life except for him. He loved the place, and hated it. The burial place of the tsars, the family he had chosen to serve, and served so well.

And the place where everything had come unraveled.

He was standing facing the iconstasis, his back to the entrance, when he heard the scraping sound of the door as it opened. The sound of two sets of leather heels on the marble floor reverberated in the huge chapel, resounding off the walls and ceilings and coming at him from every direction. He turned to face Ted Powell, Galya Starkova at his side.

"Why is she here?" Alexander asked Powell.

"She knows about this transaction and the diary. Need I state the obvious?"

"And you want me to kill her?"

"She is your problem now. Where is my money?"

"You just spent it. My fee for killing a woman! You are a fool, Powell." Alexander removed a pistol from his pocket. "The diary, please."

Ted handed Alexander the diary.

"I suggest you leave now, Ted, or I will be forced to kill you."

Powell lifted his hands as if to ward off the bullet he thought was coming and started backpedaling. The door closed with a sharp bang that quickly turned back to silence.

"I must apologize for Mr. Powell. His membership in the Guard has always been heavily jaded by his desire for money and his stupidity. There was no need to involve you."

"Who are you?" Galya asked.

"Alexander Bychevsky, leader of the White Guard."

Bychevsky opened the diary. Norwegian. He picked out words here and there, names, places. Finding Nora's drawings, he recognized them for what they were—each a clue to the vault's location. The riddle was easy for him but still brought him a smile. If all of it wasn't destroyed, someone would work it out, which could end everything. He was filled with regret and gladness at the same time. All of this could have been avoided if Volodya had left things alone. But it could all end well. Now that he had the book, he could take care of the last loose end. And the vault would be lost forever.

He reached into his pocket and withdrew a round piece of metal, placing it next to the picture in the diary. It was the same as the rounded handle of the key Nora had drawn.

"The key! But how did you—"

"It is a very long story, Miss Starkova—one I have protected for many years and am not about to reveal now."

"What happened to the rest of the key?"

"Broken. Lost. It doesn't matter."

He started to rip the picture out.

"Most museums would want it intact," Galya said.

He finished tearing it away and dropped it to the floor, then removed the photocopies Rikki had made of the six pages. Rand had put them into the diary. They joined the originals. He removed a cigarette lighter and started them burning. In seconds, nothing remained but ash.

"What do you intend to do with me?"

"You must disappear, Miss Starkova, along with this book. What you know is very dangerous to the tsar, to the whole house of Romanov."

"Rand King—"

"Is dead. Mr. Powell informed me of his meeting with Andrews. I sent someone to kill them. Only you and this cursed diary remain."

"Others know . . ." Galya said without conviction.

"Not enough. Only this"—he pointed at the ashes—"could harm us. There is nothing but you left now."

Galya felt dizzy, sick to her stomach. She had to fight to keep her balance. All of the past few days caught up with her in that moment, overwhelmed her and threatened to drive her over the edge. She felt her body slipping and reached out to balance herself against the stone pillar.

She looked through the haze in her mind at Bychevksy, who was standing a few steps away, his cold, impassive stare snapping something in her mind and filling her with a rush of hate that stiffened her body and hardened her muscles. She threw herself at him with a fury that caught him off guard. Her fist pummeled his head and face, the weight of her body driving him off balance and knocking him to the floor. She was on top of him like an animal, driving her fingers toward his eyes. He slapped at them with his hands, but her nails caught in his skin and gouged him in long streaks clear to his chin. He screamed in pain even as someone grabbed her from behind, called her name, and dragged her back, kicking and screaming. He scrambled, crawling away from her, afraid she would be let loose again, afraid her fury would take his eyes clean from his head. He felt the blood on his face, the sting of the claw marks making him wince. He sat with his back against the wall, his hands covering his face.

"Galya!" Rand said for the second time. "It's okay!" She was

fighting with fury, and it was all Rand could do to hold her arms
and keep them from scratching him as well. "Galya!" he yelled.

She opened her eyes wide, saw him, and broke into sudden
sobs that racked her body. He pulled her close, holding her tight
against him. She wrapped her arms around his neck and
squeezed, afraid she'd open her eyes and find him gone, an
apparition in a dream.

Rand rubbed her back, then ran his fingers through her hair,
comforting her until the sobs receded and she started to get control again.

Vilechenko helped Bychevsky to his feet, drew a handkerchief out of his pocket, and began to wipe away the blood.

"It seems, Alexander, that this time you have pushed too far."

Bychevsky looked at his friend, wary. "How . . . " He glanced
at Rand. "You! Both of you. I didn't expect . . . "

"No, I don't suppose you did," Volodya said. "Once I escaped
Vasily, I checked with my sources inside your closed little circle.
They told me you had plans for Mr. King. I felt obligated to save
him."

"You? But . . . "

"Do not look so shocked, my old friend. You have been careless in all this. You should have let me deal with it. It is my
responsibility, Alexander."

Rand was confused, unsure of whose side Vilechenko would
come down on. Vilechenko let Bychevsky take the handkerchief.
He removed the Makarov from his pocket and stepped back out
of reach of either Bychevsky or Rand. Rand held his breath when
the barrel swung toward him and Galya.

"Why save me just to kill me?"

"I have no intention of killing you, Mr. King, unless you
force me. I have sworn to protect the honor of the tsar and the
house of Romanov. That is my only goal. If you allow me to fulfill it, you will live a long life. As will Miss Starkova." He turned
to Bychevsky and waved him to move next to Rand. Galya was
through crying, her head on Rand's shoulder. He kept one arm
wrapped around her. Vilechenko stooped and picked up the diary.

"It must have been horrible for you when Yezhov said he had

found the diary," Vilechenko said to Bychevsky. "I am sorry for that."

"You should have left it alone, Volodya."

"I want only to know the truth, Alexander. It is all I have ever wanted. We have the diary now. Tupolev is dead. Your assassins did your bidding, and Andrews can no longer reveal your secret either. You have nothing more to fear. I want only that you tell me the truth."

Bychevsky said nothing.

"Do you mind if I try to fill in a few of my own blanks?" Rand asked.

Volodya Vilechenko made a slight bow. "Feel free to do so."

"You said that Nora escaped from the city and made her way to Bologoye. She sent you a message to come for her, warning you of a traitor."

"That is correct." Vilechenko smiled.

"The fact that she sent the message to you, instead of Alexander, leader of ALLIANCE, leader of the White Guard, was a warning. She was telling you to beware of him." Rand looked directly at Bychevsky.

"Very good, Mr. King. It was a small thing. I didn't pay much attention to it at first, but then other things happened, also little things. But together all of them began to make me wonder about what had really happened after the failure of ALLIANCE."

"Little things. Like the fact that artifacts you knew were in the vault began turning up in faraway places, in museums and private collections."

"Yes, but that came much later, after I knew Tupolev was really Robert Kitrick."

Galya's head came off Rand's shoulder. "What?"

"Oh yes, Miss Starkova. Mr. King figured it out, didn't you, Mr. King."

"He spoke fluent Russian, was Russian. All he needed was papers," Rand said.

"Easy to come by in those days. So many people dying, lying in the streets, their papers disappeared. Kitrick was selective, and he had inside help from the NKVD finding the right ones. The man who helped him the most died of an apparent suicide."

"But you think Kitrick killed him."

"I do. There were others who knew who Kitrick was, how he got to Russia, but all of them were dead by the end of 1942."

"He covered his tracks very well," Rand said.

"You shouldn't be telling him all this, Volodya," Bychevsky said.

Vilechenko shrugged. "It makes no difference now. Tupolev is dead and of no real interest to Mr. King." He looked at Rand, expecting an agreement.

Rand didn't oblige. Instead, he asked another question.

"You were trapped. He had you, and yet you both escaped. How?"

Vilechenko's face clouded with pain. "Nora was after food that morning. We had guards posted at the warehouse where we were hiding, but Kitrick had told the Red soldiers how to get past them. They were in the building before we could stop them. I, Nora, and the boy were cut off from the others. I was hit. I told them to escape while I covered for them. They refused at first, but too much hinged on their getting away, and I made them go. I was captured." Vilechenko looked at Bychevsky. "I owe Alex here my life. He had escaped, and when they started hauling me away, he saw it. Racing to a position a few blocks away, he intercepted the truck. At the time, I had decided I wasn't going to prison and that I would either escape or die trying. I was wounded in the leg, and I knew what an escape attempt meant, but I also knew that if interrogated I might give away other members of the guard. There was no other choice."

Bychevsky seemed to brighten a little at the memory. Rand was amazed at the apparent bond of friendship between the two men and caught himself wanting to know what they had been through over the past fifty years.

"At the moment I was about to make a break for it, I heard gunfire, and the truck suddenly lurched to the left and ran into a building. There was a guard at the back of the truck, and he was thrown out. The one next to me was thrown to the floor. I was able to overpower him and knock him unconscious. As I was about to exit the back of the truck, Alexander poked a gun into my face from around the side of the truck. I was relieved when I saw that it was him. He helped me get away. We fled the city and made our way to our enclave north of Moscow, in the mountains. I had lost a lot of blood and took several days to recuperate."

Bychevsky spoke. "On the fifth day, troops came to the enclave. We were unprepared, and they nearly wiped us out. Of five thousand hidden in the mountains, fewer than five hundred escaped. We found out later that it was Kitrick who had sent the troops."

"When did you find out he was still alive?"

"In 1946. All during the war he hunted us, but we never knew it was him. He had to find and destroy Volodya and me in order to live his life freely, possibly even return to his country someday. When he was unsuccessful, when we found out who he was, he knew his days were numbered—that we controlled his destiny."

"Why didn't you kill him then? Why have you let him live?"

"You cannot understand."

"Try me."

"The survival of Russia is everything. All personal wants and goals must come second to that. By the time we discovered it was Kitrick who was trying to destroy us, he had worked his way into a high position, high enough to protect us. We blackmailed him."

"That is how you received your position as curator," Rand said.

"We have many in high positions who support our movement. Tupolev was forced to help put them there."

"And for his help you let him live."

"Stalin would have personally skinned Tupolev alive had he known who he was. Tupolev had no choice."

Rand glanced at Bychevsky. "You are the one who contacted Andrews, aren't you. I had it pegged as a two-way conspiracy. Kitrick and Andrews. There were three of you."

Bychevsky didn't answer.

"One of those little things, wasn't it, Volodya. Alexander started producing money for the movement, but he never gave a

satisfactory answer about its origins. Anonymous benefactors, the
Romanov family, governments interested in your cause—none of
which you could verify."

Vilechenko nodded. "I investigated but could never make a
connection."

"You knew he was lying, even discussed it with him, but he
denied it."

"I knew he was lying. Since we were children I always knew
it, even when others had no idea."

"But you didn't pursue it."

"I was afraid of the truth."

"And the movement needed the money," Rand said.

"He used the profits wisely, multiplying many times the
assets he took from the vault. The moneys will be used by the tsar
to help the nation come out of this economic tailspin it is in,"
Vilechenko said.

"Once the people accept your claim to the throne."

"Yes."

"But you have no claim."

Galya was confused, her eyes searching those of both Rand
and Vilechenko. "What are you talking about, Rand?"

Rand tightened his grip on her waist. "I am talking about the
death of a tsar, Galya—the death of the last of the Romanovs."

Vilechenko wiggled the gun, motioning for them to move
down the center of the cathedral. The three of them walked side
by side, Vilechenko behind them, until they reached the iconostasis.

"If you're going to dispose of us anyway, do you mind
answering a few more questions?" Rand asked.

"Not at all."

"Tupolev, Alexander, and Andrews were partners. Alexander
and the movement received the biggest chunk of the money with
the other two splitting the rest, even though theirs was the greatest
risk. They had to ship, sell, handle, make all transactions. Why?"

"You are asking a question for which I have no firsthand
knowledge, but I think I can answer it: Because Alexander could
have destroyed both of them. Tupolev wasn't just selling Soviet

secrets to your country; Andrews sold many to ours as well. My guess is that Alexander blackmailed them both."

"But they had information on Alexander as well. He was selling the tsar's treasure."

"A little thing compared to international espionage, don't you think?"

"That is why Tupolev was after the diary. He thought it might tell him more, give him something to use against Alexander. Vengeance and freedom," Galya said.

"But you, Volodya, believed that it revealed more—enough to destroy your movement."

"Let us just say that I knew enough to think the diary should be found."

"How did Tupolev find out Yezhov had the diary?"

"Alexander told him," Vilechenko said, waiting for a sign of denunciation from his friend. There was none.

"It isn't a big thing, Mr. King. Alexander was just trying to protect the movement, the future of Russia. His biggest mistake was in not trusting that I would do the same thing. We could have resolved much of this together, and the result would have been fewer dead and less danger to the movement—and a better end for you and Miss Starkova."

"I am the only one who is any threat to you, Volodya. Leave Galya out of it."

"I'm afraid I can't do that now, Mr. King."

Vilechenko turned to his friend. "Alex, I know the vault is here. I know you have been inside and know how to open it. Please do so, now," he said flatly.

Alexander stared at his old friend for a long moment. The silence in the building was deafening.

Rand broke it. "Now we come to your real doubts, don't we, Volodya. If Alexander knows how to get into the vault, he must have had a chance to save Nora and William, and yet he didn't."

Vilechenko seemed bothered by the accusation but shook his head vigorously. "He discovered the vault later. The Duchess Romanov told him when we returned to England after the war."

"You don't believe it. The duchess blamed you both for the failure of ALLIANCE and the death of William."

"No, she didn't understand at first, but before she died . . . " Vilechenko looked at his friend, confused, unsure.

Alexander Bychevsky removed the metal from his pocket and looked at it, then tossed it to Volodya, who caught it. He looked it over, unsure of what it was.

"The remainder of the key Tatiana sent with us. Nora had it." Alexander gave his old friend a gentle smile, like that of an enduring parent for a foolish child. "Poor Volodya. Wanting to know but still unable to handle the hard truths that confront you. Well, my friend, I warned you. You have opened Pandora's box. It is time to see, to face all you have done with your insatiable curiosity and your fool's errand.

"You set yourself up as judge; now I will tell you the rest. Then you can judge more purely!"

He turned to Rand. "Yes, I found them. At least I found William."

"He took you to the vault?" Rand asked.

Bychevsky nodded. Vilechenko seemed to stiffen, as if suddenly hit with more knowledge than he wanted to handle.

Bychevsky started toward the elevated stand hung on the side of the first thick, wide column on the left. He mounted the few stairs and went to the top. Rand stared at the stand and realized that from this direction, its outline matched what he had thought was a scar on the hand that held the key. Suddenly the riddle made more sense.

Galya spoke softly: *"When choosing between the Savior and the tsar, stand upon high ground. It is then that the kingdom shall not be lost and the true riches found."* She changed the translation a little, making it sound more melodic, more mythical. It gave Rand goose bumps.

Galya looked over at the tomb of Peter, then up above the windows to her left, where there was a picture of the Savior, until recently covered with soot and grime. He stood with his arms extended.

The pulpit stood between the two. It was the high ground.

Bychevsky knelt before a statue. It wasn't of a child, but it did bring the other verse to Galya's mind, and she uttered it as softly as the first: *"To enter the kingdom pay homage to the Christ child."*

They couldn't see what Alexander Bychevsky did, but they felt a sudden movement in the building that made Galya catch her breath. It was accompanied by the noise of stone grating against stone, and she reached for Rand's arm, entranced.

The stand began to move, separating itself from the stairway and sliding down toward the floor. Bychevsky stood, leaning back, as a door appeared in the column. Slowly it grew as the stand moved downward. Steps appeared, descending into the column itself and disappearing into the bowels of the cathedral. As the stand touched the floor, the back of it, the part upon which Alexander Bychevsky now leaned, gave way slightly, and he stood straight. Galya could see that the middle panel of the outside of the stand had separated from the pieces to each side and was now nothing but a door. Alexander pushed on it, and it swung open to give the rest of them entrance.

Bychevsky went to the doorway of the catacomb and reached inside, retrieving an old oil lantern. Removing a package of matches from his pocket, he adjusted and lit the lamp. Rand was surprised that it still had enough oil. The flame brightened as Bychevsky twisted the knob, and an eerie shadow edged his pale, stiff features.

Volodya Vilechenko, now fearful, motioned with his gun for Galya and Rand to join Bychevsky, who was already beginning the descent. A smell came out of the hole that was both musty and putrid. Rand didn't like the prospects of such an odor. The vault looked as if it had been dug between the tombs of the tsars and their families, which were on each side of the cathedral. Possibly some of the graves had caved into the vault, filling it with the clutter of the remains of past members of the royal family. He didn't think so, but the alternative was not a pleasant one to ponder.

He followed behind Alexander Bychevsky, surprised at how bright the old oil lamp made the cavern. Galya grabbed his hand

and held it tight. He could feel the nervous quivering of her body and wondered if his own shaking was as noticeable.

The steps were made of flat stone hinged into walls of the same substance. They had a ten-inch drop to them and numbered fifteen. Rand estimated that they went down about thirteen feet. The stairway widened as they fell below the level of the floor and eventually emptied into a ten-foot-wide hall. Bychevsky lifted the lamp. Rand estimated that the wall at the far end was somewhere under the chamber behind the iconostasis on the main level, and probably thirty feet away. To his left and right were paintings on plaster, icons depicting John the Baptist in the wilderness; the birth, life, and death of Jesus of Nazareth. Their bright colors and expert workmanship nearly took his breath away.

The change of the light on the wall as the lantern moved in Bychevsky's hand cast shadows and gave Rand a chill. It felt almost as if someone else were present. He shook it off.

The light reflected from something on the floor. Rand stooped down and picked a small object out of the crack between the floor and the wall.

"A coin. Date, 1884. One ruble."

"This must have been where the treasure was kept," Galya said.

Bychevsky stepped to the side. Vilechenko remained on the bottom stair, gun still in hand. Although the man's face was filled with awe at the icons, Rand didn't think he could move quickly enough to take the weapon away. They moved further into the chamber.

Ten feet from the stairs was a cut in the wall, a small chapel that couldn't be seen until they reached it.

Sprawled on the floor was the body of a woman.

Galya gasped and stepped back, turning to look at Alexander Bychevsky. He was looking straight ahead, his face solid, impassive. He knew what they would find.

He handed the lantern to Vilechenko, who took it with his empty hand, his eyes searching those of his friend but finding nothing. Realizing he was left to make his own judgments, his jaw firmed and gripped both the gun and the lantern with renewed determination.

The light from the lantern filled the small cavity. At the front was an icon of the virgin holding the Christ child, but all eyes were on the figure prostrate on the floor.

"Who is it?" Galya asked.

Rand knelt by the woman's side. The skin was like leather, the hair still intact. He noticed her jewelry, the quality of her clothing. Tatters. The fate of a starving Leningrader during the German siege of 1941.

"Her skull is crushed." Standing, Rand moved back.

"She must have been praying when she was killed," Vilechenko said.

"She wasn't praying, at least not to them." He pointed at the icon. The others looked bewildered.

"Who is she?" Vilechenko asked.

"Anna," Rand responded.

"The woman who helped Nora and William," Galya said.

Rand told Vilechenko what he had read in the diary about Anna's feeding, saving, helping Nora and William, about their moving to the new place after Anna's son died, a place close to the vault.

"They lived in one of the rooms in the mint building across the square," Galya said.

"Who would do such a thing?" Galya asked.

It was all beginning to dawn on Volodya Vilechenko. He turned back into the main chamber and shined the light on Alexander Bychevsky. "Why did you kill her?"

No response.

"Alexander, this was an innocent girl who helped William! Why?" he said with anger.

"Because William loved her," Rand replied. "And because he had married her."

Vilechenko turned to face Rand, a confused and unbelieving look on his face. Galya stared at Rand as well, unsure of what he had meant. What was wrong with William's marrying Anna?

"William—the grandson of Nicholas II, if I am not mistaken. He was sent with you as heir of the Romanovs, the man who would retake the throne in your little coup. What was his real name?"

"Peter William III," Vilechenko said. "But marriage is no reason—"

"Peter William abdicated the throne by marrying this peasant," Bychevsky said stiffly. "He could no longer be heir to the Romanovs."

"Not to mention that fact that she was a Jew," Rand added.

Galya looked shocked. "A Jew? How do you know this? And what difference does it make?"

"Remember in the diary when her son became deathly ill? She read to him from the Torah." He knelt by Anna's side again and lifted the end of a necklace. "A star of David."

"That is why you said she wasn't praying to the icon," Galya said.

"As wrong as it may seem, her religion was an issue that changed everything for Alexander Bychevsky," Rand said, standing. "Nicholas's view on Jews was well known. So was the view of the established church of the day. To have the heir marry a Jew was tantamount to blasphemy, a reason for total banishment from the royal line."

Galya stared at Alexander Bychevsky. She couldn't help herself.

"He came back, found them, but Nora was gone. They brought him here to show him what was left of the tsar's treasure. They were a happy couple, elated to see him, to show what they had found and kept safe. And they were in love—too much in love," Rand said.

"It was a great moment for you, wasn't it, Alexander. The heir found, the riches discovered. The future bright." Rand paused. "Then William broke the news to you."

"He refused to listen when I told him he must annul his marriage to her," Bychevsky said stiffly. "The tsar of all Russia cannot marry such a one as that!" He paused. "I told him, but he refused to listen. He was not fit to sit on the throne of Russia as long as she lived, a witness to his vile crime."

The room fell silent.

Volodya Vilechenko finally spoke. "Where is Peter? Where is the tsar?" he said firmly.

No answer. Vilechenko walked to Bychevsky and stuck the Makarov into the fleshy part of his neck. "Where?"

Bychevsky looked through glazed eyes, his face still impassive. "The heir is dead! Buried!" He spat it out, each word punctuated.

"You killed him?"

"Do not question me, Volodya! You asked to know the truth. You have it! What was done was necessary—essential to the survival of the royal family. Essential to save Russia!"

A cruel smile crossed his lips. "Ah, Volodya, do not pretend you did not know! All these years you knew that the man we prepared for the throne was an impostor! You knew the real Peter was dead! Do not make self-righteous judgments about my conduct when all along you have known!"

Vilechenko's eyes flashed. "But I did not know *you* killed Peter! The siege you told me, starvation—these were Peter's killers! That is how he died! I . . . I always believed it. Now . . . now you tell me this?"

The confusion changed to hate, cold and hard. "You! You killed the tsar, Alexander! That I can judge! For it you must die!"

The sound was like thunder in the vault. Rand jumped forward, grabbing the revolver and ripping it from Vilechenko's hand as Galya screamed, then grasped her mouth in horror. Vilechenko used both arms to grab his old friend's collapsing body and ease it to the floor.

Rand glanced at the stairway and held up a hand as Sasha came into the room, his own pistol ready to fire. Vilechenko knelt next to his dying friend, the lamp casting an eerie glow across their faces. Bychevsky's eyes moved slightly, a small amount of blood gathering in the corner of his mouth and trickling down the lower side of his chin.

"I . . . I did it . . . for Russia." He smiled slightly at his old friend, reaching up and letting the fingers of his hand touch Vilechenko's cheek. "Dear friend. I told some . . . some things that are better left behind." He gave a slight smile. "Do not think too poorly of me. I did it all for Russia." His last breath pushed out the words in a barely audible whisper.

The hand went limp, the arm fell, the eyes glazed over. Alexander Bychevsky, assassin of the last tsar, was dead.

Volodya Vilechenko gently lowered his friend's head to the cobblestone floor. Standing, he removed his white jacket and placed it over Bychevsky's face and shoulders.

"I wish the body to remain here." He glanced at Rand and Galya. Then he saw Sasha. "You brought help. You are a very smart man, Rand King." He looked down at his friend again. "He was a good leader. Without him we would never have survived."

"What now?" Rand asked.

"I leave that to the council, but I would think that, once I tell them of our fraudulent behavior, their decision will be to disband."

"You told us once that you have an heir."

"As you are aware, he is a fraud. Well trained—I think even he believes it now." He smiled. "Alexander convinced me we must do it for the good of Russia. I agreed. I was convinced that Peter William had died in the siege. Alexander and I found a new tsar, a Russian of good birth who looked very much like Peter William. We lived with him outside the country for many years, training him, letting him grow older. When we returned, everyone within the movement accepted him."

"They will have you shot for your deception. The movement, the dream is finished."

"Yes. Good-bye, Mr. King. Will you allow Alexander this burial place?"

"Yes, but we'll bring a coffin for him. And for Anna. I promise we'll take care of them."

Vilechenko smiled, stepped past Sasha, and disappeared up the stairway.

Sasha was still looking things over. "I suppose you will explain all this sometime."

"Sometime. I was beginning to wonder if you were here."

"You said noon, then came early," Sasha explained.

"Things became a little rushed."

"As it was, I was fifteen minutes early. Feel grateful."

"I expected to come on my own, after a friendly chat with Samuel Andrews and a chance to pick up Galya," Rand said. "Anyway, thanks. Did you bring the package?"

Sasha handed him a small box. It was taped shut.

"Thanks again," Rand said. "Do me a favor. Find a phone. Locate three good-quality coffins. Have them brought over here."

"Three?"

"Yes, three."

Another icon, this one of Michael the Archangel, his sword raised as if to strike anyone who drew near, was painted on the wall opposite the small cut where Anna lay. Next to it was a carving, this one of the Christ child lying in the manger. Carved into the solid stone wall, it was a deep relief that seemed almost to stand by itself.

Rand stood admiring the workmanship until he was sure Sasha would be out of the building.

"What are you doing?" Galya asked.

"Bring the lantern," he said, reaching into his pants pocket for his pocketknife.

She picked up the lantern from where Vilechenko had sat it on the floor and brought it to Rand. She watched as Rand cut the thick layers of tape away and opened the box.

"The key!" she exclaimed.

"A copy. I had Sasha take a photocopy of Nora's drawing to an artisan. It is a little rough, but workable—I hope."

"But what good will it do? The vault is already open."

"Yes, without the key, remember. *To enter the kingdom pay homage to the Christ child.*"

Brushing aside the dust on the statue, he searched, rubbed, and dug at the space beneath the manger. A hole appeared. Excited, he used the knife to dig the clay plug from the hole.

"This stuff was placed in here by somebody," he said as he forced the last bit out of the hole. "Probably Alexander." He shoved the key into the opening and twisted, his hand shaking with excitement. Nothing. He twisted again, harder. This time the entire wall gave, slipping inward.

Galya yelped with amazement. Rand stood, and the two of them placed the weight of their bodies against the stone door and shoved. The wall gave more to its left, swinging on some sort of hinge on the right. Rand heard the clang of metal on stone, then was hit by a rush of stale air ejecting itself from the cavern as the door separated from the wall and swung open entirely.

He stooped and picked up the lower half of the original key. Then he picked up the lantern from the floor and lifted it above their heads as they stepped into the entrance. The light cascaded into the room, falling over the remainder of the tsar's gold. The shimmer of reflected light bounced around the room and glinted in their wide eyes. Rand slipped past an immobile Galya and stepped down into the chamber, his lantern revealing even the darkest corner.

A man, sitting against the wall, his head lying on his chest, seemed to be sleeping. His clothes were hardly rotted at all, and the flesh of his arm seemed almost alive.

Rand approached, knelt, and rubbed it. Leather. He might be less deteriorated than the woman, but he was no less dead. Then Rand saw the reason—a knife with an emerald-encrusted handle stuck out from between his ribs.

"Peter William," Galya said, coming to Rand's side.

Rand noticed the crown upon his head. Galya reached to touch the knife.

He grasped her hand gently and kept it away. "He could fall apart. For now, let's leave him alone."

Rand glanced around him. There was several million in gold and artwork in chests and crates. He walked to one of the boxes and read the words on the side.

"Hermitage. 1941."

"Hermitage? But that can't be!" Galya said.

"It could if Nora, Anna, and William brought some of this stuff from there. Remember, the Nazis had the city surrounded before they could get everything of value out. When starvation set in, a lot of the Hermitage's treasures were moved onto the first floor to make room for people trying to survive the cold by taking up residence in the basement storage rooms."

Galya started looking more closely at the items. "These are all of a later period—all from the Hermitage. But these, they belonged to Tsar Nicholas and his family. I am sure of it. These gold-embossed dishes, the jewelry, and the crowns in that chest—they were the children's. I have seen them in pictures."

Rand saw something sticking from under the leg of the dead man and knelt to pick it up. He stood with the lost half of the diary in his hand. He opened it, turning the pages until he found the last entry. It was written in Russian with a dull object. The ink was blood.

"'I am Peter William III, grand duke of Russia and heir to the throne. I abdicate as leader of my country because of my love for Anna Berstam, a Jew, and most gracious lady. I die with a clean conscious before God and men. Our God will be our judge, as only God should. May my mother understand and forgive me as I forgive Alexander Bychevsky, the man who took my life.'" Rand paused; something was caught in his throat. "Signed William Peter III, grand duke of all Russia."

"Bychevsky emptied the vault but couldn't get back in here. Why?" Galya asked.

Rand raised the piece of key that had clattered to the floor. "When we leave, I think we will find that a pressure mechanism of some kind closes the door automatically. Bychevsky didn't know. It happened so fast that he had nothing but the key to jam into the crevice to prevent closure. It broke, sealing the tomb."

"Nora must have seen him leave, then found Anna. It must have been horrible for her to see what he had done," Galya said.

Rand nodded. "She probably figured out what had happened when William didn't show up. With the key destroyed, she was locked out until, like us, she could get one made. She tried to get the message to Vilechenko without revealing what she knew." He paused. "At least she finally won."

"What about all this?" Galya asked, waving her hand over the boxes and chests.

"We'll see that the state gets it," Rand said. "But not yet. It would disappear into the hands of the corrupt, or get melted down to save an economy that, if left alone, will survive anyway. In a few years this will be a great discovery, museum pieces that millions will flock to see. Let's give it a chance to survive." He paused. "We can open the door anytime."

Galya stared at the gold and jewelry overflowing the boxes. She leaned her head against Rand's shoulder, watching the body one last moment. "He was a handsome boy."

"And an honor to Russia. When his story is told, people will revere the part he played in their history." He turned and faced Galya, putting his arms around her and pulling her close.

"I have never been so tired in all my life," he said.

"You look terrible."

He touched the cuts in her face. "Thanks, so do you."

She jabbed a sharp fingernail into his ribs. He winced.

"Come on, before I collapse next to William and never get up," Rand said. He replaced the diary next to William. It was best that it remain in the vault.

Once through the entrance, lantern in hand, Rand stepped on what he thought was the pressure plate. He was amazed at how quickly the heavy stone door slammed shut, and with what force. Now he understood why the key had broken so cleanly. He felt the edges for air leaks but found none.

They removed the lantern and ascended the stairway. Rand searched under the statue until he found the small handle that opened the vault door. He pushed it back into place, then stood next to Galya while the stand moved upward, sealing the chamber. When it finally came to a halt, he checked to make sure everything looked normal. Then he went down the steps of the stand and joined Galya. It was time to go home.

The last of the tsars was finally buried.

Epilogue

EIGHT DAYS LATER, the funeral for Dimitri Bakatin was held in the building leased by the LDS church for a chapel. Dimitri and Marina were not religious people, but Marina was very appreciative of the manner in which the branch president, a Russian, took care of the services. It was the president's first service, and he was grateful for the mission president's help. Rand thought it all went very smoothly.

Interment took place in a small cemetery near Mga, just outside of Petersburg. It was Dimitri's place of birth. Rand was glad to see Larissa there, and he and Galya accompanied her back to the hospital to look in on Nickolai, who was finally conscious, but barely. He could not speak and was blind in one eye. It was going to be a long road to recovery.

Using money Rand said was from a generous gift of Boris Yeltsin and the Russian government, Larissa had decorated the bleak room with flowers and a few pieces of furniture that gave it an air of hominess. Rand understood why. Larissa spent every hour she could there.

The "gift" was actually from Tupolev—part of the nearly $250 million sacked away in Rand's American bank account until yesterday, when all but 1 percent was returned to the Russian government along with a two-hundred-page report of what had transpired. The 1 percent was in a trust fund for Nickolai. The executor was Rand King.

As soon as Nickolai healed sufficiently, Larissa intended to have him brought to her small apartment, where they could begin a rehabilitation program. Considering Larissa's background in ballet, Nickolai was in for a painful course in recovery. Rand had kidded her about marrying the bum before she allowed him to move in. She had a serious look across her face when she told him that she would have it no other way. He hoped to be back from the States in time for the wedding.

Rand took Galya to the cathedral later that day. They stood in front of the iconostasis next to the coffin of Volodya Vilechenko. Apparently he had died of a heart attack—found in his own apartment, lying comfortably in bed. After a brief service, the casket was closed and the mourners left. Rand and Sasha moved the coffin to a special place in the cathedral—the outer chamber of the tsar's tomb, next to the coffin of Alexander Bychevsky. Only Galya and Rand knew that just beyond the wall lay the last of the tsars, his wife Anna at his side. Volodya Vilechenko would be happy with his lot in death—still a protector of the Romanovs.

Sasha had never asked where Anna's body had gone or what had happened to two of the three coffins. He knew that someday his new boss would fill him in. He now worked full time for the consulate. He was paid well; why put a hole in a seaworthy boat?

Rand took Galya back to Rustam's apartment, where she was living. Natalya had been buried five days ago, and Rustam was having a tough time. Galya was taking care of her cousin, and they were helping each other handle the grief. Discussion of religious beliefs seemed to be playing a heavy role in the resolution of their confusion and grief.

From Rustam's, Sasha drove Rand to the airport, where he would catch an American Air Force plane back to the United States. He was accompanying the body of Samuel Andrews. The official report said that Andrews had been killed in a battle by Mafia gangs over a shipment of drugs hidden on one of the tourist busses. The president expected a more detailed report from Rand on his arrival in Washington. But then, the president expected a more detailed report about everything when Rand arrived—like why he had circumvented proper authority and the Russian government. He could only hope the president would be as responsive and understanding as Yeltsin had been.

But then, Yeltsin had something to celebrate: Two of his worst enemies had been buried—with full military honors, of course. Both had been the victims of sudden ill health. Some lies never change.

And then there was Ellen. He would see Ellen while in Washington. He would meet her fiancé and congratulate them both. He really was happy for them.

He boarded the 727 and entered the small passenger section at the front after checking on Andrews' crate. Removing his jacket and throwing it into a nearby seat, he loosened his tie. Then he seated himself and closed his eyes. He hadn't slept a solid two hours in a row for several days. And there was still the report to finish, and decisions to be made about Ted Powell's replacement. Then there were the funerals and visits to the hospital.

And there was Galya Starkova.

The plane taxied onto the runway and took a position for takeoff. Rand glanced out at the hazy skyline of the distant city of Petersburg. He had fallen in love with the place; he knew he'd be back.

Exhausted, he closed his eyes. By the time he reached Washington, he'd be well rested.